ShadowShifter

Book One

Melissa D. Ellis

MELISSA D. ELLIS

Dark Woods Publishing

Dark Woods Publishing

©2009 Melissa D. Ellis

ISBN 13: 978-0996858700
10: 9-968587-0-9

Fourth Edition

10 9 8 7 6 5 4 3 2 1

Manufactured in the United States of America

Discover other projects and titles by Melissa D. Ellis at
www.MelissaDEllis.com

This book is also available in e-book through most online retailers

This book is dedicated to the women of my family. My best friends.

To my sister, Mandy, for keeping the 4 month secret about me writing this book…the longest running secret ever kept in this family. Thank you for your guidance of not only staying true to my characters, but true to my character in the writing.

And to my mom and baby sister, Jess. Your honesty and constructive criticism have been key for this project.

Between the three of you, there was enough enthusiasm, inspiration, and harassment provided for me to continue when I was ready to throw in the towel… several times.

This book is also in loving memory of my G.G.—my Grandma Perdue. Just when I thought we had caught all mistakes and it had been passed through four different editors, you swooped in and found dozens more. You never ceased to amaze me.

Acknowledgments

First and foremost, I cannot thank the independent author community for guiding me and lifting me up during this process. This group of people has not only taught me the ins and outs of publishing, but has shown me that life is not always a competition. It's a mutual adoration and benefit kind of life that bears the most success.

Others have continued to encourage me and promote this book since the beginning when I was first self-published....going through a publisher...and then claiming my independence yet again: Jessica McDonald-Layman, Jen Harley, Heather Smiddie of SupaGurl Books Blog, Katrina Whitaker of Page Flipperz, and Stacey Clifford of Sassy Book Lovers.

It would only make sense for me to thank the good people of Crossville, TN—past and present. Everything from family, friends, ex-boyfriends, high school teachers and old classmates, the Cumberland County Playhouse, Cumberland County High School, to Black Mountain—we have such a wonderful little town here and we often forget that through our trials and frustrations. I am thankful that I was raised here. My youth in Crossville was a strong foundation for this story.

A colossal appreciation goes out to my four guys for putting up with me during this long journey: My husband, Matt, and three boys. They have put up with deadlines and stress—through writing, edits, and book releases, bad publisher experiences, piled up laundry, and nights of take-out instead of cooking.

Professionally, I must give kudos to the wonderful team of people who were able to make this book what it is today. My editors, Karen Hobbs, Dana Houser, Thom Crockett, and Heather Wooten. The beautiful Mackenzie Huling for being the face of ShadowShifter. James and Heather

Crowley of Crowley Studios for the amazing and fun photo shoot. The talented Rayne Warne for the impeccable cover art.

And last, to Dark Woods Publishing. Thanks for publishing me, all the while allowing me to be independent.

Table of Contents

What a big heart I have, the better to love you with.
Little Red Riding Hood, even bad wolves can be good...

~Lil' Red Riding Hood

Preface

I closed in on the loft's edge and watched in horror as the wolf tore into his flesh and devoured the thinned meat that was left on his bones. Lucas emitted an agonizing scream as the wolf pulled back the bones of his chest, causing an unforgettable crackling sound. And within seconds of ripping out his heart with his teeth, he swallowed it whole.

I had to act quickly, because as soon as it was done with Lucas, it was sure to come for me, too—assuming I wouldn't burn to death first.

The wolf looked up to where I stood on the loft and howled. As fast as I could, I ran to the top opened window of the barn, fighting the pressing urge to collapse. I saw the wolf clambering up to where I was in mammoth bounds, bouncing from stacked bales of hay to the wall and from the ladder to the wall again. Just as I made it to my escape route I turned around to see the terrifying monster standing massively at the top of the ladder, just leaps away from me. I thought my heart was going to rupture through the confines of my chest out of fear alone, but the ache of my lost love brought me a sense of my own death.

I took in a quick breath and jumped just as the wolf drop to all fours and started driving toward me. I expected the drop to be quick, but it lasted long enough for me to panic more the closer I came to the ground. My shadow on the ground below from where the barn burst into flames projecting a great light, began to shrink and line up with my body and over my left shoulder was the wolf, hurdling after me.

Summer School

I LOOKED INTO THE rear view mirror of my car. The circles under my eyes were proof enough that my positivity was simply a façade. I didn't sleep more than three hours the night before. Instead of spending most of the night panicking over trivial matters of high school gossip and judgmental glances, I should have been resting up for my fresh start in summer school. The parking lot of the Cumberland County High School was empty. I decided to arrive early this morning to mentally prepare for my return to society. I left the driver's side window down on my 1979 Chevy Malibu to enjoy the light breeze as the sun warmed my skin.

Taking several slow, steady breaths. "I'm sure no one even remembers." But even the girl in the reflection couldn't buy that lie. Her peculiar shaped mouth smiled wryly to the side as I decided to concede the truth, "Who am I kidding?"

Everyone would surely remember, for it happened just a few short weeks ago at the end of our spring semester rally.

It was the last day of finals for the underclassmen. Seniors were graduating that night and had been in rehearsals for the ceremony all morning. The gymnasium was filling for the end-of-year rally that would not only feature a small concert by my band, The Summers, but also honor top scholastic achievers and the popular seniors who had been voted for a class superlative.

"Mr. C.C.H.S." was my boyfriend, Gavin Williams. Physically perfect in every way. Handsome, popular, and from a wealthy family. His imperfection? He had a horrible reputation for being a douchebag. His hobbies included bragging about his perfect existence and publicly humiliating those who were not in his small group of friends. Cheating was another pastime. I knew this from the beginning. Gavin and I began dating shortly *before* he ended it with his previous girlfriend, Loni Schubert. It didn't matter; the popularity status that came with dating Gavin Williams was well worth the guilt I felt. Plus, he was a challenge for me, and I never shy away from a challenge. Unlike his previous girlfriends, he genuinely liked me for who I was and not because of a physical intimacy. Simply put, I was not promiscuous. My mother drilled into my sister, Natalie, and me since the day we began noticing boys that there were the kind of girls guys wanted to date and the kind guys wanted to marry. Though marriage was *far* from my mind, I was determined to be a girl that was respected. However, rumor had it Morgan West was much more fun to "date" after he dropped me off from our evenings out together. This rumor made the circuit for the majority of our three months together, and despite the affirmation from my closest friends and peers, Gavin insisted she was merely obsessed with him, that his friendliness was being taken out of context.

As we waited for the seniors to arrive and for the assembly to begin, I sat at the bottom of the bleachers in the gymnasium so I could conveniently take the stage when the time came. Cari was setting up her drums and upon finishing, quickly took a seat next to me.

My face beamed with pride as I watched Gavin walk in with his friends. Our eyes met, and I smiled and waved enthusiastically at him. He winked and casually picked up his hand—too cool to directly wave back. He took a quick scan of the gymnasium, combed his fingers through his blonde hair, and pointed to an empty section for his group to sit. They began climbing the bleachers to their seats when I saw Morgan following closely behind, and I rolled my eyes.

My annoyance over Morgan was suddenly interrupted by the two bodies that standing over me. I looked up to see the sisters Savannah and Sydney Blythe.

~ 2 ~

"Hey, Jules, we need to talk."

"What's the problem, Syd?" The worried expression was plain on her face.

"We're not doing this to hurt you, but..." Sydney began.

Instantly, I became nervous.

"Jules," Savannah was walking on eggshells, "Syd and I just heard something and you need to know about it."

"Gavin and Morgan are getting married," Sydney blurted out and immediately relaxed as if a load had been taken off her chest.

"Because Morgan's pregnant!" Savannah braced herself for my imminent meltdown, her face frozen in a permanent wince.

I sat with my mouth open, unsure of whether I should laugh or cry. *Married? Pregnant?* I couldn't speak, couldn't breathe. I felt the whole school watching me, as if my reaction to this rumor was the first thing on the agenda. Processing.... Nope. No laughter. I was definitely on the verge of tears. Tears—the fusion of hurt and anger. After several attempts to swallow the lump in my throat, it felt as though my heart fell into my stomach.

Savannah squeezed herself between me and the boy on my opposite side. Cari remained casual, hardly showing any surprise at the announcement. She had wanted to rip Gavin's throat out since the first rumor three months ago. She never trusted anyone popular. Holding a finger, she took over the conversation in the absence of my voice. My best friend didn't care much for Gavin, but was willing to get the facts straight, at least for my sake.

"Now Sydney," her tone, condescending, "Are you sure that Gavin's aware of his impending nuptials?"

"I heard her myself," Sydney countered the question with an answer in the same condescending tone.

"Oh, come on! I could tell a group of girls the same thing and you people would take it as gospel?" Cari sounded exasperated.

Sydney was insulted. "Everyone knows they've been hooking up behind Jules's back for months now. I can't believe you, of all people, would sit here and defend —"

Cari innocently held up her hands in defense. "Devil's advocate."

Savannah interjected. "It's different this time. She's wearing an engagement ring."

This added detail even silenced Cari. Nothing ever silences Cari.

Principal Dean began taking the stage with some of the other faculty. The assembly was starting. The girls, quiet now, were all staring at me. I guess I was being invited back into the conversation. What was I supposed to say? *Hey, thanks girls. I'll take it from here.* Or should I go with a more aggressive approach like, *you girls are so full of crap!* The numbness took over and crept through my body. I wanted to be sad or hurt. Anything but the numbness I now felt. Maybe if I screamed, the adrenaline in my body would convert to some sort of an emotion that was worthwhile.

I wished I could simply crawl under the bleachers and never be seen again or disappear in a puff of smoke.

The rally was a slow, unbearable process. I wanted to confront Gavin! There was no doubt in my mind he had been lying to me all along. It was ridiculous being in denial till this very moment! After all, he *is* a douchebag! Why should I be surprised by any of this?

Principal Dean began announcing the Senior Superlatives, the last part of the rally before we were to take the stage. Being voted a Superlative was an absurdly big deal. Our school was small, and being a big fish in a small pond was easy enough if your parents made a lot of money, if you were born and raised here, or if you were simply above average at something compared to others in your class. Seniors would vote for a male and female they believed best represented each category. The winners were honored with a picture in the yearbook with their voted title below the photo, as well as a certificate and the announcement at the end of the year to remind everyone how popular they were before they had to head off and face real challenges. Before we were all to become small fish in a very big ocean.

"I'm still surprised you didn't get 'Most Individual'," Savannah leaned across mine and Cari's lap to jab at her sister, "Guess all of your liberal and hippie nuttiness got you nowhere."

"I can't compete with that!" Sydney thumbed over her shoulder at the plump Ingrid Silivasi, covered from head to toe in black as she sulked back to the top of the bleachers with the rest her crowd, holding her certificate.

"...Gavin Williams and Sophia Gregory. Our graduating Mr. and Mrs. C.C.H.S.!"

The gymnasium erupted in applause, and my eyes stalked Gavin as he sauntered up to the stage and accepted the certificate. Sophia

~ 4 ~

Gregory bounced up beside him, waving to her scattered friends, smiling brilliantly and mouthing the words "thank you" to her voting class.

"How does such a douchebag get Mr. C.C.H.S., anyway?" Savannah asked out loud.

"Beats the hell outta me," Sydney grumbled.

In a whisper, I answered. "Because he's still popular."

"Who even cares? This whole thing is such a joke," Cari responded.

The girl behind me sniggered in a snide tone, "Check out Morgan West. She's still pissed that she lost."

I took a quick peek over my right shoulder at Morgan and sure enough, she was staring daggers at Sophia. Jealousy raging in her eyes. I felt a twinge of wicked satisfaction at her displeasure. Then her eyes quickly shifted to me. Her jealous appearance changed to a smug smile, and she joined in the applause for Gavin and Sophia.

And there it was. An oversized radiance attached to her third finger on her left hand. A diamond—stabbing me repeatedly, in the heart, like a shard of glass.

Sure, I had debated on ending it with him many times based on his character flaws alone, but I wanted it to end on *my* terms, not his! To end our relationship by his call was humiliating enough without the realization that I couldn't compare, couldn't compete with other girls in this school. Girls who were popular.

Of course he doesn't want me! He wanted the tall, leggy blonde with curly hair and golden skin, whose body belonged to a Victoria's Secret angel and had a smile worthy of a tooth paste commercial. She looked like a twenty-year-old! I looked to be about twelve with a body of a young boy! So thin that the largest parts of my legs and arms were my hands, knees, elbows and feet. My upper lip was awkwardly curvy and I was incapable of completely filling out even the smallest bra size. Dating Gavin to become popular was about as realistic as me trying to fool the town into believing I was a natural blonde. Redheaded but too afraid to outright bleach it, my hair always looked strawberry. That's me. Juliana Taylor. Plain and boring. I could never be extraordinary no matter how hard I tried, and I was too afraid to ever be myself.

I didn't even hear us being introduced, I was only aware of the roar of applause and my three friends getting to their feet to rush to the stage. I remained seated for a few more seconds before Cari realized I hadn't moved. She ran back over to me, as Savannah and Sydney adjusted themselves with their guitars.

"Just get through this set and we'll kick his ass afterward." From the look in her eyes, she meant every word.

Not wanting to make a scene, I jumped to my feet and faked a smile. The heat was already creeping up my chest. *God, please don't let me cry here! Not in front of everybody. Not in front of him!* I swallowed the obstruction in my throat, determined to get through this like a pro.

I didn't want anybody's sympathy nor do I want to hear any laughter at my stupidity for trusting a person's integrity that had been in question for years. I was the laughing stock of the school. Everyone knew about his indiscretions, and I deluded myself into believing that it was all idle gossip.

Hold it together, Jules... It read in every one of my friends' glances.

My chest began feeling tight as I fought the warmth in my eyes. My body stiffened and burned from within. I warbled with venom. My knuckles ached and whitened from my grip on the microphone. The fury must have been visible to others as well, because while we were wrapping up our thirty minute set, I caught several concerned looks from many of my classmates.

The bass rang out on the last note and I stepped back from the microphone for a quick breath that never came. The applause thundered and sporadic calls for an encore echoed, but I wanted out of there.

Savannah was whispering to me.

"Huh?" I felt an oncoming anxiety attack and all noise was muffled in my ears

"Let's do *Don't Dream it's Over.* It's your favorite, Jules!" Savannah suggested.

The girls argued and debated over encore songs as I felt the mass of emotion climb its way out of my stomach and into my throat. My eyes widened—the *monster*—my mother's accurate term for my temper. I tried keeping the monster down but it waited restlessly in my throat, refusing to be pushed back down.

It sounded as if Savannah won, or that the other girls agreed to do me this one favor. The introduction to *Don't Dream It's Over* was playing behind me.

"We're going to sing one last song before we take our last exam and start our summer vacation, but I want to take time to thank you all," I started my goodbye, playing it cool through my quivery voice. "... For your support and energy this year. We had a lot of fun and..."

The monster ferociously clawed its way to the exit and I found the warmth in my eyes overpower me. My tight jaw began to slide forward as my mouth seethed with the acid to be spewed. I was losing it.

No. I had *lost* it.

"... And... Who the hell do you think you are, Gavin Williams! You dirty, son of a bitch!"

I heard three distinct gasps behind me and then others throughout the innocent bystanders in front of me but saw nothing. Everything was a wash of red, framed with a black engulfing haze. Was this a nervous breakdown? Was I passing out? I was keenly aware of some of the faculty frantically trying to control the sound board to turn my microphone off. I heard the popping noise of the sound equipment being turned off one by one. Yet, my voice echoed. We have great acoustics in here—unfortunate for this day.

I continued my tirade, but remember not one detail of the words I uttered. A few giggles erupted but were quickly hushed. My eyes were gaining focus now, and I could see Gavin smirking at me like it never even affected him. He rolled his eyes and snickered with a few of his friends. Morgan's smugness had slightly converted to a look of embarrassment.

"Girls, you're done here." Mr. Dean's strong hand clamped down on my shoulder. "Miss Taylor, we need to have a meeting with your parents immediately," he bellowed as he led me out of the gym, down the hall, and into his office.

I was suspended for the last three days of school, unable to take my last final exam—Algebra II—and therefore received a failing grade for the year. To prevent having to repeat Algebra II my junior year, I had no choice but to take second term summer school. And because of my appalling and obscene conduct that I argued was well deserved under the circumstances—I was grounded throughout the summer break. My parents wouldn't even buy my plea of insanity.

In one sweep I had managed to lose my boyfriend, my freedom, my summer, and my dignity. I was empty.

Today, however, the emptiness was filled with anxiety.

I took a glimpse at my phone to see all of my daydreaming had left me five minutes before class was to start. The school parking lot had filled considerably. I grabbed my notebook and slipped my purse strap across my skinny body as I crossed the parking lot. Fumbling to shut the door behind me, I picked up the pace to escape the halls where many were still mingling, in hopes that no one would remember me or my catastrophic outburst that landed me in this place for the summer.

Upon reaching Mr. Muir's Algebra II class I took a moment to collect myself before opening the door and walking in. I inhaled a jagged breath and blew out all the tension I possibly could from my body.

As I walked in, I realized the suffering I was going to have to endure for the next four weeks. I was the only girl in this class.

Boy Next Door

I TOOK THE FIRST seat inside the door. My chest was warming and I was sure that a blotchy redness wanted to make its unsightly appearance up my neck. Mr. Muir was studying the class with speculative eyes then shifted slightly to the clock on the wall. He set his coffee down and jumped to his feet lightly. This little man was obviously a morning person. His expression was rejuvenated and fresh.

"Question: who would be opposed to getting out of class at ten instead of noon?" he asked.

I heard a high five and a few excited whispers coming from around the room behind me.

"Before you answer," He continued, "keep in mind that you will still pay your debt of four hours a day; you would just be starting the sentence two hours earlier."

This time a few groans were muttered.

"It's up to you as a class. You can come in at eight; leave at noon, when a good chunk of your day has been spent within these walls or you can drag yourselves in at six and leave at ten, giving you pretty much an entire day to do whatever it is you do to waste your summers."

As much as I would like to stay in a comatose state until ten every morning, the earlier class time was appealing to me. Still, it didn't really matter to me because I was still grounded and my "daylight" was wasted anyway. After we all voted to start class at six, I braced myself with the understanding that I would have to start going to bed earlier. Although I may not have a life outside of my own home, I still couldn't get myself to sleep before midnight. It just wasn't in me; I have always been more of a night owl.

Mr. Muir went through the class list. Most of us, he was familiar with.

"I see we have…" he scanned the list first then would search for the face that went with the name. "Mr. Overby, how good of you to join us for *both* terms this summer."

"I thought you'd like that," Kevin Overby quipped.

Kevin Overby was a notorious trouble maker in our school. His long hair was always hanging in his face, which bothered me. It made me want to put a bow in his hair.

"Mm-hmm." Mr. Muir clearly was not excited to have him for eight full weeks of the summer. "Mr. King. Good to see you again, too."

The young boy casually lifted his chin and then turned back to his friends sitting behind him. Those boys, too, were noted as returning students.

"Mr. Cooper, what brings you in here for the summer?" Mr. Muir was clearly caught off guard by this name on the class list. It caught my attention, as well.

Broderick Cooper, who could be easily called a next door neighbor if it weren't for the patch of trees and small creek that separated our properties, was now sitting two rows over and two seats back. Often I would see him jogging in the neighborhood or mowing yards and landscaping, a summer business he started with his best friends Jackson Pugh and Joey Burnett. He was well known in our town for being an athlete. Often, I would hear my dad's prediction that Broderick Cooper would someday play major league baseball. He also excelled in football and basketball. I, along with every other girl at our school, lusted after him, though he was practically untouchable. Providing a scandal almost as big as mine last year, he dated beautiful Taryn Green for a few short months before she hooked up with his best friend, Jackson, behind his back. Since then, he hadn't been seen with anyone and yet still continued to be friends with both of them. It baffled all of us.

His puppy dog brown eyes, that always seemed to beam, were lined with thick lashes and brows, and his boyish appeal was made more apparent by the way his perfectly shaped lips smoothly pulled back into a smile emitting two very defining dimples. His brown hair always had that tousled look and his bangs hung lightly over his forehead as he tried sweeping them off to the side with his fingers as he spoke.

"My GPA, sir," he sheepishly admitted.

This appeared to only please Mr. Muir according to the nod he gave. To me, it was odd that anyone would put forth an extra effort beyond a simple passing grade. I couldn't imagine a school GPA being so important that you would take a summer class to rectify it, especially when you were consistently on the honor roll like Broderick Cooper.

I found myself staring at him. He obviously felt my gaze because shortly after Mr. Muir resumed his checklist of students, he glanced over at me. He turned his lips back into a small and kind smile. As much as his smile encouraged me to smile back, I refused to share any of my smiles with him. I wouldn't give him the satisfaction of openly being another girl added to his likely inventory of broken hearts and foolish affections; I had already been on someone else's inventory for that. Besides, guys like Gavin and Broderick were of the same mold. They were popular. Cari was right never to trust them. I knew that now.

My brows began to furrow at him and I could feel my imperfect lips push upward into a stubborn pout. *I will never allow a guy to make a fool of me again. Never again, will I…*

"Miss Juliana Taylor." Mr. Muir was standing over my desk.

"Sir?" I twisted around facing forward in my seat again, only to catch a glimpse that my expression must have insulted Broderick.

"Can we be expecting any repeat performances from you this summer?" He was partly joking, I could tell. His tone wasn't degrading, but I was humiliated just the same. If no one remembered before, they certainly did now.

"No sir." I shifted uncomfortably in my seat.

"Are you sure?" he continued to rouse, "I wouldn't want to hinder any of your artistic output."

"No, sir," I quickly answered, hoping he would move on to his next victim and forget about me if I played polite and quiet.

"No, you're not sure or no, you don't feel the need to express yourself?" He wasn't letting up and his question made me flustered. I was willing to answer the question as long as it meant that he was willing to let up on the aggravating, but a voice two rows down became my sudden saving grace.

"Sir?"

"Yes, Mr. Cooper?"

"I was wondering if we were meeting for class on the Fourth of July?"

Mr. Muir's shook his head. "Absolutely not. I'd rather spend that day with my family just as most of you would probably prefer spending that day groping young girls in their bikinis by the lake."

The boys in the class laughed in agreement as Broderick smiled in appreciation. "Thank you, sir."

"You each will be allowed one sick day," he announced to the class. "Anything beyond that will result in a drop of a letter grade and possibly failure if you're only holding a D at that time."

Broderick caught my stare again and smiled awkwardly at me. I got the bizarre feeling that he distracted Mr. Muir on purpose to save me from any further harassment. Whatever the reason, I was grateful because I was already long forgotten and the next student on his list was now being tortured.

Steering my eyes to the front chalkboard pretending to be deep in thought, I could still feel Broderick's gaze upon me. My back stiffened and my lungs became more like full iron vats instead of balloons. My head slowly edged back over my left shoulder. Just one more peek. Real quick. Broderick's eyes were burning holes through me. He wasn't smiling this time, but he didn't seem upset, either. His thick brows were pulled together and his eyes narrowed in a studious manner as if I was the hardest algebra equation he would be confronted with this term. Was his expression supposed to threaten me or was he genuinely confused by me? Maybe he was puzzled by my bipolar hair color? Maybe I really hurt his feelings with the way I looked at him. I didn't mean to; I just wanted him to know where he and I stood. We would not be friends. Not even close.

The first week we spent our mornings rehashing over the basics of Algebra II and getting used to the routine of waking up at an ungodly hour. I wasn't the only one in there struggling with the early morning hours; others were regularly walking in five minutes late every morning. However, Broderick Cooper was always seated and relaxed by the time I arrived.

I had already built up a resistance to Broderick Cooper's lingering glances and was able to ignore them altogether—well, at least when he was looking.

I chose to spend Mr. Muir's allotted fifteen minute classroom breaks away from class in the solitude of my car. It was a sure way to avoid any unwanted conversations with the boys in my class. Sneaking out of the side door of the school with cheese crackers in hand, I darted in the direction of my car and wasn't even half way there when I heard my name being called.

"Jules! Jules, come over here for a minute." I looked over to see Kevin leaning against an old truck surrounded by a few of the guys from class, his blonde hair, for once, was pulled back behind his ears.

I dragged myself over to him in an effort to be friendly though I was far from trusting.

"So why are you in this class? I thought you were smart?" Kevin tactlessly asked.

I was a bit offended. "Well, I was passing until I chose not to take my final exam."

"You *chose* to skip the final?" he raised an eyebrow with a smirk on his face.

Maybe the word "chose" wasn't the appropriate term to use?

"Yeah!" one of the other boys chimed in, "I heard you got suspended after you freaked out on stage."

I tried to be light on the issue. "Well, I made that choice leading to the suspension, didn't I?" I really hated that the words *I* and *suspended* were in the same sentence together without the words "never have been" between the two.

"They didn't let you finish that last exam?" Kevin asked.

"Nope."

"That sucks," he said, chuckling a little under his breath. I seriously doubted that if Kevin had been in that position last spring, he would hardly be devastated. "I thought you were pretty funny freaking out like that."

The guy standing next to Kevin was laughing heartily and a few of the others were starting in as well.

Another boy was shaking in laughter. "That had to be the funniest damn thing I saw all year!"

"Glad you enjoyed it," I muttered in sarcasm as I walked back to the school. I could hear the boys behind me bellowing over my humiliation.

Jerking the door open in frustration, I made a straight path to Mr. Muir's class. Eyes glued my feet, I dropped into my chair inside the quiet classroom. The break seemed to be more insufferable than the class itself, today. At least during class, your classmates couldn't just start up a conversation about life's most embarrassing moments. I tore into my crackers and shoved the first one into my mouth as a whole. Resting my head on the desk, I slowly chewed the cheese cracker. I didn't want to cry from the anger and humiliation, so I concentrated instead on not choking on the sizable portion of food in my mouth.

The sound of a chair scraping against the floor and the light sound of squeaky sneakers stepping toward me, caught me off guard. *I thought that I was alone in here?* I braced myself for a repeat of my most recent chat. Instead, the person just sat at the desk next to me and took a deep breath. I didn't even want to look up and see who it was. Maybe if I acted as if I were unaware of his presence or that I was napping, he would go away?

"We live next door to each other." His voice was deep, but friendly.

Slowly sitting up, my mouth full of cheese and cracker, I gazed into the warm, brown eyes of Broderick Cooper and I immediately began to thaw, despite my instinct not to do so.

"Do you need a drink with that snack?" he quietly offered.

I began to answer with my mouth full, tiny crumbs trickling out from my lips, but he held out his hand in a gesture.

"Go ahead and swallow first. No hurry."

I chewed quickly and swallowed loudly. "I'll be okay." My dry throat screamed at me for being so stubborn.

I took the time to reaffirm my guard in silence, and make sure that I could continue this chat unaffected by any of his natural charm.

"Oh, well… the machine accidently gave me two cans of soda and I thought you might want one of them… Are you sure you won't need to wash that down?" He smiled in a last hope to rid himself of the extra beverage.

"I should never turn down a free drink, now should I?" He placed the drink in my waiting hand and I popped it open after tapping the top to prevent it from spewing all over me in case he was setting me up for disaster by shaking the can beforehand. "Thanks."

"No problem." He hesitated for a moment then put his hand out. "I'm Broderick Cooper."

I found this manner somewhat amusing so I took his hand and shook it. "Yeah… I know who you are. Everybody does."

"It's Jules, isn't it? Or do you prefer Juliana?"

"My friends call me Jules."

"It's a small high school; I can't believe we've never had a class together in the two years you've lived here." Broderick tucked in his lips as if he were unsure of his words.

"Well, you're getting a full dose of summer school with me now, so you can check that off your bucket list." In a goofy move, I used my finger to check an imaginary box in the air.

He emitted a small grin. "Maybe summer school won't be so bad now. How come I haven't seen you around this summer?"

I took a small swig from the can and choked a little. He waited for my answer as I grabbed another cracker from the pack, this time only taking a small bite. I was uncomfortable with the direction his friendliness had taken and couldn't imagine that anyone of his caliber would notice my absence.

"I've been grounded," I replied.

He made an empathetic, playful grimace. "When do you get *un-grounded*?"

I laughed half-heartedly. "Good question. Probably when I turn eighteen and move out."

He was leaning toward me with his elbows resting on his knees, near enough for me to catch a faint trace of his scent. Like soap. Clean. Natural. I loathed the strong colognes that most guys at our school apparently swam in.

"A whole summer…that's a letdown." He sat thoughtfully for a moment.

I could tell he was holding back on something in our short talk as he bit his lip and cleared his throat. Quietly I sat enjoying the cracker, drink, and his presence. He was soothing to be around, even in silence.

"Don't Dream it's Over," he finally spoke.

"Excuse me?" I was confused.

"It's one of my favorite songs."

I could feel the encouraging tone of his voice edged with reluctance. He had no intentions to drudge up an impossible-to-forget memory; he was trying to be nice.

"Mine, too." Finding a common interest almost brought a smile to my face, but my lips fell lopsided instead as my recent memory of the song seeped into the forefront of my brain. "Sorry you didn't get to hear it that day."

"I'm sorry you didn't get to sing it. Your voice is absolutely mesmerizing." He gave me his most stunning smile, emphasizing the dimples in his cheeks, which left me breathless. Captivated. "And I know you would've really…" he searched for the appropriate words. "…you would have really been amazing."

The other students began to enter the room to finish our last two hours of class for the day, so he got to his feet. "I'll talk to you later, Jules."

"See ya," I said softly as he loped over to his desk again.

I felt absolutely alone as he moved back to his seat. Then I was overcome with the self-inflicted anger at my foolishness for allowing myself to be caught up in his faux-friendly behavior. Frustrated with my own naiveté, I couldn't understand why I wasn't more aware of dishonest approaches. Like Cari. My heart of ice burned with reaffirmed coolness. Furious at my own imprudence, I wanted to bang my head on the desk in front of me.

Drowning

MY PARENTS WERE MERCIFUL enough to grant me temporary parole for the Independence Day celebration at the lake in town. A day packed with games, live music, inflatable play areas, junk food concessions, and water fun at the lake. The majority of the town would be there. Savannah and Sydney lived in one of the nearby lake homes and could always be relied upon to allow friends to park on their property avoiding the heavy traffic at the park. It also made a great headquarters for free snacks, a place to rest, and clean bathrooms, outweighing any inconvenience that the five block walk around the lake to and from the park appeared to be.

My dad was quick to remind me that I was to return to my imprisonment first thing upon my *early* curfew. This meant I would not only have to drive separately from Cari, but also leave immediately after the fireworks display, missing the after party shenanigans many of my friends would partake in back at Savannah and Sydney's.

After trying on three different outfits for the party, I finally optioned for comfort instead of style—my black full piece swimsuit to wear under my clothes, in the event I actually decided to get into the lake. I cringed at the idea of anyone seeing me in a bathing suit, though.

"Jules, if you went any slower to get ready, we'd be going backwards." Cari muttered impatiently as she sat at the window seat in my bedroom, hanging her head out of the opened window while smoking a cigarette. I was pretty anal about smoking; it was unhealthy and it smelled horrible. "I want to get a great spot for the show at noon…I can't wait for you to see this guy! He's an *amazing* musician."

She finished her cigarette and ducked back into my room, grabbing the air freshener, and spraying erratically as she studied my latest look. In spite of her efforts, I could still smell the stench. Before I could complain, her face twisted in disapproval. "You look like a hobo. If you're trying to get everyone to believe that you're drowning in misery over the break up, you're off to a bang-up start." Cari was never subtle in her thoughts. "And you're going to have a heat stroke in that hoodie."

My goal for the evening, other than avoiding any discussions about my crucified love life, was to stay out of the water and to keep my bathing suit-clad body covered. The ridicule of my flat physique was tough enough when I was fully clothed. Standing next to Cari's well-endowed body only added insult to the injury. She donned a pair of short denim cut-offs and a black tank top, unsuccessfully trying to conceal her god given gifts that were at an overflowing point in her purple bikini top that peeked from behind the thin, black fabric. Her shoulder donned a tattoo similar to the Jolly Roger but in place of the cross bones were drumsticks.

By the time Cari and I parked our cars at Savannah's and made our way to the park, the celebration was in full swing. With nervous butterflies in my stomach, we walked through and entrance that held endless possibilities for a girl who had spent her summer cooped up at home and in school. I was excited to see familiar faces, reacquaint myself with school friends…maybe even see Broderick?

As I looked out to the crowd of people, a friendly pair of blue eyes swept into my line of focus. Blue eyes that belonged to Joey Burnett. "Hey, Jules! Is Nat here too?"

Joey became like a brother to me ever since we were lab partners in Chemistry last fall. When I was struggling, he came to my rescue. During that time he had also became a best friend to my younger sister, Natalie. His unspoken affection for her was clear to everyone but her. She had a knack for being one of the guys, but her natural beauty eventually compromised her friendships with the opposite sex. Joey knew that if he ever made his feelings known, she would bring their friendship to an abrupt halt. So he hid his affection, hoping someday she would return those feelings.

"Sorry, Joey. She's spending the afternoon shopping in Cookeville with Amber and her mom." His enthusiasm was immediately crushed as the words left my tongue. "*But*," I continued, "She plans to be here tonight for the fireworks."

"Awesome!" He grinned. "A friend is letting me borrow his jet ski for the day and I was hoping to get her on it… Maybe you and I can play a game of volleyball later? They're setting up the net right now over by the…." I glanced behind Joey as he prattled on and saw a red Jeep slowly roll by the park with Broderick Cooper at the steering wheel. My eyes were locked on Broderick as he maneuvered his vehicle through the pedestrians and onto the grassy knoll that was being used for overflow parking.

Joey began snapping his fingers in my line of sight. "Hello? Jules?"

I blinked and returned to the person in front of me. "I'm sorry. What?"

Curious, he looked over his shoulder to see what had pulled my attention. I winced hoping he wouldn't realize it was Broderick Cooper who had stolen my concentration from him. Instantly seeing Broderick, he shot his hand up to wave him over, my preoccupation completely forgotten. His wave provided no success, then pointed to another car parked a few spaces away from Broderick. "Jackson and Taryn are finally here. Took them long enough. I wonder what changed Broderick's mind about coming…" He turned back to me. "I'm going to go over there and flag them down. You wanna come?"

Cari grabbed my arm. "Jules, we have thirty minutes before Isaac Philetos takes stage. I want to get a good seat."

I shook my head at Joey. "I promised Cari that we'd watch this guy play at noon. We'll catch up later." Joey waved as he jogged over to Broderick, Jackson, and Taryn in the grassy knoll.

Cari and I made our way to the amphitheater and found a spot close to the front while the previous act was winding their set down. "We'll grab the very front as soon as these people are done and the audience thins out," she assured me.

Sure enough, within minutes of the last song being played, the audience began thinning and Cari pulled me to what she deemed as the most perfect spot. Savannah and her boyfriend, Tripp, joined us moments later. She, too, had been scouting the area for the most perfect spot to watch the noon show with Isaac Philetos.

I was unfamiliar with him and his music, but Cari and Savannah had caught his act a few months back when they were in Atlanta. For weeks after, I heard nothing but his name.

Cari suddenly leaned in to all of us and started speaking in a husky and rushed whisper. "Oh my God! There he is, there he is!"

My mind was still centered around Broderick—hoping I would get a chance to run into him, whilst also wishing that I'd quit thinking about him altogether—so when I looked up and saw the person Cari was referring to, I felt traitorous to my current obsession. Isaac was godlike in his startling beauty. I locked my eyes onto him as he confidently crossed the stage, guitar case in hand. Keenly aware that I was foolishly gaping at him, I tried tearing my eyes away, but they betrayed me and resisted. His fully developed muscles pulsate under the tanned skin of his tattooed arm as he shook the hand of someone on stage offering to help him set up. His body was sculpted flawlessly, strong and muscular; the clothes he wore couldn't veil it. As he spoke, his bright white teeth seemed to sparkle in a smile framed by his smooth, perfectly shaped lips. His thick black hair was neatly swept and arranged in a spiky fashion found on the young heartthrobs of movies and television. And despite the danger I found in his icy blue eyes, lined with thick black lashes—a look that could easily be found in the eyes of a mysterious and tortured rebel—I saw a distinctive twinkle dart from them. He released a stunning and confident manner as he strolled over to set down his guitar case and retrieve a stool from a girl who was also helping him set up on the stage.

"Ingrid Silivasi!" Savannah hissed like a snake as she glared at the girl on stage. The recent graduate from last spring was wearing a long skirt and a denim jacket over a bust enhancing black leather corset. It was too hot for that sort of outfit, in my opinion, and the medallion that dangled from a chain around her neck looked to weigh about as much as the denim jacket. I broke out into a sweat just watching her... or from my own overdressed outfit as I stood under the noonday sun in a hoodie.

Isaac thanked Ingrid for her help and she turned to join Lucas Reiser off to the side of the stage where he waited for her. Tall and too thin, I always thought Lucas Reiser looked as though he walked on stilts. His skin was pale white against his oily black hair.

"Ew," Savannah cringed at the two outcasts from school, fueled alone by their division of classes.

"Isn't he delicious?" I turned to Cari in shock only to realize in relief that she was referring to Isaac and not Lucas.

I opened my mouth to respond but only air escaped. Was I blushing at him? And as if he could hear her through the bustling energy of the park and through my skull into my own thoughts on his undeniable beauty, he looked directly at us. Narrowing his eyes on us, he pulled his lips back into an entrancing and arrogant smile and then seductively bit his bottom lip. Cari's throat made an awkward creaking sound, as she tried to catch her breath in response. An audible sigh was heard throughout the already growing audience. I shuddered as my heart thundered in my chest. *I'm not breathing*!

Savannah was also deeply captivated with him. She uttered breathlessly, "Wow."

"Yeah," I heaved a sigh and finally looked away.

"What did I tell you?" Cari grabbed my arm, still watching him closely. His focus was already diverted elsewhere. "Now, I want you to listen to him with critical ears, Jules." I'd never seen Cari so obsessed with anyone before.

"Oh, my ears will be critical, alright," I assured her.

"I wonder if I can get him to meet me tonight at the fireworks show or afterwards, for a bite to eat or something?" Cari mused out loud.

"This guy is far too old for you! You're crazy!" I chewed on a realistic age for him. He sure didn't look under the age of eighteen; twenty-five, maybe.

Savannah stated in her know-it-all tone, "Actually, I saw him registering for classes yesterday at the school offices when I went to change my schedule."

"This guy?" I thumbed over to the stage in question, certain she was wrong.

"What grade is he in?" Cari demanded as she leaned further across the table to her.

"I think he's a junior. At least that's what I was able to gather without being too obvious."

I looked back at him in disbelief. "No way."

Tripp's insecurity was getting the best of him, I could see as he began pulling Savannah closer to him like a family dog begging to remind everyone of his existence. Reaching back, she patted him softly on his cheek as she continued to gape at the musician like the rest of us.

Isaac smoothly spoke into the microphone. "Happy Fourth of July, Crossville!" He began with a devilish grin and eyes scanning the entire female populace in the amphitheater. "My name is Isaac Philetos and I'd like to thank each of you for coming out today." His teeth shined brightly against his olive skin and I heard many female snickers, on the verge of giggles. Cari was right. He was *hot*, indeed; enough so, to get my blood pumping faster.

Without any further words he began picking gracefully at the strings, creating some pop/jazz fusion piece. His fingers glided up and down the neck of his guitar, moving so quickly and fluently that they only seemed to flutter across, just tickling the strings. His concentration in the act was infinitesimal, for he didn't fixate his mouth like many others did while they were playing. Occasionally he'd bite his bottom lip, more in an act of seductive drama I was sure, but for the most part, he gave his audience a good amount of attention. He was one hundred percent, completely relaxed through this instrumental song.

The audience wasn't exactly a core market for what he played. Our small town consisted of people who enjoyed listening to top 40 pop or country, not indie and acoustic music; but nonetheless, we erupted in applause the second his last note rang out.

He humbly nodded his head in appreciation. "Thank you. That was a little piece I composed called *Waiting in New Orleans*."

I was impressed, within reason; unwilling to give in to my inferiority to him. *So what? He can play guitar*, I casually thought to myself as I studied him with skepticism. Anything was "amazing" compared to my clumsy strumming. But could he sing? *That* was my forte. Cari's faith in his vocal skills was surely blinded by her acute attraction to him. I used to be the same way with a few actors until I finally looked past their charming good looks and found only a mediocre talent in each of them. It was common for women to do that.

Again, he started a new song. The intro was short, but gave enough time to blow me away with how much he could make his guitar sound more like a symphony than just a single guitar. But nothing could prepare me for the beautiful sound that flowed from his mouth. Although the song was a bit upbeat, he was somehow able to incorporate a soft, breathy voice to contrast and compliment the song. His voice at first was smooth and sensual, like a melodic whisper. Then, his voice grew so sure and thunderous—almost like a tuneful scream—yet remained tasteful and harmonious. Never did he strain; never did he fall from pitch. He was impeccable. I shuddered as I felt his tortured lyrics and dramatic voice grab my soul and squeeze tightly.

"Breathe, Jules," Cari laughed in my ear. She nudged me. "What did I tell ya?"

I was determined not to give in. "He's not bad."

"*Not bad?* He's a freakin' god of music is what he is! You are *so* jealous!" She was getting a kick out of the envy I was so desperate to conceal.

"I agree with Jules," Tripp threw in, obviously hoping to deter his girlfriend's attention from the musical Romeo. "He's okay, but he's not phenomenal," he scoffed.

"Sounds like someone else is jealous as well, but for completely different reasons," Cari laughed.

I was rendered hopeless as he continued singing, the guilt from my attraction pulsing through my veins. It was hopeless to be rescued from the clutches of my envy and unfortunate lust of Isaac Philetos.

"He's perfect in the face and his body reminds me of a soap opera actor!" Savannah gushed, "But there's something about him that seems a bit dangerous. Like a rebel."

Cari countered excitedly, "Every girl has a thing for the bad boys; it's completely natural."

"It's the tattoos on his arms," I explained in theory.

"I love a man with ink," Cari smiled.

"I don't have a thing for bad boys," Savannah stated self-righteously and she twisted around to kiss Tripp.

"*Every* girl does," Cari corrected her. "Even when they're not willing to admit it. Take Jules for instance. She's yet to take her eyes off of him."

"That's not true!" I exclaimed, frustrated that she was spot on with her assessment. Cari looked at me with a wicked smirk on her face.

"Gavin was Jules's bad boy," Savannah said quietly with reluctance.

Cari pointed to Savannah in agreement. "Good point! See? Everyone has a thing for bad boys!"

"Gavin wasn't a bad boy; he was a *mistake*," I corrected her. "And I didn't go out with him because I thought he was a bad guy either."

"Whatever!" Cari's voice started getting louder and louder to the point others could hear her over the music. "You were warned that he was bad news. Just admit that you have an attraction to bad guys. It's okay. It won't make you any less of a Christian if you do!" She sighed, turning back to the stage. "I cannot believe he's going to going to school with us!"

After Isaac Philetos had finished his set, a gang of girls began edging their way closer to him, while he began packing up his equipment—Ingrid Silivasi assisting him with the task. The quickest one to reach him was Loni Schubert in all her bleach-blond glory. Never had I seen a girl move so fast to get near a guy.

"Well, that's a deal breaker," Cari muttered as she watched Loni standing at the edge of the stage looking up at Isaac and chatting along as he wound up his microphone cord up; her clothes consisting mainly of a skimpy tank top that scooped low enough for her cleavage to make a statement and denim cut-offs that would provide as much cover as my bikini bottoms would.

"Forget about it," I told her. "He'll see right through that trash if he has any character. Let's go do something fun. I think Joey said something about playing volleyball."

The four of us decided to join the group of people dividing themselves into teams for a volleyball match. I ended up on the same team with Joey. Unfortunately, Savannah, Tripp, and Cari wound up on the team with Kevin Overby.

As the game ensued, I would take moments to search for Broderick among the festivities. Sure enough, I found him sitting on a camping chair with a small, energetic group near the lake that included Taryn and Jackson. Despite the laughing and talking among the intimate and private circle of friends, Broderick seemed distant. Although he sat listening and occasionally laughing with the others, he often stared into the middle of their circle, his eyebrows puckered and his eyes filled with deep thought, as though no one was really around him and he were sitting completely alone. Only during the raucous laughter was he brought back to the entertainment that surrounded him.

Thwack! A spiked ball from the opposing team slammed into the side of my face, knocking me to the ground. The booming laughter followed instantly as I hit the ground.

"Jules! Jules! Are you hurt?" Joey's voice was strained as he tried to hold back his own laughter.

"Only my pride," I groaned in embarrassment, dusting myself off and taking Joey's offered hand to get to my feet. I sheepishly looked over my shoulder and saw Broderick blankly staring at me; a couple of his friends chuckled in my direction and then turned back to their own discussion again. But Broderick continued to stare. "Brilliant, Jules," I muttered to myself as the heat rose to my cheeks.

The laughter by the volleyball net hadn't let up, and I looked over to see Kevin on the ground rolling with laughter, the rest of the team equally in throws. Cari was covering her mouth with her hands, but her eyes had welled up in tears from her suppressed laughter.

"I didn't mean to hit you that hard," Kevin chortled as he got to his feet.

"You meant to hit me?" I instantly caught his choice of words.

"Well if you'd keep your head in the game..." he continued to taunt. The rest of the laughter was slowly dying down now.

"You *meant* to hit me?" I gritted my teeth as my blood began to boil.

Kevin straightened his face and held up his hand as if to hold a group back away from me. "Uh–oh, everybody. Hide the microphones. Jules's having another meltdown."

"Back off, man" Joey warned.

"Shut up, Kevin; that's enough." Cari angrily scowled at him.

"What? Can't she take a joke?" he asked.

"I'm warning you. Lay off." Joey stepped closer to the net.

"What are you going to do about it?" Kevin came toward Joey.

"Joey, forget it. He's an ass. Just ignore him." I pulled his arm as I felt the stinging on the side of my face.

A girl on Kevin's side of the net was looking a bit perturbed. "Can we play, already?"

"Yeah! Shut up, Kevin," Savannah called out.

Joey and Kevin continued to stare each other down as the game continued. I decided to raise my competitive streak and hopefully snuff out the memory of the most recent mishap instead of walking away with my tail between my legs. Joey and I played well off each other and made a great team. No matter how tough the play was, I was always prepped to set him up for one of his unforgiving spikes to the other side.

By the third game, I was overheated by the sun and became sluggish.

"Jules," Joey was concerned, "why don't you take off the hoodie? You look like you're roasting."

Imagining my unshapely stick figure ungracefully moving across the volleyball playing field, I grabbed the zipper on my hoodie as if preventing Joey from unzipping it and leaving me completely exposed. "No, I'm fine," I insisted.

Cari could see the dread plainly on my face and like so many times in the two years we've been friends, she came to my rescue. "Hey, Jules, why don't we take a break from volleyball and grab a bite to eat barbecue over at the tent?"

I wasn't hungry, but was thankful for the exit she gave me. She quickly made up her sandwich and found a spot on the lawn to picnic with Tripp and Savannah. I stood over the meat, trying to decide whether I wanted the pulled chicken or the pulled pork when I heard Broderick's smooth, deep voice.

"How are you doing, Jules?" He stood across from me at the food table.

"Fine." My forced disinterest hovered in the distance between us.

"You look nice today."

Dropping my jaw, I looked to him with disbelief. "Are you kidding me?"

Two sets of female eyes from beside the corn on the cob tray watched closely with perked ears. I could see in my peripheral that it was Loni and her best friend Casey.

"No, really." He cleared his throat and furrowed his brows trying to make his point. "You look good."

Loni and Casey, with their sun-streaked blonde hair, stood behind him and started snickering at my homely appearance, rolling their eyes with unreserved disapproval in his choice of words. My self-consciousness kicked into overdrive with the stares and stifled giggles, so I zipped my jacket up to my neck.

"Have you been on the lake any today?" He thumbed back to the water, unmindful of our small audience.

"No," I answered, thinking about my unappealing bathing suit-clad body that resided beneath the suffocating hoodie I was wearing. "I don't plan on getting in the water at all. It's not my thing. It would be a bad idea…if you catch my drift."

Again, despite my comfort around him, I fought to become *un*comfortable, hating myself for allowing Broderick to be a distraction from my goal of self-preservation.

Loni finally spoke up as she coldly stared at me. "Could we please move it along so that *we* can eat?" She leaned into Casey and whispered loudly, "Not that my appetite isn't ruined now anyway…"

Normally, my monster would retaliate with hostility to the offending party, but at this moment I was willing to play the peacekeeper to rid myself of my current weakness—Broderick Cooper. I bit my tongue, turning back to Broderick and shrugged in relieved defeat.

Like a gentleman, Broderick apologized to the girls for holding up the line. He then turned back to me and smiled. "Talk to you later, Jules."

Desperately, I wanted to partake in all the action that so many were enjoying on the lake. I actually loved being in the water during the dog days of a Tennessee summer. My thoughts began to linger on the idea of sharing a jet ski with Broderick. How it would feel to wrap my arms around his waist as he skidded across the water, jerking the handles to spin out of control, as others had done so many times today already. I marveled at the thought of pressing my cheek to the bare skin on his back as I would cling tightly to him; the spray of the water cooling my exposed cheek and my long hair whipping in the wind. *Oh, how he would smell! Would he mind if I sat closely behind him? Is that what he wanted—to use the excuse of preventing me from slipping off as an alibi to hold him tightly?* I knew Joey did that when he and my sister went four-wheeling. I was truly enjoying these thoughts until my insecurity kicked in.

Would Broderick be repelled by my long skinny arms? My boney body would look like a gaunt zombie, a creature parasitically attacking his lean, muscular physique. The disgust would fill the expressions on everyone's face on shore. On his face, too.

It was ludicrous of me to even daydream about this unrealistic scene. He wasn't even remotely interested in me; he probably felt sorry for me—for my lack of judgment on those I trusted, people I've dated. I needed to stay far away from Broderick Cooper. His very presence preyed upon me like an endangered species.

My stomach recoiled in knots from the realization that that my ignorant weakness for beautiful and popular guys at our school was still intact. The knots tightened as yet another popular guy at our school, Erik Peterson, grinned and winked at me when he reached across the table to grab a napkin from the stack in front of me.

What's his game? Erik was the kind of guy to flirt with an ugly girl just to get a laugh. I thought as I reached up to feel if anything was hanging out of my nose. I closed my lips tightly in a quick smile back just in case there was something in my teeth.

My cheeks flushed as I felt humiliated by my own assumption—that Erik was flirting with me for a laugh. For a bet. The anger I still felt toward Kevin Overby wasn't helping, either. My cheek was still stinging from where the ball made contact. *I can't breathe!* The humidity was cooking me. The sweat began pouring in streams down my back and dripping from my temples. My eyes began to burn from the sweat's salt. No. It wasn't sweat. I could taste the salty tears as they trickled down to my lips. My head dropped in defeat. Self-pity was going to devour me until there was nothing left; I simply could not fight it.

I ran out of the tent and toward the entrance of the park. This day had turned sour for me and I felt I was better off just going home instead of ruining everyone else's day. I made my mind up to just walk back to my car parked in Savannah's yard and call Cari once I was already driving away, that way she couldn't talk me out of leaving.

I was already on the road that wrapped around the lake and led to Savannah's when I heard Joey calling after me. I turned around to see him sprinting in my direction.

"Jules, where are you going? It's not even sunset and you're leaving?" He caught up to me and kept pace at my side.

I groaned. "Joey, I don't want to be here. I'm miserable and—"

"Well, take the jacket off."

"It's not the jacket; it's me. I'm just in a bad mood..."

Joey frowned. "Is this because of Kevin Overby? Ignore that pansy-ass rich boy, Jules."

"He's only part of the reason." I rolled my eyes at the memory of being hit in the face with the ball. "I think Erik Peterson is making fun of me, too. It was weird. He winked at me and..."

Joey laughed. "*That's* what's bothering you? Are you kidding me? He probably really likes you—in his own sick twisted way."

"What? You know as well as I do he does that to some girls for laughs."

"Yeah, but you aren't just *some girl*. You're Jules Taylor—singing extraordinaire! But watch out for him. He's almost a bigger douchebag than your last choice of boyfriend." Joey put his arm around me and began turning me back around to walk to the park. I couldn't fight his endearing behavior to get me to stick around.

"And Broderick Cooper?" I asked.

"What about my boy, Broderick?"

"I think he's trying to make me look like a fool, too."

Joey shook his head. "No, ma'am. Broderick wouldn't know how to do that even if he wanted to. He doesn't have a mean bone in his body."

"I guess I just have a hard time trusting guys right now. Well, all guys, except for you." I chuckled and rested my head on Joey's shoulder as we continued to walk.

"Who can blame you?" Joey's mood shifted immediately in an apparent attempt to pull me out of my depression. "Hey, why don't we jump on one of those jet skis?"

"I think I'm just going to go home." Dreading the idea of exposing my body, I tried rolling away from him and walking back toward the car, but he grasped my wrist.

"Oh, come on! Have fun! You're at a celebration. Besides, this may be your last night of freedom for a while."

"That's true." His reminder of my impending return to my jail sentence sealed the deal for me. "Can I leave my jacket on?"

"Suit yourself, psycho, but it's going to get wet," he muttered. "You and that stupid jacket."

We walked back into the park and over to the lake where the Jet Ski that Joey had borrowed was docked.

"Do we have to wear a life vest? I'm gonna get hot."

"Take that stupid jacket off!" Joey exasperated while climbing onto the Jet Ski. In a silent protest, I twisted and grabbed the zipper to protect my outfit. Joey resigned, "Whatever. Just get on."

Eagerly, I hopped on as I heard a deep voice bellow in alarm, "Shouldn't you wear a life vest?"

Broderick was ripped from the group he sat with, standing tall. The engine of the Jet Ski erupted and I decided to pretend that I couldn't hear his request. Joey was oblivious to Broderick's concern as he tore off and darted across the lake toward the park. Although the current situation was nothing like I had imagined with Broderick, it was still enjoyable. As Joey maneuvered across the water in a weaving motion causing the sides of the vehicle to dip into the water, my toes clutched tightly onto my flip flops just as my fingers held on to the front of his life vest.

Joey slowed for a moment to turn around and shout over his shoulder at me, "Let's see how fast this thing goes."

I gave him the thumbs up and then reaffirmed my grasp onto his vest. The wind felt cool as the summer evening fell upon us. The rush was exhilarating. Joey twisted the vehicle in figure eights and tight three-sixties. We both leaned along with the force of each turn as he would gun the vehicle forward at an accelerating speed. He turned his head slightly to the side and shouted something inaudible to me.

"What?" I shouted back. My eyes followed his pointed finger to the center of the lake where Kevin and some girl recklessly maneuvered their jet ski.

Joey pushed the vehicle into the large ripples in the water left behind from a small boat. I could feel ourselves become airborne for a split second and then crash back into the water causing me to giggle nervously, giving him the encouragement to do it again. This time the landing was smoother and my grasp eased. Joey punched into another wave, lifting us back into flight and slamming us into another wave. My hair tie became loose on the impact and flew out into the lake, leaving my long hair to fly sporadically.

The sun was setting and the party lights on the park's dock glowed in the growing twilight. The sheriff's department began marking off the area of the fallout zone for the fireworks display. Joey redirected us back to the dock for the show. As he took the turn, my long, strawberry tresses smothered our faces. I quickly reached my hands around to the back and began twisting my hair and stuffing it into the hood of my jacket. As I locked my legs firmly onto the seat for a little security, I heard Joey curse over the roar of the motor. We had become unwitting participants in Kevin's game of chicken. Joey quickly twisted the vehicle to prevent a collision as I let go of my hair and fumbled for a grip on Joey. And just as I heard the slicing scream of the girl riding with Kevin, my own body began soaring through the air. I was only aware that I was no longer attached to Joey or the Jet Ski when I saw them both flip under and vanish into the murky lake water. The impact of my back slamming into the water felt more like I was being rammed into a brick wall; my long skinny arms and legs reaching and kicking still as I sank into the dark water.

My head filled itself with insurmountable dread as my gangly body awkwardly twisted and my flailing limbs tried to keep from plunging into the lake. It seemed impossible to avoid a scene when I resurfaced. In a snap decision, the idea of attempting to swim to the other side of the lake, closer to Savannah's house where my car was parked. As ridiculous as I knew it probably was, I still found the plan brilliant. The lake wasn't big and I was positive that I had the energy to make the swim. I could easily drive home and avoid a spectacle. Sure, Joey would notice that I never resurfaced, and he would freak out for a little while until I called him to let him know I made it safely home. It was worth the shot.

The hood of my jacket caught onto a sunken branch of a tree and I reached behind me to untangle without much luck. My arms and torso felt heavy from the soaked jacket that weighed me down. Suddenly, I felt an iron grasp around my torso. The panic of drowning rushed through me as I envisioned either an incompetent swimmer or a masked madman chained to a rock holding me under water. I fought to wriggle free of the grasp, my jacket twisting awkwardly around me and hindering my strongest push to free myself and swim away. I began kicking at the shape and readjusting my jacket. His large hands grabbed the front of my jacket and in one strong, vicious jerk he ripped my jacket at the zipper and pulled the material off my arms. Carelessly, I tried screaming at him for ruining my favorite jacket but instead inhaled a large amount of the nasty lake water. I tried to cough and expel the unnatural inhalation but I only managed to refill my lungs with more water.

Between the violent contorting and grabbing of my body and the lack of air in my lungs I fell limp, like a rag doll. His arm wrapped ferociously around my flat chest and pulled hard to bring me to the surface. Like a vise, the arm squeezed me tightly causing my chest to heave and breathe in the night air. My throat felt like a meat grinder as I continued to cough lake water out of my lungs. It felt as though they were filled with fire. I had become weak from the underwater struggle and the fight to breathe.

I could hear the moans and murmurs from the nearby audience. Certain that it was Joey swimming me to shore, it confused me to see him racing by on the jet ski and jumping off onto the dock. I was pulled up to the flat surface, scraping my back against the rough grained wood of the dock.

My body was thrown on its side and the meat grinder that once was my throat completed its course of driving out the fluid I was heaving from my lungs. The warm water rushed out the side of my mouth and spewed out my burning nose.

Broderick! Is she okay?" I heard Savannah's voice shake.

Broderick? My mind tried to comprehend the name to the question. I looked over to see a small crowd of people pulling a very soaked Broderick Cooper away from me, over to a chair and draping him with a towel. His friends hovered over him asking him questions in awed voices, but he sat silently staring at me, his eyes were wide with alarm.

As I stared back at him, the anger and humility brewed within. He must think I'm a hopeless cause to drown after being thrown from a jet ski and because of his unnecessary rescue, I nearly *did* drown! Not to mention that he shredded my favorite hoodie like an animal! I wanted to storm over to him and punch him in the face.

Joey pulled me up to a sitting position and held my face in his hands. "Jules! I am so sorry."

"Are you okay?" Erik Peterson leaned in—a little *too* close for my taste.

"I'm fine," I growled as I stood up and pushed my way out of the overbearing crowd of onlookers.

"Your family is going to kill me…" Joey said nervously as he remained close by.

The angry monster inside of me began clawing its way up again, like last spring and a thousand times before when my temper got the best of me. I tried swallowing him back down.

"My family doesn't need to know."

"God, Jules! You don't think they're going to hear about this?"

I broke away from Joey only to be met by an onsite medic. The medic led me to over to the medical tent where I sat on a rickety chair. I needed to be alone. I didn't want to tempt fate; recreating another meltdown in front of spectators. There was never a forewarning of my inner monster's appearance.

Unfortunately, of all the doctors in the community to be working there, it was Savannah's dad—Dr. Blythe. Savannah entered the tent and quickly stepped over to me, wrapping a towel around me and rubbing my shoulders. Dr. Blythe twisted a chair around to face me and began examining me. My eyes burned as he tilted my face toward the tiny flashlight he held in his hands. He moved behind me and placed a stethoscope on my back.

"Take a deep breath, Jules," the doctor requested. He was apparently content with what he heard, because he packed the stethoscope back in his bag and looked me over. "You feel okay?"

I nodded my head though I felt furious and embarrassed.

He looked up at his daughter who was standing behind me. "She's fine, Savvy." He then shifted his eyes to me. "You're fine. Next time wear a safety vest."

I bit my tongue as he smiled at me.

"Savannah, let's give Jules some privacy." He led her out of the tent.

For a few seconds, there was peace. Then an angry onslaught of sobs began climbing its way out of my burning chest. Before I could release them, I heard his voice again.

"Are you going to be okay?" I peered over to see Broderick Cooper standing in the entrance, his clothes drenched while he remained wrapped in a towel.

My face burned with the resentment I felt toward him. This was the perfect opportunity I was waiting for to strangle him. I felt my body tremble from the fury I held inside.

"Yeah, no thanks to you," I practically hissed.

"Are you suicidal or something?" he angrily asked. "You nearly drowned!"

I spun at him. "You *attacked* me! You freakin' tore my jacket off of me like some animal! *You* nearly killed me!"

"I thought you couldn't swim!" he sputtered with confusion.

"Wh-What?" I stammered. "I can swim just fine..."

"No..." He shook his head, his eyes fogged over in confusion. "You said that you couldn't swim."

"I never said that!"

He continued to shake his head. "You said that you weren't getting in the water, that you didn't want the others to make fun of you."

"I was talking about my body!" My raspy voice shrieked and I fought tears.

The realization of his folly sank into his expression and broke through the fog in his eyes.

Holding off a crying jag that was desperate to ensue, I gritted my teeth. "You made me look like a fool." He reached out and touched my shoulder to comfort me but I swiftly knocked it away. "Don't! You are not allowed to touch me."

"I'm sorry," he whispered. "I didn't know. I misunderstood…."

I looked out from the tent to see everyone setting up their chairs and claiming their spots for the fireworks show. My Fourth of July was ruined.

"I don't want you to regard me as some heartless bastard you've apparently already mistaken me for."

I felt the tear in my heart at the truth of what he'd said. Already I'd tossed Broderick into the mix with Gavin and all the other douchebags of the world. Broderick's intentions were questionable. There was never any doubt in my mind that I liked him, but I just didn't have it in me to trust him. Once burned…

He stepped closely behind me. In the corner of my eye I saw him raise his hand to reach up and touch me again, but he stopped short. He released a ragged breath and stared out at the groups of people enjoying the twilight as it began to fall.

"What do you want me to do?" He quietly spoke.

I stared ahead, never giving him eye contact. "I want you to stay away from me, Broderick." I left him standing speechless and alone in the tent.

Cari, Savannah, and Tripp were sitting on a blanket with Natalie, Joey, and Amber when I found them, waiting for the fireworks to begin. I refused every plea they made for me to stay. My sister offered to come home with me, but I declined. I didn't want my anger and hurt to ooze onto her holiday enjoyment.

Leaving the park, I saw that the red Jeep was missing. Broderick had already left. I guess I ruined his evening, as well.

I was equally thankful to see my mom and dad were still out of the house when I returned home.

My shower consisted of a quick lathering and shampoo to rid myself of the dirty lake water. Even a long and leisurely hot shower couldn't relax me tonight.

Lying in bed, I could hear the boom of every firework explosion from across town and the footsteps of my family when they finally came home. My mom opened my door to check in on me and I closed my eyes to appear as though I were sleeping so I wouldn't have to talk.

After hours of tossing and turning in bed, I decided to grab my favorite red hoodie and shuffled to my front facing bedroom window and onto the roof. Positioning myself securely on the dormer of my window, straddling the sides, I leaned back, and gazed up. The moon was almost full and offered an overwhelming brightness against the night sky. Occasionally, I would see a rogue firework in the sky or hear a bottle rocket screech in the midnight air. My mind danced around the many horror flicks I had watched over the years—movies of zombies, witches, vampires, and werewolves. I always enjoyed the classics.

A gust of wind rustled the leaves on the tree at the corner of our yard rendering me anxious and restless. The eeriness was darkly stimulating and I sat up to let it envelope me. My heart rate increased as my eyes locked through the swaying trees and onto the lamppost that sat near the Cooper's detached garage behind their house. My breathing became slow and deep while I tried to glimpse movement from any of the windows. The entangled memory of Broderick pulling me out of the lake swept through my mind again and the claustrophobic sense of drowning set my heart to pounding.

"Ugh!" I moaned as I leaned back against the roof. A booming sound cracked the silence as a red shower entered the night sky. I let out a long exhale and whispered through my burning throat, "Broderick." My stomach tightened as his name fell from my lips.

The wind blew harder and through the leafy rustle, a man's scream shattered the darkness only to be choked off instantaneously with a gurgling howl.

"What the hell?" My voice shook as I scrambled to my knees and then struggled to my feet. Like loose ropes, my arms erratically grappled unsuccessfully for support. In my fear-induced state, I slid jaggedly down the joint of the window frame; twisting my body at the last minute to leverage my weight through the open window, praying that my grasp was secure enough not to let me fall.

My ears were tuned solely for the cry that no longer sounded but still echoed in my mind. I ricocheted off the window seat and onto the floor, flipping onto my backside in one strong jolt and expecting to see the predator that howled into the night.

Nothing.

My shallow breaths and thundering heart became the central resonance to the ensemble of the faint swoosh of wind. The billowing eyelet curtains bordered the now quiet night sky.

I stared at my bare feet and wiggled my toes; one of my sandals was gone. I couldn't force myself to peek over the edge of the roof to see it lying on the dewy ground below. I imagined some, creature was at that very moment climbing to the roof for its eventual assault. I jumped up and shut the window and steadily backed away from it, my eyes never leaving the malice that waited beyond the pane of glass.

Instinct

THE DROWNING INCIDENT WAS the first thing my mother brought up at breakfast the next morning before my 6 a.m. class. "Good gravy! Does *everyone* know?"

"Juliana Irene, did you really think we wouldn't find out?" she said. "It happened in front of the entire town during a national holiday celebration."

"I just didn't want any of you to worry. Nothing serious happened," I assured her as I dowsed my cup of coffee with sugar.

"Julie, you nearly drowned. That's not considered serious?" Her voice was tense with concern.

"Mom," I assured her, "I was fine, everything was under control. *Really*. It was just a small misunderstanding."

"And Joey saved you?" she asked.

I frowned at the memory of Broderick and his heroic act and how I had treated him afterward. "No, it was someone else. And the other guy didn't really *save* me; he just kept me from swimming to the other side of the lake."

"And *why* were you trying to swim to the other side?" she asked with a tone of incredulity.

I groaned. In hindsight, I could see that attempting to swim across just to save face was one of my most ignorant ideas ever. "I didn't want everyone making a big deal out of it. It was embarrassing. I was mortified! I was just going to swim to the other side and leave the party, hoping no one would notice."

Mom cackled as my dad shook his head in disbelief.

"And this other boy made you swim back to the party?" She then asked.

"Well, not exactly. He practically dragged me back." I sipped the coffee and contorted my face realizing I forgot the vanilla creamer.

My dad, who had been eating in silence at the breakfast table listening to our conversation, spoke up. "What did you say his name was again?"

"I didn't." I replied flatly.

Natalie slipped in the kitchen without us taking notice. She, too, had an early appointment this morning—cheerleading practice. Easing behind me to grab a piece of bacon my mom had just fried, she answered for me. "It was Broderick Cooper."

"Our *neighbor*? Evelyn's grandson?" My mom was bursting with interest.

"Thanks a lot, jerk." I whispered to Natalie. She grinned widely in response.

I was unwilling to divulge any more information, afraid my face would say too much to my parents—especially my mother, who knew me all too well. She would immediately catch on that I liked Broderick, although I was still working hard to convince myself that I didn't.

"But instead of thanking him," Natalie continued, "she bit his head off."

"Jules, why would you behave so ungratefully?" My mother was appalled.

I became defensive. "Because, I told you—he really didn't *save* me, mom. He nearly killed me is what he did. I was fine until he decided to play Superman."

"You mean Aquaman," Natalie corrected in a witty fashion.

I conceded dryly, trying to downplay my interest in Broderick Cooper. "He was about as effective. All Aquaman ever did was talk to the fish."

Natalie was shaking in laughter at my dry humor. "Really, Jules, he was trying to save you."

"Talking to the fish," I repeated.

"Savannah said that she had never seen anything like it before." Natalie announced with excitement. "She said it seemed like he was making his way to the lake before the collision even occurred. Nobody on shore was even aware of anything dangerous going on until he sprung to his feet! It caught everyone's attention. Like, totally intense. She said that before anybody could even register what was happening, he was swimming across the lake like a mad man to get to Jules." She chewed silently on a thought before raising her eyebrows and adding, "It sounds hot. Wish Amber and I had gotten to the park a few minutes sooner to see it."

Mom rolled her eyes with a laugh. "Oh, Nat."

"It was stupid. I didn't *need* his help," I reminded the family sourly, ignoring the butterflies in my stomach as I heard the heroic account. Secretly, I thought it sounded incredibly romantic.

"So," Natalie paused dramatically. "Is there something going on between you and Broderick?"

I was shocked at the forwardness; it could only mean that she was aware of my feelings. "No! I hardly know the guy." It wasn't completely a lie.

"He lives *right next door*!" She bellowed with incredulity. "And you have summer school with him."

I shot a glance to the clock and was thankful to see I had to leave for school. "I gotta go. See you guys after class."

I grabbed my purse and book bag then reached for the door handle just as my dad called out to me.

"Wait a second, Jules." His voice was always so commanding.

"Yes, Daddy?" I worried that somehow I was about to be in trouble for trying to keep the incident a secret.

"Your mom and I were talking last night after we'd heard what had happened. We saw that you even came home much earlier than your curfew..." he began.

"Am I in trouble?"

Mom smiled as Dad continued. "No. Actually, we feel that you've paid for your irresponsible actions last spring and that it's time to lift your punishment permanently."

My eyes widened as a smile grew on my face. "Really?"

My parents nodded in reply.

I ran over and hugged Dad's neck, then did the same to mom as I made my way back to the door to leave. "Thank you so much! You have no idea how much this means to me!"

"Just show Broderick the same appreciation when you get to school," my mom requested. "I raised you better than that."

"Yes, ma'am. I will. Thank you! Love you." I edged out of the door as they said their goodbyes to me. I was on cloud nine, having every intention of holding up my end of the bargain—to thank Broderick for his good deed.

This would also mean that I would have to apologize for how I treated him, too. That was going to be a hard pill to swallow, but worth it if it meant I could be near him and talk to him. I also wanted to ask him if he had a dog—to put my mind at ease over the startling howl I had heard last night.

But in class, Broderick never even looked at me. He didn't seem angry, just distant and involved in something more interesting. Algebra. I reminded myself that this is the result from what I had asked of him, but that didn't put me at ease. Because of that, those four hours of class felt like an eternity. In that time I built up my confidence and beat down my pride enough to decide I was going to have to speak to him before he went home. If I didn't, I would have all weekend to talk myself out of it by Monday.

Because of Kevin Overby's lack of tolerance for staying awake in class, Mr. Muir kept us in class five minutes later to inform us that if any of us slept through his class, he would count us as absent from now on. As he finished this warning, he dismissed us, and Broderick was the first one out of the door. Throwing my books and papers into my book bag, I scrambled to get to catch up to him. He was stepping through the exit as I entered the hallway and burst into a sprint toward him. Slipping through the double doors for the hall exit, I scanned the parking lot for his red Jeep; however, what I zeroed in on was the sandy blonde male standing next to my car. Erik Peterson.

Broderick said hi to Erik and continued strolling past him to his Jeep. He watched Erik over his shoulder for a few paces with frown knitted upon his brow then got into his Jeep. I wasn't sure why Erik was at my car or if he even meant to be standing so close to my car, but at this minute I didn't really care. My goal was to get to Broderick before he drove off—before I lost my nerve.

"Jules, can I talk to you for a minute?" Erik stepped forward from my car.

I stopped in my tracks to tell Erick to wait for a moment, but he was already moving toward me. I glanced over at Broderick as he sat behind the driver's wheel and turned on the engine. I took a step closer to the Jeep and opened my mouth to ask Erik to wait a moment.

"Isn't this your car?" Erik asked with a chuckle. I must've appeared confused to him—with a nervous look upon my face and walking *away* from my car.

"Yeah, it's mine...I just..." I was trying to find a nice way to excuse myself.

"I wanted to talk to you yesterday at the park, but you left before the fireworks," Eric continued.

My cheeks became warm as he mentioned yesterday's almost-drowning incident at the park. I was certain Erik was about to tease me over it.

"Oh, well...I had a curfew," I told him, giving most of my attention to Broderick as he sat in the Jeep watching me and Erik. I wondered if he was trying to listen in to our conversation.

Erik raised his eyebrows. "That's an early curfew. The fireworks started at nine thirty."

"Well, I...uhm...had school this morning."

He laughed upon my awkward response. "Is your curfew always that early? How late is your curfew on Friday nights—specifically, tonight?"

My voice carried a high level of uncertainty. "My curfew depends on what I'm doing."

Erick flashed his beautiful smile and playfully raised an eyebrow. "...And what are you doing tonight?"

I scouted the area of any of Erik's friends, to see if I was being set up for a joke. It was clear of anyone in Erik's group. "Nothing," I told him.

Broderick put his Jeep in reverse and moved out of his parking spot.

"Would you like to go to the movies tonight?" Erik asked confidently.

Watching Broderick's red Jeep pull out of the parking lot lit a fire of frustration inside of me. What I *wanted* to do was jump in my car and chase him down; what I did instead was stupid and unexpected.

"Sure. What time tonight?" I asked.

No! I screamed internally. What was I thinking? I wanted to smack my head in that instant. I didn't want to go out with Erik. I never have! However, now that the damage was done, there wouldn't be any take-backs. I would just have to make sure that this was a one-time deal only.

Cari and Joey were hanging out with Natalie when I got home and I dreaded having to admit to them my folly of agreeing to go out with Erik tonight. The three of them were in the family room, with a semi-fierce rivalry over a video game. I stood in the doorway, listening to their playful banter.

"I can't maneuver my car from this angle!" Natalie lamely excused as Joey heartily laughed at her. "I usually play from where you're sitting. I quit."

Cari rolled her eyes. "You always quit."

"Quitter!" Joey leaned back in the recliner and relaxingly continued to defeat her. "Yup. I'm in the chair of power."

Natalie dropped her control and stared at him in disbelief. "That chair is pink! How powerful can it be when it's pink?"

Cari continued concentrating on her game against them, but dryly remained in the conversation. "The pink chair of power…sure."

He scowled. "You're just jealous."

Natalie was beautiful, inside and out. Only fifteen, she easily befriended everyone because of her calm nature. She was compassionate and laid back. Her smile was always sure to light up a room. Unlike mine, hers was perfectly shaped. Her teeth would glisten against her sun kissed skin. We were both thin; she, however, had enough weight on her to give her the curves that belonged on a young woman. She always looked healthy and glowing.

Joey suddenly jumped up. "Ooh! Yeah!" He danced victoriously at Natalie and Cari. "In your face!"

Natalie looked over to see me in the doorway and rolled her eyes. "Catch that? The pink chair of power just helped Joey win."

I laughed at her dry humor.

Cari jumped up. "So, rumor has it that you were just ungrounded." she probed curiously.

"The rumors are true." I grinned as I let my book bag and purse fall from my shoulders.

"So what are we doing tonight to celebrate?" She asked.

I winced. "I sort of already made plans."

Cari dropped her jaw. "With who? Savannah?"

"I wish," I hesitated. "Not quite…"

Joey's head jerked knowing the sound of my tone. I was clearly hiding something. "You have a date or somethin', Jules?"

"Sort of. It's no big deal," I replied embarrassed.

"Whatever!" he laughed tauntingly as a big brother would, tossing his control onto his 'pink chair of power'. "Who's the guy?" He was crowding around me with a sly grin on his face.

"Is it Broderick?" Natalie asked eagerly.

Cari laughed and wrinkled her nose in distaste. "Broderick Cooper? Boo! He's such a boy scout!" Cari clarified with criticism. "You have *got* to be kidding me."

If she hated the idea of me and Broderick together, she was really going to hate the truth. "No. It's Erik Peterson."

A bewildered hush filled the room. Joey opened his mouth to say something as Natalie reached over to cover it. Natalie looked stunned as Joey scowled.

Cari broke the silence.

"You. Are. A dumbass."

"I second that." Joey crossed his arms as if he were waiting for me to give a viable excuse for my decision to accept this date.

Natalie raised her hand, asking for permission to speak, but Joey pulled it back down. She asked anyway. "*Why* Jules? It's *Erik Peterson*. He's a complete douchebag; just like Gavin. He uses girls. Jules, you *know* better than this."

"I honestly don't know what happened. I was actually in hurry to go somewhere when he asked and I think I just said yes so he would leave me alone." My tone was whiny.

"You can't trust him, Jules," Joey stated.

"He's after one thing and one thing only. You need to cancel," Natalie pleaded.

"Well, I can't cancel now; I'll look like an ass if I do."

"You look like an ass already," Cari informed sourly.

I looked at the other two to see if they agreed with her. Natalie looked worried. Joey shrugged. "I just think you should follow your instinct on this one. That's all," he said.

Pouting, Cari grabbed her purse and headed toward the door, leaving. "Don't call me when he breaks your heart like Gavin did. That was a dumbass move on your part and I'm not picking up the pieces."

Her chastising words cut deep. I would've canceled the date in a heartbeat if I thought I wouldn't be judged for it later. I felt like I had taken on enough judgement thrown in my direction lately. Good guy or bad guy, breaking plans with someone at the last minute just felt wrong so I was willing to suffer through the evening.

Date from Hell

MY NERVES WERE SHOT by the time Erik arrived.
Standing in the hall just outside of the living room, I watched Joey torture Erik with asinine questions and sarcastic remarks. Joey must have felt that the proverbial intimidation torch had been passed onto him since my dad was working late. However, this was not at all how my dad would handle Erik. My mother couldn't get a word in edge-wise and Natalie stood in the kitchen door stifling giggles as she sipped her soda. I cleared my throat and took a few steps forward to break it up. Joey, my mom, and Erik all twisted around to see me enter the room and Natalie began gulping her drink to hide her laughter.

Erik stood up and walked over to me in his confident and tall stature. "Wow! You look absolutely breathtaking."

Oh, brother! I felt my eyes roll as I dropped my head in embarrassment at his remark. I was well aware of what I was wearing and there was nothing *breathtaking* about it. A polo and a pair of shorts. Joey, however, chuckled and I slapped him on the back of the head.

"What movie do you two plan on seeing?" Mom was finally able to squeeze in a few words as Joey continued his chuckle.

Natalie immediately jumped on the subject at hand. "Jules hates comedies," she warned.

Smiling at Natalie, I internally thanked her, for I hated today's comedies and wasn't about to spend an evening that included the two hour torture of an unintelligent, vulgar comedy. They were the next worst thing to chick flicks, in my opinion.

"I have no intention boring your sister this evening," Erik assured Natalie. I became rigid as he rubbed his hand on my back, but he remained oblivious.

"Erik, one more thing…" Joey started back in, but my mom was quick to cut him off.

"You kids should get going so you don't miss the movie and aren't late getting back."

Erik shook my mother's hand and led me to the door. As we passed Joey, the two boys exchanged a heated and intense stare.

When the door shut behind us, I could hear Natalie burst into laughter and Joey start a rant on his opposition to my date. My mother spoke in response to both of them, but was so calm and quiet by comparison that her words were muted.

"Sorry about that in there. Joey had too much sugar for lunch or something," I said to Erik as he walked me over to his car, parked in front of the house in the circular drive.

He opened the door for me and I sat on the leather seat. Erik sat next to me and buckled his seat belt quickly before starting the gentle purr of the engine. His poor choice of music thumped and boomed in the car, rattling the windows. It was a slow and sensual beat of a bass, and I hated it.

"Isn't this hot?" He cocked his head over to the side to grin slyly at me.

I cringed at his use of the word *hot* and at his undeveloped taste in music. It was far from *hot*. My eyebrows raised in response, hoping it would relax my face. The words "baby" and "woman" were warbled a countless number of times, causing me to squirm in my seat.

As Erik decided to bore me with tales of his football greatness, I slid down into my seat like melted butter when I slowly began allowing my mind to wander to Broderick. It was the only thought that could block out the bad music and self-centered company. I wasn't as angry as I had still planned to be with Broderick. In fact, I wasn't angry at all anymore. For the first time ever, I was incapable of holding a grudge against someone.

Erik knew I hated comedies, thanks to my sister. Guys hated chick flicks, and that simply left *Battle over the Pacific* and *Secluded* and both movies were on my wish list, so I thought that my chances for a good movie were pretty strong.

In line for movie tickets, he reached for his wallet as we approached the ticket booth. "Two for *Forget Me Not*."

The misery rushed in. I hated chick flicks in general, and this one in particular was about a married woman being cheated on and after her divorce, she finds true love again. Not an original storyline. Not an original actress either; This was the same actress that had done the same movie at least three other times in the last four years, but with different titles and leading men.

Erik grabbed my hand and whispered intimately. "I bet you weren't expecting me to pick this movie, were you?"

My smile was like plastic.

Idiotically encouraged by my false approval, Erik tightened his grasp on my hand and pulled me closer as we walked past the concessions. I looked at the popcorn and candy display like a lost puppy. The smell of butter lingered around me as we entered in screen number two, where the two hours of torture would ensue. He led me to the dark corner of the back row and sat down. The surrounding couples were too busy locked at the lips to even notice us. Erik wrapped his arm around my shoulders and pulled me close to him. He clearly had no intention of actually watching the movie. My brain worked hard for a valid excuse to avoid Erik's intentions.

Distraction mode.

"I'm going to get some popcorn and something to drink. Do you want anything?" My voice shook from nerves.

He was obviously taken aback by my preference to eat instead of make out. "Uh, sure. I'll have a water."

The lobby was like a ghost town. Screams were coming from behind the doors of *Secluded* and loud, thundering battles rattled the doors where *Battle over the Pacific* was screening. *What I would give to slip away into one of those movies!*

"Why are you so distressed?" a voice from behind the counter called.

Chase Montandon, the theater's assistant manager, was my go-to guy for all my movie needs. On several occasions he was counted on for free movie passes and concessions. He appreciated my taste for masculine movies as well as slasher films.

I grunted as I pulled out my ticket stub and showed him the title.

He laughed. "You lose a bet or something?"

I groaned, "Feels like it. I'm on a date."

His expression was confused for a moment till he realized that I was not happy to be on said date. "Tough break, kiddo." He laughed as he began grabbing a bucket of popcorn. "You want the usual?"

"Yes. And add a water to that."

Chase slid the bucket over to me and I began nibbling on the butter drench popcorn. "How's *Secluded*?"

Chase threw his head back in feigned rapture. "Awesome! You're missing one hell of a movie in there. Do you two want to sneak over?" he offered.

It was debatable, but I resigned from any idea to escape. "Nah. I don't want to be rude." But I wasn't ready to join Erik yet. "Can I leave my stuff here while I go to the restroom?"

Chase waved me off and I left the lobby to hide out in a restroom stall for a few minutes to buy me some sanity. When I was mentally prepared to retrieve my concessions and rejoin Erik, I walked back over to Chase who was busy with a customer.

"You gonna be okay, kiddo?" he asked as he handed a beverage over to the guy at the other end of the counter. I dropped my elbows down on the counter and huffed in response. "Then go to one of the other movies, Jules." Chase walked back over to the other guy to hand him his popcorn.

"I don't want to be rude."

"How is *Battle over the Pacific*?" I toyed with the idea of sneaking off, trying to forget about who and what was waiting for me in the *Forget Me Not* screening.

Chase shrugged. "Not sure; I haven't been able to see it yet. I'm working two jobs now. I was lucky to catch *Secluded*," he lamented. "This guy's watching it right now." He looked to the opposite end of the counter. "Hey man, how's the movie so far?"

My heart leapt at the very sight of Broderick's smile. I couldn't control the smile that spread across my face. Forgetting who was waiting for me in the other movie screening right at this moment, I couldn't remember where I was or why I was here. I was just here with Broderick. That was all that mattered.

"Hi, Jules." He gave his closed-lip smile pulling his already tight jaw even tighter. He was tentative in his approach to me.

I was equally tentative. "So, the movie… is it good?"

"It's great." He stood tall over me—at least a foot taller. "What are you watching?"

Chase interrupted in laughter, "Jules has turned into an actual girl tonight. She's watching a chick flick."

Broderick looked confused with Chase's remark, so I explained as I crinkled my nose, "I don't like girlie movies."

Chase chimed in, "She's the only person I know that isn't a forty-something year old, overweight man who reads comic books and still lives with his mother while spending his free time surfing internet porn that lives for a good horror movie."

Broderick and I both laughed at his stereotype.

"You like *horror*?" He was intrigued.

"*Love* it." I corrected him with a mischievous grin and immediately became animated. "I love being scared. The adrenaline rush is like a drug to me! War movies and action movies are a close second. In fact," I pointed to the entry of the third screen "I'd rather be in there with you." The minute I said it I blushed. My hand flew to my mouth as I immediately tried to back pedal. "I didn't mean with *you*… I meant, uh… the *movie*. I would rather be watching the movie that you're watching."

"I know what you meant," Broderick chuckled.

Chase passed an awkward glance in my direction and eased over to another oncoming customer, clearly wanting an excuse to duck out of our uneasy turn of conversation.

"I saw Savannah out here earlier. Are you here with her and Tripp tonight?" Broderick asked.

"I *wish*. I'm actually on a date." I felt guilty to admit to Broderick why I was there.

Through his bangs, I could see his eyebrows raise as he nodded his head. He appeared to be well aware that I was on a date. I'm sure he heard Erik ask me earlier when we were in the parking lot. He set his drink on the counter and shoved his hands into the pockets of his jeans. "So does this mean that you're ungrounded now?"

"Yes! Thank goodness. My parents ungrounded me this morning after what happened at the park." I cringed at my sudden mention of the park, remembering of our horrible parting of ways. "Who are you here with?" I changed the subject.

He sounded almost apologetic. "I'm here with Jackson and Taryn."

"*You're* a third wheel?"

"What makes you think that I'm not the first wheel and *they're* not the second and third?"

Being a third wheel with Taryn and Jackson was confusing to me. It was beyond understanding for me how he could be so forgiving to them after betraying him the way they did last year.

We began to speak at the same time.

"I'm sorry, you go first," he said ruefully.

I hate apologizing; it made me feel like a weaker person. But I regretted what I had said to Broderick and how I treated him last night. For once, it felt okay to apologize. "I'm sorry for the way I treated you at the park last night. I had no reason to be so angry. I was so hateful…"

"Please, don't apologize. I jumped to conclusions. You didn't need that kind of stress; you've been through enough already and had every right to be angry with me. I have this hero-complex and I —"

"A *what?*" The phrase caught me off guard.

"My hero-complex," he repeated sheepishly. "I always feel the need to be a hero, assisting a person stranded on the side of a road with a flat tire or helping a little old lady with her groceries… or saving a drowning girl who isn't really drowning."

"*Hero-complex*," I said to myself and looked up at him approvingly. "I like that."

Chase hissed at us and motioned his eyes to something behind me. Before I could see what he was looking at, I heard Erik bellow from behind me, causing me to groan.

"Cooper! What's going on, man?" Erik strolled up and wrapped both of his arms around me. I cringed at the contact and immediately realized that Broderick undoubtedly saw my reaction.

"I was just talking to Jules before I head back in and watch the movie." Broderick held out his hand to shake, subtly pulling Erik away from me. Still after they broke apart, Erik seemed almost desperate to touch me in front of Broderick. Territorial.

"Thanks for saving my damsel in distress last night. If it weren't for you we wouldn't be here right now having such a great time, would we, Jules?" I lifted my eyebrows in silent response.

Broderick began to explain. "Actually, she's a great swimmer, I had just assumed—"

Erik laughed. "Did she tell you to say that?"

Broderick shook his head vehemently as his frown increased.

Erik ignored Broderick and tucked his head in the crevice between my neck and shoulder and whispered heavily. "Are you ready to go back to the movie?"

I sure as hell didn't want to go back to our seats, but I felt cornered and was determined not to cause a scene, as I often did. I had made it this far in the date with my talent of diversion, I could make it until ten o'clock without being pressured into anything I was unwilling to succumb to. I looked at my watch. *Nine o'clock! This is the longest date ever in the history of dates!*

Broderick lingered behind watching us walk back to the movie. I said goodbye to him over my shoulder, wishing that the hero could figure out a way to keep me in the lobby. He watched us closely until we passed through the doors and I wondered if he waited for me to give him a signal to save me—careful not to cross me again with any assumptions.

Once again, Erik trapped me in my seat, instantly putting his hand on my knee. In fact, he didn't hesitate with anything. He twisted around in his seat and smoothly ran his hand to the inside of my thigh and wrapped his other arm around my neck. He pressed his fingertips to my jaw line and turned my head to face him.

"I have never felt this way about anyone before," he whispered breathlessly into my ear.

"I'm sure you haven't." My sarcasm bled through, wondering how many girls he's given that line to. Wondering how many have actually fallen for it.

"Let it go. Let it all go," he purred as he ducked into my neck again, this time pressing his lips to my skin.

The greasy bile sat in my throat, waiting for its entry into my mouth, creating even more tension in my neck. I could feel pieces of popcorn kernels scratching my insides as they made their way back to the entrance.

"Erik, I'm n-not..." I stuttered at first, then gained my full composure. "I'm *not* going to do this with you."

He lightly nibbled my earlobe. "Jules, don't be like that. Gavin is not the only guy that can show you a really fun time."

The claim was sobering. "What? *Gavin?*"

Erik continued kissing my neck. I felt his tongue slide up to my ear. This was a nightmare. I thought about pulling back, but worried that maybe, somewhere in the evening I gave the wrong impression and had invited this in. My blood ran cold and I felt numb and unmoving. Erik was under the impression that I was an easy lay and it was clear who gave him this false information—Gavin Williams.

"Erik, stop. I don't want to do this," I warned. This time I was firm.

His hand slip from the back of my neck, down my arm, then under my shirt. "You won't regret this," he whispered. His thumb brushed the underside of my breast and I snapped.

Pissed off, I was disgusted and I was tired of being groped. Given no prior indication that my evil monster had crawled and nestled its way into my bile-filled throat, it scraped and clawed up the back of my tongue, bringing with it the hell that burned within. I tightened my fist and in a piercing silence, I saw my skinny arm shakily reach from far right of my peripheral, moving center and crushing into Erik's nose. His head snapped to the side as he cussed and held his face with his hands. I stood over him ready to throw my next punch, slightly aware that we were getting far more attention than the movie screen from those surrounding us.

Shaking, I grabbed my purse and began climbing over my seat, feeling the cool air of the theater on my exposed upper thighs as I inelegantly threw my leg over the back of the chair. Erik continued to hold his face, moaning explicit names at me as I started up the aisle. Regretful of my silent escape,

I turned back quickly to stand over him again and speak exactly what was on my mind.

"If you ever speak to me or touch me again, I will freakin' kill you. You got that, asshole?" My voice was rough and gravelly.

As I walked out of the theater, I could still hear the sarcastic sounds of awe and the muffled giggling from the back corner of the witnesses who sat nearby.

My face was hot and my legs wobbled like a newborn fawn. I rounded the corner to the concession to see Chase handing a large bowl of popcorn to a small group of girls who had just arrived for a late show. He looked up and immediately responded to my expression of anger and embarrassment.

"What the hell did he do?" he demanded as he came around the counter. Chase's normally pale skin was flared.

"I took care of it." I wasn't willing to share the embarrassing details of my horrible date with anyone.

"*Omigod*! What did you do to your hand?" Chase was already trembling with laughter.

I looked down to see a small cut on my knuckles from where his teeth must have made contact—I must have missed the target. The cut itself was very small, but the swelling and redness from the impact were intense.

"Do you need some ice for that right hook?" He figured it out.

"I just need to find Savannah and Tripp so I can get a ride home. Someone said they were here tonight." I was still trembling from the rush of adrenaline.

"They were here but their movie let out ten minutes ago; they're gone."

"Can I use a phone then? My phone took a swim last night."

He turned over his shoulder to see another line forming at the counter. "Just give me a few minutes and I'll get you in the office to make that call."

I plopped myself down on the bench in the lobby, thoroughly disappointed in my behavior. I should have been more assertive earlier. If I had drawn the line when I first felt infringed upon, I wouldn't be feeling so low and dirty as I do right now. I should've declined the date altogether.

Broderick suddenly came barreling through the theater doors, close on Taryn and Jackson's heels—concern and determination on his face. My head dropped in shame, hoping he would simply walk by me, afraid that he may have heard of my rumored promiscuity with Gavin as well. My desire to be hidden from the world became yet another unanswered prayer as I saw Broderick break away from his two friends and walk over to me and sit on the bench beside me. Relief oddly covered his face now. I kept my head lowered, avoiding eye contact.

"How was your chick flick?" He forced out a chuckle, a contrast to the alarmed look he had only seconds ago.

I sniffled with my misery. He leaned over and peeked around the draping of my strawberry hair.

"Jules, what happened? What did he do?" Aggravation grew quick in his voice. He touched my injured hand and I quickly pulled away as a guarded reaction to his touch. "Where is he?" Obviously, Broderick wanted to hunt him down.

"I left him in the theater and he never came out."

"How are you getting home?"

"Chase is going to let me make a phone call as soon as he's done over there." I pointed to the overwhelmed spiky-blond, buttering two popcorn buckets at once.

An idea flash in his eyes and he stood up and walked over to Taryn and Jackson who were patiently waiting for him. He spoke to them briefly then strolled back to me with Jackson and Taryn on his flank.

"We'll give you a ride home, Jules," Broderick said.

I didn't want to trust him. He made it too easy for me to feel at ease with him, and I wasn't even close to being ready to let my guard down, especially after a night like tonight. I shook my head. All of my free passes for being stupid had been used as far as I was concerned.

"No, I couldn't intrude. I'll be fine as soon as I call home."

"Jules, it would be no problem," Jackson spoke up, his arm around Taryn.

"You wouldn't be intruding. Let us take you home," Taryn insisted. Despite the strange smirk on her face, her tone was concerned and sincere.

"You live right next door so, it's not out of the way," Broderick persuaded.

"You still need that phone?" Chase asked suddenly.

I sighed quietly in relief, "Yes, thanks."

"We really don't mind making sure you get home." Broderick was adamant.

A smile broke at the corners of my mouth. "No thanks. I'm okay."

I quietly waved at the three of them. Taryn and Jackson began walking out and tugging Broderick by his shirt as he continued to watch me. I walked swiftly to the office with Chase, without looking over my shoulder, fearing that I would change my mind and carelessly place myself with Broderick.

Chase handed me the phone and I immediately began dialing my home without thinking. It rang once before I hung up. Chase looked at me as though I had lost my mind.

"I can't tell my family what happened tonight. It's far too embarrassing." I sat thoughtfully before I came up with a better plan—to call Cari, despite her request not to call her.

I walked back to the front lobby to wait for Cari and was stunned to see Broderick waiting by the bench.

"What are you still doing here?" I asked him.

He grinned. "I thought I should stay here with you until your ride arrives. I'm not sure if I'll rest easy tonight until I know you're home," he explained, filling me with a glowing satisfaction.

"So, how are you going to get home now?" There was no way Cari would let him in her car. He was popular and to Cari that deemed him as an 'untrustworthy douche-bag'.

"Jackson and Taryn are just across the street eating."

"Please don't miss dinner on my account," I pleaded.

He laughed. "I just downed a large bucket of popcorn and two drinks. I'm *not* starving." He was so easy to be around. Comforting, to the point I almost forgot why I was waiting in a movie theater lobby for a ride home. "Besides, I think they enjoy being alone. I hate third wheeling it."

"Wait a minute; I thought you were the *first* wheel?" I reminded him causing him to smile shyly. "All jokes aside, why are you with them?" I bluntly asked.

He shrugged with a chuckle, making himself comfortable beside me on the bench. "They regularly drag me out of the house. They think I'm too much of a homebody these days."

I couldn't understand how he wasn't actively pursuing anyone at our school; it wasn't like he was going to be rejected. And I was confused as to why he continued torturing himself by hanging out with his best friend and ex-girlfriend. Maybe that's why he wasn't pursuing anyone; he wasn't over her.

"And you're okay with them being together in front of you?"

"Jackson's like a brother to me, Taryn's good for him. They're great together. Why wouldn't I be okay?" He must have seen the confusion still on my face. "Oh, I get it. You think they're being inconsiderate with my feelings, don't you?"

I gave a small nod.

He leaned into me slowly. "Can I let you in on a little secret?" He leaned in closer to me and I could once again smell his clean, fresh scent. His breath warm against my cheek as he turned in toward my ear. "Sometimes...Correction...*Most* times—things aren't exactly what they seem to be." I flashed my questioning eyes at him and he pulled back, smiling with his smooth lips. "Only believe half of what you see, and *none* of what you hear, Jules." He nudged my knee playfully with his fist.

I said nothing, only stared at Broderick with credulous eyes.

He broke the silence and stood up. "I think your ride's here."

"Wow, Jules. Where have you been hiding your friend?" I heard Chase call out in awe as I looked out the window to see Cari tapping at the window of the ticket booth.

Spinning around to face Chase, I fought to keep the corners of my mouth from turning upward at his approval of my rebellious friend.

He spoke softly, in case she could hear through the glass. "Does she have a boyfriend?"

"No." I was no longer able to hold my composure. I was giddy for Cari even though I could tell Chase was far from her type. She'd never shown interest for clean cut guys like Chase. "I'll put a good word in for you."

I pushed the door open with my backside and faced Broderick, who was walking out with me. "Bye, Broderick. Again, I'm sorry about last night.

And thanks for…" I was grateful to him for so much, I didn't know what to say. "…for sticking around with me until my ride got here."

"I had fun. We'll have to hang out again during one of your other bad dates." I laughed as he smiled widely—dimples on each side of his cheeks.

Cari was walking slowly around to the driver's side of the car, watching us with a speculative glare.

"I'll see you on Monday." I waved casually.

"See you later." He shoved his hands into the pockets of his jeans and watched as we pulled out of the parking lot.

Cari didn't hesitate even a second when he was out of sight. "What happened with Mr. Wham-bam-thank-you-ma'am? And what the *hell* is going on with you and Broderick Cooper? And don't tell me that you just have a class with him or it's because he lives next door. I'm not stupid; I have eyes."

"But that's what it is; we just have a class together."

"I'm not buying that. I saw how you two were in the lobby. I wouldn't have been able to wedge a piece of notebook paper between you two," she hissed.

I couldn't help but marvel at Cari's perception. Did Broderick and I come across as friends? Maybe even something beyond that? I blushed at my wondering mind, thankful the thought was private and not on public display.

I explained to Cari about what had happened with Erik and how Broderick and Chase stayed with me, keeping me company after I had left my date. She especially loved the part where I punched Erik and was sorry that she missed it.

We were pulling up to the front of my house five minutes before my curfew when I decided to put a good word in for Chase.

She put her small car in park and turned slowly in a quick realization to face me.

"Are you kidding me, Jules? *Him?* I don't think so." She crinkled her nose and shook her head fervently.

"He's cute," I defended. "He's older, actually has a job, unlike the other losers you've dated, and he's got a great sense of humor—"

"That's code for 'dork'," she said under her breath. "He's too squeaky clean." She dismissed him without a second thought, and I sank in disappointment for my movie buddy.

"Your loss," I teased her. "Thanks for the ride," I said as I shut the door.

She leaned toward the passenger window. "Just remember, you owe me."

"I just tried to fix you up with Chase, what more do you want?" I chided her lightheartedly. She waved me off and drove away.

Cherry Cokes

JOEY'S BIRTHDAY WAS SUNDAY, so after church Natalie and I, with our narrow budget, decided to treat him to a cherry coke at Main Street Drug Store. It was one of the few remaining businesses still standing in downtown Crossville from a time long before mine. It carried that old-timey environment of the old man working the back pharmacy and the younger man working the front counter selling milkshakes and sodas. It was there I discovered the awarding efforts of actually adding cherry syrup to the coke as opposed to buying it premade in a can.

As I changed out of my church clothes into something more comfortable, the gentle afternoon wind whipped through my room from the dormer window beside my bed. My eyes drifted to the small window on the other side of my bedroom facing the woods separating our property from the Cooper property. My mind immediately wandered to Broderick.

The sensation that Broderick had an ulterior motive for befriending me was unshakable. Still, the draw to him was absolutely tenacious in every sense. But after what I just endured with Gavin, and now Erik, I could never trust Broderick.

Closing my eyes in resolution, my eyelids became a painted canvas. A perfect depiction of Broderick Cooper. In my mind's eye, I saw his strong and tight jaw, flawlessly sculpted, and his perfectly shaped lips. The endearing dimples he always seemed to subconsciously try to hide as he kept his beautiful, smooth lips together when he smiled. I was irresistibly enthralled with the steady thoughts dashing behind his brown eyes, emphasized by the thick brows that furrowed during his deepest thoughts. Broderick Cooper—the popular boy who didn't quite replicate the in-crowd. A flawless creature to me, and yet somehow he didn't appear comfortable in his own skin.

By the time I got to my car Natalie and Joey were already sitting in the front bench seat waiting for me.

"Just think, Joey, maybe after a few more landscaping jobs you'll be able to fix up that truck of yours and take *us* out to get cherry cokes," Natalie said cheerfully.

He grinned, his blue eyes beaming at the thought. "I'm actually thinking about taking the driver's test tomorrow—*finally*. Hope I pass," he thought aloud.

Unlike the friends he ran with, Joey's family didn't have a lot of money. His dad was town sheriff and his mom was a homemaker, so Joey resigned himself to rebuilding an old truck for transportation. He'd been working on it since before his sixteenth birthday, starting a landscaping business with Jackson and Broderick to pay for the parts he needed.

"Jules sucks at driving and she passed with flying colors," Natalie chimed as she unbuckled her seatbelt so she could lean closer to the mirror and apply lip gloss. I narrowed my eyes and stuck out my tongue.

We just entered city limits when I became distracted by the very familiar musical intro to a song on the radio as the DJ announced it, "... peeked at number two on the charts in the spring of 1987: *Don't Dream it's Over* by Crowded House..."

I love this song! I thought quietly to myself and instantly remembered the other person who claimed this song as their favorite as well.

As I looked down and reached for the volume knob, I felt a tire drop off the shoulder of the road and in a panicked split-second decision, I jerked the wheel back onto the road. Suddenly, a high pitched screech ripped through the walls of my head and pierced my ears. As I tried to make sense of the noise, I saw in slow motion the straight road before me slide to the left and around to my side window replaced by a small white house and large oak tree. I felt the odd sensation of swinging as I involuntarily leaned to the left—the warm window pressing against my head. Joey leaned hard on my right side, as well. The picture screen in front of me became a blurred image again of the road and then an even larger view of the white house with the tree.

With a hard gasp, I stared frozen in complete horror of the oncoming impact. I couldn't breathe. My short suffocation was interrupted by the sound of crushing metal and the explosion of glass. My body jerked forward, slamming my torso into the steering wheel. My disorientation was complete as time stood still for an insurmountable amount of time. *Has it been a full minute? Where am I?*

A light whimper came from my right and the engine sputtered to a final stop. I could hear the passenger door open but I still couldn't open my eyes. I began squeezing my lids closer together in hopes that would offer a springing reaction. I needed to *see* what happened.

"Jules." The weak voice shook to a moan.

Natalie! My eyes flew open at the sound of her voice to find the large oak tree was only a few feet in front of us, in the middle of the hood. Joey was picking his head up, reaching out to the dashboard for support.

My dazed eyes shifted frantically to my far right. Natalie was standing in the opened door. Her bewildered eyes, full of pain, rolled slightly and her body went limp. She disappeared from my view and my bewilderment intensified until I heard her body thump to the ground. In that moment, my brain snapped out of the fog that constrained my reactions. My hands were uncontrollably shaking as I fumbled with the door handle. I kicked the door open and wobbled to the other side of the car. A lump rose in my throat as I saw my younger sister lying helplessly on the ground in throes of obvious pain, but I couldn't see anything physically wrong with her.

Joey was shuffling out of the passenger door when I heard a voice call from the other side of the car.

"Is everybody alright?" A hefty woman soon leaned over us, assessing the damage.

Joey knelt beside Natalie and began talking to her as he battled his nerves.

The woman continued, "I've already called 9-1-1." She focused on Natalie, and her voice was gentle but urgent.

Within minutes, I heard the sirens approaching from town.

Natalie listened attentively to the older woman who remained close. I listened to her calming voice, never detecting the words. It was obvious Natalie had sustained the worst injury and the woman was trying to keep her calm. I just sat beside her and extracted my own comfort from the old woman, whose tree had just defeated my car.

I wiped my hand against the stream coming from my forehead, smearing blood on my hand and into my hair. My ears throbbed from noise of the sirens as the lights filled the peripheral of my vision.

I squeezed out of the group of crowding paramedics surrounding my sister and watched from a distance as I sank in guilt.

"Looks like the left clavicle is broken," one of the paramedics announced to the other.

I wanted to throw up. *I hurt my sister! I broke one of her bones!* My vision blurred and I felt faint.

"Ma'am" The young medical technician put her face in direct line of my eyes. "Let me help you." I must have nodded because she immediately assisted me onto a gurney and maneuvered a neck brace under my chin. I stared mindlessly for a moment, and slowly closed my eyes as the white clouds danced across the deep blue sky of this sunny Sunday afternoon.

The wait at the hospital dragged on until evening. It was confirmed that Natalie had a broken collar bone. Like her bone, my heart was completely broken for the pain I caused her. All I sustained was a few bruises and a small gash on the left side of my forehead from where I must have banged it against the window. Joey had a matching job done to his forehead after his head forced the rearview mirror through the windshield. His gash, however, warranted a couple of staples in his head and reminded me of Frankenstein's monster.

It was widely assumed by the police on the scene that Joey's right shoulder prevented Natalie from going through the windshield but inadvertently broke her collar bone. Joey would forever be Natalie's unwitting hero.

Upon returning home, I went straight to bed. Drowning in guilt, my hope was to let sleep separate me from my consciousness. Instead, the remorse woke me throughout the night, just enough to extend the torture. It didn't help hearing Natalie's sobs down the hall throughout the night as she tried finding comfort with her new limitations. She couldn't even escape the pain in her drug-induced sleep.

I knew it wouldn't make the pain go away and I was too ashamed to face her, but I so badly wanted to go to her room and apologize.

And hitting me almost as hard as the car had crashed into that large oak tree was the realization that I no longer had a car, making my misery intensify. *You're so selfish, Jules.*

My eyes flew open at the startling sound of laughter. I continued to lie in my bed trying to decipher the voices from downstairs in… *the kitchen?* Laughing with such force, they were too noisy and too chipper for this early morning, especially a morning that followed a day like yesterday. Then I heard the familiar guffaw from Joey. He was probably worried sick about Natalie and wanted to check on her first thing this morning.

I pulled my hair into a sloppy ponytail and slowly descended the stairs. Everything on me hurt. Soreness had set into every muscle of my body and I stiff-legged into the kitchen to see the commotion.

"Good afternoon, sleepyhead," mom called from the other side of the kitchen island. "Would you like a sandwich?"

Beaming through the windows, the sun reflected brilliantly against the pale yellow walls of the kitchen. My eyes strained as they adjusted to the brightness. Sure enough, Joey was leaning attentively toward Natalie at the kitchen table. She was donning a navy blue sling for her arm. He looked over and gave me a sly, loaded smile as Natalie stared at me with a confused and frozen smile on her face that I couldn't begin to decipher.

My mom waited for my response. It was then that a shockwave jolted through me as I noticed *another* person sitting in the kitchen with us. A body that was quite familiar, but not within these walls, not in my home. He turned slowly on the bar stool to catch my horrified gaze, smiling an eager boyish grin, his thick brows framing his caring eyes. His brown hair was not overly styled, but laid in an appealing windblown manner. He sat comfortably on the stool, stretching out his long and muscular legs on the stool next to him.

"Hi, Jules," Broderick shyly welcomed me.

"H-h-hi, B-Bro-Broderick?" I stuttered mindlessly as my hands subconsciously pulled the top half of the unzipped sweatshirt together to prevent his noticing that I wasn't wearing a bra. The astonishment of having Broderick Cooper sitting in my parent's kitchen was overwhelming. "What are you doing here?"

His cheeks turned a slight shade of pink at the forwardness of my question. "Well, we missed you in class today, so I thought I'd bring your homework by so you wouldn't get behind."

Speechless.

"I appreciate you looking out for Jules that way, Broderick." My mother smiled approvingly at me before she shifted her eyes back onto Broderick. "That's so kind of you."

"It's no problem, Mrs. Taylor."

My slow thought process finally caught up to the conversation. "Oh, crap! I missed class!" With a feeling of defeat, I leaned on the counter. I had missed a day of school which will inevitably prevent my absence this Friday for my girls' weekend getaway. "Why didn't someone wake me?"

"You needed your sleep. Did you want a sandwich, Jules?" she asked again.

"Um... turkey." Slowly, I walked over to join Natalie and Joey at the kitchen table—cautiously staring at Broderick.

"We were just talking about your Wonder Woman days, Jules" Joey grinned mischievously.

"What?" I was horrified as I shot a glance at my mother.

My mother, unaware or simply unconcerned of the embarrassment I would suffer from my past preschool years, just smiled and nodded. I shot a quick glance at Broderick to see his reaction to the story. He offered a consoling smile and seemed willing to forego the subject but Joey, apparently, was dying to give me a replay.

"So," he boomed, "did you really wear your grandmother's dress boots and aluminum foil around your wrists like Wonder Woman?" His roar of laughter was like nails on a chalkboard to me.

Looking at Broderick, I attempted to laugh it off, but it came out awkwardly. "I guess I had a hero complex as a kid?"

Joey continued barreling through. "Can you still fit into your Wonder Woman pajamas? What was it she called her again?" He asked my mom for a recap. He was having too much fun with this information; all at my expense.

"Wonn-o, Wonn-o" my mother repeated for the amusement.

"Ugh, you all hate me." The flame of humility burnt from my chest to my face. Only death could make this humiliation go away, and I didn't think it was coming soon enough to save me. Moaning, I buried my head into my arms as they were folded on the table.

At the age of three, while other girls were dressing as their favorite princess, I was enthralled with the idea of being a hero. Too difficult for me to pronounce my all-time favorite hero's name, Wonder Woman, I said *Wonn-o Wonn-o.*

A plate scraped across the bar top and I looked up the see Broderick thanking my mother, then taking a bite of his sandwich. *Oh, my gosh! He's eating here, too?* I quietly watched him chew as my mom continued to talk his ear off. *Why is he sticking around and getting to know my family?* I was just thankful that it was only the five of us, and not —

My dad. My heart sank as I heard the door in the basement slam shut. It just got worse. Groaning, I slid further down into my seat. My mom walked over and placed a turkey sandwich and a glass of milk in front of me. My nerves were shot and I was pretty certain that everything I swallowed would soon reappear. There was no possible way I could eat now.

My dad was still in his work uniform, but in his socks, not shoes. Mom hated when he tracked ink through the house which was often.

My dad stomped in the room, obviously trying to intimidate our new guest that was joining us for lunch. My mother, who was always more sympathetic to the boys that were subjected to my dad's subtle torture, enthusiastically made the introductions.

"Mike, this is our neighbor, Broderick Cooper. He brought Jules's homework over from class today." She was clearly delighted over Broderick.

Broderick bounced up from his seat and closed the distance, taking the initiative to shake hands. My dad was real familiar with the name and immediately became animated. "Broderick Cooper. It's good finally meeting you. Are you ready for your last season of high school football?"

If there was anything that could bond two men in this town, it was football. Natalie and I rolled our eyes simultaneously at the turn of their conversation.

"Yes, sir, we anticipate a good season. Isn't that right, Joey?" With his mouth too full to speak, Joey held up his fist victoriously to agree with Broderick.

Broderick was completely at ease with my dad, and that pleased me. As they carried on their discussion of football, I began to really notice how tall Broderick was. My dad was six feet and two inches tall, and Broderick was an easy inch and a half taller. He was relatively muscular and yet still lanky. Lean. His long legs and arms were perfectly sculpted with toned muscles. I was never drawn to guys that were too beefed up or scrawny and Broderick was neither. He was perfect.

I interrupted their football talk to ask, "Broderick, didn't you say that you brought over some homework for me?"

"Yes. I left it on the table downstairs."

"Let's get started on it then. I'm sure you have other things you would rather be doing today."

He turned back to his sandwich and glass of milk and began racing to consume them.

I immediately felt bad for being so brisk, and added, "No hurry, I need to change out of my PJ's, and I'll be right back." I also wanted to brush my teeth and fix my hair. Maybe I would even have enough time to apply some makeup as well?

"Just let me know when you're ready." He smiled widely, this time exposing the cutest dimples I had ever seen.

Walking out of the kitchen and toward the stairs, I could hear Natalie scoot her chair against the floor. "I've got to ask Jules something real quick," I heard her say.

Her steps were light, but closely following mine up the stairs and into my room. The butterflies in my stomach made it nearly impossible to concentrate even on the smallest task as taking steps. My heart was pounding so fiercely that I thought it would burst through my chest. I dug through my dresser in a frenzy looking for something to wear. Something casual enough that it wouldn't appear I had dressed to impress Broderick, yet that was exactly what I intended to do.

Natalie slipped into my room and quietly closed the door behind her; a squeal on the verge of breaking through her self-control.

"Jules! You've been holding out on me! What is going on?"

"I swear there's nothing going on. He just showed up to give me homework," I answered nervously as I dressed, not fully positive of my own answers. "I hardly know the guy."

"Give me a break!" She eased herself on the edge of my bed, trying not to jar her injured side. "A friend would just stop by randomly after class and drop the stuff off. He's sticking around. And let's not forget when he so heroically saved you from drowning…"

I pulled the rubber band out of my hair to brush it.

"I wasn't *drowning*," I retorted in my most nonchalant tone.

Natalie rolled her eyes. "He is into you, Jules."

I laughed it off. "Sure, sure…just like Gavin and Erik…" I was too short on time to straighten my hair so I placed it back into a neater ponytail and ran to the bathroom to brush my teeth.

Natalie stood silently studying my face in the reflection of the mirror. She then, chuckled delicately as she whispered in astonishment, "Broderick Cooper is into my sister."

Quickly, I hushed her nonsense. "How do I look?"

"Eh. You look like someone who's about to spend time with a *friend*," she sarcastically joked. She got up slowly and walked back toward the door.

"Nat?" I called to her. "How's your arm?"

She laughed wryly as she turned to face me in the doorway.

"Great right now, with the heavy duty pain killers I'm on. I am feeling a bit drowsy though," she added sleepily.

"I am *so* sorry. I just feel absolutely sick over what happened…" I said, dripping with remorse.

"It's not your fault." She paused for a moment as she started back to the stairs. "I mean, I had just stated before you did us in, that you were a horrible driver. No surprise here. Maybe it was instant karma." She pointed to the sling. She gave a lopsided grin as she left the room and returned downstairs to the kitchen.

Grabbing my Algebra book, I sprinted down the stairs to find Broderick still in the kitchen visiting with my dad, Joey, and my mom.

Natalie was sitting back at the table and observing Broderick closely, though she was clearly ready to succumb to the drowsing effects of the pain killers.

"I'm ready if you are," I called to him.

He stood up and shook hands with my dad again. "It was nice meeting you all. Thanks for lunch, Mrs. Taylor."

"Thank you for bringing Jules's work over." Mom was in heaven.

Dad patted him on the shoulder, "Don't be a stranger, Broderick." I couldn't believe it. In the three months while dating Gavin, my dad made it a point to steer him out of the house since day one.

"I won't sir," he warmly replied.

Broderick waved to Joey and Natalie and strode around the corner shyly pulling the corners of his mouth into a smile. He followed me down the steps to the family game room where I pulled two chairs out for us to sit at the small table.

"So what did I miss?" I asked. The pencil in my hand anxiously tapped an obnoxious rhythm as I waited for him to begin his "lesson". Today was supposed to be a review before tomorrow's test. *Who does he think he's kidding?*

His long and lean arms stretched across the table and his fingers interlocked. The uneasy smile on his face slowly developed into an impish grin that could have belonged to a person with a funny secret or an inside joke. He contained his composure, but the glint in his eyes gave him away as a guy who knew he hadn't thought his plan through well enough. Relishing his discomfort and the boyish charm of the whole act, too, I decided to increase the intensity for him, by drumming my pencil louder and staring him in the eye with immense impatience. I knew I had hit the nail on the head when he couldn't hold eye contact with me. His adorable performance had me on the edge of giggles, but I was determined that he would be the one to crack first, so I released a sigh of annoyance to evade the oncoming snicker. His irritation was even more alluring to me but I figured he'd suffered enough.

My mouth curled at one corner and his poise visibly withered. At this point, he knew I had caught him in a lie. He was merely playing along with me. He closed his eyes in one last attempt to control himself but a snicker escaped and all composure was lost.

"Y'got me," he admitted with a shrug. "There's nothing; it was just a review today."

"Why are you doing this?" I pleaded with seriousness.

"I was worried when you didn't show up for class." He drew a deep breath before answering. "I wanted to see if you were okay. Joey said you guys were in an accident?"

His confession of noticing my absence gave me a jab of satisfaction. I felt giddy and my stomach tightened as I was rendered speechless for a few short seconds before I gained the tenacity to play indifferent. I would not allow myself to foolishly fall for such a line that could be genuinely platonic or even worse a trap.

"Well, I'm still in one piece." I gave him a smart smile.

"What happened yesterday?" He leaned forward; his thick brows were puckered in concern.

"I simply lost control of the car." My recollection of the actual event was blurry; like trying to focus on an object through a window, during a heavy rain storm. Then I remembered the song that was playing just before the crash and how it had made me feel. *Who* it made me think of.

I gave him a rundown of how the accident occurred.

"Wow!" He leaned back and released a breath he apparently had been holding. "Your sister's lucky the worst she got was a broken bone. Without a seatbelt—"

"No joke!" I agreed. "Joey's bruised up and she's broken from the impact, but if they hadn't of clashed shoulders..." I trailed off, astonished at how truly amazing it was that no one was more seriously injured. "I can't think of what could have happened to her. I just can't go there."

He shook his head in amazement. "What happened to your car? I mean, not that it's more important than your sister, but *jeez*, Jules. It was a classic! I think every guy in town coveted that car." Gloom crept through his voice at the thought of my car no longer in existence. I was pleased that he was even aware of what I drove up until yesterday afternoon.

I replied back in a playfully regretful tone, "I killed it."

"No!" He threw his head back in feigned agony causing me to laugh. Broderick made it easy to relax despite my underlying paranoia and persistence to stay at a distance. "So, how are you going to get around, now?"

I shrugged. "We haven't given it much thought yet." Pressing the eraser of the pencil to my lips, "I'll probably end up having to rely on friends and family to get around." I dropped my head. "Ugh, I'm totally dependent on others now."

He simply nodded at my dilemma while his eyes appeared deep in thought. "Yesterday was Joey's birthday you know?"

Joey's birthday was a grimace-worthy reminder. "We were actually on our way to Main Street Drug Store to treat him to a cherry coke when we had the accident."

Without deliberating he pressed to his next train of thought as if the information I had just shared worked well with his arrangements. "Would you be opposed to me tagging along with the three of you for a cherry coke? I'll drive."

"Don't you have anything better to do today than play chauffer?" I stated suspiciously.

He reasoned, "We're neighbors."

"You hardly know me," I argued.

His mouth broke into a tiny smirk. "Can't we change that?"

I was willing to accept the idea of Broderick wanting to get to know me. We did, after all, have a class together. But the problem was that we had already been neighbors for a couple of years! Why would it matter now if we became friends? That didn't make a whole lot of sense to me. In addition to his questionable timing to be friends, there was still the impending fear that there was an ulterior motive.

My brain wouldn't stop turning: *Why does Broderick Cooper want to waste his efforts on someone like me? Maybe he doesn't think it will be a wasted effort? Not if he believed the rumor that Gavin undoubtedly started. Erik believed it to his own misfortune.*

I looked at him with suspicious eyes. "I guess. If that's what you want to do."

Natalie interrupted my confused scowl, holding her phone to her chest. "Cari's on the phone for you." She handed me her phone and left the room.

"Jules?" Cari's frantic voice rushed in the earpiece. "Are you okay? I heard you nearly killed Little Bits in a car accident."

Bad news travels fast. I cringed at the knowledge that my accident was already talk among some circles in town.

"I'm fine, just a little banged up." I heard a sigh of relief on the other end. "Natalie's fine, too. She broke her collar bone, though."

"I heard that it was a one car accident. Damn! Can't you drive?"

My confirmation was reluctant. "I just lost control."

Cari's excitement rang through. "Why don't you tell me all about it over coffee? I can come pick you up right now."

It took no debate. As much as I hated myself for my weakness toward him, I *had* to be with him. "I have plans right now." Broderick's face broke into a wide grin as he stared at his algebra notes.

"Doing *what?*" She pressed aggressively.

I didn't want to reveal my visitor, so I deflected her nosy question. "We can get together later. Is that okay?"

"When?"

"Hold on, let me find out."

I dropped the phone to my shoulder and turned around to face Broderick. "When do you think we'll be back?" I kept my voice low so Cari wouldn't figure out why I was currently unavailable.

"I don't have to be anywhere until three," his voice boomed louder than I expected and I wasn't entirely sure that he hadn't done it on purpose. My attempt to keep him a secret must have been obvious.

I placed the phone back to my ear. "How about some time after class tomorrow? I have a test and need to study—"

"*Who. Was. That?*" Cari asked.

I played ignorant. "I don't know what you're talking about."

"You are such a liar! Who do you have over there?" Cari was pushing hard now.

"Joey," I stated without lying.

"That was *not* Joey Burnett. Try again." Her voice was now playful.

"No," my answer came quick and shaky as I blushed.

"Come on, Jules! Who is it?" I could easily picture Cari in my mind, sitting on her bed and smiling as she bit her pierced tongue, trying to keep from laughing.

"No one," I insisted.

"Jules, I'll drive over there right now and —"

"Okay, okay!" I nervously rubbed my forehead, pressing the bandage against the stitches.

"Broderick Cooper." The name was light and inaudible through my low voice, clenched teeth and unmoving lips.

"Huh?"

Is she trying to make my life hell or is she really that deaf?

I tried again, just a notch louder, mouth still frozen. "Broderick Cooper."

"*Who?*"

"Broderick Cooper!" I shot a quick glance at Broderick, and he stifled an airy chuckle while I heard Cari burst into laughter through the phone. She was so loud he must have heard her, too. It was clear that she had set me up, and I fumed over the deceit. "Are you done?"

After she regained her self-control, she started giving me the third degree. "What's the story with you two? And you better come clean this time."

The last thing I wanted to do was explain the complex start of our unidentifiable relationship in front of him. "I'll fill you in about the *movie* over coffee tomorrow. Bye."

"*Movie?* Wait, what movie?"

Before she could ask any other convicting questions, I hung up. Broderick looked up and his eager expression changed my entire view of the room. Everything seemed brighter.

"So… cherry cokes?" he tempted in a reminder.

The four of us loaded up into Broderick's red Jeep Wrangler with the top down and each took private pleasure from the whipping wind. Broderick drove cautiously down the highway toward town—he didn't want to startle any of us after our accident yesterday.

Joey gently assisted Natalie out of the backseat of the Jeep when we arrived. In spite of her pain and need to rest, she insisted on coming along.

After ordering cherry cokes, we sat in a booth. Joey slid in the seat in front of me, giving Natalie an open space on the left side to keep her from getting her arm bumped. Broderick insisted on staying at the counter to pay for the beverages.

Natalie leaned as far over the table to me as her slinged-arm would allow. "You're not mad at me, are you?"

"Why would I be mad?" It was then I noticed that she appeared to be hiding something. "What did you do, Natalie?"

Joey nudged her with an I-told-you-so look, but she just giggled.

"I called Cari to see if she knew anything about you and Broderick." She looked over at the counter to see Broderick turn and wave at us. She then lowered her voice. "She was clueless, Jules. I'm impressed; you've done quite a job at keeping this a secret."

My eyes widened with the comprehension that the phone conversation with Cari earlier was only a conspiracy between her and my sister to gain information about the supposed relationship between me and Broderick. Information I didn't have. Nothing lost there; I hope they had fun.

"I'm mad now," I huffed. "You should've never confessed. I already told you that there wasn't a secret!" I sat stiffly in my seat and frowned at my sister while she rambled on.

"Jules," she pleaded "I wasn't trying to interfere." She shrugged apologetically, "We were just curious."

"Well, we're not dating. We're not anything!"

"Calm down, both of you," Joey jumped in. "Jules, try seeing it from our side. He has class with you, he's hanging out with you at your house today, the incident at the park, and according to Cari the two of you were hanging out at the movies, too—sharing loaded glances? Somehow we're all supposed to believe that you don't even know each other? I think the lady protests too much," Joey joked aside.

I leaned across the table to Joey with a threatening glare. "Do you really want to start talking about loaded glances and undeclared love, Joey?"

Panic swept Joey's face as he turned to Natalie. "But, I'm willing to admit that we could have blown all of this out of proportion."

To his relief, Natalie ignored Joey and focused completely on me. "Jules, I'm not trying to make something out of nothing, but what *I* see is that he likes you, and more than just a friend."

Broderick was now strolling to the booth where we sat, the four cherry cokes being carried on a tray.

"We're nothing more than friends. Hardly even that."

"Fine. Become friends and see where it goes from there. That wouldn't hurt anybody, now would it?" She quickly whispered the suggestion then added one more thought before he approached, "*He* is different."

Start out as friends. I still wasn't completely sure if I could do that. It was so natural being around Broderick, but I wasn't one hundred percent ready to trust him. On the other hand, I couldn't see how having a male friend around could hurt anything, especially if it was clear up front that that is all it would ever be. Joey and Natalie were best friends—even though Joey had aspirations for a more romantic relationship—and I envied their relationship in a way. I wanted that with Broderick.

"Did I miss anything?" Broderick said as he sat beside me.

Three hands, including my own, flew out to grab a drink from the tray. We immediately began sucking on our straws and avoiding eye contact with Broderick, unwilling to answer his question.

"O-*kay*." His face twisted when he realized that he was the topic of it by our reaction.

"So what put you in summer school?" Natalie asked Broderick bluntly. "Joey told me that your grades have been perfect since junior high."

There it was again—Broderick's 'hidden agenda face'. Trying to control his shifty eyes as he tucked in his lips, he quickly shook off the evidence on his face by frowning and clearing his throat. "I need to get my GPA back up for a good college. It dropped quite a bit last semester."

"I had no idea it had dropped that much," Joey said with a surprised expression.

Broderick was clearly uncomfortable and I wanted to take the focus away from him. "Well, that's a better reason for being in there than what I have." Joey and Natalie laughed in astonishment. It was the first time I had mentioned my reason for having to take summer school in such a light hearted fashion.

"I think a lot of people would have handled it the same way you did, if not worse," Broderick defended.

I smiled at his insistence to take my side in the matter. "Thanks, but I doubt that."

"Jules has a short fuse." Natalie winked at me.

"Hot headed," Joey added.

My head slowly nodded in acceptance of their accusations. I knew who I was, and I couldn't deny that I was ill-tempered. Well, he wanted to get to know me...

"I don't believe that," said Broderick, clearly being facetious.

"I'm just misunderstood." I played innocent to the accusations.

"*That's* what you are," Joey bellowed in laughter.

Broderick took another sip of his beverage. "These cherry cokes are good! It's no wonder the girls wanted to treat you to this for your birthday."

Joey gave us all the thumbs up.

I laughed at Joey's response and then explained, "I was introduced to this place by some of the cast during last year's play. We had our promotional photo shoot for the play here."

"Do you plan to do the school play again this year, Jules?" Broderick seemed genuinely interested.

Before I could answer, Joey groaned, "I hated last year's show." He was unaware how his comment could have offended me, until Natalie nudged him with her good arm. "But *you* were great in it, Jules!" The four of us laughed at his sudden change of heart.

"How come you've never done the school musical before?" I asked Broderick.

"I limit my singing to the shower," he confessed with a grin. "Besides, I stay booked up with football during the fall." Broderick explained, and then was once again swinging the discussion to me. "Do you and your band still play together?"

I wasn't the only one aware that his eyes had stayed glued on me through most of our time here. The toothy smile and bright eyes splashed on Natalie's face made it apparent that she had noticed as well. She loved this. Broderick had a fan in her that was for sure.

"No," I started, "our last performance was... well, you were there. Sydney starts school in Roanoke this fall and already moved there last month, so we've been shorted a bassist. You wouldn't happen to play bass, would you?" I teased. He shook his head smiling at me with his smooth lips. "Then I guess I have to take my act on the road alone," I joked.

"You're better off," he assured me.

Our chatter remained light throughout our stay. Broderick continually tried to keep the conversation on me. I tried spreading the direction of talk to everyone at the table evenly, but Joey and Natalie were his unfailing assistants in his quest to get to know me better. They would always turn it back onto me.

When we returned to the house, Joey hopped on his four-wheeler to go home promising Natalie that he'd be back tomorrow. As he took off down the driveway, Natalie loyally waved goodbye until he disappeared over the hill.

"Thanks for the cherry cokes, Broderick. And thanks for not killing us like Jules tried to yesterday," she said to Broderick as she walked to the house. I curled a side of my upper lip at her remark.

"I had fun. We'll have to do it again soon."

She grinned widely and walked into the house, closing the door behind her.

"Well, I guess I'll see you tomorrow morning." I began walking backward in the direction of the house as I spoke to him. I didn't want our time together to end, but I couldn't come up with anything useful to keep him around—not without blowing my cover. I turned to pick up the pace and get in the house.

"Wait, Jules," he called out to me.

My eagerness palpable, I spun on my heel to face him. "Yes?"

He opened his mouth to speak; deliberating whether he was going to say what he had spontaneously started, but then he closed his mouth and exhaled loudly, deciding against it. "I'll see you tomorrow morning."

"Bye," I whispered as he climbed into the jeep.

He backed out of the driveway and drove off, waving as he pulled away. I sulked into the house, consumed in thoughts of Broderick. Before I could even reach the stairs to sneak up to my room and continue that obsession, mom and Natalie had me cornered.

My mom sat at the computer turned toward me. "He's a nice boy, Jules!"

Natalie oozed of fervent anticipation as she sat on the pool table. "So, what did he say?"

"He said goodbye," I answered Natalie casually.

Natalie's face fell. "*Goodbye*? That's *it*?"

"What did you expect? A marriage proposal?"

"No, but at least you two could have exchanged phone numbers!" Natalie exclaimed in frustration.

"Why? He lives right next door. Why do I need his phone number?" I asked dryly.

Natalie hopped off the pool table, holding her injured arm stationary in the movement. She walked swiftly to the steps. "I'm feeling drugged. I'm going to my room to rest. Mom, will you talk some sense into your daughter?"

Mom and I stared at each other for a few seconds in silence as we heard Natalie stomp down the hall to her room.

"Your sister just wants to see you happy. She likes Broderick," she finally said.

I frowned. "Do I have to have a boyfriend to be happy? Can't I just be happy on my own? Because, I am!"

"You *sound* happy." My mother smirked at the contradiction in my voice.

I gave her an incredulous look. "You know what I mean."

"I do." She smiled warmly at me with understanding eyes. "Do you like him?"

"Yes," I answered before I gave it a thought. Quickly, I tried back peddling. "I mean, no. I mean... not like that." I took a surrendering breath. "I don't know." Groaning, I walked over and sat at her feet, as I commonly did when I needed advice or to vent.

Mom knew me far too well. She could see my heart and mind warring with one another and she began to lean in to me as if she were sharing an important secret with me. "Having your heart broken is a part of life. It happens to everyone at one point of time or another —"

"Mom..." Embarrassed, I whined in low grunt.

"Listen," she urged, "Relationships are learning experiences. No one should blame you for being untrusting. But there's a fine line between being cautious and paranoid. Broderick didn't cheat on you nor was he the one who put you in an awkward position the other night. That's not to say he never will, but don't hold him accountable for the stupidity of others. Okay?"

My mother's wisdom was well received by my sister and I, but actually having to sit through it was pure torture. Uncomfortable with conversations about my feelings, I didn't even like hearing the word "love" in the privacy of my own head.

"What Gavin did to you was wrong, no question about it. Same goes for Erik. But did you learn anything from your experiences with them?" She asked.

Once again I nodded. "Men are not to be trusted. Leggy blondes that pursue other girls' boyfriends are sluts. If a guy compliments you, he's trying to have sex with you. And last, but certainly not least, I have very poor judgment." She chuckled at my reply which wasn't really supposed to be humorous. I was serious.

She sighed. "Don't worry about what Natalie or I want... or even what Broderick wants. But remember, he is a human being with feelings, and you know what it feels like to be treated badly. Don't treat someone else that way. Show that you have learned from your time with Gavin and Erik. As much I didn't like those two boys, they were in fact, learning experiences. I'm proud of you for staying on the path your father and I have set you on. Don't ever stray from it, Jules."

Silently, I stared at the floor and nodded my head. I *would* have to do right by Broderick; I just wasn't sure what right was. My mind—instinct— told me that everything he did was motivated by something I shouldn't be willing to surrender to. My heart told me that he was and could always be my light in the darkest shadows. I didn't know which was right, and both frightened me greatly.

I dwelled on that fear for the remainder of the day and long after everyone went to bed that night. Escaping through my bedroom window and laying out on the roof, I listened for the unknown noises of the night— waiting to hear the wolf's howl. But again, nothing came. I was beginning to doubt I'd ever heard it to begin with.

avin

H E CONQUERED EVERY ONE of my dreams last night and the minute I opened my eyes, he was all I could think about.
Broderick Cooper.

I couldn't wait to see him. No longer some silly school-girl crush, it was quickly becoming so much more to me. The continuous pull to him was becoming an unrelenting battle against my determination to remain wise when it came to matters of the heart. Every little thing about him, from his undignified way of befriending me to his *hero-complex* stirred my soul. And through it all, I resented my weakness to see him and be near him.

In spite of her newly acquired injury, Natalie had to be at cheer practice by six, so mom loaded us into the van and out of the driveway before fifteen minutes to the hour. Unlike me, she and Natalie were reliable with schedules. I had a habit of either being late or rushed to get anywhere on time.

Natalie stepped out of the van with apprehension when we arrived at the school. Her mind was completely focused on cheering with one arm in a sling and while still in pain. Her face was full of concentration as she said goodbye. I quietly waved at my mom and wished Natalie good luck.

I walked slowly to class since I arrived earlier than usual and had the time to enjoy the coolness of the morning before the humidity kicked in for the afternoon. When I arrived in class, I found only five others, including Mr. Muir waiting patiently.

All the guys in the room, including Mr. Muir, winced at my revelation that my car was no longer in existence. I was beginning to gather the feeling that if my car had survived and I hadn't come out so well, it wouldn't have affected them as negatively. Normally, I would have dwelt longer on that insulting thought, but this morning, the anticipation of seeing Broderick was practically sweeping me into the air. Would he walk in with the pretense that nothing had changed between us? Would he say hi to me with our mutual classmates as witness or try to keep our new friendship private?

Five minutes before the hour, a few more students walked in, but there was no sign of Broderick. Kevin Overby walked in just before the hour. He was usually late, Broderick wasn't. I glanced at my watch. Two minutes left. I opened my Algebra book and pulled out my notes. As the seconds slipped by, my shoulders dropped in defeat and I stole a quick glimpse over my left shoulder at Broderick's empty seat when I heard the door to my right fly open. Broderick walked in hastily.

"Sorry that I'm late, sir," he apologized.

"You're just in time, Mr. Cooper," Mr. Muir assured as he began reviewing for the test.

My heart leapt as Broderick slid into the empty seat directly behind me.

"What time did you leave your house this morning?" he whispered as he leaned into his notebook.

I was caught off guard by the question. I kept my eyes locked on Mr. Muir at the front of the class but twisted my head slightly to speak over my shoulder. "Huh?"

"Did your mom bring you?" he asked.

"Of course she did. I don't have a car."

"I thought you'd need a ride this morning, so I went by to pick you up; I waited for ten minutes." Instantly, my body went languid at his confession. "I assumed that you were just running late and couldn't answer the door. You almost made me late. I'm blaming you." He chuckled in a hushed whisper. Amused at his little blame game, I let a small giggle escape.

Frowning at the insight that I was losing my self-control with Broderick, I faced forward and tried to listen to Mr. Muir. His lesson was in a hollow box outside my ears. This class, like so many others, had become a wash due to my long winded daydreams and reflections. I zipped through the test absorbed with Broderick's proximity, sensing every sudden movement behind me. Every time he made a sound—clearing his throat or heavily sighing—I fell further into a realm of pleasure, enjoying the low electrical hum that covered my back, literally feeding off of his presence.

I was sure I was going to fail the test. *Why did I even bother showing up today?* The answer was known before I had even finished the question. Like most students, I didn't come to class to learn. I wasn't interested in furthering my social agenda, and I wasn't intimidated enough by my parents to fulfill my obligation to pass the final. There was only one reason to come to class. The expectation to see Broderick again; the moment that I most looked forward to.

"Whoo!" Mr. Muir cried out as he dropped a large book to the floor. The slamming noise ruptured through the room in an attempt to wake Kevin from his slobbery slumber. Kevin sat up wiping his mouth and blinking in a daze from his apparent snooze.

"That's an absence counted against you, Mr. Overby. Wake up and go take a nap somewhere. It's break time," Mr. Muir sarcastically suggested as he walked out of the class.

Slowly, the roomful of boys emptied as they drifted into the halls and parking lot to stretch their legs leaving Broderick and me alone in the room. The haunting cry emitted from Mr. Muir that woke Kevin Overby up sounded more like a howl. An all too familiar howl from two weeks earlier that rang in my memory causing me to shudder at the unnecessary fear.

I turned questioningly to the beautiful boy that sat behind me. "Do you have a dog?"

He was amused by my random and odd question. "No, Jules, I don't. Do you *want* me to have a dog?"

It must have been a neighbor's dog that I heard howl, but that didn't explain the scream. I paused. "I thought I heard a weird noise last week—late after the whole park incident—and it sounded like it came from your house or maybe in the woods between us."

"What kind of noise?" He turned serious, puckering his brows in concentration.

"I'm not sure." I shook my head, dreading having to use the word *werewolf.* He seemed genuinely concerned and waited for my explanation. "Well, my first thought was that it sounded like a man's scream." I waited to see his reaction. When I saw he wasn't looking at me as the next-door-lunatic, I continued. "And then it turned into something like a howl or something. Maybe a dog or a... *wolf.*" I carefully omitted *were*wolf. That certainly would have sealed my fate as a total nut job.

He seemed to be in deep thought and I held my breath waiting to see his reaction. I was starting to feel foolish when Broderick surprised me with his own theory of what I may have heard that night.

"I've had some pretty vivid nightmares, lately. I suffer from dream anxiety disorder. You may have heard me scream. Some of my nightmares are just too much and it's the only way I can wake myself." He shrugged in embarrassment.

It sounded like a rational explanation to me; the terror in the scream itself was agonizing to recount. Its sound still haunted me. I've had my own share of bad dreams, and not surprising since I avidly watched horror movies. But now I felt a cold chill as I tried to imagine what horrifying dream could cause Broderick to scream like that.

"But what about the, uh... howl... uh, the animal sound?" I asked.

"My scream probably woke every dog in the neighborhood." He attempted to lighten the conversation.

"No. It was definitely a *wild* animal. Besides, I didn't think any of our neighbors had a dog," I said.

"The Boston's have a Chihuahua."

I chortled. "There is no way it was a Chihuahua. This sound came from a much larger animal."

Broderick shrugged again, seemingly apologetic that he couldn't help figure out the mystery. "Then aside from the growing population of coyotes in our area, I'm out of theories, but it adds to the whole creepy element of the discovery this weekend."

"What discovery?"

He grimaced. "I guess you were too busy having a car accident to hear." Broderick winked. "A body was discovered in Roane County, two miles from our county line. I heard it was pretty brutal."

"I hadn't heard anything about it," I admitted.

Broderick smiled to ease the tension in the air. "It's just as well. We don't need to be worried by things that are out of our control, right?"

I nodded as I shrugged out of my denim jacket and draped it across the back of my chair.

Suddenly in a low gasp I heard him marvel, "What is that?"

"What is what?" I asked in alarm. Starting to feel self-conscious over my skinny arms, I started to pull them inward and closer to my body, wishing I had never taken my jacket off.

"*That.*" He brushed his warm fingers over the spot in question, causing me to tremble in delight.

I took a deep breath to get control of myself. "Oh, that's just a birthmark. They call it an angel's kiss," I explained as I slowly turned around hoping that I wouldn't see a look of revulsion on his face. He was nothing but intrigued and deeply taken with his newest discovery that set on my shoulder, which caused me to relax again.

"But yours looks just like a real print of lips…" He trailed off in amazement. This wasn't the first time I had heard this. He drew in a ragged breath. "That's just…" he held his fingers out as if he were about to touch it again, but then tucked both hands in closer to him as if in restraint, "…just remarkable."

My angel's kiss. Never had I seen someone react to my birthmark with such reverence. It was amusing to say the least. "Thanks. I guess." Shutting my book, I faced him again.

"Do you need a ride home today?"

I shook my head as I swallowed another sip of my drink. "Nat has cheer practice all this week, so mom's taking us. But, again, thanks."

"I can take Nat, too. It wouldn't be a problem at all."

"I don't know…" My mind wouldn't work quickly enough for me to come up with a strong enough defense against riding to school with Broderick other than trying to protect myself from vulnerability because even that reason was slowly losing any ground.

"Are you afraid of me for some reason, Jules?" he asked.

"Of course not!" I quickly defended in a tough manner.

He smiled, unbelieving. "I don't bite."

"I just don't want to inconvenience you."

"I live *right next door*," he reminded me in a lighthearted chuckle.

"My mom lives in the *same house* with me," I countered.

"Jules, let me drive you." Broderick's intense brown eyes melted into mine and I found my head slowly nodding in acceptance like I was being hypnotized. I could see the enthusiasm pressed on his lips as he smiled.

"Good. Now that that's finally settled… what are you doing this weekend since you're finally ungrounded and not going out with Erik?"

My mood changed immediately. "Gavin's getting married so, the girls and I made plans a little over a month ago to go out of town for the weekend. That way I can save my face and my sanity.

He deflected any talk of my ex-boyfriend. "Where do you girls plan on going?"

"To the mountains. But I'm fairly sure that I won't be able to go now since I missed class yesterday and they're planning on leaving Thursday night. It's the usual bad luck I tend to run into," I grumpily added, but as I silently dwelled on recent events that would prohibit me from leaving with my friends, I realized that I didn't feel quite *un*lucky. In fact, I wasn't sure if I wanted to leave town at all anymore. Deep down, I knew it was because of Broderick.

"I can take you after class on Friday so you won't have to be here this weekend," he suggested.

"No! You don't need to do that. It's not your problem. I'll handle it."

"Let me help you."

"Broderick! Why are you doing this?" My frustration seeped through, as I tried to figure out what he thought he could gain out of helping me.

"What? It's wrong to help someone? I don't understand you. You have a problem, I have a solution, but it seems you don't want a solution. Or am I wrong?" He forcefully tried to reason with me.

"I just don't want you to feel like you need to come to my rescue. I'm a tough girl. If I can't go, then I just can't go. You shouldn't trouble yourself by becoming solutions to my problems." I turned around to cut off eye contact before I gave into him again.

Blankly staring at the chalkboard in front of me, I tried to calm myself, but his deep whisper was so close to me that his breath brushed my neck and blew a few of my dangling hairs in a tickling fashion. "Are you against anyone helping you or just *me* helping you?"

I sighed and twisted back around in my seat to face him. He was leaning in, resting his chin in his fisted hands that lay on the desk, his face closer to mine than I had imagined. "It's not that I don't want help." I paused to keep my cool.

"So you like making things harder on yourself?" he asked.

"No." But the more I thought about it, the more I realized he couldn't be any closer to the truth.

A thought seemed to click on in his head. "What if I told you that I was going to be in that area that afternoon anyway? No inconvenience there. Plus, I'd appreciate some company on the drive there." Then he slam-dunked me by adding, "*Your* company."

"First, I would say you're a liar, because I know for a fact you have a scrimmage Friday afternoon and wild horses couldn't drag the co-captain away from that." I narrowed my eyes as I slyly called him out. "And second, I still wouldn't go with you."

Confused, he sat his head up and turned his palms up in question. "Jules, do you think that I'm trying to hurt you or take advantage of you?"

My eyes widened in shock and my cheeks burned. He saw right through me and I felt guilty for not trusting him. I incoherently stuttered, desperate to collect some rational thoughts and tactful phrases. "No! I...I..."

"I'm sitting here because I want to be your *friend*. I'm offering my help because I want to be your *friend*. Do I need to prove myself loyal and trustworthy to you before you'll even give me a chance?" He stared deeply into my eyes.

Mr. Muir briskly walked in and a few students trailed in after him. I swallowed the tight lump in my throat as I realized my salvation. I turned to face forward again and opened my book, eager to start class and pardon me from this conversation. Sensing him patiently waiting for my answer through the dragging minutes before the second half of our class officially began, I never answered.

The minute ten o'clock rolled around, I grabbed my folder and book and stood up, ready to bolt out of the room and avoid a repeat of our earlier conversation, but he was already speaking.

"Look, I'm sorry," he humbly started. "You hardly know me, and you have every right not to trust anybody right now. We've lived next door to each other for two years and I have never made an effort to get to know you before, and I can see how that would make you question my motives..." he cautiously paused, "especially after your recent track record."

Now, I felt even guiltier. "It's not your fault. I tend to be grouchy in the mornings. I didn't sleep well last night." I lied. I slept peacefully, swimming in dreams of him.

"Are you still going to let me make it up to you by taking you and Nat to school tomorrow?" he smiled.

My tone was light. "I'll run it by my mom when I get home."

"I'll walk you out and offer it myself." My stomach fluttered in excitement. "You're a hard customer to please, you know?" he teased.

"Yeah, I know," I conceded.

Broderick waved me off with a smile. "That's okay. I think I can handle you."

We walked to the front of the school where Natalie had already claimed the front seat in mom's van and waved to us.

"Hey, Nat, how was practice?" he asked as I climbed into the back door of the van and sat down.

She pointed at her gimped arm. "It sucked."

"Natalie..." my mother's tone warned of her use of the word *sucked*. She turned to Broderick. "Hi, Broderick, are you coming over again today?"

"No ma'am. I've got to work today," he explained. "But I'd like to offer to take the girls to and from school for the next few days."

My mother's delight radiated in her tone as she shot a quick, but obvious glance at me, causing me to blush. "That's so sweet of you, Broderick."

"Is five-thirty too early?" he asked me.

Natalie and my mom jumped right in before I could answer. "Not at all."

"You're welcome to have breakfast with us, too, if you want to come earlier," my mom continued.

"Thank you, ma'am. I just might take you up on that."

The idea of seeing Broderick first thing in the morning, before I even reached school, was like a dream come true. I would just have to make sure I was presentable before breakfast every morning now.

Since I bailed out on Cari yesterday, I figured I should try to make up for it today and make plans to go to the Java House with her. Nearly noon and she was still asleep in bed when I called. By the sound of her groggy voice, coffee was definitely at the top of her list.

She bombarded me with questions about Broderick the minute I sat down in her car.

"We're just in a class together, Cari."

"Is he your tutor?" her sarcasm was clear in the question.

"I don't need a tutor. He was only dropping off my homework yesterday. Don't read more into it than what it really is," I cautioned.

"I'm not," she tried to assure me. "I'm just wondering why you never mentioned your *friendship* with him before. It makes perfect sense to me now—why you two were so tense around each other at the park last week and why he was hovering over you at the movies."

I rolled my eyes at her subtle accusation. "Things were tense because he nearly drowned me and made me look stupid in front of the whole dang town. He also ripped my favorite jacket which pissed me off." I rolled down my window to clear the smell of cigarettes in her car. It was useless, though. "*And* he just happened to be there when I went to call you for a ride from the movies. He was offering me a ride home, but since I don't know him all that well I called *you* instead." I worried how I was going to smell like smoke when we arrived at the Java House. "Gosh, don't you have an air freshener in here or something? This smell is killing me."

"Quit trying to change the subject." Desensitized by my constant complaining of her smoking habit, Cari ignored me. "Do you like him?"

"Why does everyone keep asking me that? If I ever feel the need to be screwed over by another guy, you'll be the first to know, okay?"

"Good to hear you're still using your brain. Broderick's too popular. He'll take advantage of you; you know that," she pointed out. "Popular guys are only interested in three things: Themselves, money, and a piece of ass. Erik and Gavin should be enough proof of that for you."

"That's really not a fair accusation to pin on someone just because they're popular." I couldn't believe the words that were coming out of my mouth. Broderick had a stronger influence on my way of thinking than I had realized.

"You're sticking up for him now?" she asked.

"No. I'm saying you don't know him."

"But *you do*," she concluded.

My frustration level began to rise. "No."

"So you don't really know what motivates him then, right?" she challenged.

I twisted around awkwardly in my seatbelt to face her. "Can we change the subject? I don't want to fight."

"Fine," she replied shortly. "I just don't want to see you be made a fool of again and have to hear about it for months on end when you could've prevented the whole thing from the beginning. Just remember, I warned you."

Changing the subject quickly, I wasn't ready to discuss the matter of the howling wolf, but I figured it was the biggest distraction from the current conversation. Besides, I knew Cari would appreciate my story. She was as enthusiastic about horror as I was.

"By the way, you're going to laugh at me for this, but—"

"I'm going to laugh at you anyway, but go ahead."

I gave her a wry smile. "Last week I think I heard a wolf howl from the woods beside my house."

She stared straight ahead with a blank stare for the longest moment before busting with laughter. "Up too late watching werewolf movies that night?"

"It was the night of the Fourth—after I nearly drowned. I didn't watch any TV and I was wide awake when it happened, too. Besides, werewolves don't scare me." My words ran fast together as the adrenaline from the memory rose. "I promise you, one second I heard a man scream and a split second later it ended abruptly in a howl... the howl of a werewolf." I dripped in ghost story narration mode, to prevent myself from looking like I was taking this too serious, though I was serious.

"There are coyotes all around this area. That's what you heard. I guarantee it."

Cari laughed at me all the way to the Java House. The aroma of freshly brewed coffee flooded our noses as we entered the establishment. The wooden floors and earth toned walls brought back a familiar comfort. Unable to enjoy a coffee here since before Gavin and I broke up because I was grounded, I was elated to finally be able to enjoy the atmosphere as well as my favorite coffee beverage.

"Jules, you came to see me." I heard a familiar voice call from behind the steam that blew from the machine on the counter.

I looked up and surprisingly found Chase Montandon behind the counter wearing a crisp white dress shirt and khaki pants with a Java House blue apron draped around his neck.

"What are you doing here?" I asked him.

"I told you I had to get another job, didn't I? Well, here I am." He handed a drink to the girl beside him who in return handed it to the customer.

"You told me you were working another job, I just didn't think it would be at one of my other favorite places." I smiled. "We're going to become *real good friends*, Chase."

His eyes shifted to Cari and I immediately saw the opportunity to introduce him to my friend. I kept it casual, though, to avoid another argument with Cari.

"You're the one who picked Jules up the other night at the movies, weren't you?" Chase asked Cari, completely aware that she was.

"Yeah, that was me." Cari remained disinterested and jumped ahead of me to order. "I'll need a large black coffee with a little extra crack to help start my day."

I gave Chase a lopsided smile in apology for her actions. "I'll have a large vanilla latte, Chase. Hold the crack, though; I'm trying to quit."

We made our way to a secluded table for two in a quiet corner. We'd just sat down and she instantly started in. "I saw right through that, by the way; I told you I wasn't interested."

"I was just introducing you to him, so he wouldn't spit in our drinks," I claimed as innocently as possible.

"Sure you were. And I'm the pied piper," she laughed.

"Speaking of leading rats with music, have you got a new band together yet?"

"Funny you should mention rats..." she smirked cleverly. "I still need a singer."

"Forget it. Mr. Dean will never let you play in the school as long as I'm fronting your band. You know that," I reminded her.

"Still need a bass guitarist, too, but I think I might be able to swindle Savannah into doing it," she said.

Chase appeared over Cari's shoulder with the beverages and set them down on the table.

"Chase, you wouldn't happen to play an instrument, would you?" I asked him sweetly.

Red faced, Cari looked as though she was going to come across the table and strangle me. However, aggravating her was a great payback for the phone call from hell she gave me yesterday when Broderick was present.

"I played guitar in a high school garage band back in Jersey. And I can play a little percussion. Does that count?" he asked.

Cari's cold stare never left me, but she spoke to Chase. "No. We already have a drummer. Thanks."

"Can you play bass?" I pressed.

Her eyes got even larger as she stared straight at me. "That's taken care of, too."

Chase's eyes were questioning me, but I simply smiled in satisfaction and waved him off cordially. He shrugged and returned to the espresso counter.

"What the hell's your problem?" She narrowed her eyes, heavy with makeup. I laughed so hard at her discomfort that I couldn't even breathe, only snort.

"Played drums, my ass," she muttered under her breath. "He probably plays tambourine for his lame Praise band in church."

"Not cool. Quit knocking Christians and their music." I scowled and turned a sharp tongue. "He may be a pretty awesome drummer. What makes you think that's the kind of music he plays anyway?"

Cari gave an incredulous stare. "Are you kidding me? Look at him." She shifted her eyes over to the counter where Chase stood making another coffee beverage for another customer. "That guy reeks of door to door salesman for Jesus. White button up shirt, khaki pants—yup, he's winning souls alright."

"That's his work uniform! I hate it when you say crap like this. It's insulting." I held up my cup and took a deep inhale to absorb the aroma of coffee and light vanilla; it calmed me instantly.

"Then *you* go for him. He's more your type, anyway. Or would that cause a conflict with Broderick?"

I let it go. Unable to ever win an argument against her thick sarcasm, I steered our conversation, away from boys in general and onto music instead. This topic kept us drinking coffee there for hours.

When Cari finally took me home, I spent my evening doing homework and hiding in my room. Impatiently, I waited for nightfall to possibly recapture the sound that trapped me in a mystical state two weeks ago. The howl of the wolf. I didn't really believe it was a *were*wolf. They didn't exist, but my over-exposed-horror-movie brain wanted to enjoy and entertain the idea. It was a morbid thing to confess, but I relished the sense of danger of a wild creature, only witnessed in the movies, tracing a territorial circle in my neighborhood. But when the night showed to be silent, I was again questioning whether I had heard it at all. The sound seemed a far off fantasy now due to its unlikely existence, and I wish I had never mentioned it to Broderick or Cari. Still, I was vigilant in my mission to hear it again, leaving me to a restless sleep.

Broderick was eating breakfast with Natalie by the time I was dressed and ready to join my family in the kitchen the following morning. He sat, muscular legs stretched out from his chair, across from my sister as they conversed passionately about their common interest of four-wheeling. Although, we had never owned one, she had become quite fond of Joey's and their rides together.

"Do you ever go four-wheeling, Jules?" he asked, inviting me into their conversation. I quietly shook my head observing their interaction. I wanted to remain as removed as possible with him without being too obvious that I was on guard.

"Jules doesn't have an adventurous bone in her body," Natalie informed him.

"Sure she does," Broderick pleasantly argued. "She's courageous enough to sing in front of crowds, isn't she? That's one adventure *I* wouldn't have any part of."

"That's because you can't sing," Natalie joked. He simply grinned as he took another bite of the scrambled eggs my mother had given him.

I wanted so badly to take part of their conversation, but found a small insecurity and paranoia tugging away at the notion. My sister and her ability to feel secure when talking to others more popular or older than she was amazed me. It was that very ability that made her conversation with Broderick so natural. She never concerned herself with saying something stupid or too honest or worrying about what others thought. Natalie was secure with herself because she was popular. There wasn't any way to deny that her attachment to the cheerleading squad would catapult her into the high school limelight. I was secretly disappointed in the fact that popularity was something I would never fully get to experience aside from the occasional singing opportunity or public meltdown on stage.

Gathering my stuff for class, I slipped out of my chair at the table. Broderick and Natalie followed in step as I walked out to the jeep. As Broderick opened the door for us, I quickly scrambled in the back seat.

"I was going to let you sit up front, Jules," Natalie said.

My response was premeditated. "I'll sit back here. You'll be less likely to bump your arm up front and you need to get out first, anyway." I had hoped that my resistance to sitting up front near Broderick would come across as helpful to my sister and not guarded, but Broderick's head dropped slightly in hurt and my chest ached. Natalie shrugged as he assisted her with climbing up into the jeep.

Listening to their exchanges on the drive to school nearly extinguished my desire to distance myself from him. They lightly carried on about cheerleading and football. Often, Broderick would turn to me with a question about the flag corps and I would reply in short basic answers. Even by extracurricular school activity standards, I was inferior. Being a part of the flag corps and the Jet Theatrix drama team was nowhere near as impressive as football or cheerleading, despite his effort to equalize the two in importance.

We dropped Natalie off by the football stadium and then proceeded to the parking lot closer to the math wing entrance. He assumed the seat behind me again in class and I glowed inside with satisfaction at his determination to remain close to me.

After class, we walked out to the parking lot and saw Natalie leaning against the Jeep, already waiting for us.

"Why aren't you going with the girls this weekend?" he asked as we made our way to her.

What would I be doing in the mountains, anyway? Shopping? Laughing? Playing music? I can do all that at home. The trip felt like a waste of time and effort. I didn't feel the need to be protected from Gavin's impending wedding at all. I hated sleeping in any bed other than my own anyway. And what if I missed that howling sound this weekend while I was gone? I needed to hear it again just to confirm to myself that I never imagined it. Also, *Nightmare Theater* was going to be hosting the movie *Friday the 13th* on the Horror Channel this Saturday night. Such a classic! I wouldn't want to miss that. All of these reasons worked against any plan for me to leave town Friday, but deep down one reason stood out, greater than the rest. The one I didn't want to admit to myself: I didn't want to be separated from Broderick.

"I just want to get this class over and done with. I think leaving town would only distract me."

"What are you going to do this Saturday without your friends?" Concerned, he grabbed my arm to get me to face him. "Jules, talk to me."

The sudden closing of our physical distance took me off guard and I pulled my arm free from his grasp. "I'm not a coward, Broderick. Gavin can't run me off or make me hide from his mistakes."

But the irony was that I was becoming a pro at "hiding". I continued to hide out in the backseat of Broderick's jeep during our rides to and from school. Though I wasn't sure either of them bought it, I used the convenience of Nat's limited mobility as an excuse. Occasionally, I would participate in their conversations, but still made great strides in keeping my distance.

Thursday afternoon, before my friends left town, Savannah decided that it was her duty as a good friend to take me out for coffee and offer a shoulder for me to cry on since I was no longer going with them. Although

I had no need for a good cry over the matter either, I appreciated the coffee and quality time.

"So, what's going on with you?" she finally asked before she took a sip of her iced coffee. "I heard you went out with Erik Peterson and it ended in disaster." She laughed.

I fidgeted with my coffee cup, turning it carefully around in a circle by the ceramic handle. Erik was the last person I wanted to talk about. Instead, I blurted out the next big thing that weighed heavily on my mind. "What can you tell me about Broderick Cooper? The two of you run in the same crowd and you know *everything* about *everybody*."

Savannah straightened her back. This was not at all what she was expecting. She started, a little puzzled, "What do you want to know?"

"What's he like?" I frowned as I saw myself open wide, exposing too much. My tone was a strictly business manner, hoping it would keep speculation down to a minimum.

"He's tall, hot looking, the cutest dimples I've ever seen, co-captain of the football team and will probably go to college on a baseball scholarship or academic scholarship…"

"I know all that," I reminded her dryly.

"Well," she began slowly, trying to make a mental list of things to tell me about him. "He's really smart and everybody likes him. He's not overly social like the rest of us. He doesn't go to parties often or anything else like that. I was surprised to see him at the park on the Fourth of July, actually."

"Why's that?" I asked.

"Well, since his sophomore year, he became more of a homebody. He's just very private." She shrugged. "He fits in with us, but doesn't really fit *in* anymore like he used to. You know what I mean?"

I shook my head.

She sipped her drink thoughtfully and then tried to continue to explain. "He's different. Really *different*—almost to the point of being weird. On second thought, he is weird. I guess we all just overlook it because… well, he's one of *us*. He's popular, smart, talented, funny, friendly… *hot*— you name it."

"What do you mean by weird?"

"Like I said before, he's unsociable."

Her vague explanations were killing me. I needed something more. "You mean *shy*?"

Savannah laughed. "Hardly. He's quite confident. He's funny at times and real easy to talk to. He's just private with his home life. It's like Broderick-at-home is hiding behind Broderick-at-school as if they're two different people… just no one knows who the guy is at home or anywhere else for that matter. Not even Taryn."

She twisted her face as she tried to understand who Broderick was. "Oh! And he doesn't date much either."

"But he dated *Taryn*," I pointed out.

She frowned, clearly confused as to why I was being so inquisitive. "Yeah, for like two seconds. It wasn't very serious though, because when she cheated on him with Jackson he didn't seem too broken up about it." She spoke self-righteously in disgust. "Talk is that he had his eyes on someone else, anyway."

"Who?" My interest was piqued.

Savannah loved school gossip and now was very animated. "Taryn claimed that he had become detached and that's what pushed her to Jackson." Savannah rolled her eyes. "Her defense is lame. It doesn't excuse her for banging Jackson long before they broke up and *everyone* knows they were," Savannah said matter-of-factly. "But… it's also common knowledge that Broderick was interested in someone else, too. We just never figured out whom; just another one of those things that makes him weird."

"How do you know he had someone else on the side?" I asked dubiously.

"I never said that. I said he had his eye on someone else. Completely different. He was probably rejected by this girl and decided to keep it on the down low."

Savannah's comments were absolutely ridiculous. It amazed me how much everyone talked about people, when they didn't have the slightest clue and facts to back up their statements. "But how do you know it was another girl?"

"Taryn had a hunch. She said that shortly after their breakup, he started dressing differently, like he was trying to impress someone, and that he no longer took normal routes to his classes in the halls. Going out of his way, in fact. He was secretive about it and Jackson warned her that they should mind their own business. She did follow him once or twice though, and found him leaning against a set of lockers just staring down the hall, but she couldn't see who it was he was staring at because the hall was so crowded. You know how tall he is; he practically towers over almost everyone at school. It would be easy for him to zone in on one person. I just can't get why he was never caught stalking them."

"You think he was stalking someone?" I asked.

"Of course he was! But he's a *hot* stalker so that makes it okay," she giggled. Savannah whispered secretively, "And why are you asking? Do you have a thing for your personal hero?"

I turned up my nose and pretended to shudder, reverting back to my kindergarten ways of covering up a crush. "Absolutely not." Quickly, I came up with an entertaining alibi that didn't involve 'the cooties'. "I think Cari has a thing for him. She's been asking a lot of questions lately." I smiled devilishly as I glanced over to the entrance to see Gavin step inside with two of his friends.

It was the first time I had seen him since the rally last spring. Something I wasn't prepared for. My expression must have changed because Savannah's face twisted in concern and she peered over her shoulder to see why there was a lump residing in my throat.

"Oh my god…" She whispered.

Savannah quickly grabbed her purse, rose out of her seat, and crossed over to me. She pulled my arm, leading me out of my seat and over to the door. Passing like two ships in the night, he and I paused for a moment and locked eyes. Unlike the last time I saw him, with an arrogant light in his eyes, this time he was softer.

"Hi, Jules." He said quietly to me.

Stunned and speechless, I walked out the door and allowed Savannah to cram me into her car.

"Changed your mind about going away with us tonight?" She asked angrily. I was at a loss for words.

Sitting on the roof of my house that night, while listening for the howl of the wolf, it was hard not to notice Gavin driving slowly by my house several times. He never stopped and he never called out to me and for that, I was thankful. I was not ready to see him again. Now that I had a period of peace and the time to process the event of running into him for the first time in months, I know that something strange had happened tonight.

Seeing Gavin was like being rammed into a brick wall. There were clearly some unresolved feelings on my end, but none of them resembled love or even a broken heart. I was overcome with the dreadful feeling—a *strange* feeling—that a confrontation or a conflict was on the horizon, because of this weekend and I prayed that it wasn't because of a hidden emotion that lingered over Gavin. This weekend was a turning point for me. I could feel it in my bones.

The first thing that entered my mind when I woke up Friday morning, was that dreadful feeling of conflict again. Something was on the horizon. I groaned as I lay on my side rejecting the sun from any power over making me want to hide. I opened my eyes to stare at its intimidating rays peeking through my eastern window, but I was unable to focus on their bright streams. I only saw the summer green leaves of the trees that physically divided Broderick and me.

I just needed to make it through the weekend, then I would be fine. I would continue my life as it always was, and everyone would see the proof for themselves—that Gavin Williams was no longer in my heart or on my mind, and he hadn't been for some time. That, I was certain. After school, I planned to simply stay busy in my room studying for the upcoming final or any other homework assignment I may have. That would save me from any need to face my mom or dad, or even Natalie for the rest of the day— to hear someone tell me they're sorry Gavin Williams was getting married. I didn't care he was getting married, I was mourning the death of the girl he once dated. I knew the minute he made Morgan "Mrs. Gavin Williams" I would be free from the cloud of doom he placed over me when we started dating.

Yes, I just needed to get through this weekend without studious eyes upon me.

There was no way around facing Broderick, though. I grabbed my sunglasses from my dresser. There was a wicked security in hiding my eyes from him.

Fortunately, the need to suck in my courage to face my entire family was almost unnecessary. This morning my mom was the only one in the kitchen, reading the newspaper. As I walked in she quickly folded the paper and placed it in the trash compactor. She blushed ever so slightly then stood in her usual spot behind the kitchen bar top, like a waitress in a diner.

"What would you like for breakfast this morning?" she asked.

I hated the idea of adding food to the knotted mess that already lay in my stomach. "I'll just have a slice of toast."

"That's it? Are you sure?" Her concerned look was plain and I decided it would be best for me to avoid eye contact before I cracked. I scurried over to the last slice of bread and placed it in the toaster. I crumbled up the bread's empty plastic sleeve and opened the trash compactor to throw it away, when I saw Gavin and Morgan's smiling faces staring back at me on the ink laden page of the wedding announcements. My gasp echoed in the kitchen and saw my mother grimace in my peripheral. I slammed the door and walked away from it.

"I didn't want you to see that," she said soothingly. "I know it must hurt, but think about how far God can see in your future…"

"I'm not really that hungry. I'm just going to sit outside on the back deck until my ride gets here. Tell Nat to get the lead out and hurry up or she'll make us late." I started out of the room.

"Oh, she doesn't have practice this morning."

"Why not? She *has* to ride with me," I panicked.

"They just don't have practice today," Mom said, taking notice of my sudden worry. With my sister playing the part as a buffer all week, I was nervous at the impending ride alone with Broderick today… of all days.

"Are you okay?" she asked. My mother knew something was wrong. Despite my unraveling seams, I was determined to hold it together.

"I'm just sidetracked with studying right now." I started out the door.

"Jules," Mom called out to me, "Everything happens for a reason. This hurt will pass. I love you." She spoke with persuasion, as if she knew firsthand what she said was true.

It was this very thing I wanted to avoid this weekend. Unnecessary condolences and encouragement. *Just get through the weekend, Jules.*

Broderick was pulling into our driveway when I walked out onto the deck, so I just kept right on down the stairs and placed the glasses on my face.

"Good morning, Miss Jules Taylor." He beamed as he practically sang my name. "Where's Nat?"

Despite my apprehension to be alone with him, I was keenly aware of the calming effect he had on me. "She doesn't have practice this morning, so you're stuck with me."

"Great!" He seemed happy at the news.

"Something's wrong..." He looked at me as I silently climbed into the Jeep. "S'everything okay, Jules?"

I stared straight ahead through my glasses. "No. It. Isn't."

"You want to talk about it?"

I buckled my seat belt and crossed my arms. "No. I. Don't."

He released a heavy sigh and began drumming his fingers on the steering wheel, far from the rhythm of the song that played on the radio. He allowed me to reflect quietly on my own and I appreciated that.

In class Broderick claimed the seat behind me again, keeping me comforted with his closeness. Feeling him behind me—the way he moved and shuffled, his breath, his voice—it was soothing even with the constant fluttering in my stomach. I liked him. I loved the sensation his presence gave me. He was so easy to be around, as long as my cynicism wasn't preventing the flow of our natural harmony. Truth told, since yesterday when Savannah filled me in on the oddities of this young man, I felt even *more* at ease with him. He was every bit as different as I was from the other kids at our school, making him normal to me. We didn't really fit in.

During the class break, Broderick rested his head on the desk. I wanted to talk to him, like we had for the past few days during our breaks, but as I twisted around to open up a conversation, I found him catching a quick snooze so I left him alone. Slow breaths with his eyes closed, looking peaceful. He probably had nothing to say to me anyway. I had been so standoffish from the beginning that he had probably grown frustrated and tired with my fickle attitude. I couldn't blame him. I wish he could read my mind and see my turmoil, because it was difficult to talk about; saying it out loud made it sound unreasonable and senseless. *I* should know—I had practiced the monologue close to twenty times alone in the bathroom mirror. It was unreasonable and senseless, but that didn't make it any less real to me.

After class, we made our usual trek to the jeep. The day was gloriously bright and beautiful.

"It's really turning out to be a nice day, huh?" Broderick finally broke the silence.

"Yeah, it really is," I said, jealous that that my attitude couldn't reflect the beautiful weather.

"Are you going to be okay?" he asked as he opened my door.

"Sure. Why ask?"

"You seemed to be having a rocky start to the day. I was worried it might have something to do with the fact you're missing your girls' weekend."

I shook my head.

"So what *are* you doing tomorrow?" Doom was in his tone.

"I'm going to the wedding." I said nonchalantly.

Broderick spun his wide eyes and horror stricken face in my direction. "What?" his voice cracked.

I laughed uncontrollably at his shock. "What kind of moron do you take me for, Broderick Cooper?" I said his full name out loud to get a taste of how it felt on my lips. It left a heavenly vibration on them that made me smile.

He climbed into the jeep and drove off, shaking his head with a smirk on his face as I was still laughing.

"So why have you decided to speak to me today?"

My smile instantly vanished. "I *have* been speaking to you," I quickly tried to argue.

Now it was his turn to laugh. "Please, Jules. What kind of idiot do you take *me* for? You've done everything in your power this week to avoid me like the plague."

"I have *not*," I lied.

"Is that why you've worked so hard to sit in the back? That excuse about Nat's arm—that was the best you could come up with?" He continued to laugh.

He knew what I had been doing all along! *This* is why I wore the sunglasses this morning; I was far too easy to read. I began pulling the glasses back out of my bag to hide. Thinking hard to come back with a witty remark hoping to prove him wrong, I was distracted with the song that played quietly on the radio.

"Hey, it's our song!" Broderick said mindlessly as he turned up the volume. Suddenly he realized what he had just said and I saw his body strain to face forward and his face flushed a bright color of pink. "I didn't mean *our* song. I just know it's one of your favorites, and I love it too and..." he trailed off in embarrassment.

"It's okay. I know what you meant." I smiled sympathetically at him as he exhaled in relief.

"You look tired. You slept through our class break today," I stated, wanting to keep the conversation going as I felt my guilt of the day before begin creeping back in. "Studying late last night?"

"I *wish*." He blinked his eyes viciously to wake his face up and then yawned. "I had a really bad nightmare early in the night and I couldn't go back to sleep."

"Must've been some nightmare," I thought aloud.

"It was." He shuddered. "It probably wouldn't bother you since you're so used to watching horror movies though."

"Just because I watch them, doesn't mean they don't scare me. I watch them because they *do* scare me. Fear is exciting," I explained. "Everyone has a fear that haunts them, whether it's reality or from a movie screen."

"Is that supposed to make me feel better?" he asked with a chuckle.

"Eh." I shrugged. "Can't say I didn't try."

We stayed relaxingly silent, listening to the song. As long as I kept my mind off from the tightening knots and the gnawing dread, I was content in his presence.

"I saw Gavin yesterday." He was plainly uncomfortable breaking the silence with these chosen words. "He was driving around our neighborhood last night." He pulled the corners of his mouth back, not into a smile, but more of an expression of disappointment. "Did he come to see you?" he asked.

I squeezed my eyes tightly together as the illness overtook me. "Just get me home."

"I don't understand. I just asked a simple question. I know it's none of my business, but..." he scrambled.

"You're right. It isn't any of your business." I rolled my head over so he couldn't look at me.

As we bound over the hill, I could see the safety of my two and a half story Cape Cod on the corner and I placed my hand on the handle of the door. My door was already opened before he came to full stop in my driveway. I jumped out and ran to the door fighting the tears that were ready to spill over.

"He's not good enough for you, Jules. Jules!" he yelled for me, but I slammed the door behind me and prayed that he wasn't as bold as to follow me inside the house.

Natalie and Mom were in the kitchen but I couldn't face them so I simply announced that I was going to my room to study and planned to stay there for the remainder of the day. No one came to check on me or to press themselves on me. They knew I wanted to be alone.

Near midnight, I threw on a pair of jeans and wrapped a hooded sweatshirt around me, in case the night air was cool. Shoving my feet into my tennis shoes and lazily ignoring the laces, I was in a hurry to climb onto the roof to clear my head. I opened my window to feel the cooler night air.

Confrontation is on the horizon. I winced at the thought.

At the edge of my lawn, near the woods, a car flashed its headlights at me. My heart stopped in the shock of familiarity, only to speed up hard the minute I recognized the person stepping out of the parked car and walking across my lawn. It wasn't my neighboring hero in his red jeep. Nor was it Savannah or Cari.

Gavin.

"Jules! Can we talk?" he whispered up to my bedroom window.

I dropped my head and shoulders in unreserved defeat. *The confrontation.* My instinct hadn't failed me.

"Come on down here and get in the car, Jules. Let's drive around so we can talk."

A dream-like veil fell over my eyes, making my life seem completely unrealistic. I couldn't answer. I wanted to conceal myself from the confrontation we were fated to have.

"Jules, please. Just get in the car," his voice pleaded.

"What are you doing here?" My throat closed tight so that my voice sounded raspy. I covered my face with my hands.

"God, Jules," he spoke loudly as the wind picked up, "It wasn't supposed to happen this way… Please, can we go somewhere to talk?" he asked as he turned the heat on.

"I'd rather not." I worried that my family would catch me sneaking away with him. The consequences were quickly piling up in my brain, making me nervous. Although I wished we could just sweep the broken pieces under the rug and move on, my curiosity to hear him out was getting the best of me. "I'll climb down to you. I don't want my parents to see you here. You're also whispering too loudly."

I quickly tied the laces of my sneakers and climbed out of my window and down the tree that loomed over the corner of our roof.

The idea of someone driving by and seeing Gavin's car parked at the corner of our property made me uneasy. Although getting that news to circulate through town until it reached Morgan was appealing, my family would be angry and disappointed. But that didn't compare to how I ached from the possibility that Broderick might see us together.

"We can drive down to the end of my road where they're doing construction. I don't want anyone to know you are here," I said, knowing that the unfinished cul-de-sac of my road would be the last place anyone would see us.

We pulled into a clearing behind the patch of trees—well hidden, but good enough for me to keep watch of my house in case my parents realized I was gone.

"I was desperate to see you. I came here at the first opportunity I had." He unbuckled his seat belt and turned to face me. "You have to hear me out," he started.

I nodded quietly, numbed by his presence.

He rubbed his head and closed his eyes. "This is not supposed to be happening. I don't know how things got so out of hand… I don't want to marry Morgan. I just couldn't let you stay behind and wait for me. I love you too much for that."

"Wh-what?" I brokenly stammered. This was not what I expected.

"I said I love you. *Still.* I can't forget you. I think about you all the time." He placed his hand on my hand that rested on my leg and his blue eyes became shifty. "I messed up. I know that, but I would do anything to get you back."

Completely floored, my head started shaking in a delayed denial. He could never be trusted.

He leaned his head back against his seat. "Sydney Blythe had a few choice words for me that evening at graduation; she got in my face about five minutes before we lined up." He closed his eyes again, like he was in torment. "I never meant to hurt you, but I couldn't get rid of Morgan."

Her name, falling from his lips, ignited a wicked fire in my brain. "Get rid of her? You were screwing her! That's why you couldn't get *rid* of her!"

He looked at me pleadingly. "What was I supposed to do, Jules? I'm a selfish bastard who can't control his hormones. You never gave it up and I was tired of the cold showers."

True to my masochistic nature, I had to know. "How did it happen?"

His face reddened as I gained control of the interrogation. He looked away at first—out into woods, and then he settled his eyes on me. "She would leave me over twenty text messages when you and I were together. I'd drop you off to go home and I would always find myself passing by her house." He paused to collect his thoughts. "I would drive by several times, telling myself it was the wrong thing to do, but I always wound up parking the car in her driveway…"

"Like you're doing tonight? How many times?" I pressed, fighting to overpower all of my emotions. I was like stone, but the stone was cracking.

"What do you mean?"

"I mean how many times, how many dates, how many times? How many times?" My voice rose to a scream as I dramatically threw my arms up in fury.

Silence.

"How many times?" I demanded again.

"It probably *didn't* happen more than… twice," he admitted slowly

I dropped my jaw at the cutting truth. He had been cheating on me more than I had ever imagined.

"I hated myself after every time," he concluded. "I wished it had never happened. It didn't mean anything."

"Then why are you marrying her? Because she's pregnant? Because adding another mistake will make it better?" I asked. "Never mind; don't answer that. I don't even care. Your excuses are lame, they don't make any sense, and I'm not buying them."

I glanced at my house to see if any lights had come on, so I could excuse myself. Unfortunately, the house was still dark. Everyone was still sleeping soundly.

"I just thought you deserved better…" he trailed off.

"I *do* deserve better."

Silence. I could only hear the sound of our breathing. "... I realized though, that I can't go on without you. I need you in my life one way or another." He grabbed my face desperately and pressed his lips to mine.

Shocked, I sat numbly and let him molest my lips, unable to move. My heart throbbed in protest. Everything was different now. I no longer wanted to be with Gavin—not even out of the mad challenge to win him in the end, beating Morgan. Popularity was never worth being with him. My heart was being pulled elsewhere and logic reminded me that I was kissing a practically married man. A man that not only had lied to me about who he was, but had also lied to others about who *I* was. A man that I was certain was lying to me now.

Pulling away, my eyes were full of scorn as I wiped my lips of his kiss in disgust. "What sort of bullshit have you been spilling to Erik Peterson about me?"

Gavin's eyes faked confusion. "I don't know what you're talking about."

"Don't play stupid. You told Erik that we had sex!" Clenching my teeth during the reminder, it was finally dawning on me how dirty he made me feel. It made me angry and I felt strength in my anger. My monster was deep inside of me, growling to be released.

"Jules, I'm insulted. Even if we had been intimate, I would have never shared the details. That would be something special and private, just between us. Being with you like that... it's all I ever dreamed of..." He reached over and brushed my cheek with his fingers, causing me to cringe.

I jerked my face away and looked over at my house again. "So, she would text you and you would drive by her house. Hmm... Do you know what the difference is between then and now?" He didn't answer, so I turned around to face and him and give him the answer myself. "I didn't text you. I don't even want you here. Go home." I grabbed the door handle and pulled it open slightly

"Don't do this. Don't turn away from me." He grabbed my wrist to keep me from leaving but I sternly jerked out of his grasp.

I looked at my house again and kept my hand on the door handle. "I'm going to walk home now and I don't want you to feel welcomed anywhere near my home again."

I tore loose of his grasp and walked down the dark street back to my home. Although I could hear Gavin's footsteps behind me, the knots in my stomach became unraveled. I had conquered Gavin Williams. I was victorious even though he was relentless in his pursuit of me, calling after me in a hushed voice as I walked down the dead end street. His footsteps sped up as I edged my way into the yard and across my front lawn.

"Jules, no one would ever have to know about us..." He said grabbing my wrist again.

I turned to face him, furious that he would even think that I would agree to an affair with him. How dare he question my character! The venom in my mouth soon dropped into a lump in my throat as my words were cut off by the sudden haunting howl echoing from the woods around my house.

Gavin's eyes widened in terror at the sound. "What the hell..."

Ripping my wrist free of his grasp, I sprinted toward the corner of the house, and scrambled up the tree to my window. My body shaking frantically with every step. By the time I reached my bedroom window, I looked over my shoulder to see Gavin was bolting out of my yard and down the street where he left his car. I would have laughed if I wasn't panting so hard from fear.

It was too close to our homes whatever *it* was. My eyes focused into the woods, hoping to catch a glimpse of the predator. It clearly wasn't a dog and there was no way it was a coyote, either! It was a freaking *wolf*! Mimicking the sound that has resonated in over a hundred horror movies, I could never be convinced otherwise now.

Climbing inside to the safety of my house, I heard the sound of Gavin's tires screeching against the road as his car sped away. Slowly creeping closer to the window, braver than I had been before and slightly relieved it was never a figment of my imagination, my hands trembled as I placed them on the edge of the window for support and stuck my head outside. The howl rang out again.

The Shape in the Shadows

THE SOUND OF THE howl was still resonating in my ears, chilling my blood when I woke the next morning. Fate had intervened, the confrontation was over. I could move forward, at last. Gavin's wedding was not a concern of mine. I wasn't concerned about deflecting questions over the wedding this weekend anymore either. It was the last thing on my mind. The chapter of Gavin Williams was finally closed and a new path beckoned. A path that beckoned forcefully to me this morning. I had to see evidence of the wolf! A footprint, a trail. Anything!

Upon dressing and doing my morning hygiene duties, I told my mother I was going to take a walk in the woods. I stood with hesitation at the head of the trail leading into the woods at the side of my house. It wasn't just what awaited me in the woods that made me anxious, but what waited for me on the other side of those woods, as well—Broderick Cooper.

I stepped slowly on the worn path, careful to not trip on any tree roots or get my clothes snagged on thorny bushes. I thought of the howling I had heard last night and how the sound echoed from this vicinity. The memory brought a sudden fear and a cold sweat. Passing the pines and scrub oaks, I walked into the vegetation and thickets, stopping as I came to a bubbling creek. I put my hand on the dogwood tree that stood beside it as I took in the view. There was nothing here that gave proof to the wolf's existence. Puzzled, I turned back to view the path that had dipped and twisted and had led me to the creek. Only a handful of times had Natalie or I traipsed through these woods, yet here was a well-worn path leading straight to the creek that divided our properties. I studied it for a few minutes and came to the ultimate conclusion that someone made regular trips to this very spot, creating a path. Looking up I could clearly see my secret sitting spot on the roof of my home—a perfect shot from where I stood.

I stepped onto the large rock embedded in the creek and made a quick plan of attack to cross. The water was shallow. A moderately sized rock rested dry, perfectly between the larger rock I stood on and the even grander rock that jut from his side of the property. I cautiously hopped onto the center rock and to the other side.

"Piece of cake, Jules," I congratulated myself for not slipping and landing in the creek.

I then gasped at the equally worn path from this side of the creek that would lead me to his house. Swiftly through the woods, I ran to the edge of the leafy shadows and onto the soft green grass of Broderick's side yard.

Subconsciously, I walked along the edge of the woods to the front facing road, and started down the broken sidewalk to Broderick's front door. Now, more than ever before, the pull to him was undeniable as I knocked on the front oak door of his two story brick home.

I prepared for the door to be slammed in my face, but then Broderick stood in the doorway smiling from ear to ear. The surprise of my presence was clear in his expression. "Jules!"

Smiling, I gave a resigned sigh, a small lift and drop of my shoulders; I was finished running from him.

"Would you like to come in?"

I laughed nervously at his eager bearing. "Thanks."

He closed the door behind me as I stepped into the foyer, and stared at me for a moment in disbelief. He cleared his throat. "Come this way. You have to meet my Grandmother, Evelyn."

In a formally set living room, most of the furniture looked to be antique and I felt it was only meant to be appreciated not actually used. The frail, old lady sat in a floral winged-back chair reading a book.

"Grandma," Broderick began "I'd like you to meet our neighbor, Jules Taylor. She's the one I've been telling you about."

"Hi," I said pleasantly, trying hard to disguise the desire to know exactly what all he had been *telling* her.

Her face twisted in such a way that I was unsure if she was shocked to see me or scared of me. Regardless, she didn't seem too thrilled to have me in her home and I couldn't understand where I had already gone wrong with this woman.

"Pleased to meet you, Jules," she curtly spoke as she turned away from me.

Broderick quickly came to my rescue and patted me on the back. His outward show of affection took the sting away from her rude regard toward me.

He spoke to her warmly, "We'll be around back. Call me on my cell phone if you need anything, grandma." She nodded quietly and picked her book back up. He kissed her on the cheek and as he led me out of the room, I felt her eyes burning me from behind her book into the back of my head.

Broderick blushed with embarrassment and whispered, "She doesn't trust people she doesn't know yet. Give her time." As long as I could avoid being in her presence, I would be fine, but I knew I would obsess over her behavior toward me until the day I die.

I followed Broderick through to the back of the house and he stopped in the kitchen for a moment to pour us two glasses of sweet tea. I was about to sit at the table, when I saw him gather the glasses of tea and walk over to the back door.

"Whoa! Where are we going?"

"Come on." He motioned his head as he grinned.

I trailed behind him out the back door, off the back porch, and across the expansive driveway to the garage that had a large, circle-top window over the garage door. We walked up a flight of stairs on the side of the garage that led to a door and a small front deck. He handed over my tea and then opened the door with his free hand. I hesitated entering in at first, for I knew my parents would throw a fit if they found out that I was in a guy's room. He waited patiently, his face innocent of any wrong doing. Nervous, I walked into the large room which had the appearance of an efficiency apartment. To the far corner was a full size and neatly made bed—a desk and a dresser on either side. Over the bed were two windows;

in one of the windows was a small air conditioning unit that was throwing out as much cold air as possible, giving me a chill. On the opposite wall was a door I could only assume was a bathroom. A futon was placed at the foot of the bed and a television set a few feet in front of it. The supremely large, circular shaped window in the center of the front wall made the room burst with sun light. The window would probably give a clear shot to my back bedroom window in the fall when the trees lost their leaves.

But it wasn't the size of the room or the envied privacy it provided that amazed me. Near the large window were countless canvasses—paintings—that either sat on an easel unfinished, hung on walls, or leaned against the wall in stacks. Some were vibrant with colors and beauty and a few were dark and fierce, full of torment.

"You did these?" I asked as I stepped closer to them, fighting the urge to touch the one that was covered in silver, gray, black, and red. It looked like a dark shadow of a tall thin man in a dark corner of a room. A spot of light sliced his face and the man's black hair was dipping over part of his face. It was hard to make out any details of his face, but what was visible was chilling. It looked as though the man had fangs and blood was trickling from his lips. Eyes so pale, they appeared silver.

"Yeah," he answered sheepishly.

I couldn't tear my eyes from the tormented painting. Despite the fear it was supposed to project, I couldn't shake the feeling of amazement and beauty with it. His paintings were incredible.

"They're amazing," I said in a hush as I glanced over at another painting, of a young girl in a red hooded jacket, standing in the shadowy woods at night. The only light came from the full moon and its reflection in the bubbling brook that ran under a bridge on the path. Though her face was hidden, her long tresses were auburn—like my natural hair color. In the light mist that rose around her, a human face was scarcely seen looking over her shoulder, blending in with the light smoke that enveloped around them. But what chilled me was what I saw between them in the bushes. Two topaz eyes darting from behind the leaves—eyes that belonged to an animal. The fear in seeing this painting was nearly debilitating. I was hypnotized.

"It relaxes me after nightmares."

His voice made me jump back. "*This* relaxes you?" I asked wide eyed and in disbelief as I pointed to the first painting that told a tale of danger that crept in the woods.

"It's therapeutic." A corner of his mouth pulled back into a lopsided grin.

"Did you paint this one after that nightmare you had the other night?" I asked curiously.

"Yes and no. Like the nightmares, it…" he thought for a moment before continuing his words, "it's a work in progress. I've been painting that one for a while." I couldn't decipher if he was scowling at the painting or the memory of his nightmare.

"Wow, Broderick. Your nightmares are all sorts of jacked-up if they inspired these paintings."

He nodded in agreement.

"I heard the howling again last night." I said changing the subject. "Did you hear it?"

"No, I didn't. What time last night?"

"*Late*. That's how I ended up here. I went into the woods to see if there was any sort of evidence left behind. That I'm not going crazy. I wonder if you're hearing it in your sleep, causing you to have these nightmares."

"I don't know," he confessed. "Maybe…"

He stood at the easel gathering a few of the paintings, trying to straighten things up as he watched me drift from place to place in his room. The pleasure of my presence covering his face quickly disappeared, turning to nervousness when I walked over to his dresser to get a better glance of the pictures sitting on top of it. There was a picture of his grandmother wearing a straw hat and a floral dress in a meadow sitting beside a tree full of leaves. She didn't look anything like the woman I had just met. This woman in the picture was happier, smiling broadly. The other picture was of Jackson giving Taryn a piggyback ride.

I turned to see Broderick biting his bottom lip and narrowing his eyes at the pictures as well. "Did you take these photos, too?" I asked him with awe.

He smiled at my reaction to them, gaining confidence in his work. "Guilty."

"You really have a great eye for this stuff!" I exclaimed. "Why aren't you in the art department or on the yearbook staff?" I waited for a moment then gave a spicy after thought. "Or are you *too cool* for that?"

He laughed. "No, I'm not *too cool* for that," he repeated mimicking my sarcastic tone. "I just stay busy with so many other things; I haven't found the time. Besides, what if no one liked my work?"

"Are you joking?" I asked incredulously. "If anyone ever told you they were bad it would be out of pure jealousy."

I strolled over to his entertainment center and saw on top of the TV three DVD cases with a local rental kiosk logo. I picked them up. "*Friday the 13th, Halloween, An American Werewolf in London...* You watch these kinds of movies?" My excitement of the possibility of our common interest was far from hidden.

"I haven't seen any of them yet."

"John Carpenter's *Halloween* is my all-time favorite horror film..." Beside the movies was a large ceramic popcorn bowl and a few bags of microwavable popcorn tucked inside. It suddenly occurred to me that he had plans today—possibly to invite a friend or a date over to watch movies. "I'm sorry. I came over uninvited."

Flustered, I walked over to the door, but he trailed close behind me. "Wait, Jules."

I handed him my drink and began stammering my goodbye. "Thanks for letting me come by to see you and showing me your room. I only came over for a bit to talk to you about the howling sound and to apologize about yesterday." I started for the door.

"Hey, you don't have to go. Please, stay."

"No." I shook my head. "I really should go. You obviously had plans and I don't want to impose."

I pulled the door open a few inches only to have him gently press it shut again with his hand. "You wouldn't be imposing. Please. *Stay.*" He leaned in close to me, towering over me as he leaned against the door, his dark brown eyes smiling back at me. I thought of trying to re-open the door but really didn't want to leave. I was dizzy with exhilaration over the effort he had shown to get me to stay already.

"If you insist..."

"I *do*."

I slowly walked back over to the futon and wondered who he had invited over and if it would be someone I would enjoy being around. Or worse, hated. What if it was Taryn?

"So who'd you invite?" I asked.

"I haven't exactly invited them yet..." He looked away and blushed. "...but she showed up anyway."

Astonished with his confession, I was sure that my foolish grin mimicked his. *I was meant to be here.*

"I assumed you would want a distraction today with your friends gone..." He stood straight and brushed off the embarrassment. "...I wanted to invite you yesterday, but I said something stupid to upset you and I am really sorry about that."

"You didn't upset me," I assured him.

"Then what was it?"

I dropped and shook my head in dismay. "It's silly."

"Do you think I won't understand? That I would judge you?"

"Yes. Actually, I do."

He smiled gently at me. "I wouldn't judge you any more than I want you to judge me."

"But I *have* judged you."

He leaned in just a couple of inches away from my face. "And?"

Admitting my misgivings was something I often tried skirting around. "I *may* have been wrong about you," I finally answered after a long pause.

"You thought that I had hidden motives for wanting to be your friend," he concluded for me. "I'd lie to you or about you. Is that how you saw me?"

My body tensed to the point that I was barely capable to nod my head.

"Let's lay the cards out on the table then, shall we?"

I chuckled, only partly joking. "I don't think I'm playing with a full deck."

"Jules, my intentions with you are completely honorable. I have a strong..." he narrowed his eyes as he delicately chose an appropriate word. "... *instinct* that you and I should be very close friends."

The truth of his words frightened me; it was too close to my own instinct. "How can you even say that?"

"I have a knack for knowing these things." He winked. "No judgments, Jules. I promise."

"I saw Gavin the night before while I was out for coffee and it affected me a lot more than I thought it would," I confessed in embarrassment.

He stood there silently in full composure, nowhere close to shock. "He must have really broken your heart."

Wrinkling my nose, I shook my head. "It was only a scratch."

He sighed heavily. "I knew that he was preying upon you. I had hoped that maybe by mentioning it to you that I could prevent him from taking advantage of you or at the very least, warn you. Guess I was a tad late."

"*Prey* upon me? Broderick, I'm not a victim."

He shook his head earnestly. "You're a victim, I assure you."

With a small laugh, I gave him an incredulous look and shook my head. "And you can't save everybody, Broderick. No matter how big of a hero you are, it can't be done."

"So, what happened?" he asked.

I groaned. "He had the nerve to show up at my house late last night. He proposed that I be his side girl while he remained married to Morgan." I shook my head. "It was insulting."

Broderick finally relaxed at my words, exhaling a long breath that he had been holding.

"He's not special to me, Broderick." I assured him further. I paused as I grasped the courage to continue. "It was always about status with him. The fact that he showed any interest at all, from the beginning, it made me feel pretty and important. Being his girlfriend made me popular. And I liked it." If this didn't run Broderick off, I didn't know what would. I turned around and saw Broderick attentive and patient with no hint of running. "Things ended so abruptly and without closure, that for the last two months I've just been hanging by this invisible thread that was somehow, still attached to him. I couldn't cut it loose, making it impossible for me to cope. And the *way* he did it—my gosh! Everyone knew! *Everyone*—but, me. I ignored everything—my friends' warnings and even the proof I saw with my own two eyes on numerous occasions. It was humiliating! And I did that to myself! You have no idea what it's like to be the punch line in a joke that the whole school is in on. But last night... I felt like I finally got my closure and *I* got to be the one to do it. *I* made the choice." I smiled with joy. With relief.

Broderick tucked his lips in and pulled the corners of his mouth back into a small smile. "I'm proud of you."

"However, it would have felt good to get revenge on Morgan. Thank goodness I heard the howling before I had a chance to change my mind, right? I nearly jumped out of my skin when I heard it! And you should have seen Gavin's face!" I laughed and looked over to see Broderick shaking his head and chuckling. "I can't believe I just told you all of that. You must think I'm horrible or crazy… or… *something*."

He shook his head. "No, I don't. I've been there; I know what it's like to lose yourself during less-than-appealing situation or a permanent change in your life."

"You're talking about Taryn?"

"Possibly."

He chuckled as if he carried a private thought. My eyes drifted from his face to my feet. I felt that I had overstepped a boundary.

"Look," he began again. "Maybe who you were before isn't who you were meant to be at all. The person you are becoming is who you're supposed to be. There is something greater out there for you. Greater than just being popular in school, or singing in the best band, greater than this town—greater than Gavin Williams. You're better than all of that, Jules." He quieted then he whispered, "You were too good for him. Always have been."

"After dating the likes of Gavin and Erik, I'm pretty sure I'm not good enough for anybody honorable," I countered, keeping my eyes glued to the floor.

He lifted my chin with his fingers and leaned in closer to me. His eyes smoldering. "Are you sure of that?"

I couldn't answer, for I didn't really want to believe that.

Our faces were aligned to close in and my breathing became heavy as I anticipated our first kiss. Closer. Closer…closer…hold…

The moment suddenly became awkward.

Broderick released my chin and stepped away, His cheeks reddening with embarrassment. "So which movie would you like to watch first?

Halloween? You said that was your favorite. I had you pegged for a classic-horror kind of girl." Broderick went over to the stack of DVDs and I grinned. He was great at moving on from an obviously uncomfortable moment though he was still feeling heated from it. "Is it too hot in here for you? I can turn the air on a little higher if you'd like." Broderick fanned his T-shirt and I caught a glimpse of his tight, rippled stomach and for that split second, I *felt* hot.

"Actually, I'm cold natured." I fought for composure.

He dashed over to his dresser and pulled out his varsity football sweatshirt. He held the sweatshirt out to me and I, without hesitating, grabbed it from him. I was eager to wrap my body inside of it and take in his scent again. Though too large for me, I enjoyed the warmth it provided.

"That's a good look for you." A dimple peeked through on one side of Broderick's cheek.

Throughout the movie, it was so easy to be around him. Once in a while, we would playfully toss popcorn at one another. We would laugh when one of us would shudder, jump, or even scream during the intense movie. I couldn't be sure, but I had the distinct feeling that he was flirting with me, or at least testing the waters to do so. Nonchalantly, at times I sniffed the fragrance of his sweatshirt and fell into the fresh spirit of its aroma. My peripheral would do me the justice of catching him staring at me and smiling endlessly as he thought I was locked into the movie. I wanted badly to know what he was thinking and what he was feeling. How did his eyes perceive me? Was he drawn to me as I was to him?

Before I could give those questions too much thought, my phone vibrated in my pocket with a text message. I pulled it out to read it.

"What is it?" Broderick asked.

I flipped it over for him to glance at as if my word wouldn't be enough for him to believe. "It's my mom. She and Dad are getting ready to leave for a company dinner and she wants me home so she can feed me before they leave." I chuckled, shaking my head with a slight embarrassment at her insistence to baby me. "I think I'm full on popcorn though. Moms...you gotta love them."

"You're lucky to have one."

Heat rushed to my face as I realized my insensitive gaffe. Sighing, I pulled his wonderfully scented sweatshirt off and draped it on the back of the futon before jumping up to make my way to the door. Broderick hurried to my side to let me out.

"Do you want to get together again and finish these movies? Maybe tonight after your dinner?"

"No, you go ahead and watch them. You'll like *American Werewolf*. It has a bit of humor in it."

"Maybe tomorrow then?"

My instinct told me now to solidify plans with him but my heart warned that it would be that much easier to see that I was a fool if he broke them. "Maybe. See you later."

He opened the door and I hurried down the stairs before I had a chance to change my mind. I so badly wanted to stay with him.

The house was strangely quiet when I entered. Standing still for a few short seconds, I finally heard the faint tapping sounds of my mom moving things around in her bathroom. To comfort myself from the eerie silence of the house, I noisily stomped up the stairs until I reached my mom's bathroom.

Sitting at her vanity with rollers in her hair, she immediately saw my reflection in the mirror. "That was quite a long walk in our small neighborhood. Where have you been? It would have been nice to know where you were and that you weren't lying in a ditch somewhere." She gathered the last lock of hair and rolled it up with a heated cylinder and clipped it into place.

"I was watching TV over at Broderick's," I replied cautiously.

Forgetting all about her worry about where I had been, my mom's approval was hardly concealed. "Jules, I like him. He's such a nice boy."

"Yeah, he's really great."

"Do you like him?"

I shrugged in reply.

"Well, you can act as flip about him as you want. I *know* you." She gave a wink.

"Where's Nat?" I changed the subject.

"Spending the night at Amber's."

I scowled. "Great. I'm stuck here *alone* tonight. No friends, no car..."

"You should invite Cari or Savannah over then," she suggested.

"Mom, it's a Saturday night. Savannah and Trip are more than likely on a date and Cari works late."

"You can have your dad's truck tonight. Would that make you happy?" She began applying her base makeup as I shrugged in response. "We'll be leaving here in about an hour and won't be home until late—closer to eleven."

I sat quietly and watched her line her eyes with a dark brown pencil accentuating her icy blue eyes. "Wow! That *is* late for you old fogies," I teased.

"Are you hungry for dinner? I can make you something real quick before we head out," Mom offered.

I shook my head. "I filled up on popcorn." She frowned at my choice for a meal. "Well, I'm exhausted. I'm going to go to my room and lay down for a bit."

"Okay, sweetie," she said. "I'll let you know when we're ready to leave."

My emotionally charged week finally crashed down upon me as I walked into my bedroom and sank into my bed. My head was having trouble wrapping around the possibility that Broderick could very well like me. I was almost positive he was flirting with me—that there was some sort of chemistry between us. The mystery, though, was why someone like Broderick would waste his efforts on a *nobody* like me. Also, I couldn't put my finger on it, but he behaved differently from other people; as if keeping a secret from the whole world. And what was his fascination with me, anyway? I wanted to ask him, but felt that I was being too presumptuous in my theory. Still, there had to be an explanation for the worn path in the woods between our homes and the most logical and appealing suspect was Broderick. Nevertheless, the eerie truth was that someone or some*thing* was creating a trail out, a straight line between Broderick's yard and mine. My mind was quickly directed to the howl I had heard again last night.

As I closed my eyes and let sleep envelope me, the paintings and photographs by Broderick burst through my mind. He was so gifted. His art was amazing and terrifying at the same time. If his nightmares were anything close to the unfinished painting of the fanged man in the shadowy corner, then I understood why he suffered through so many sleepless nights.

Sleep was short lived by the tapping at my bedroom door. I clumsily trampled to the door and rubbed my face to stimulate my senses. When I opened the door, I saw my mother dressed in a classy black dress walking down the stairs. "Your dad and I are heading out."

Nodding, I followed her down to the family room. My dad sat in front of the flat screen catching the score of a baseball game before turning it off. "You ready, Leah?" he asked.

"I just had to let Jules know that we we're leaving," she explained.

My dad stood up from the couch and straightened his suit. "No plans tonight, Jules?"

I wrinkled my nose. "I could use the study time. My algebra final is Friday so..." I made a sour expression.

"Go to the movies and see that one movie you've wanted to see. What was it? *Serenity*?"

"*Secluded*, Daddy." I grinned as he shook his head in response to my choice of movies. Mom kissed me on the cheek and headed out the door behind Dad.

Still a little disoriented from my nap, I decided to grab a coffee from the Java House when they left. A quick pick me up. Then get a movie from one of the local DVD rental kiosks. My goal for the night was to watch a movie and then at the first sign of twilight, I would wait on the roof to listen for the howling. Maybe I would even see the animal this time.

By the time I returned home with my coffee and a movie, it was just before sunset. Despite my preference for horror movies, I was really a coward. After locking every door in the house and even the door to my bedroom, I peered out of my side window for life in the woods—life on the other side of the woods. It was too dark to make out anything other than the thick, overgrown vegetation. Everything was in dark shadows. They appeared sinister.

As the movie started, I settled comfortably on my bed. Before long, my overactive mind conjured up sounds—things that go *bump* in the night—outside my bedroom window and on the roof, leading me to sit tense in my bed and turning the TV off with the remote. Without leaving the relative safety of my bed, I glanced out my side window facing the woods again, but with no lights coming from Broderick's garage apartment,

I could scarcely make out his window through the trees. This made me feel even more nervous. With a quick twist of the knob, I turned off the lamp on my night stand allowing the darkness to conceal me, protecting me from who or what may be watching me through the woods. With my cell phone in hand, lighting my way and ready to dial the emergency number, I rushed over to open and look out the front two windows facing the road. Night was falling fast. My eyes shifted from side to side for several minutes, waiting for any tangible proof that someone was watching me. No matter how paranoid I may have seemed, I knew that paranoia did not blaze that trail in the woods. Still, I saw nothing. I shuffled quietly over to the small lamp on my nightstand and flipped it back on a dim setting.

A breeze whipped through my room and I was unsure as to whether I shivered because of the uncharacteristically cool night or because of fear. A fear that both shook me and thrilled me at the same time. Being a fear-junkie, I was experiencing an adrenaline rush like a rollercoaster ride or cliff diving. It was why I enjoyed watching horror movies so much. I had to be outside! Closer to the assumed danger that lurked in the woods, but not too close. No. I would watch for it from the safety of my roof.

I shoved my skinny arms through the sleeves of my red hoodie. Before I grabbed my coffee, I plugged my mp3 player up to the speakers in my room and turned the volume up loud enough for me to hear it outside, providing just enough comfort to keep me brave.

The noises were all in your mind. You haven't even heard them since you turned the movie off, silly.

Not to spill any of my coffee, I maneuvered myself carefully out the front dormer window and onto the roof, placing myself in my regular spot. As if in a watch tower, I sat perched, hoping to get a hint of what was howling in the night and what was creating a visible path to and from mine and Broderick's houses. Surely I was safe at such a high distance from the ground. Wolves can't climb houses, so unless it was a rabid bird or a squirrel, I should be safe from any animal attack.

The eastern sky was darkened with a deep hue of dark blue, sporadically lit through the clouds by a bright star or a passing plane. The far west was brushed with light sweeps of pinks, yellows, and blues—painted perfectly, like one of Broderick's artistic creations; the sun dipping behind the wooded pines across the street. Shadows of the dividing woods were no longer confined to their own daytime existence but had reached over to pull my house into its eerie and mystical fortress. My eyes slowly adjusted to the darkness. I listened for the howl, the slightest rustling of branches or leaves in the woods to compensate my sanity. I had heard the call of the wild animal, there wasn't a doubt in my mind what it was.

My latte had already cooled enough to drink it without burning my tongue, so I popped the lid off and tossed it to the side, hoping that it wouldn't slide right off of the roof and into the yard where I'd have to pick it up later. It landed by the A-frame of my window and I made a mental note to grab it on my way back inside.

The moon glowed around the edges and the western sky no longer held the sun. I leaned back to rest my eyes upon the evening sky as it darkened further to a hazy black. The shadows loomed over me from the tall oak trees that lined along the corner of my house with the blackest of black. Like a cloak, it covered the entire roof and a large portion of the yard. The mp3 player inside my room shuffled songs again and it began playing the familiar melody that was beginning to carry so many meanings and memories for me. I sighed at the one particular memory—the one where it played in the jeep and Broderick referred to it as *our* song.

"Broderick," I sighed breathlessly—*longingly*—letting every consonant and every vowel have purpose on my lips as they created his name.

A low and nearly inaudible moan came from the corner of the roof by the oak tree and I shot straight up, nearly spilling my latte that I held upright on my stomach. Studying the roof closely, I saw only the black shadows from the overhanging tree at first, but as my eyes adjusted my mind projected a figure standing among the shadows—a part of the shadows. The blood in my veins ran ice cold and my breathing became shallow. Logic fought hard to convince me that what I was seeing was simply branches, leaves, and shadows shaped like a human figure, much like the clouds in the sky resembling animals or faces. Still, my confidence in the safety of my location had wavered and I decided to crawl back through the window. Slowly, I got to my feet and stepped to the steep front side of the roof. Then I heard a snapping sound, like a twig had cracked only feet from where I stood—where the figure stood. With wider steps quickly toward the presumed safety of my window, I hoped that I could make it inside before I was attacked by whatever imagination preyed upon me on the roof.

The latte splattered on my hand and sleeve as I shuffled quickly to the crease between the frame of my window and the steep roof for a more secure footing.

Suddenly, I heard and felt the crunch of plastic under my left shoe, causing my leg to uncontrollably slide forward and down the slope of shingles. I dropped my drink and fell back sliding forcefully closer to the edge of the roof.

"Oh, shit!" I choked.

I twisted on my stomach in an attempt to use my knees and palms as friction, desperate to grab anything, but the steep roof, the momentum of my fall, and the plastic object that had crunched under my left shoe, was working against my resistance, making the surface smooth and slick. The grain from the shingles scraped my palms, and elbows like sand paper. The split second my feet slid past the gutters I screamed, aware that falling was imminent. I tucked my head closely to my chest, preparing for the painful impact that waited for me below, rubbing it against the rough surface beneath me; my chin burned from the shallow abrasion. As my body slid from the grainy surface, I made one last grab for something to hang on to and my fingers hooked over the lip of the gutter.

I closed my eyes tightly as my body jerked to an unexpected stop. My heart thundered loudly as my right arm was being held tightly and pulled by a powerful and fleshy-feeling vise that wrapped around my wrist. I opened my eyes to see a black shadow slide up my arm and pull harder from above my elbow. Like the same black mass around my wrist, it too pulled firmly. The shuffling sound in front of me was the sound of something struggling against the slope of the roof, but still I saw nothing realistic through my tears of trepidation. Just blackness. The shadowy figure.

My fingers tightened around the gutter of the roof.

"Jules, grab one of my arms and pull your feet up!" The deep, familiar voice strained.

I whimpered and shook, confused as I searched for an arm and a face—a *body*!—to save me, debating quickly if I favored better by dropping to the ground from a two and a half story roof.

"Jules, I can't pull you up if you don't help me!" The voice pleaded.

I blinked erratically and recoiled as the black shadow that held me like a vise took shape. It wasn't an animal; it was a *man*! Within seconds the shadow was absorbed into flesh, and became a visible human form. The dark shadow faded away giving light to the face of comfort and salvation. Broderick Cooper!

The gutter began bending and pulling from the roof.

"Jules! You're slipping!" Broderick panicked. "I need you to pull your legs up before we *both* fall!"

My heart shuddered violently and I let go of the gutter to grab his arm that held onto my tiny wrist. I grunted pulling my left leg to the gutter and planted my knee into the trench of it for stability. It gave way and he growled as he strained to pull me closer to him, off of the gutter. I scrambled to where he stood when my feet were finally able to gain some friction against the downward slope of the roof.

His arm wound tightly around my waist and he looked hard through the darkness into my eyes. "Are you okay?"

I couldn't find the courage to speak, staggered with what had just happened. With what I thought I had just witnessed. Carefully, he climbed around the frame and into the window, never once letting go of my hand. I was shivering when he pulled me through the window.

And there he stood in my room, dressed in black from head to toe and holding my arms, studying my face closely. He lifted my face to the faint light from my night stand.

"We need to clean that," he said referring to the small abrasion on my chin. "Do you have a washcloth and some ointment?" His voice quivered as if he, too, were shivering.

I moved my mouth to answer him, but my words fell short of my lips. My mind was unable to catch up to the danger I had just faced. My perception of reality was not accepting what my eyes had just witnessed. The unnatural and impossible change I had seen in Broderick.

What just happened? What did I see?

Broderick walked over to my closet door and opened it only a crack before shutting it in conclusion that it was not the door he was looking for. He turned to me in question. "Where's the bathroom, Jules?"

My hand trembled as I limply pointed to the small bathroom in the hall on the other side of my locked bedroom door. He immediately dashed to the bathroom and I could hear him rummaging through my medicine cabinet. The water came on and then was shut off shortly before he reappeared. He walked me over to my bed and sat me down on the edge.

He knelt at my feet and placed the cold, wet cloth on my chin. Peering at me through the strands of hair that had fallen in his eyes, I could see his own fear at the danger he, too, had witness and the bizarre change he had revealed to me. I stared hard at his face, wanting answers, but was still unable to speak the words to even ask.

Am I crazy?

He handed me two aspirins. "Take these. You're going to need them when the pain hits you. I couldn't find a glass for you to wash them down…" he trailed off. I slipped them between my lips and swallowed.

He looked me over, at my scuffed palms and the worn holes in the elbows of my hooded shirt. He pulled and twisted my arms lightly to get a better view of my elbows. When he saw the tears in the material and the abrasions on my skin he began pulling the sleeves over my wrists to remove the hooded shirt. "

What happened out there? What did I just see? My mind continued to scream these questions over and over again.

As he pulled the sleeves over my elbows, I sucked in my breath through gritted teeth and he winced at my pain. The shock of the stinging sensation not only solidified my recent experience, but brought me back to a shallow disappointment over losing my favorite red hoodie.

"You're bleeding." He placed the cloth on my elbow. "Are you hurt anywhere else?"

I shook my head and continued to gaze at him in bewilderment, stoically staring at him. *Did I really see what I thought I saw? He's dressed all in black… maybe I only imagined what I saw?* I questioned whether I should be frightened of the boy who saved me.

Broderick continued his visual assessment of my minor scrapes and bumps avoiding eye contact as much as possible unless he wanted a response from me. His ragged breaths betrayed his act of calm authority. His face was red from the exertion and tension yet, every touch was smooth and tender.

"I'm sorry I hesitated out there," he whispered.

I shook my head in confusion. Finally, gravelly words jittered from my trembling lips. "What just happened?"

He shifted his eyes far from mine and continued preoccupying himself with mending me.

"You slipped on that lid from your coffee cup," he mumbled.

I never stopped shaking my head, unwilling to accept any excuse he would give me. I was well aware of *my* clumsy move and for once, embarrassment was not even in the vicinity of my concerns. I was trying to make sense of what *he* did—what he *was*. I fought back my tears, scared that something dangerous would come of my knowing, but was deeply curious and full of wonder. "What did you do?"

He stopped moving instantly as I could see the weight of defeat rest upon him. He took several deep breaths and shot a glance at the window; probably debating on whether he would answer my question or leave.

He frowned as he dropped his head. "What did you see?"

My mouth remained open as I waited for my own answer. I couldn't comprehend enough to even ask; I couldn't make sense of it. "I… I don't even know."

He rubbed his eyes with the palms of his hands like he was trying to blot out the visual memory. "Your mind is in shock…" he began.

"I couldn't see you." Tears dripped from my wide eyes as the memory finally brought me out of one shock and into another.

He saw I wasn't going to give in to his theory of trauma. "I was standing in the shadows."

His simple explanation didn't mesh. It was something further. I pushed the recent memory completely to the front of my mind. I swallowed hard, refusing to allow him to convince me that I was losing my mind, that I didn't see what my memory swore to. "No," I said firmly.

Broderick stood up from the bed and walked to the window to look out.

"I was in the shadows… I didn't mean for you to see that."

At last, my vigor began to return, and I demanded an explanation further. "You didn't mean for me to see *what?*" I panted. "You were black as the night one minute and then you, you… changed into… *you.*" There was absolutely no logic to what I had just seen! "How did you do that?" I swallowed the hard lump in my throat before I ultimately pressed, "What are you?"

He stood at the window. Waiting. Hesitating. Silently, I dared him to deny what I saw, yet terrified from the answer I may receive. He took a deep breath.

"Broderick," I whimpered in fright.

"For months now, I have seen you sit on your roof, gazing at the sky. I was drawn to you, your silent thoughts—your sadness. *Everything.* I wanted to know what it would be like to sit near you on that roof...to be part of that with you," he confessed. The muscles in my stomach tightened beyond comfort as I realized that he had, indeed, sat with me on the roof without my knowledge on numerous occasions. "I don't know what I was thinking..." he trailed off. "I was wrong; I'm sorry."

Broderick blew out a deep breath again and threw his head back as if in debate to continue with his confession. Despite his nervous bearings, at last, he surrendered and looked square at me as I sat shivering on my bed.

"I'm not like everyone else, Jules. I'm different," he warned. His hands shook, like his voice, as he spoke softly to me. "I absorb shadows. I stand in them and I *become* a part of them."

"I don't understand." My brows furrowed in hard concentration. It was nothing I had ever heard before; unbelievable, even though I saw it with my own eyes.

"I'm a shadowshifter. My body can appear as a shadow. The darker the shadow, the easier it is for me to hide in." He was careful with his words, trying not to scare me with his revelation.

"Are you... *human?*" I asked.

"Yes!" he instantly defended. His words became rushed. "It started about two years ago. I've only learned to control it in the last year. I can choose to be visible or remain hidden. Like tonight, when you couldn't see me, I made myself visible to you."

Resolved as I touched my stinging chin with my finger, like pinching yourself in a dream, the slight pain reminded me that I was experiencing a very fantastic reality. "You saved me. Thank you."

He was clearly disgusted with himself. "Don't thank me. I'm revolting. I hesitated because I didn't want you to know. You could have been killed and all because I was too selfish."

Never had I felt an inner aching so intense before, seeing his pain. I wanted to take it away from him no matter what the cost would be. I stood and unsteadily walked to him, closing the gap between us.

"You *saved* me," I repeated. It was all I could muster again as I continued struggling to grasp his revelation.

He frowned and ground is teeth. "Jules, I'm different."

A smile broke onto my face. "But I already knew that."

We stared at each other for the longest moment swarmed by an overabundance of mixed feelings: awe and fear, vulnerability and humility, anger and affection.

I needed to see it once more. Proof that not only was he here with me now, but that everything he said—everything I saw—was true. "Can I see it again?"

He contemplated the request, tightening his lips. He unabashedly grabbed my hand and I firmly latched onto his without a second thought.

"Turn off the light."

Careful to keep my hand in his, I leaned around him to turn off the lamp beside my bed. The light from the hall bathroom angled through the room and crossed half of his face as the other half set in the dark.

His shaded eyes, holding strongly to my gaze as my eyes readjusted to the darkness of the room. "Are you ready?"

"Yes," I said, though I trembled with the debate that I was not ready. My eyes stayed glued to his face, waiting for the slightest change.

The darkness slowly overtook his shaded side, leaving but a black nothingness. I couldn't see through him; I couldn't see anything but a standing shadow where half of his beautiful chiseled face once was. His piercing pair of brown eyes and thick dark brows, only visibly on the right side where the light from the bathroom behind me glowed upon his face.

The pain of this secret was seared deep in the side of his face that was still visible to me. There was an irresistible beauty in his sadness. Slowly reaching up to touch the darkness of his face, to *feel* it since my eyes had failed me, I stopped in uncertainty as the small portion of his face that was still visible suddenly faded out like a smokescreen. I gasped at the change and my hand recoiled, shaking with indecision. He placed his warm hand over mine and slowly guided my white skin to the black mask. I heard him sigh as my hand traced down his jaw line to his chest. Our breathing was the only sound to be heard. Even as I thought I could literally hear the nervous drumming of his heart from beneath my fingers, I saw nothing but a dark, shadowy figure standing before me. I closed my eyes, wishing that we could stay in this one moment until the end of time—where I finally understood the depth of his eyes and had entered into his secret world of mystery and shadows. A place no one else seemed to be a part of. I no longer felt lost in this lonely world.

Shortly, the darkness seeped into his skin, like a faded black mist and I clearly saw Broderick divided again by the light of the bathroom and the darkness in my room. But it wasn't the mysterious change that grounded me to my guarded reality, it was the image of his hand on mine, placed comfortably over his heart that jostled me and I pulled my hand back in response. Broderick was tense with my reaction, his face dropped in hurt and panic.

"I've scared you. I'm sorry. I never wanted you to see me like this. And I should have never spied on you in such a way. *Please, don't tell anybody,*" he begged as he turned away and walked back and began climbing to the window, resigned to leave.

I rushed over to stop him. "I'm not scared. I'm just... it's overwhelming for me. Can you try to understand that?" He stopped pulling himself to the window. "You're the most fascinating... *person* I've ever met." He turned to me with an incredulous front. "Okay, I'll admit it. I'm a little spooked. But, I won't tell a soul."

"I'm not ordinary," he reminded me. He was clearly troubled with me knowing his little secret.

I gave a tiny smile. "You say that like it's a bad thing."

"Isn't it?" he pressed begrudgingly.

I shook my head; my smile grew as wide as my bewildered eyes. "I don't want you to be like everyone else."

The moment I said it, I felt as though I had placed my feelings under a spotlight for him to see, which frightened me just as much if not more than Broderick's gift of casting himself as a shadow.

"Jules, you've got to swear on your soul that this will never leave this room. I don't know what would happen to me if —"

"It's going to my grave." I made a crisscross motion with my finger over my heart.

His voice shook nervously as he stepped closer to me. "Tonight changes everything. If we're to be friends, we need to trust each other."

If I was to be as honest as he was demanding me to be, I'd admit here and now, that *just being friends* would never be enough for me.

"I have so many questions…" I began awkwardly in a desperate attempt to get him to stay just a little longer.

"Not tonight. Your parents will be home soon and I'm pretty sure they wouldn't be thrilled to find me in your bedroom."

"I'll keep your secret if you keep mine," I said with a breathy chuckle.

"You've got a deal." He held out his hand to shake on it and I firmly grabbed his hand to confirm our pact.

Broderick backed to the window never loosing eye contact with me. "So, I guess this is goodnight, Jules Taylor," he announced while opening the window.

"Why don't you just go out the back door? My parents aren't home yet," I asked confused.

He emitted a boyish grin, "Because this is far more exciting. I feel like *Peter Pan*."

"Then think happy thoughts before you climb down," I teased as he sat in the opened window ready to climb out.

With a smile, he hopped himself out the window and onto the roof. I darted over to the window to make sure he made it safely down the tree, but instead he stuck his head back through the window, startling me to a scream.

He cleared a laugh from his throat, "Can I see you tomorrow?"

"I get home from church around noon."

He ducked back out. "Sleep well, Jules Taylor," he whispered in the dark as he shifted over to the tree.

I stuck my head out the window to watch him grab a branch and swing closer to the trunk. His smiling face faded to a blanket of black and I heard him scurry down the tree. Each branch shook as he proceeded down the tree and then a sharp thump on the ground sounded from below.

"Goodnight, Broderick!" I whispered into the shadows.

Broderick Cooper

EVERY WORD HE SPOKE last night, his low and tender voice echoing in my mind, pulled me out of an adrenaline induced sleep. His confessions kept me light as air throughout every dream and in between. Giving up any memory of my near death experience, I couldn't get passed my thoughts of Broderick. My eyes opened with a fresh glimmer in them, and I could feel the warmth of the sun as it beamed through the windows, beckoning me to join the day in a renewed sense of life.

I couldn't wait to see him again.

My parents overslept from their night out, so church was no longer on the agenda this morning. Instead, true to my natural procrastination, I reminded myself of the marching band practices that would start tomorrow, and I figured it would be a good time to rehash a few flag drills before we learn a new routine for the upcoming football season.

After a quick shower, I got dressed and brushed my teeth. Looking into the mirror, my chin wasn't nearly as bad as I thought it was going to be. It was pink and raw. I dabbed some ointment on it, then headed to my parents' bathroom in search of two bandages for my elbows.

The entire morning was spent running through flag drills on the front lawn until I felt prepared for the week ahead. It was like riding a bike.

Tossing the blue and yellow sickle shaped flag with a simple flick of my wrist and catching it with rhythmic ease had become second nature. Keeping time by lifting my heels in tiny movements, I maneuvered the flag in graceful twirls and spins until I decided to take a break for lunch. On the way inside, I stopped to retrieve the coffee lid laying in the yard by the house; the one that nearly caused me to meet my maker the night before.

Mom and Dad were sitting in the kitchen rehashing their night out together, sharing a pot of coffee. "Good afternoon!" I chirped.

"Well, you're in a cheery mood." My mother smiled brightly.

"What's that on your face?" Dad asked.

My hand quickly popped up to touch the graze on my chin. "Oh! That?" I grasped for an easy lie. "I tripped and fell in the driveway last night." I began pouring a bowl of cereal.

"Is that what happened to your elbows, as well?" my dad raised as he stood up and made his way to the back door.

"Yes. I was in a hurry to get in and start the movie I rented," I answered, hoping to change the subject. "You know me, Dad. I'm just that talented." He shook his head and walked outside to enjoy his cup of coffee while sitting on the back deck. I chuckled softly at my clumsiness as I pulled a spoon from the drawer and sat down at the table.

"So what are your plans for today since we're out-of-church heathens?" Mom winked playfully.

"Broderick and I are going to hang out for a bit today," I stated nonchalantly as I finished my cereal.

"A date?" my mother asked with a curt smile.

"Just friends," I insisted, hoping my face wasn't betraying me.

"Cari called to check on you while you were outside."

"You didn't say anything about where I was yesterday afternoon, did you?" I was panic-stricken.

"Why does it matter?"

I shook my head. "I'll never hear the end of it from her. She doesn't trust Broderick because he's popular."

Before my mom could offer some advice over the matter. Natalie walked in from her overnight stay at Amber's wearing a cute lime green dress with tiny white polka dots that didn't match well with the navy blue sling she sported on her left arm. She stood in the middle of the kitchen with her free hand on her hip. "How was church?" Her tone was thick in sarcasm.

"Your dad and I slept in this morning," Mom said as she walked back over to the coffee pot to pour another cup.

"No kidding." Natalie slanted her eyes at me. "And what's *your* excuse?"

"No car? Didn't want to go alone?" I offered lamely.

She gave us the tsk-tsk and shook her head. "Y'all are going to hell…." she accused in her beautiful southern drawl.

"Joey called," my mother said to her.

"Really? When?" Natalie plopped over to the bar.

"A little over an hour ago. You two getting together today?"

"Eh. Maybe." Natalie's disinterest was forced. "It's been forever since I've been on the four-wheeler." She nudged her broken wing for emphasis. "I don't know what we can do today though."

Mother chuckled, "You've only been in that sling for a week."

"And I'm sick of gimped-up pool and playing video games with one hand. I lose all of the time! It sucks."

"Natalie…" my mother warned. "There are better words to use."

"Ew. What happened to your face?" Natalie suddenly asked, taking notice of my chin.

"I tripped."

"Good to know gravity is working." She laughed.

Giving Natalie a false-recount of what happened, I noticed that it was already one o'clock and I became restless waiting for Broderick to show up. Worried that he wouldn't. Miserable and feeling foolish with the notion I had trusted the wrong person again; I really believed that after last night's revelation that Broderick and I had a strong bond. Even after Joey arrived, his foolish antics couldn't provide a strong enough distraction.

I was almost able to relax when my phone rang, hoping it was Broderick.

"Hello?" My voice rang through as a girl on pins and needles.

I heard the familiar laugh on the other end, that didn't belong to the boy who had so desperately begged for my friendship last night. "Well, it sounds like you survived without us this weekend. We sure did miss your gloom-n-doom ass, though."

Sighing, I could hardly conceal my disappointment. "Hi, Cari. I missed you girls, too."

"We're going to swing by the Java House before heading home to unpack. You game? I need to talk to you about a certain *something*." I could literally hear Cari's spiteful grin on her face as she spoke. I cringed with the imminent repercussions of the lie I told Savannah—of Cari's supposed attraction to Broderick.

I considered her offer. Broderick clearly wasn't coming.

"What time do you think you'll get here?"

"Uh..." She hesitated as she clamped her hand over the mouthpiece of her cell phone to ask. "Thirty minutes, max. So you're in?"

I was ready to throw in the towel, when suddenly I saw the red jeep pull into the driveway. As he stepped out of the jeep casually in his usual strong form, he pulled his sunglasses to the top of his head. Beautiful.

My mind was made. "I can't. I have plans."

"Plans? Doing what? With *who*?" her tone was testy.

"I have a final this week. Bye." I hung up before she could argue my excuse and hurried out to the deck before he entered in the downstairs door.

"Broderick, I'm up here!" I called over the rail.

He took each step up to the deck where I waited. I fell into a daze at the first sight of his bright smile.

"I'm so sorry; I ran into some heavy traffic on the way back from Cookeville." He grinned sheepishly as he handed me a shopping bag from a popular clothing store in the nearby town. "I didn't know what size to get you, but I assumed extra small?"

"What is this?" I looked into the bag to see two neatly folded cotton items: one red and the other white. I closed the bag immediately in refusal. "What's this for?"

"I believe I owe you two hoodies," he answered. "I massacred your white one at the lake and then your red one last night..." He shifted his weight at the memory and grinned embarrassingly. "You wore the red one often so I figured it was a favorite."

I looked up at him, astonished that he had been so observant. "You didn't have to do that. You weren't to blame for the red one," I said as I pulled the thin material of red out of the bag.

"I shouldn't have been up there like that. It was creepy of me. I scared you. I am so sorry..."

"If you hadn't been up there, I would be lying dead or busted up in a hospital right now," I gravely assured him. "What happened was my own doing. You saved me. I owe you big time."

"That still doesn't excuse me from being there in the first place," he said flatly.

"And it still doesn't explain why you feel the need to replace my red shirt. I fell; you didn't push me. Or did you?" I laughed to lighten the mood.

"I like you in the red hoodie." My heart quickened with his words. I hesitated only a moment before pulling the red shirt out of the bag. Unlike the faded old one, this one was a deep, brilliant red. I loved it. "I would have gone to Knoxville for a wider selection, but I didn't want to keep you waiting. Sorry I was late anyway. I would have called, but I don't have your number," he admitted.

I felt vulnerable at his assumption that I missed him. "Oh, actually I forgot you were coming over today." I lied.

He pulled the corners of his mouth back in a small grimace, as if my words had cut him, but I couldn't let him have the upper hand between us. I needed to keep control, or at least let him *believe* I was in control.

"Do you want to take a walk?" he suggested. I poked my head through the door to set the bag of clothes inside and tell to my parents that I was going out for a walk.

We walked in silence to the unfinished cul-de-sac of my road and continued down the hill on a dirt path—early efforts of lengthening the dead end road and expanding the subdivision. I buzzed with the excitement of walking by his side, yet kept a safe distance from him, allowing no physical contact. Broderick walked in sure, relaxed strides. Unlike my usually long and quick steps that were my trademark, I strolled slowly along with him, trying to prolong every minute. We walked leisurely for quite some time with small talk about the expansion efforts and new construction of our neighborhood.

I scanned the area to see a clearing where a set of trees were laying across the dirt path. We walked over to the clearing and sat on the trunk of a large fallen tree.

"What did you call it again? That thing you can do?" I nervously asked.

"I don't know if there's a technical name for it. My grandmother calls it shadowshifting." He said.

"Like *shape*shifting?" I asked.

"What's that?" his head tilted to the side as if he expected me to have more information on his abnormality that he did.

"It's when you change shapes. Like a werewolf."

"I know I'm a freak." He frowned. "But I am not some Hollywood monster, Jules. I am *human*."

"I didn't say you were a werewolf, and I certainly don't think you're a freak of any sort. I was simply drawing the connection from shadowshifting to shapeshifting. Sorry," I swiftly reconciled. "Are there other people like you?"

He shook his head. "I don't know, but apparently my mother could. That's how my grandmother was able to cope with it so well when she learned I had the ability. She'd already been through this once before with my mother."

"And you've been shadowshifting for two years?"

He nodded as he took a long breath. "I didn't handle it well in the beginning. It was at night during football camp at a nearby college. We were going to a party in the upperclassmen dorms. Only a small group of us underclassmen were invited to come. We had to sneak out that night from the other side of campus, and I was uneasy about the whole sneaking out bit, so I hung back from the rest of our group. I was so anxious about being caught out after curfew…" He chuckled at the memory. "One by one, we started slipping in at the back entrance of the dorm. I remember watching Joey and Jackson slide through the back door as I hid behind a dumpster. When I thought the coast was clear, I dashed over to sneak in the door behind him.

Then I heard some man yelling and I froze." Broderick laughed at himself then grew serious again. "I saw campus security and knew I'd been caught. I already had the door open and knew the light from inside had exposed me, it was then I noticed my hand was cast a dark grey—almost black. My whole body looked like that, the color of the shadows around me. I was so shocked I forgot I was being chased by security." He shook his head as he stared off into the woods that surrounded us. "He never even saw me. That security guard only saw Joey and Jackson."

"What happened then?" I could literally feel the fear of his first encounter with shadowshifting. My own experience was still fresh in my mind; I understood what it was to be traumatized by the reveal.

He glanced up at me, finally returning to the present day. "I ran. I never returned to my room; I remained outside throughout the entire night, nearly collapsing from exhaustion the next day during drills." He paused and smiled wryly at me. "That party was busted and all the players were suspended for the first several games. Joey and Jackson never made it to the party and were never caught. They slid into a laundry room while the party was being raided, then set out to look for me. They gave up after about an hour and returned to our room hoping I'd show up."

"What did they think of your disappearance?"

Broderick released a breathy chortle. "I simply told him that I was out. I think they have always thought of me as a peculiar person. But from that moment on, I became very careful when it came to hanging out at random gatherings at night, sweating bullets during football and baseball games— never have I been more thankful for the invention of stadium lights. I was always the last one out of the locker room after the parking lot would clear, the first person to call it an early evening when out with friends."

He sat silently in thought, and I remembered how Savannah said he was unsociable at times, making his story even more credible.

"I spent my entire sophomore year in near seclusion. I hated it. No parties, no dances. I never dated. Only for night games of football and baseball would I risk being out. That's when my grandmother figured it out. She was emotionally prepared for my little inconvenience—for lack of better words, explaining that my mother was also a shadowshifter; and my grandfather, before her.

"She explained that my ability to control the shifting was somewhat linked to my emotional state of being, so I spent every night last year outside in the dark trying to control my emotions and my shifting while sitting under a street lamp in our front yard. I learned quickly that the calmer I was, the better I was at controlling it—which is easier said than done when all you do is stress out over completely blacking out and never being seen again."

My eyes widened. "Can that happen?"

"I couldn't see a reasonable explanation for any of it to begin with, so why *wouldn't* that make sense at first, right?" I nodded as he emitted a lighthearted laugh. "No. I can't disappear. How it works is that I have to have at least a piece of a shadow on me to absorb it—I'm kind of like a chameleon—but I have to admit that the fear was still there at first.

"Anyway, I worked at it nightly in the front yard and occasionally throughout my late night walks in our neighborhood until I finally learned to control it. I learned that I just have to find a small bit of peace within me, let that peace consume me and eventually gain control," he explained in a simplistic tone.

"So you were at *peace* last night on the roof when I nearly plummeted to my death?" I asked with insult, but partly joking.

"Not at all!" His eyes grew bewildered at the question. "It scared the hell out of me, Jules. I came apart at the very idea of you falling. I just had to find that small part of me that was in a state of peace."

"Like what?" I curiously asked.

"*You*. In that red hooded shirt, like a beautiful modern day *Little Red Riding Hood*." He tucked his lips in, nervous that he had said too much. Quickly, he changed the subject. "I'm amazed that I've made it this far in high school without being completely blacklisted for my reclusive behavior."

"Far from it!" I said incredulously. "You're still popular! I don't get it. You have pretty much shunned an entire crowd—*the* crowd—and they still accept you. They'd treat me like a disease even if I *paid* them to be my friends."

He cleverly grinned at my naiveté. "Being popular simply means to be well-liked or well-known. Too many people chalk being popular up to going to parties and hanging with a large group of friends that aren't really your friends at all. It's not all what it's cracked up to be. Some of the best advice my grandmother ever gave me was that a person should be able to count their true friends on one hand alone."

Despite my lingering desire to be accepted among the in crowd at school, what he said made perfect sense to me. I had my few reliable friends, easily counted on one hand with two fingers to spare, and the rest were simply acquaintances of casual friends who I would never make an effort beyond school to keep in touch with.

"And for the record, I'd like to point out that you're speaking about popularity like you're invisible to the school. Everyone knows you! You're Jules Taylor! The best singer in town! Many genuinely like you and some are insanely jealous of you. You did that on your own, Jules—before you ever dated Gavin. Can't you see that?"

"No, I can't," I said flatly.

"Well, that's only because you see yourself only with your own clouded judgment. You can't see what everyone else sees or what I see." He looked up at the sky and saw the gray clouds start to roll in from the west. He inhaled slowly. "It's about to rain. Can you smell it?"

I quickly sniffed the rain-scented air. "Yeah, we better start walking back before we get soaked."

We started back to the dirt path that led to our houses on the paved roads. "You never explained to me why you think you remained popular during your sophomore year, though. Do you have any theories on that, smart guy?" I teasingly broached the subject again in a lame attempt to figure out exactly how he had managed to stay above the curve. It totally befuddled me.

He laughed jubilantly as he rolled his eyes. "Because I play a mean game of baseball and I'm not too shabby at football or basketball, either. That's all. Neither of us were born and bred here or born with a silver spoon in our mouths, so popularity or entitlement wasn't handed down to us, Jules. If we had never found our niche, we'd be nothing to our peers. If I quit playing ball and you quit singing, we'd have nothing to set us apart from the rest according to popularity standards."

"And that doesn't bother you any?" I asked concerned. It bothered me.

He didn't miss a beat. "I don't care if I'm accepted by a crowd. All I want in life is to belong with someone special. Someone who can understand me and accept me for who and what I truly am. That's what life is all about. Happiness and hope, not baseball or popularity."

"So why do you keep playing sports if it's not important to you?"

"Because, it makes me happy right now. It gives me a focus to direct my aggressions. If it ever got to the point where I was miserable with it, I'd quit in a heartbeat."

"Really?" I was in disbelief.

"Oh, absolutely."

His level headed and honest approach to life was healthy and agreeable. I was unequivocally impressed with his clear sense of thinking and confidence—more than I had ever imagined I would be. He was real, nothing like other faces in the crowd I had assumed he ran with. Broderick Cooper blew my mind out of orbit with his beautiful face and beautiful heart.

As it began to sprinkle, he grabbed my hand to pull me farther along, to keep up with his jogging pace. His hand consumed mine with warmth.

His touch alone was electrifying to me as we ran through the rain to our homes.

The Home Stretch

MONDAY MORNING, BRODERICK SHOWED up at my house at five o'clock on the dot, but instead of staying for breakfast, he offered to take me on an early run for coffee before class. It was going to be a long day—a long *week*—with football and marching band practices immediately following our summer class. He wanted us to be prepared.

"We just have to make it through the week, Jules. Practices all week this week and our Algebra final this Friday. This is the home stretch before we start a new school year." He grinned, charged with excitement. Now, I can't promise fancy coffee like the Java House, but I can promise caffeine and a good sugar high."

He grabbed my flag and bag that had my change of clothes in it and threw them in the backseat with his football gear. We drove through the dark morning hour to the local breakfast diner, Donuts 'N More. He saw my apprehension that all the lights inside appeared to be off.

"I know the owner and I'm willing to bet that she's been here since about three this morning getting ready for the breakfast crowd." He put the jeep in park and walked to the back entrance as if he'd been doing it every morning for years. He knocked until a middle aged woman appeared smiling at the door, her gray and faded blond hair pulled back into a sloppy bun.

"Broderick!" she reached her arms up to hug him. "Taryn said you'd be by this morning. Who's your friend?" She eyed me as she allowed us inside the building.

"This is Jules Taylor," he introduced us. "Jules, this is Taryn's mom, Sarah Green, but we all call her 'Mama Green'."

"Nice meeting you." I smiled; still in a minor sleep state, trying to wake up.

"Same here." She thrust her hand out after wiping most of the flour onto her apron. Her down to earth manner quickly relaxed me, reminding me of my own mother.

"I have plenty of original glazed and chocolate icing ready for you two to grab." She walked us to a kitchen area with a tray full of fresh doughnuts. "The coffee is up at the front of the diner by the counter."

Broderick handed me a small plastic container. "You get the doughnuts. I like chocolate, so get me at least three of those. What do you want in your coffee?"

"Two creams and six sugars, please."

"Are you sure you don't want *seven* sugars?" he teased as he disappeared through the swinging doors that led to the front of the diner.

I placed one glazed doughnut for me and then three chocolates for Broderick into the plastic to-go container. Continuing with her work, Mama Green positioned at least a dozen more in the industrial sized fryer. Broderick breezed through the doors and set down the two cups long enough to grab another one of each doughnut—a glazed and chocolate— and added them to the original four.

"Mr. Muir may want one." He winked.

I narrowed my eyes and laughed. "You are such a suck up!"

He walked over to the fryer with the two drinks and set them on the empty tray that was waiting for a fresh batch of donuts. He reached into his pocket and pulled out a small wad of cash and stuffed it in Mama Green's side apron pocket.

"Thanks, Mama Green!" He kissed her swiftly on the cheek and swooped up the drinks as he dashed toward the door, signaling me to follow him quickly.

She turned and glared at him sternly. "Broderick Cooper, you come back over here and take this money, right now!"

"I can't. My hands are full. You've been very generous, ma'am."

"You use this money to take this pretty girl out sometime or buy her something nice," she lectured as I blushed at her suggestion.

Laughing, he handed me the coffee, then used his free hand to quickly grab me by the elbow and rush me out the door. "Bye! Thanks again, mama!"

"It was nice meeting you," I sputtered, hoping that she heard me as the door slammed shut.

Broderick was still chuckling when we reached his jeep. "She has yet to make me keep my money."

Thankful for the doughnuts, Mr. Muir made it a point to inform us that he preferred chocolate. As usual, Broderick sat in the chair behind me. The night faded away and welcomed the morning sun. Swirls of orange and yellow dominated the sky by the time class began. The coffee wasn't my usual overpriced, five-star quality I order at Java House, but it did the trick. On what Broderick referred to as a sugar high and my normal caffeine fix, I was able to stay focused through class and still have enough energy to take on marching band practice.

My insecurity, once again, closed in around me as Broderick walked me back to his jeep for my change of clothes and my flag. I searched warily through the school grounds, in the parked cars, and in the small lingering groups that hung close to the building for wandering eyes that would catch on to our friendly pairing, worried that they would see the exact thing I feared most—a striking young man humoring a gangly young girl with her delusional ideas of romance. I panicked more over the chance that Cari would see us together. My lack of self-confidence was going to snuff us out before we even started, but still, I caved.

I stared blankly at the crowd I was about to join. A group of musical misfits, nerds, and overweight nobodies of the marching band. If I belonged to any crowd at all, this was one of them and I was suddenly ashamed of it. I was ashamed he would see me in my inglorious role on the flag corps and not with the cheerleaders or the dance team like the popular girls. The flag corps was deemed to many as the cheerleader-rejects. I never even tried out for cheerleading.

My anxiety began to overtake me as I saw more and more students walking by us and watching and nudging each other.

"Broderick…" He seemed keenly aware of my mood swing, he looked concerned. I gulped; already feeling the regret that I was going to push him away again. "… Please go to practice and don't walk me to the band room."

He stopped walking. "Are you embarrassed to be seen with me?"

Shocked by his words, I came to an abrupt halt. "It's not y-y-you; i-i-it-it's… me," I stammered with the worst excuse ever recorded, stumped for a good explanation.

He frowned with hurt in his eyes, stinging my heart. "That is lame, Jules." I shook my head at the cluster of negation that weighed in my brain. Speechless at my stupidity. "Just meet me at the jeep after camp." He appeared defeated as he sulked over to the stadium on the other side of the parking lot.

I couldn't shake the guilt of what I had said. Throughout the entire marching band practice, my heart hurt from the memory of Broderick's expression when I suggested us not walking together. It was a small request that I didn't want to ask for anyway, and I never thought it would affect him the way it did.

Mom dropped Natalie off for cheerleading practice as I was finishing marching band practice. She caught up with me at Broderick's jeep not looking in any better form than me.

"I feel like a total idiot. I just found out that while the other girls are cheering, I get to yell through an oversized megaphone until I can get this sling off. This season sucks," she pouted.

"Sorry. I feel like it's my fault."

"Well, let me set your mind at ease, sister. It *is* your fault," she chortled.

In the parking lot, Cari's mouth dropped open when she noticed me by Broderick's jeep, then her eyes quickly became slits as she hurried to her car and sped off. Just how I expected her to behave. I groaned at the realization I would have to face her eventually. The question was, would I be up front about my friendship with Broderick, or would I cower like I did earlier today?

"She doesn't look happy," Natalie said under her breath.

"She's disappointed that I've become friends with Broderick." Natalie's face twisted in confusion, so I explained further. "Because he's popular." She nodded in understanding.

"She'll get over it. She always does." Natalie loved Cari like another big sister and saw her for the person she was, like I did.

Here come the guys," Natalie said. "Looks like you're giving Joey a ride home today." She waved and skipped off." I gotta go to practice. See you this evening."

With the impending doom to face Broderick and having to somehow apologize for being a creep again, I winced.

"How's the arm?" Joey asked as he ran over to Natalie and hugged her real quick before she reached the gymnasium where her practice was being held.

"I'll tell you about it later, after I get this joke of a practice over with. I'm too grumpy to talk about it right now," she warned. "Bye, Brody!"

Broderick waved to her and then drew a tense filled breath as he approached the jeep where I stood. "I think everyone's bags and flags will fit in the backseat with Joey."

Joey and I threw our bags in the back and he then situated himself into the backseat with our equipment. Quickly, I scurried over to the driver's side, in hopes I could apologize without an audience, but saw that the driver's side window was down. Joey would hear everything.

Broderick, still obviously stinging from my earlier rejection, smirked as he tried to joke through our earlier dispute. "Is it your turn to drive, Jules?"

Joey shot a nervous glances in my direction, knowing that I had never driven a stick shift. Plus, he was still recovering from my most recent accident behind the wheel.

"I-I-I was just going to offer to hold your bag for you," I stuttered foolishly, reaching out to take it. It was the best I could manage as an indirect peace offering.

"I'll just cram it in the backseat with the rest of them," he said curtly.

"Please, let me do this." My Irish-blooded temper pulled my face into a frown and I grabbed the strap of the bag; my fingers warmly wrapped around his knuckles.

Joey's voice drifted from the backseat of the jeep. "Why don't you two just rock-paper-scissors for it?"

"No!" we both growled.

I huffed, "I'm trying to be a friend."

Joey leaned closer to the opened window. "Actually, Jules your lip is doing that snarl-thing again which isn't friendly looking at all."

"Shut up!" I quipped.

"You want the bag?" Broderick challenged.

"Give me the stupid bag, Broderick," I told him.

"Then take the bag!" He released the bag into my hand, causing me to lean to the side from the unexpected weight of his gear.

"Fine!" My tone was angry.

"Fine!" His was final.

Joey stifled laughter as I huffed and puffed, situating the awkward size and weight of his bag. Broderick started the engine and faced forward, never batting an eye. His knuckles were white as they curled around the steering wheel. Our clash was not only extremely exhilarating for me, but oddly arousing.

We remained silent on the drive through town and to our homes. I moped. Broderick seethed. Joey forced a normal conversation with us from the back, though I could feel his wondering eyes shift constantly between me and Broderick which confirmed there was nothing normal about the current atmosphere. Joey was quick to jump out of the jeep as soon as we pulled into his driveway. He was eager to leave us alone to our own silent treatments.

Upon arriving home, I lingered behind in the jeep, wanting to apologize. As soon as I was able to free my small bag from the backseat, I stepped out of the jeep and turned to shut the door. His silence punched me in the gut as he shifted gears and left without glancing at me.

However, five o'clock the next morning, Broderick and I were making our way back to Mama Green's shop and then to the school. It was already becoming an easy routine. Throughout the thirty minutes we spent in and out of the jeep before we entered into the school building, I waited for a sign that Broderick was still upset. He no longer seemed angry, but did mention that he was exhausted from another sleepless night. Although I, too, had a sleepless night over our argument, we carried on as if yesterday had never happened, which was perfect for my already bruised ego.

Despite the fact that the whole hour of class content was a nonstop review, I felt like it wasn't long enough. The minute ten o'clock rolled around, I realized my time with Broderick was up—at least for the next four hours while we were at our respective practices. We walked out to the jeep to retrieve our equipment and I saw Cari zoom by, parking closer to the practice field near the band room. I needed her to accept my new friendship with Broderick and I refused to be a coward about it.

We stayed busy through practice. I wasn't able to speak to her, so I waited for her by the percussion room when practice ended.

"Hello, lover," she quipped breathlessly as she strode past me to go to her car and I hurried after her.

I immediately began explaining as I walked alongside her. "I know you're mad about me riding with him." I was afraid I would blush if I even said Broderick's name. "And you're probably pissed because I told Savannah you had a thing for him, right? That was intended as a joke."

Cari played dumb. "I don't know *who* you're talking about."

"Yeah you do," I accused her. "Don't be like that. He's a ride to and from school. I totaled my car two weeks ago. Remember?"

She narrowed her eyes and stepped aggressively toward me with her finger pointed accusingly. "You *like* him!"

I shook my head in a speechless denial.

"Jules, do us all a favor and just admit it. You've got it bad for that guy. Who, by the way, is totally out of your league, but I'm sure he's *totally* different than the last two winners you hooked up with. You're a dumbass if you really believe he is."

"Thanks a lot," I replied bitterly. Her words hurt me, and I didn't have anything clever to fire back, so I stomped off. If there was any doubt left about Broderick, Cari had just nurtured it.

In spite of the lingering distrust I had for Broderick, he and I continued on our week's routine of an early morning stopping off for doughnuts on the way to school and enduring Algebra until marching band and football practices. With every new minute together, I began to question if we were surpassing our originally intended friendship. With each minute apart, my heart ached to be near him.

Practice came to a close and the band walked past the football team running drills on their practice field as we made our way to the band room to pack up our equipment. I stopped momentarily, my eyes sifting through the sea of dirty, faded blue practice uniforms of the football team. Frustrated for not knowing Broderick's jersey number, I searched for him on the field and soon found him. I couldn't see his face, but everything about his body and the way he moved was familiar to me. Number eighty-six. More agile and more coordinated than the others, he was muscular but appeared lanky due to his height. I watched him, waiting for him to remove his helmet. Seeing him in this role—in this uniform—he became the untouchable guy in school again and no longer the boy next door. I desperately needed to see his face and his eyes for reassurance he was still the friend I was growing accustom to. The boy I was growing to love.

The team began exiting the field, heading toward the locker-room showers as he lingered behind with another player to speak to the head coach. The other player removed his helmet, revealing Jackson's face. Hot and sticky, his black hair was soaked with sweat from the workout. Jackson was intense as he spoke to the coach and then motioned at jersey number eighty-six, bringing him into the conversation. Eighty-six lifted the helmet off and gave his head a quick shake, slinging the sweat from his rich brown hair. *Broderick*. My heart was racing as I watched Broderick carry himself with such certainty and authority while speaking to the coach. Standing a few inches over the other two with his helmet tucked under his arm, Broderick looked up and saw me. His serious expression quickly faded to a boyish grin. He lifted his hand in a small wave as the other two peered over the clipboard. Shyly, I waved back. Finally the three of them began walking off the field.

Broderick's eyes remained locked on me until the coach took the clipboard and banged him on the back of the head. "Get your head out of your ass, Cooper. Flirt with girls on your own time."

He made a playful grimace at me and turned quickly to the coach. Cari's eyes trailed along with Broderick. With a pursed grin on her face, she was obviously pleased with his concession to acknowledge me and even foolish enough to get caught, but there was something else in her eyes. Maybe it was a jumble of her usual cynicism and disappointment that she was more than likely wrong in her judgments about him?

The late July sun had left us all drained of sweat and had all but sucked the energy out of our youthful bodies. I struggled to skip ahead to talk to Cari. Her drum sticks were humorously stuffed in her abundant cleavage from under her tank top, and she rested her arms on the snare strap. She stared at me through her shades, then pulled them up to rest on top of her head. Her face was neither scornful nor angry, but amused with my hurried procedure of rolling the fabric of the flag around the pole to keep from getting twisted in it.

"What's the story, morning glory?" she asked.

"You still think I'm stupid?" I asked her.

"I never said you were stupid; I said you were a *dumbass*. Huge difference," she corrected with a smile. "But I love you anyway. Mainly, because you make me look smarter. Everyone should have a dumbass friend."

I saw Broderick stroll toward the locker room at the stadium and my head throbbed with the thought of what I was about to do. Without a second's hesitation I grabbed Cari by the arm and directed her over to Broderick.

"What the hell are you doing?" she griped.

"Just come on," I begged nervously. My voice strained from the tension of what I was about to do. I just wanted to get this over with and move on. I dragged her right up to Broderick. He smiled as we stood before him.

"Broderick," I began, "this is one of my best friends, Cari Patterson. Cari, this is my neighbor…" I swallowed hard. "…My friend, Broderick Cooper." I blew out a long full breath that I had subconsciously been holding.

Cari looked at me as if I had lost my mind. "I *know* who he is, Jules," she stated dryly, leaving me to sink deeper in embarrassment.

Broderick didn't waver a bit. He thrust out his hand immediately to her and spoke cheerfully. "Our paths have never really crossed before. It's nice to finally get to meet you, Cari."

"That's one way to put it," she tartly replied, cautiously taking his hand. A smirk grew to the side of her face and her eyes became calculating. She was waiting for one false move on his part to tear into him, to prove her point to me.

Seeming genuinely interested in her, Broderick was quick to keep her talking. "Jules says that she's not in the band anymore, so do you have a new band now?"

Her eyes widened slightly with her smile. "Actually, I'm still searching. You don't play anything do you?"

He shook his head. "Not at all. I'm surprised Jules isn't sticking with the band, though. You girls were great together," he said enthusiastically.

"Cari is a good singer, too," I assured Broderick.

"Well, I can't wait to hear you sometime," he replied. "What exactly are you looking for so I can keep my eyes and ears open for you?"

She balked for a moment at his desire to help her. It was quite amusing to see her disheveled in such a way "Uh..." she blankly said. "I need a bassist. I have a potential lead guitarist."

"Oh?" This was news to me.

"Isaac Philetos. We ran into him Sunday night when you stood us up at the Java House..." She closed her eyes in total bliss and trembled in delight from her memory, before prattling on about music and ideas for the new band.

I waited impatiently for the drive home to hear his thoughts on Cari, curious to know if his friendliness to her was all just an act. "Well, she's just as unconventional as I had imagined." He smiled, "She doesn't trust me much yet, but I think she doesn't because she's watching out for you. That's what makes her a good friend. You're lucky to have her." I pursed my lips tightly together to keep from smiling.

All the way to my house, he laughed at her sharp attitude, and how she and I were like night and day, but he was also quick to point out how we balanced each other.

Broderick lingered behind at his jeep, fidgeting as I walked up to my house. I slowed my pace to buy him some time, assuming he had something to say to me.

"Jules?" He sounded unsure. I turned to see him approach. "Are you doing anything tonight?"

My mind ran wild as I shook my head.

"Come to the stadium with me. A bunch of us are playing football together and hanging out." He looked anxious as he invited me.

I never hesitated over the answer, "I'm in."

I was anxious to see if I would fit, worried about the reception I would run into at the field—a group of popular football players and their equally popular and high maintenance girlfriends. He picked me up that evening looking ragged from a day full of landscaping. He masked his exhaustion with a smile though, as we drove to the school. I was too nervous to really talk, so we drove in silence. Maybe he, too, was nervous about his friends' response to my appearance beside him.

As we walked into the stadium, we saw a group of about twelve guys standing out on the field throwing a football, talking and cutting up. Their girlfriends and their friends were sitting together in a staggered clump on the bottom concrete slabs of the stadium seats for the private game. I looked over to see Jackson hold up his hand to wave at Broderick, catching Taryn's attention.

"Broderick!" she excitedly called out to him from the stadium seats.

He waved at them and began drifting away from me and to the field. He looked back at me, "Are you going to be okay?"

"Yeah," I nervously smiled. "Go have fun. I'll cheer from the stands." I looked over to where the girls were sitting, some whispering and pointing. My heart sank as I assumed that I wasn't fully welcome in there gathering.

"I'm not leaving you alone, until I know you're all right," he stated.

"Jules, it's so good seeing you again. Come sit by me." Taryn waved me over cheerfully as she made her way to us. Hope must have washed over my face, because Broderick winked at me and started jogging off to the football field.

Although I recognized most of the girls from school, I had never really spoken to most of them before. Everyone was friendly to me. All but two. The same two who scrutinized me at the lake when Broderick spoke to me before the drowning incident—Loni Shubert and her friend, Casey Barnes.

Taryn sat next to me, cheering for Jackson and talking to me about her summer, the upcoming school year, as well as the discovery of the body pieces in the woods from earlier this month. Everyone seemed convinced it was an animal attack. I thought of the howling.

She would interrupt our talk often with a *"Way to go, baby!"* and then jumped back into the conversation at hand. I was clueless with this whole game, so I was grateful that Broderick and Jackson were on the same team. I quickly learned that when Taryn cheered, I cheered.

"Broderick was worried sick about you that night after the movies." She giggled. "Jackson and I finally just took him home and left him to worry on his own." She paused for a moment. "He's a sweetie, though, isn't he?"

"Yeah," I agreed as I watched bodies slamming against one another, grime and dirt covering their clothes. Watching Broderick speeding across the field—unstoppable and unable to be caught—excited me.

"Jackson and I haven't seen much of him this summer." She was fishing for answers, I could tell, but I kept my mouth shut. It was uncomfortable to talk about Broderick with anyone, especially his ex-girlfriend.

Loni, who had spent most of the evening scowling at me with her friend, decided at that moment to speak to me. "I enjoyed your melt down on stage last year," she snickered. Her friend, Casey, doubled over in giggles.

My eyes, despite how out of place I felt, narrowed in anger. My voice shook, "It wasn't a meltdown. It was an accusation."

"Oh shut up, Loni," Taryn said without looking at her, keeping her eyes on the field the entire time. Loni gave me the middle finger and I wanted to crawl under a rock. I didn't belong here.

Taryn must have felt my discomfort, for she frivolously began talking again. "You know Broderick and I dated?"

This didn't take my discomfort away at all. The question only made it worse. I silently nodded.

"He was a good boyfriend," she said with adoration. "We just didn't click like Jackson and I did."

"I see," I replied uneasy.

"I wish he would find someone that could make him happy though. He really deserves it." We sat in silence as I squirmed in my seat. She stood up to cheer for Jackson again and then she finally sat down and turned to me in dead seriousness. "So, what's going on between you two?" She barreled through.

I stuttered carelessly, looking for words to make a simple sentence. *Any* sentence. "We're just friends."

"Oh." Her disappointment was clear. "I thought that maybe… I'm sorry." She hesitated as she watched the surrounding girls, making sure they were not listening to us; they were too caught up in their own private conversations and boyfriends on the field to care. She motioned her head for us to move back. We slipped back two rows up the stadium and she began talking.

"I fell in love with Jackson long before Broderick and I even ended things. It was wrong of me, but you just can't help who you fall in love with, you know? But I *never* cheated on him, Jules. I couldn't do that to anybody, especially Broderick. When the rumors started, it spread like wild fire and there was really nothing we could do about it. You know how that is?" She smiled a contagious smile which I returned. I knew all too well how rumors could be completely out of one's control.

Half of the girls stood up to cheer their team of boyfriends while Taryn booed them in a teasing manner. It was enjoyable how she took her role seriously as Jackson's ever present and personal cheerleader.

"Anyway," she continued without missing a beat, "the way he carried on over you that night after we left the movies, and then after Jackson mentioned to me that he was in summer school with you…well, it just became clear to me… or at least I thought it did."

I wanted to cunningly remind her that she was the reason he was in summer school. That their break up had devastated him to the point where his GPA had dropped drastically, but I let it go. I was in a den of lions and the last thing I needed was to piss off their apparent alpha.

"When my mom mentioned meeting Broderick's 'new girlfriend', I just knew it was you. And to be honest, I had felt for quite some time that he was into somebody." She stood up and clapped and I clapped mindlessly along with her. "You show 'em, baby!" She turned back to me. "Are you *sure* there's nothing going on between you two? He's such a great guy."

Before I could answer her or even ask another question in return, another blonde sitting three rows down from us turned around to speak to me. Her face twisted in question when she noticed how far back Taryn and I had moved. I smiled, trying hard to make a good impression on these girls, terrified how she was going to treat me.

"Are you still singing in that girl band with Savannah Blythe?" her two friends beside her turned around to wait for my answer.

"No." I wiggled uncomfortably, keeping my answer short and sweet as I started fuming under the collar.

"That's too bad. I *love* your voice!" Her two friends nodded in agreement. She stood up and dusted off her bottom before climbing the two steps of concrete to sit closer to me and Taryn. She introduced herself and her two friends that followed before bombarding me with compliments on my singing. In no time, the question of mine and Broderick's relationship status was asked again.

"We're just friends," I explained, trying to keep my disappointment down to a minimum.

The other girl spoke, "But you two look so cute together."

"And he's *so sweet*," another gushed, trying to sell me on him.

They chatted endlessly about the upcoming school year with eagerness: prom, homecoming, and superlatives. Eventually the discussion of the neighboring county's recent murder came up again. One of the girls had more insight to the gory details because her father was a detective on the case. Taryn would throw in her two cents a couple of times in between her cheering. The end of the game brought the talk of the murder to an end. Taryn and I stood up to meet Broderick and Jackson down on the track as I saw Loni welcome Erik in a disgusting display of affection. *Why am I not surprised that she's with him?*

As we approached Jackson and Broderick, Taryn leaned toward me and in a secretive tone asked, "So if he does ask you out, are you going to say yes?" She almost had me popping out answers, but I was quickly saved by Jackson's impatience. She held up her finger at him to give her a second. "I really hope to see you again, Jules," she said, hinting that I could be a regular presence with Broderick.

I waved to her as Broderick closed the gap between us and looked down at me. "Did you have fun?"

I teetered my hand like a see-saw and crinkled my nose. "It was okay. Taryn's pleasant." I hated to admit it, but she was.

"I hoped that the two of you would hit it off. Sorry, you didn't have fun, though. I just promised the guys that I'd be here tonight and I thought that maybe you'd like to come and watch." We started walking out of the stadium. "You're not a football fan, are you?"

I shook my head apologetically. "Not really. But I *love* baseball!"

"Cool! Then maybe I will appease you next spring when it's baseball season."

He dropped me off in time for dinner and as soon as I was sure that my parents were asleep, I climbed out to my usual spot and made my usual mistake of getting my hopes up at seeing his house through the trees. The night was breezier than usual, but the air was humid.

I started to lay back to look at the stars and the crescent moon, filling my lungs with air as my mind raced through the events of my day.

"You have room up there for anyone else?" his voice echoed from the darkness below. Broderick stood dressed in dark clothing and standing on the ground below my window. "No longer snooping," he declared innocently.

"Come on up!" I whispered in excitement.

He scampered lively up the tree with ease and dropped lightly onto the roof from a high hanging branch. He was full of energy as he sat close beside me on the roof. "Nice night, huh?"

I nodded, just happy to have him with me again.

"You're not getting tired of me yet, are you?" he asked.

"Nope; I'm having too good of a time with you." Thanks to the comfort the darkness provided me, I had no problem admitting it.

He paused for a moment. "So, I was never able to figure it out. What brings you out here almost every night?"

"It's my thinking spot," I said into the air, listening to my voice travel in a hush through the night sky. I lay back against the still warm shingles and Broderick lay back beside me causing me to shudder in delight as I felt his arm brush against me. He left it there stretched out against mine as he listened to me and I couldn't help but wonder if it was because he was unwilling to move it away. That maybe he had this growing need to touch me. "I'm kind of a daydreamer and this seems to be the only place I can do that without it hindering real life or everyday conversations." I laughed aloud as I thought about my daydreaming habits around my friends and how I would occasionally blank out on them to dwell in my thoughts.

"What do you daydream about, Jules?"

"If I told you, I'd have to kill you." I gave him a sly look. I wasn't about to share the secret that *he* had been the root of all of my dreams lately. "I imagine myself in the role of a movie character or sometimes I plan my singing career." I continued to talk, marveling at the night that enveloped us, "I also like to just sit under the sky. Don't get me wrong, sunsets and sunrises are quite beautiful, but the night sky is just—*wow*! To me, there's nothing more amazing than seeing the moon light up an otherwise hopelessly dark sky."

Suddenly, off in the distance we saw a quick flash in the sky and then a low rumble. We both sat up and saw the oncoming storm clouds make their way to us. The storm would break up our time together. It was nice while it had lasted.

"Lightning lights up a dark sky as well," Broderick chuckled. "We're going to get drenched."

I tried not to look too disappointed that our time together was already over.

"You want to watch a movie?" he asked all of the sudden.

"Seriously?"

"Sure."

"In my room?" Nervous about getting caught—it was forbidden, making it even more appealing. The butterflies in my stomach agreed. "What movie did you have in mind?"

Smiling sheepishly, he reached in the large pouch pocket in the front of his sweatshirt and pulled out the *An American Werewolf in London* DVD that he had rented last weekend. "We didn't get to watch this the other day and I thought…"

Oh, my gosh! He planned this! I thought excitedly to myself.

"If it's too long, we can spread it out over the next several nights if we have to…" he trailed off in uncertainty. "Unless, you have other plans."

I laughed, "My schedule's pretty clear after ten o'clock every night."

We carefully scaled down the side of the roof and into my window. I kicked off my shoes, grabbed the DVD from Broderick and I slid it into the player, turning on the TV. As I walked back to the bed, I saw Broderick claiming his seat, respectfully on the floor at the foot of the bed. I leaned back on the bed and debated long about allowing him next to me. *We're just friends. Innocent enough,* I justified.

"You can sit with me."

"Are you sure?" He twisted around to look at me. "I don't want to come across as inappropriate."

"Well, I don't want you uncomfortable on the floor. What kind of hostess would that make me?"

He stood up and kicked his shoes off, placing them neatly in my untidy closet. He gently sat down on the bed beside me and leaned back against the head board. My arm pressed warmly next to his. He looked adoringly down at me, pulling his lips back far enough for one of his dimples to appear. He smelled wonderful, too. Clean. I took such pleasure from it. I wanted to nestle next to him and inhale him, feel his warm skin against my cheek.

As we heard the rhythmic downpour outside and the low rumble of thunder, he leaned over to whisper in my ear. "I love thunderstorms?"

His whisper brushed my neck and I heard him draw me in as he lingered momentarily in my hair. I closed my eyes and shivered with excitement, even as he pulled away. It was impossible to concentrate through the movie; it couldn't hold my attention like he did. Slowly, I felt the day's energies drain from me, the adrenaline of having him near wear me down. I rearranged my pillow to appear as though I was sitting upright when I was in fact becoming more dependent on a place for my head.

"You're sleepy." He reached for the remote and flipped the movie off.

"I'm still awake," I tried arguing through my exhaustion. I popped my eyes wide open, only to see my lids draw slowly shut again within seconds. I felt his body shift to a full sitting position.

He chuckled, "You can't even keep your eyes open."

"Don't leave," I begged drowsily.

"You want me to stay?"

Barely moving my head in a nod, I was still awake, but unable to open my eyes from their heaviness. "Stay until it stops raining so you don't get wet."

My eyes remained closed. There was no energy left in me to open them. He spoke my name as if to check if I was asleep. I was too tired to communicate and continued to lay still. He hummed softly along as he flipped the pages of either one of my music magazines or last year's yearbook. His deep voice was on pitch for the most part, and he occasionally forgot the words to the songs, but I was too tired to giggle. A small smile spread across my face as I fell into a light sleep.

I never heard him leave, but he was gone early the next morning when I awoke and parked in my driveway at five, ready to conquer the day. Algebra review was all we did in class. Tomorrow was our final. My last day of summer school. I was concerned if that would also mark the end of my friendship with Broderick.

Marching band practice ran over its usual time because of a miscalculated blocking on the field. With a major traffic jam between the woodwinds and the brass sections near the thirty-five yard line Mr. Grayson, our band director, was left with no other choice but to re-map his halftime show. He had spent so much time on the one particular section that a small group of us remained near the fifty yard line almost the entire last hour of our field time just waiting to continue. Mr. Grayson continued tweaking the formations by moving us slowly from point to point on the field. Killing time on the forty-five yard line, I fidgeted with my flag, twirling and tossing it to keep me occupied. I began twirling the flag double time, revving it up for an obnoxious toss. I flicked my wrist high, pointing with my finger where I deliberated it to fly and then caught it with ease. By the time it landed into my hands I felt Cari's drum stick slap me in the back. I spun around with a scowl on my face. Her devilish grin greeted me instantly as she pointed to the track.

"What? That hurt!" I asked sourly.

"Guess who's looking at you?" Cari spoke loudly for everyone within earshot to hear.

I played it off, secretly dying to swing a glance over to where she motioned.

"Jules, he's blatantly staring at you with hunger and undressing you with his eyes," Cari raised her volume. I blushed, slanting my eyes at Cari. She simply grinned and waved at me.

My eyes drifted inconspicuously to the track to find Broderick, indeed, staring at me with a smile, patiently waiting for me to finish with practice and take me home. I returned the smile of the same sort and initiated a wave to see if he'd even wave back, which he did instantly.

I heard a small laugh escape from the drum line. "Mm-hm. Undressing you with his eyes," Cari sang tauntingly.

I spun quickly to gain control of her before she embarrassed me any further. "Would you shut up?" I threw her drum stick back at her.

She playfully growled with a sexual undertone. I was just pleased to know that somehow she had come to some sort of acceptance of him and was now teasing me about him. She made me self-conscious of every movement I made on the field. His eyes never strayed from where I stood. Even when I casually carried on as if I was done being aware of his presence, he continued his stare and smile.

Finally, Mr. Grayson ordered all of us to make our next mark on the field.

"So… are you two more than *friends* yet?" She asked, standing at attention only steps behind me.

"*Just friends*, Cari," I reiterated, staring forward at attention.

Broderick continued watching us and I prayed that neither he nor anyone else nearby could hear our conversation.

"I don't know, Jules. Ol' long and lanky is a bit too hot to just be friends with, don't you think?"

I shrugged, "He's not ugly, if that's what you mean. I guess it's a matter of taste."

"Then I suppose you wouldn't mind if I asked him out."

"What?" I dropped my flag and twisted around at her, staring at her in horror. I couldn't accept it. He was hardly her type. He was what she would degradingly call 'squeaky clean'.

"I could use a boy scout like that and according to Savannah, I'm already into him. I can't imagine where she heard that," she laughed.

Giving her a cold stare, I scooped my flag back into my hands and returned to attention. I couldn't understand why I was so angry with her. She was always giving me a hard time about something.

Sneakily, she moved in close behind me and smacked me in the back of the head then quickly returned to her spot on the field a few feet back. "What the hell are you thinking?" she scolded.

"What do you mean 'what am I thinking?'" I huffed.

"I just wanted to see your reaction," she said. I shot her a questioning look—still quite angry. "To see if you'd get jealous, and I tell you, Jealous Jules definitely made an appearance," she laughed.

I scowled at the name I was often referred to in my worst moments of jealousy. She was right, I was so jealous in that split second I couldn't even see straight.

"It's okay, you know? To be jealous?" she started. "If I had someone like him at my side all the time, I'd rip any girl to shreds who thought she was could step in between us."

"Why are you saying this?"

"Because, I might have been wrong about him. *Might have been.*"

I was shocked. "Surely you're not apologizing..."

"Oh, hell no! I would never apologize for looking out for one of my chicks. And I'm still not fully trusting of him, but he's definitely fond of you and he's not in the least bit ashamed to show that. So, either he's in love or just pathetic. And I hate to think that one of the hottest guys in school was pathetic, so I'm going with *love.*" I could hear the grin in her voice.

"Please, don't say that word." The anxiety started bubbling like a shaken soda in my stomach.

"I'm curious though. What do you think is going to happen if another girl *does* decide that she wants to place herself where you're standing?"

"Where? On the forty-five yard line?" I asked in a joking manner.

She ignored my remark. "The flirting between the two of you is only going to keep him at bay for so long. What are you going to do?"

"He's not flirting. We're just friends. I'm not cool or popular enough to be his actual girlfriend."

"You're right; you're not cool, but he'd be lucky to get you." It was the nicest thing she had ever said to me.

I attempted to study for my Algebra final during dinner. Joey stayed to eat dinner with us since my dad had to work late, again. He and Natalie talked about cheering and football, and couldn't emphasize enough about how sad they were that we only had one week left of our summer break before school was back in session.

"I have some news," my mother interrupted.

"You're pregnant!" Natalie accused as a joke.

This got my attention and I raised my head up from the notebook I was studying from. Joey ceased in his quest for chewing his food and let it set in his mouth, his cheeks full and puffy.

Mom gave Nat a dry smirk. "No. I got a job."

"*Why?*" I asked. My mother had taken pride in the fact that she was a stay at home mom since I could remember. In almost seventeen years, she had never worked outside the home.

"You're going to college in two years and Nat's going in three. We're going to need the extra money." She smiled proudly at the mention of college. "So, I'll be working for a doctor as a medical secretary. Her name is Dr. Renata Kowalski…"

"What if I don't want to go to college?" I loathed the idea of school beyond another two years of high school.

"Jules, we've been through this. Try it out for at least one semester," she suggested.

At the mention of college, I pondered on what the future held for me and Broderick. He would be graduating at the end of this coming year, then he'd be gone. I wouldn't be leaving for another year after that. With that in mind, spending so much time with Broderick and secretly hoping for a relationship with him seemed pointless.

Friday morning began like all the other mornings. Broderick picked me up, we went to see Mama Green to pick up some doughnuts (for us and Mr. Muir), and then we arrived at school.

"You ready for this final?" he asked.

"I hope so. I actually studied for it," I said nervously. "I'm going to be upset if I don't pass this exam like I thought I would last spring."

"You'll do fine." He nudged me with his elbow as we walked over to our seats.

Mr. Muir thanked us for our doughnuts and immediately plunged in to a two hour review. He handed us a five page exam as each of us returned to the classroom from our midway break in the schedule.

"This is a two hour exam. As soon as you finish, you're free to leave. Grades will be posted this evening online. Have a great rest of the summer and I will see you all in one week when school returns." His words were uttered dryly and without enthusiasm, sounding as if this speech was recited and forced. Mr. Muir thrust the five page exam at Broderick. "Cooper, I will never understand why you've wasted this summer taking a class you passed two years ago."

I shot my head up at Mr. Muir's sudden reveal. Of course! Algebra II was typically a sophomore class! Betrayed by his dishonesty, I shot a nasty glance over at Broderick. He shifted uncomfortably in his seat as he scrambled for words. "My GPA, sir, it had dropped —"

Mr. Muir let go of the exam and dryly sighed. "A 3.9 is hardly a drop in GPA. You know, Cooper, even a fantastic four-year university will accept a 3.9," he reminded him as he walked over to his desk, shaking his head. "But to each his own, I guess."

Flustered at this revelation, Broderick stared at the test on his desk, never once looking at me. My mouth dropped open and I furrowed my brows at the betrayal I felt. The irritation was so overpowering that I was panicking over my lack of concentration on the exam. My brain throbbed with rage and I aimlessly gazed at the pages in front of me.

Barely an hour had gone by when Broderick stood up and placed the test on Mr. Muir's desk. He gathered the notebook up in his hands and began walking to the door.

"Do you want to stick around while I grade this so you can see your score, Cooper? I'm pretty sure I have time to do so before the others start turning in their exams." Mr. Muir offered.

I looked up to see Broderick catch a quick glimpse of me staring darts at him. Seemingly resigned to the truth, Broderick admitted grimly as he slouched out of the door, "No. I aced it."

I was able to focus better after he left the room, but still could feel the boiling anger in my veins. My exam took exactly two hours after I had started. I handed him my book, thanked him for the summer class and left the room.

Broderick was waiting for me just outside the door and was hot on my heels as I stormed past him. "Jules. Jules, wait. We need to talk."

"I have nothing to say to you," I heatedly replied as I continued walking.

"Please give me a chance to explain."

"Explain what? That you're a liar? No thanks, I get that." I pushed through the doors that led to the parking lot, making my way to marching band practice.

"It's not like that."

"A 3.9! Really, Broderick? Because last I checked, I have 3.0 and even *that* isn't low enough for me to waste a whole freakin' summer in a class that I aced two years ago." I continued to storm away from him.

"Jules, please, listen! You've got to give me a —"

Interrupting him, I spun on my heel and pointed a finger directly at him. "I don't have to give you a damn thing! I refuse to be friends with a liar. You came barking up the wrong tree... *literally*! From here on don't talk to me, don't call me, don't even look at me and we'll pretend this summer never happened."

My mind was already planning ahead for a ride home. Cari was my best option though I'd have to listen to her proverbial "I told you so". It would be worth it, not digging myself further into Broderick and avoiding any additional hurt.

"Jules!" I could hear he was no longer following me, but standing in the middle of the parking lot yelling for me in front of a swarm of students that were passing by, heading to their respective practices. "I lied about my GPA! I didn't need to take the class!" Defeated, he announced to all that would listen.

My legs could no longer walk away from him, but I kept my back to him for a few seconds more, clenching my fists. I wanted to turn around and punch his lights out for making me feel like a fool. But I also wanted to look at his beautiful face and strong features that made my knees weak. And I *wanted* to believe him. Slowly, I dropped my hands to the side as though I had given up any fight against him. He jogged over to me and stood in front of me.

"I signed up for second term Algebra II this summer after learning that you were denied the final exam. I wanted to meet you. If anything, please believe that because *that's* the honest-to-God truth!" His eyes begged for my acceptance, but I fought against them.

"I don't know what to believe anymore."

He was impulsive, "Come with me right now; I'll tell you everything."

"We can't skip practice; we'd get in trouble. You'd probably have to sit out the first home game…"

"It would be worth it. Come with me, Jules."

His words lingered in my ears like beckoning echoes as I stood in a long, silent debate. Doubt forbade my feet to step toward him and our freedom. Walking away from me and toward his jeep, my heart ached as I watched the distance between the two of us grow. I couldn't stay away from him; I didn't want to. He climbed into the vehicle and started the engine. He shifted the gears. My nervousness made me queasy and anticipation, like ignited sparks, burned me from the inside out from the top of my head to my toes.

My voice broke through without warning, "Broderick! Wait!"

He slammed on the brakes and smiled in relief as I ran and jumped into the door he had opened for me, and we sped away from the school. My heart thundered in my chest at the risk I was taking. I didn't care what torture it could possibly bring me, but only dwelled on the forbidden bliss of running away with him.

Premonitions

DRIVING THROUGH THE COUNTRYSIDE, he clearly had no intentions of bringing me back any time soon. I should have been at least a little frightened that I was with someone who seemed obsessively desperate to get me alone and away from where I was normally accounted for, especially someone who seemed to carry a bundle of secrets about himself.

No one knew where we were; *I* didn't know where we were. Far outside the city limits, I could see more farm land ahead. We drove down a winding road and eventually broke off to the left starting up a steep incline. The valley below was completely drenched by the morning sun. My ears felt muffled and I tried yawning to pop them again.

We ended up on a road that was blocked with thick cables looped through cement posts, marking its end. Upon parking, he ripped the keys from the ignition and leaned back in his seat, drawing in a deep breath. He opened the door and stepped out to stretch his legs. I shrugged into the red hoodie I had left in the backseat from earlier this morning when the air was cool. Somehow it offered protection. Protection from what? I didn't know, but I needed that security.

He opened the passenger side of the door, "I want to show you something."

"You still owe me an explanation." I scowled at him and crossed my arms, determined to not take a step out of the jeep.

"I just needed to come up here to clear my head before I get started, that's all." I hesitated; my eyes scrutinizing him. "Come on, Jules. It's only a bit up the trail. I promise I'll tell you everything once we get to the bluffs." He held out his hand for me to join him.

"The *bluffs*? You plan on pushing me?" I stepped next to him, stubbornly folding my arms and ignoring his hand.

We walked side by side down the dirt path covered by a canopy of trees. "I wanted to tell you the truth last Saturday, but after learning about the shadowshifting, I felt that anything beyond that would be overwhelming for you. By the middle of this week, I'd convinced myself that keeping the truth from you couldn't hurt especially since things between us were finally coming together. But you deserve to know how deep my need to be your friend is. What it's rooted from."

We moved through the tall canopy of trees until we came to a bright overlook. My eyes widened at the sight of the rocky bluffs that stretched out before us. Grassy Cove, in all of its green beauty, sat thousands of feet below us. Farms and tiny homes were scatter throughout the valley. To my right another rock shelf was separated from the one that I stood on by a crevice only a few feet wide. The drop had to have been close to a hundred feet, and I shivered at the thought of plummeting.

Broderick stepped closer behind me and whispered, "Welcome to Black Mountain. Breathtaking isn't it?"

I opened my mouth to speak but didn't want to interrupt the peace and beauty with my noise. Nodding, I stared off into the magnificence until Broderick stepped beside me and began talking. His voice was the perfect tribute to the scenery. "I come here often when I need to get away from everything, to clear my head. Like you, when you're on your roof."

I sat down on the bluff edge and securely wrapped my arms around my legs to shield them from the chilly morning air. The sun cast a brilliant orange across the sky. Broderick sat down next to me with one of his legs dangling off of the edge and the other propping his arm up, in which he rested his head. He looked at me good and hard, debating on whether to continue his confession. He stared at the sunrise and breathed deeply. "Do you believe in divine intervention?"

The closest to *divine intervention* I could think of was the howling noise I heard in the woods near our homes on the night Gavin came to see me. "Yeah, I do."

"Mama Green had a heart attack last year and I saw it happen." His voice coursed through, gravelly and dazed.

"Taryn's mom? You were *there?*"

"I said that I *saw* it happen." He wasn't making any sense to me but I could tell he was hesitant on continuing the story. I pressed my eyebrows together in confusion. His face became flushed as he surmised if he had already said too much. "I saw her have the heart attack weeks before she actually had it."

Shaking my head ever so slightly, I wasn't certain if I was more shocked at his declaration or at the possibility that he was lying to me yet again. "How?"

His eyes stayed glued to the brightening horizon. The disgust on his face was thick. "I see things in my sleep."

Air escaped me as a tingle climbed up my spine.

"I saw her lying face down on the floor of the shop. No one was there to help her." He never once looked at me, and his voice was grave, "I ignored it for a while, but it was relentless every night I slept. The memory of the visions haunted me almost every hour of every day, and that was when I wasn't obsessing over the impression I had that Taryn and Jackson were falling for each other.

"Then one morning I woke from the same reoccurring dream but this time a feeling of imminence came with it. I knew I had to check on Mama Green at the shop. These images are dreams, yet they're more than that. The physical feelings and the emotions that come with those pictures go beyond reaction to what I've seen and they grow with intensity every time—

the closer I come to the actual event. I can't explain it; it's as if I'm actually *there*." He shook his head; embarrassed and defeated.

"When I got to the shop and knocked, there was no answer. Donuts 'N More opens at five and it was already four-thirty. Her car was parked around back, so I knew she was there. I was terrified; so much urgency in my thoughts, and so much doubt with logic. So I did what anybody else would have done and called the police."

"What happened then?"

"The police showed up to check for anything out of the ordinary, and apparently the only thing 'out of the ordinary' was the fact that I was at Donuts 'N More at four thirty in the morning, trying to get in the back door. I told them I was dating the owner's daughter and they recognized me from a few of the high school sport teams; that got me off the hook long enough to talk them into trying to bust into the shop. Sure enough, there she was, just as I had seen her in my dreams. Face down and barely breathing. A heart attack."

He finally looked at me and my tension eased. "So you were right about one thing. I am a liar. The last thing I want is for people to figure out just how different I am. I don't want to be taken from my grandmother, trapped like a lab rat, and studied as a freak." The treachery was evidently crushing him by the look on his face. "I'm a hypocrite, acting like I don't give a damn what others think—the same *others* who are my friends— because I *do* care about what they *know*. I can never let them know about me. I could lose everything I love in my life."

I was speechless.

"The precognitions happened again and again—every one of them panning out, just as I saw them in my dreams. It was hard to cope with because at that same time, I had become aware of the mutual feelings between Taryn and Jackson. I'd be lying to say it didn't bother me, but neither of them acted on it, and they both seemed content with enduring the current situation. Nobody was making a break for it, so I kept my mouth shut and stuck it out. I wasn't miserable with her. Taryn's a sweet and beautiful girl, but something was always missing between us. I needed her; I needed her friendship. I wanted so much to have someone I could rely on. I was desperate to get a grasp on the dreams and the shadowshifting. I was being so selfish. Jackson could see that I was draining her and he became the friend that she needed in return.

"I learned quickly I couldn't control the dreams like I could the shifting. Some dreams were good, others pointless and then there were those that shook me to my core. It's a curse. I didn't know what to do with the information they provided, and I gained no personal benefit from them. I questioned my sanity, wondering if this is how it feels to be stark raving mad. My dreams started really throwing me for a loop, when I saw Jackson and Taryn together in my dreams. They were telling me that they were pregnant. Apologizing for it. I didn't know if it was happening, already happened, or was going to happen…or if it was just a regular dream. Instead of approaching the situation responsibly, I freaked out and my jealous rage pushed her right into his arms."

Bowled over at the truth of what had really happened, for the first time I felt sympathy for everything Taryn had gone through.

"I ended things pretty bad with both of them that evening. My ego was bruised and so I pushed away two of my best friends." He sighed and shook his head at the memory. "Jules, that was the loneliest I'd ever felt. I prayed for a sign—anything that would help me understand just what the heck was happening to me. And then that night I had two of the most defining dreams of my life. The first one gave me a palpable feeling of hope and peace. But the second one… it was a nightmare that still haunts me to this day. I woke up screaming, dreading to close my eyes again. I still have them both often. "

He dared a glimpse in my direction and took a deep and choppy breath. It occurred to me at that moment that he had revealed more than he'd ever intended. I also knew that he was truly desperate to share this with someone.

He struggled to finish his story. "I couldn't go back to sleep, my mind couldn't rest; I was terrified with what the second vision showed me and anxious to see the first one play out. I don't know how to explain how I felt that night. My thoughts were focused and excited one minute then scattered and horrified the next."

He dropped his head and shut his eyes to the anguish he was remembering of that night. "So to clear my head, I decided to take a walk that night instead of drive up here since it was snowing pretty hard outside. I found myself migrating toward our woods. It was a subconscious pull from a higher power—*divine intervention*, if you will. I cut my way through the woods, not really considering where I'd end up and stopped when I came to the creek. Looking up through the bare branches of the trees… It would have been a beautiful picture to paint—the moon was high, a bright white and it stood directly over your house. Snow was falling in large, puffy flakes all around. And that's when I saw you sitting, bundled up in a blanket, on your roof. *Crying*."

My eyes widened. "I remember that night," I softly choked out. "It was the first time I had heard the rumor about Gavin and Morgan. I decided to cry outside as it snowed, hoping that the burning cold would distract me from how badly my heart hurt."

"I sat on that rock beside the frozen creek and watched you cry for over an hour, Jules. I completely forgot what it was that led me out that night in the first place. I even watched your house a few minutes after you crept back into your window and turned off the bedroom lights. I wanted to make sure you didn't slip."

His face changed to a regretful one. "I had been oblivious to you for the two years you'd been there and I'm sorry. I didn't know a whole lot about you—beyond singing. But something about you that night intrigued me. It triggered something in me. I went home and all I could wonder about was what could make such a beautiful girl so sad and if there was anything I could do to take away that sadness." Now Broderick flashed a dimple and a lopsided grin. "Hero complex, remember? Anyway I was actually able to sleep then. I guess in a roundabout way, I owe you for that. You helped me to move beyond that nightmare for one night." He smiled warmly. "Even better, I got to see that first vision again that night." His mind seemed to marvel at the memory of the dream.

"Seeing you that following Monday, was overwhelming. It didn't take long to find out who you were dating and what was going on behind your back. I could tell that you weren't completely ignorant of Gavin's cheating and that he was probably the cause for the night I saw you crying. Of *all* the nights I saw you crying."

It floored me to know that he had been watching me for so long.

He heaved a big sigh. "But that last day of school… Jules, my heart broke for you. I could see in your expression that you were finally wise to that creep, and you were falling apart little by little with every word you sang. I felt every bit of your humiliation and anger. I can't explain *why* or *how*, but I did and it wasn't just out of sympathy. When you exploded, I wanted to explode with you. And when Mr. Dean pulled you away, I would have done anything to go in your place. It lit a fire under me to set things right for you. I was determined for us to be friends. It sounds strange, but I saw how different *you* were from others at school, too, and I hoped that I would get a chance to know. I wanted to save you that day, like the way you saved me that night when I stood watching you from the woods."

I began to breathe deeply like I was actually filling my lungs with clean air for the first time and not simply sustaining life as he described the girl I knew in the mirror. He knew me and he could see me.

"By the end of that day, everyone knew you had been suspended and denied your final. So, I took a gamble and signed up for the same summer class, in hopes that we would connect like we were supposed to."

"Like we were *supposed* to?" I whispered.

He lowered his head and laughed at himself quietly. "I know that it must sound crazy, but it's the truth, and I don't know any other way to explain it. Like a gravitational pull. Divine intervention"

My heart hammered loudly in my chest. There was nothing underhanded about anything he had done. I saw nothing but sheer innocence and honesty. I didn't know what to say as I was still taking everything he had said in. Completely preposterous, yet, I believed him!

Curiosity was getting the best of me. "So what was the first dream?"

He leaned his head back in a soft laughter-filled sigh, reveling in his private remembrance. "Ah… *That*. I'm going to keep that one to myself, at least for a while longer."

I pressed my eyebrows together in what was becoming a familiar frown. "Secrets don't make friends."

He continued to laugh. "I promise. *Someday*, I'll tell you."

He reached over and lightly pulled a strand of my hair. My body tingled at the slight pressure on my head from where he pulled. I began to panic, wondering if he was realizing that my hair was colored—that I was a natural red. He released the lock and sighed. "I believe that in life we're given a path to follow and then we're left with the free will to choose that path—that we're brought to a crossroads and make our decision: Do we become hell-bent on fighting that gravitational pull toward the path we're called to or do we follow our fate? I'm following mine," he said profoundly.

His resolution alone was brighter than the sun in front of us. I was no longer angry with him for deceiving me and only felt something stronger than anything I had ever felt before in my life. I just didn't know how to direct the overpowering essence of my affection for the boy next door. A guy whose popularity reached to the ends of our county line and yet nobody knew him.

"So what do you want to do for the rest of the day?" he began. "You want to go swimming?"

I grimaced as the horror of him seeing me in a bathing suit permeated. "Maybe another time." I was far too curious about his dreams to just let the conversation die and desperately needed a change of subject. "Have your dreams ever changed? I mean, God gave us free will and all, so surely not all you see is set in stone, right?"

He thought for a moment and finally spoke. "I never saw you angry with me for 'saving you' in the lake." He quoted with his fingers to assure me that he didn't consider it a rescue, and he chuckled at the reminder of our earlier interaction.

"Is that why you were so quick in the water?"

He nodded sheepishly. "I misread the dream but I knew you were going to be under water. And I sure as heck didn't see you decking Erik."

"What do you mean *Erik*? You saw that, too?" I was shocked.

"I saw it the night of the lake incident. That's why I was at the movies that night, to protect you," he confessed in a regretful tone looking out to the glowing horizon. Broderick's face scowled. "I'm not a violent person, Jules, but what I *saw* was *my* fist slamming against his skull, not *yours*."

There was nothing but satisfaction at the prospect of a man coming to my rescue; I had to smile. "You and your hero complex."

"I kept second guessing what course of action I should take, worried about how much more damage I would do in a relationship between us. I was revved up and ready to go by the end of my movie, well on my way to break things up, but that's when I saw you on the bench. I had waited too long and you had already done the deed yourself. Although I was impressed, I was also disappointed I hadn't saved you. A lady should never be left in that kind of position to defend herself."

"That's not your fault," I assured him. "Anyway, it felt kind of good to take control like that. I needed that sort of anger release." I shook my head in astonishment at how it all connected and made sense to me now. "Gosh, I remember seeing you bolt out of that movie like a man on a mission."

"And now you know why." He grinned.

"Now I know." I grinned back, taking a few breaths as I prepped myself for the inevitable question that had me piqued from the moment he had mentioned his nightmares.

"What *can* you tell me about the second dream? The nightmare?"

"You really don't want to hear this." His pitch was warning as he rubbed his eyes with the palms of his hands.

"Yes, I do." I waited patiently for him to tell me.

In preparation, he drew in a deep breath, blowing it all out in one big release. He shivered in remembrance, and then began his story.

"I'm in a barn, and I feel challenged by someone in the shadows. A dark figure with pale skin. I can barely see him, except for his pale skin. He begins to charge me at superhuman speed and as he gets closer, I see his teeth. Like fangs. The whole thing flashes in my mind so quickly my view gets choppy, like a strobe light. He's moving so incredibly fast I can't really make out what happens, just focus on the colors. I can see his black hair in contrast to his skin that's white as a ghost. His mouth and lips are blood red. His eyes are such a pale blue, almost silver looking." Broderick's shoulders dropped in exasperation. "I can't really see anything useful..."

"The painting in your room!" I threw my hand to my mouth as I gasped. He nodded. "Ew," I shivered as I remembered the horror induced painting.

"I thought you liked that stuff?" He chuckled with a raised eyebrow as I shivered. "Anyway, the dream ends the minute I hear a high pitched scream. I don't know where it comes from, but it's so high and loud, it almost sounds like a whistle. My ears continue ringing from the shrill long after I'm finally awake...The whole dream happens in just matter of seconds, from start to finish, but it's vivid enough to get my blood pumping and get me to dodge sleep for the rest of the night." He then added, "And sometimes several nights afterward."

The painting continued to enter my mind. Too scary. It was hard to accept. "How can you tell a vision from a regular nightmare?"

He frowned in concentration. "That's the whole problem; I can never be fully sure. Usually, I feel the imminence of the event when I wake the day they are set to happen. But this nightmare is so much more like a horror movie that I have difficulty accepting it as a vision. It's just unrealistic. But there are urgent emotions that come with it just like the visions. For example, I know I'm in danger, and it just feels real when it happens. I can't fully explain it," he grimly admitted. "I become so terrified that I tremble in my sleep, literally shaking the bed I sleep on. And there's so much rage inside of me, practically overpowering the fear. More rage than I've ever felt before, but I have no clue as to why I'm so angry." I waited. He didn't seem finished with his thought. "And then there's the power I feel...."

"*Power?*"

"I feel this unstoppable power within me every time I awake from it. As if I'm an unbeatable force. I've never felt anything like that before, not even in the heat of a game. In the dreams though, I'm practically invincible."

"If you feel invincible, then why is the dream so frightening?" I asked him.

He swallowed hard and leaned in closer to whisper. "If I want to be completely honest right now… In my nightmare, I can't decide if I should be more terrified of the monster in the shadows, or the anger and power within myself." He shook off the seriousness of the subject and pressed on in a lighter tone. "Painting about it has really helped. I've been using it as a therapy. If I paint it, I can eventually get enough of it off my chest for the night and get a few hours of sleep."

We sat quietly on the bluff listening to the birds sing and the wind blow by. The sun warmed my skin.

"Broderick," I began my quest to understand his living arrangements. "Why do you live with your grandmother?"

He slowly started, "My mom died of breast cancer when I was young."

My face became hot with guilt for ever bringing it up. "I'm so sorry."

"I hated losing her, but looking back, I couldn't imagine her suffering any longer than she already had. I wouldn't want that." His eyes clouded over with a distant gaze, before he pressed on with a false lift in his voice. "When she died, my grandmother wanted me, so I moved here to Crossville when I was ten and that's basically it."

"What about your dad?" I asked. Though I was pretty nervous asking these things, he seemed willing to share.

"I was almost two when he died," he said.

"My gosh!" I exclaimed. "*Both* parents?"

He tucked his lips in, causing his dimples to appear. "It was harder losing Mom. I don't even remember my dad. I've only seen him in a few pictures."

"What happened?" I was sure that I was sticking my foot in my mouth by merely asking, but I couldn't ignore the persistent curiosity.

"All I know is what I've been told. My dad was a detective in Louisiana. He apparently got a lead on a serial killer and tracked the suspect to an abandoned shack near some swamp. He acted alone—without any backup—and only the evidence left behind at the scene could explain what happened. The killer got away and my dad was dead. Everyone tried to shield me from the details, but as the years passed…well, a little boy isn't always noticed when people are having adult conversations. I heard bits and pieces, but not everything I heard made sense to me, like, his body was never found or…" Broderick shook his head as if to clarify the memory. "At least not all of my dad's body was found. His clothes and blood samples were identified."

I sat momentarily in shock. My mind instantly turned to the recent discovery of the dead girl in our county.

"I guess you get your hero-complex from your dad then." He emitted a small smile at my words. "And your mom—she could shadowshift, too?"

"From what I've heard."

"What did she do for a living?"

"She was a kindergarten teacher." I heard him release a small breathy laugh, probably from a memory. "My mom was an only child. She met my dad in high school. They married the day she turned eighteen and had me seven months later. I can do the math, so I know the motivation behind their marriage," he chuckled.

Suddenly, our solitude was interrupted by footsteps coming up behind us. A couple old enough to be our grandparents emerged from the woods and the woman smiled at us.

"Beautiful morning isn't it?" she asked cheerfully.

Broderick gathered himself to a standing position. Looking intently down at me and holding out a hand to help me up he said, "Yes it is."

I took his hand and never let go of it until we reached the jeep. We spent the rest of day together at Main Street Drug Store chatting over cherry cokes and seasoned fries, seeming to never run out of things to share with one another. We finally parted ways when it came dinner time and he took me home.

Resolved to my usual thinking spot on the roof after lights out, my mind was in hyper drive as I recalled all of what I had learned about the boy next door and all the events that led to this very day. It all made sense now, coming together like one giant puzzle.

"Hello, Jules," his voice projected from the shadows behind me as he sat in the tree. I loved the way my name sounded when he spoke it. And I was pleasantly surprised to see him again so soon.

"What are you doing here?" I asked.

"I saw that your light was on and I wanted to come by and ask if you wanted to do something." He dropped onto the roof and made his way closer to me as I climbed to my feet.

"What did you have in mind?" I considered suggesting a movie again, but knew it would be more of a diversion from talking and getting to know each other better, which was what I really wanted to do.

"Actually, it's been ages since I last took a midnight swim. You game?" He appeared nervous as he chewed on his bottom lip.

My brain was scrambling for an excuse not to go despite the combination of excitement and fear that ran through my body. "I don't think so…"

"You promised."

"When?"

"Today."

I vaguely remembered; he had twisted my words, though. "I said *another time.*"

"This *is* another time, and the weather is perfect. It's too dark for anyone to see you in a swimsuit if that's what you're worried about," he tempted.

I gave a strong consideration, leaning more toward a yes at every passing second. "What if we get caught?"

"Our chances of getting caught are slim to none, but there's still that small risk factor to make it exciting." He added confidently, "I promise to keep you safe, Jules."

I bit my bottom lip in contemplation.

"Come on, Jules, be impulsive." He snapped his fingers playfully, frazzling me as I tried making a rational decision.

Impulsive! Without a word, I left Broderick on the roof and rushed into my window. I locked my bedroom door to prevent my parents from checking in on me and grabbed my red bikini—still not fully sure if I would even get in the water, but just in case.

As I began reaching out the window where he now waited for me, I playfully smiled. "Well, help me out of here."

"We're going?" he asked eagerly; I could hear the smile spread widely on his face. He gently took my hand and guided me out of the window as he darkened to a shadow.

"Yes," I announced boldly, staring in amazement at his shadow; I wondered if I would ever get used to that.

He held tight to me as we eased over to the branches of the tree and down. His free arm never releasing from around my waist, he was delicate in his maneuvers, making sure that I safely made it to the ground even though I felt quite confident in my tree climbing skills. As soon as I touched ground, I darted toward the sidewalk along the street and he grabbed the hood of my shirt jerking me back.

"What do you think you're doing?" he asked.

"Going to your house where the jeep is."

He shook his head and gave a small laugh. "Not by the street, silly. That's how we'd get caught. Through the woods," he pointed.

My eyes filled with fear. I cringed as I thought back to the echoing sound of the wolf. "Seriously?"

"It's just the dark. You're not afraid of the dark are you, Jules?" He emitted a low moan like a ghost.

With determination, I rolled my eyes and took his hand that he offered. He led me through the woods effortlessly, taking his routine path. He took extra special care as we skipped over the creek and onto the sandstone that sat on his side of the property.

Soon enough we were in his back yard. Following him up the stairs and into his loft, his air unit was cranked up too high, and a chilly burst of air slammed into me as I walked through the door. His room had easels and canvasses strewn about, essentially making it seem unorganized. His bed was tangled and unmade.

He strolled over to his dresser to retrieve his swim trunks and I set my bikini down on the small table just inside the door before migrating to his paintings. Looking desperately for the painting of the pale man in the shadows, I wanted to see it again now that I knew the root for its inspiration. I couldn't find it. He grabbed his swimming trunks and snatched the keys from his desk. He opened the door for me and I gave him a playful look as I walked past him. The night was eerily silent as we made our way to the jeep.

Night Swimming

W EAVING RIGHT TO LEFT, he sped down the highway with the top down. The warm, humid air whipping my hair into a mess, so I pulled my hood up to contain the frenzy. The moon was hanging low and the fireflies had already retired for the night. Broderick was clearly at ease with the whole sneaking out bit. As he drove under a canopy of trees he shifted into the shadows that were cast upon him. I giggled in amusement as the steering wheel appeared to maneuver itself at times.

He took a few turns off the highway and we entered into an eerie, backwoods area I was unfamiliar with.

"We're swimming in the boonies?" Alarm was thick in my voice.

"We're going to a swimming hole I know."

I had seen way too many movies. "Um, Broderick?" My nervous demeanor bled through, "Did you ever watch *Friday the 13th?*"

He just laughed while he looped us through the country roads until we reached a dirt path. "Jules, how is it you can watch all those horror movies and still be terrified of real life?"

"Are you kidding? I think it's for that very reason I am so cautious at times. Granted, those movies may make me a bit skittish, but they also make me street smart," I quipped.

"How do you figure that?" he asked with a laugh.

"Well," I began to explain, "I know to always check underneath the car before I approach it in a parking lot and the backseat before I get in it at night."

"Okay..."

"And I know to never investigate a strange noise outside."

"True," he chuckled.

"And to never go walking on the moors during a full moon," I said quickly. His laughter ricocheted through the surrounding woods. The noise was unsettling.

"If you think that's funny, wait until I fill you in on my contingency plan for surviving the zombie apocalypse," I quipped.

He parked the jeep in a small cove of trees and helped me out of the jeep to make our way down the path toward the water. The moonlight that was able to peek through the mass of trees glittered in the water as it rushed by. Sovereignty. Me and him. The night and the moon.

We walked over to a large rock that jutted from the bank and sat on it. He stayed quiet for a moment as we listened to the light rush of the stream.

"So, are you ready for school to start in a little over a week?" he casually asked me.

Shaking my head, I gave an exaggerated shiver. "I hate school. I lose interest easily in class and I'm sick of the drama and gossip that circulates during the school year." I paused as I reconsidered my last statement with a mischievous grin. "Okay, I hate the gossip about me; I actually do enjoy listening about everyone else." I laughed.

"Remember what you said about my photos? Do you think they'd actually let me on the yearbook staff?" he asked thoughtfully. I found his insecurity over the matter amusing and very attractive.

"You're actually considering the yearbook staff? I think you're extremely talented, Broderick. They'd be crazy not to see what I see," I encouraged.

"I've secretly always wanted to do it," he admitted.

"You need to do whatever makes you happy," I informed him. He looked over at me and I silently reiterated, pointing a finger at him.

"And what makes *you* happy, Jules Taylor?"

I wrapped my arms around my knees and looked up at the moon as I sighed dramatically. "Music, movies, good friends, walks on the beach, vanilla lattes, autumn leaves, the smell of carved jack-o-lanterns at Halloween—"

"Other than because of what happened last spring, why aren't you singing with Cari's band this year?"

I humbled myself. "I've decided to focus more on theater this year."

"Is that what you plan to study in college?" he asked.

"If I had my way, I wouldn't go to college at all. Making it as a singer or an actress takes dedication, talent, and pure luck; college can't guarantee those things for me."

"But it could give you skills and experience you otherwise wouldn't have," he remarked.

I curled my upper lip in response. "I hated my first thirteen years of school. Why would I put myself through four more? What about you? What are you going to do after this year?"

Here was the moment I dreaded. He was going to share with me his grand plans of shaking the dust of this town off his feet and never looking back.

"I don't think I'm really college material, either," he confessed. "I have toyed with idea of enlisting in the military... my hero-complex and all." He smiled at me. "But, I think I'd rather study photography and art somewhere. Possibly at a small arts college."

"Seriously? No baseball scholarships? No Fraternities?"

"Those are my friends you're referring to, not me. If I could make a living out of painting or photography I'd be a happy man," he disclosed. "I would like to find a nearby school to enroll in some classes that could point me in the right direction, hone my craft, and then set me free to start my life as I see fit. I don't want to go far. My grandmother is here and..." He chewed on a thought for a bit. "Well, this is my home."

"What about Jackson and Taryn?" I probed. "Why wouldn't you try to go to a school near them?"

"He'll study law and Taryn will go wherever he goes, even if she doesn't get accepted to the same school. In all my years with him, though—and he is like a brother—I could never talk to him like I talk with you."

"So if he was like a brother to you, that would make me... a *sister?*" I winced internally.

He laughed and evaded the question. "What do you want to do after you graduate, Jules?"

"I just want to travel! I think doing theater would provide me with that opportunity as well as a small paycheck."

He leaned in with interest. "Where do you want to travel to, Jules?"

"Everywhere!" I announced excitedly. "I'd love to see all of the states first, of course. But most of all, I want to see Ireland."

"What's in Ireland that interests you so much?"

"It's my heritage. And my grandmother's there." My smile fell to one of a bittersweet memory.

"You're grandmother lives in Ireland. That's pretty cool."

I shook my head in correction. "No. She doesn't live there; her ashes were scattered there."

He dropped his head in shame. "That was clumsy of me."

"She died last November from bone cancer," I sadly spoke. He reached over to lightly rub my back. "She went quickly, like your mom. I guess that's why I have so much sympathy for your loss. But you lost your *mother*, I lost my grandmother. It's not nearly the same. But she and I were close..." My thoughts became distant.

"Tell me about her."

I laughed nervously trying to understand how anyone aside from family could find interest in my relationship with my deceased grandmother. "Well, she introduced me to Frank Sinatra's music and for that I will be forever grateful. She loved musicals, which was part of the reason I decided to take up theater in the first place, and it turns out I love it." I thought further. "And we watched *An Affair to Remember* together every time it was on." I relished in that memory.

"You actually like a chick flick?" His tone was disbelieving.

"That and Gone with the Wind are the only chick flicks I like. Since they're classics, I don't really count them as chick-flicks," I assured him.

We sat quietly for a few seconds before he snapped his head up with enthusiasm. "Let's go swimming."

He stood up from the rock. My heart leapt with alarm as I realized that I couldn't find my bikini. Mentally retracing my steps, I remembered leaving it on the table inside of the door of Broderick's bedroom before we left and realized that I must have left it there! The fear must have been plastered all over my face. He frowned down at me, just before he slid out of his T-shirt. Kneeling down to get eye contact he whispered. "What movie excuse are you going to use this time, smartass? *Jaws?*"

"No excuse. I just don't know..." I was almost whining as I warred with my own inhibition.

He devilishly grinned, a laugh emitting from his throat. "It's a perfect night for it. Come on, Jules," he quietly beckoned. "Are you worried about me seeing you in a bathing suit, really?"

"Actually, I think I left my swimsuit in your room."

"So?" He was apparently unconcerned with retrieving his own swim trunks from the jeep, yet I could feel his nervous energy fill the gap between us. Staring at his strong, lean body standing before me in only a pair of jeans as he kicked his shoes off, my deliberation weakened as desire slowly triumphed over responsibility.

"Oh...." My thoughts became scattered. "I've never been skinny dipping," I confessed with a nervous giggle.

"Me neither." He laughed with a sudden surge of liveliness in his voice.

"Wouldn't that be weird for us to be doing? I mean...as *friends* and all?" My heart jack-hammered in my chest.

He suddenly stepped out of the light of the moon and disappeared in the dark shadows from the looming trees above, leaving nothing else for me to see, but his jeans. I heard the zipper slowly unzip to the right of me. "You don't have to skinny dip. You can sit here and keep me company from the bank."

Never in my life, not even in my bursts of anger, had I ever felt so out of control! My inner-monster had nothing on what Broderick could do to me! I could hear him shuffle out of his jeans and saw them slowly scrunch down to the ground, his boxers with them. He uttered a low grunt and I was suddenly speckled with a splash of water. Immediately, I saw the ripples grow in the moonlit path of the stream. Then he appeared again, treading water, his tan skin, glowing in the light.

"It feels good in here," he tempted.

"That's not fair. I can't hide in shadows." I gulped, fighting my yearning to join him.

Jittery but determined to meet his challenge, I climbed to my feet. My heart could burst out of my chest. I wobbled, with rubbery legs to the corner of the tree, tingling with pins and needles all over my body as I pulled my body behind the trunk. My anxious fingers fumbled the button and zipper of my jeans for what felt like minutes until I was able to slowly shimmy out of my jeans. Clumsily forgetting my tennis shoes, I couldn't pull the jeans off over them and I nearly toppled over from the lack of strength in my legs. I stood anxiously behind the tree in a hooded shirt and my yellow briefs.

"I'm not looking, Jules," he called with his back turned to me. The echo of his voice ricocheted from the other side of the bank where he faced.

"Okay," I said timidly. My hands shook with so much anxiety that I was hardly able to grasp the zipper of my jacket, but eventually I was able to pull it down and shrug out of the sleeves. Crossing my arms in an unnatural way, I tried to cover my body and my mismatched underwear.

"Broderick?" I called out to him.

I could hear him chuckle which slightly relaxed me. "The sooner you get in, the less likely it is that I'll see you."

I wanted to be out there with him, just unsure as to what he would feel about me, compromising myself in such a way. I panicked more about where this would lead my emotions. I was no longer feeling as timid as I thought I would, but a stronger instinct took over. I was out of control. I quickly dashed from behind the tree and jumped into the water before he had a chance to turn around and see me.

"Okay. I'm in." I breathed a sigh of relief as I came up from under the water.

He turned around, his teeth gleaming from the reflection of the moonlight. "Come out here," his deep voice made the invitation more enticing.

I moved my arms sinuously in the water as I swam to him. I imagined myself looking as graceful as a mermaid or one of those synchronized swimmers in the Olympics, I felt angelically beautiful in the moonlight. The tepid water rippled softly against my body as it ran with the current. My confidence overthrew any fear until I saw that he, too, worked in slow strokes to close the gap. Finally we treaded water roughly two feet from one another.

I tilted my head back into the water to keep my hair sleeked away from my face. I jumped to attention as I felt him reach over to my shoulder and snap the strap of my bra.

"You're still wearing your bra?" he bellowed out in laughter.

"So?" I whined as I defensively grabbed my shoulder. "What's the difference at this point?"

He smirked at my determination to stay dressed in something, even if it would be see-through at this point from being wet. "You hold up pretty strong, Jules Taylor," he said proudly. He searched my face for a moment. "What are you thinking about?" he asked quietly.

"Well," I started, uncertain if this was the time and place to actually question the positions we were putting ourselves in. "This probably isn't a good idea for us. It doesn't look good, I'm sure."

"Doesn't look good to who? No one else is here and I'm not going to say anything to anybody," he whispered.

Scared for my reputation but more for my heart, I continued to fight the pointless battle that I had already surrendered in. "This isn't something we should be doing with just anyone," I said solemnly.

"You're right." He swam a small distance around me as I tread water to keep my eye on him. His face matched his voice with a matter-of-fact tone. "But I'm not doing this with just anyone; I'm swimming with you."

I spoke not a word, unsure of what I should say next.

"Did I pressure you into something you didn't want to do?" His tone became serious and his remorse was clear. "I told you that you could just keep me company from the —"

"I didn't feel pressured, just felt nervous."

"And you don't anymore?"

"Uh…" I hopped around my dizzy thoughts. "Do you do this often with your other friends? Like Jackson or Joey?" I set my mouth in a sharp little smirk.

"Only my pretty friends," he quipped.

"I thought you said you've never done this before," I reminded him.

"Well, I didn't lie." He smartly replied back, "You're the prettiest friend I've ever had."

"I'm telling Jackson…" I said in a sing-song manner.

Broderick swam out of the moonlight again and vanished in the dark. I could hear him splash sporadically around me, but by the time I would turn toward him, he was in another spot, but hidden in his cloaked shadow. I heard him pull under the surface to sneak up on me and I poised myself for the imminent attack. The splashing in front of me stole my attention away from his intended assault from behind me. Grabbing me firmly around my waist; he gave me a quick jostle. I emitted a deep and bellowing scream. His laughter echoed in my ears and my heart thumped loudly in my chest at the adrenaline rush and his arms wrapped tighter around me—his chest firmly pressed against my back. My legs bouncing off of his as he stood and I continued to tread water, since I was too short to touch the bottom. My stomach and groin tightened with an unfamiliar anticipation.

Resisting the need to collapse in his arms, I spun around to face him, only to find a dark shadow holding tightly to me in the moonlight. I could feel him panting on my neck.

"Let me see you," I said. Regardless of my growing trust in him and my astonishment with his mystical ability, it made me edgy if he remained phased over an extended period of time. I was dependent on the expressions of his face to better read him.

"What?" he whispered. I felt him pull back suddenly, letting go of me to look at his hands and arms. Slowly he became visible, with shock and fear on his face. His face twisted in a mask of confusion. "I couldn't shake it off of me for some reason."

This alarmed me. He didn't seem completely undaunted with it, so I let it drop. He began to close in on me again and I entered full panic mode. "Where were we?"

"Well, I was going to jump out and put on my dry clothes," I said as I swam to the bank. "Don't look," I reminded him in a threatening way.

I heard him duck under the water behind me as I tried swimming to the shore. Suddenly, I felt his strong hands cup from underneath my upper thighs and bottom, causing me to jerk in shock. My body was forced out of the water and into the air. My arms and legs began kicking sporadically as I soared through the air squealing with delight. A split second later, I was plunging back into the water, a few feet from where he had tossed me. Laughing and coughing from the water I had taken in while I was screaming, I came to the surface.

"You okay?" He guffawed.

I pushed back my hair and wiped my face. "Are you trying to kill me?" I shrieked in giggles as I began swimming back to the bank.

He swiftly caught up to me by grabbing my leg and pulling me back into the water. Twisting me around by the leg, he pulled himself closer to me, trapping me on every side by his arms and the rock behind me. His eyes traced my face—full of hesitation and energy—and slowly trailed down to my lips.

This was too much. His constant grabbing and touching me. The way he looked at me. *Am I imagining this?* I wanted to scream into the night air as frustration tingled every inch of my body, begging for some sort of release. I wanted to kiss him and see where it would all lead. I didn't know where or how to focus any of my wild energy.

"What has gotten into you?" My chest was heaving in deep breaths and I scowled at my emotional battle.

He stopped short of moving any closer—as close as he could be without kissing me—and appeared guilty as he seemed to snap back into reality. "I was…" he pushed off from the rock and gave us some space. "I was just playing. I'm sorry if I made you uncomfortable. That wasn't my intention." He tucked in his lips, producing deep dimples on each cheek that told of regret. "Go on. I won't look."

He turned around again and faced the other side, giving me the privacy to climb up onto the dry land—leaving any graceful quality I had behind in the river. Quickly, I pulled my panties off and put my jeans on. I wriggled myself out of my wet bra after I had already put on the protective cover of my T-shirt.

My heart never once steadied. Only thundered louder.

"Okay, all clear," I told Broderick as I pushed my arms through the hoodie I was wearing on top of the T-shirt.

He faded into the shadows again and I could hear him climb out of the water. I saw the boxers and then the jeans miraculously begin to pull upward off the ground and be shaken out. I was squeezing my wet feet into my tennis shoes as I bent over and retrieved my damp bra, but my hands became frantic as I realized that I couldn't find my underwear. I groaned.

"What's wrong?" I looked up to see him again, pulling his shirt on.

"I can't find my underwear." He stepped over and began trying to focus on the ground; I was horrified that he wanted to help me look. "No! I don't want *you* looking for them!"

"Why not?" he asked innocently.

I stumbled through the words in my head, "Because… It's my underwear!" I lamely explained as if that would be reason enough for him not to help me in my search. "I don't want to leave them for someone to find them. The thought, alone, creeps me out."

"No one will even know they're yours," he chortled.

I deliberated what he said, remembering, too, that they were in fact my least favorite pair to wear. "You're right. Let's just go."

We climbed into the jeep and silently listened to the night on the drive back to his house. The air had dropped a few degrees and actually felt chilly with my wet hair, so I pulled my hood back on my head. And as he had promised, we had gone completely unmissed. He walked me slowly back through the woods and climbed the tree to my roof, being sure that he would be able to catch me if I fell. I slipped my fingers under the window that I had left cracked open and lifted it with ease. He helped me in the room all the while staying on the roof, ready to part ways for the night.

"I'm sorry if I made you uncomfortable tonight," he softly spoke.

"I wasn't uncomfortable. I just didn't..." I bit my lip, unsure of what to say without revealing myself or coming across presumptuous. "We're still friends, right?" I smiled at him as he nodded his head with reassuring vigor. His cheeks became a deep shade of pink, and dimples began pulsating from his tense jaw.

"Are we doing anything tomorrow night?" I asked anxiously.

He gave a lopsided grin, which already clued me in on his answer, instantly breaking my heart. Not even the next morning, and he had lost interest because I had compromised my virtue with him tonight by 'sort of' skinny dipping. My mother always warned it would happen if I ever did compromise my moral values.

"Actually, I have plans with Joey, Jackson, and Taryn to go to Chattanooga tomorrow afternoon. We're supposed to catch this band at a local spot down by the river. Taryn's been pestering us to go and listen to them for a while now," he said. "I would invite you to go with us, but they're sold out."

"That's okay." Likely excuse, I thought sourly to myself.

He grinned and started to pull away from the window.

"Oh, and Broderick?"

"Yes?" He returned quickly and with energy.

"Please, don't replace my panties like you did my hoodies. That would be...weird." I laughed.

He nodded and laughed with me. "I'll keep that in mind."

He narrowed his eyes in thought looking deeply into mine. His hesitation broke shortly and he shuffled off to the tree. He whispered goodbye as he fell into the shadows.

Summer's End

I SLEPT IN A state of euphoria that night and awoke earlier than usual for a Saturday morning. I couldn't decide if it was because I was used to getting up early these last few weeks or if it was because of the anticipation of seeing Broderick again—whenever that would be. I needed to find something to divert my obsession, so I spent the entire day cleaning my bedroom. Unlike my mother, I was a slob at heart, a true pack rat. Often, I would peer out my window to try and catch a glimpse of the Cooper residence. Quite obsessive. Time passed slowly. Painfully.

After Mom and Dad went to bed Nat and I sat silently on the couch, bogged down with deep thoughts, while staring at the television screen. She randomly flipped through the channels, looking for something of her taste. She lay lazily on the side of the couch, with her arm—out of its sling, for once—draped across her body and holding the remote; her thumb pressing the channel button.

"I'm calling it a night, Nat." I started for the stairs.

She popped up into a sitting position instantly. "Does Joey like me more than just a friend?"

Stunned with her sudden question, I reluctantly turned to her and gave her a resigned look. "I don't know, Nat. I know he likes you a lot, but he's supposed to like you a lot; you two are best friends."

"He can't fall in love with me." Her green eyes were wide with worry. Her concerns seem to come out of nowhere, completely unrooted, unless someone had said something. Maybe she was just done denying the blatancy of it all.

"Why does it matter if he does? Does that mean you can no longer be friends?"

Torn in silence, she got up and walked out of the room. I stared off in thought, worrying about Natalie and Joey, as I heard her shut the door to her bedroom upstairs.

Was the same thing happening with me and Broderick? Would he react the same way as Natalie, if he had a clue as to how I felt about him?

Broderick's absence was a harsh reminder of how badly I had let things get out of hand between us. I missed him desperately; missed his mysterious eyes and dimples that made their appearance not only when he smiled, but any time he held his lips tightly. I missed his quick wit that challenged mine.

The hands on the clock appeared motionless. It was after eleven. My heart was sinking slowly as I lay on the bed and listened to music through my ear buds. Faintly through the music, I heard a light tapping at my window. Sitting up, I removed one of the ear buds from my ear and listened intently. Sure enough, there was a tapping sound at my window. I eased myself cautiously to the window to see Broderick smiling through the glass. I slid the window open then ran to the door to lock it as Broderick let himself in.

"You're a sight for sore eyes," he said cheerfully as he unzipped his black hoodie and slipped his tennis shoes into my closet as if this had become a routine.

"How was your evening?" I asked nonchalantly, hiding my enthusiasm with finally having him near again.

"I wish you could have been there," he said. "You would have loved it. Good music, good food, and even good coffee, or at least that's what Taryn said. I can't drink the stuff."

I strolled over to my bed and sat down. The anticipation of seeing him again finally wore me down. I could somewhat relax now that he was here.

"So, what have I missed today?" Broderick sat next to me.

"I think Nat's onto Joey's feelings for her," I said.

He made a face. "Yikes. How's she handling that? Better yet, how's he handling it?"

"He doesn't know yet. He would never jeopardize their friendship for something that probably wouldn't last anyway. Blah, blah, blah…" I spoke in double meanings, hoping he would catch on. I needed a sign that my feelings were returned.

He lifted the ear buds that I had left on my bed and placed one of them up to his ears to listen. He smiled. "Nice."

I blushed. "Boring for a girl to be doing on a Saturday night…just listening to music in her room."

"I don't require much entertainment. Can I listen with you?" He pressed the ear bud into his ear.

I strolled over to my bed and sat at the edge then placed the remaining ear bud in one of my ears as he stretched back to relax. I leaned back and joined him.

With our legs hanging over the foot of the bed—his feet touching the floor, mine were inches off—our heads were leaning on one another as if we were cloud gazing on a grassy hill, splitting the ear buds between the two of us. I must have unconsciously emitted a sigh because while my eyes remained shut to take in the music, I felt the movement of his head turn to look at me. The longer we lay on my bed, sharing the ear bud pieces, the more I became aware that something was, indeed, going on between us. It was the same thing I felt last night. He and I claimed to be strictly friends, but here he was, spending a late summer night in the trappings of my bedroom instead of out on a date with some beautiful, popular girl from school. The tension loomed over us like a storm cloud ready to unleash its fury. It wasn't exactly something that could easily be ignored and it caused my heart and head to ache from the battle against its recognition. It was no longer some delusion I had secretively conjured up in my mind. It was very real.

The calming music morphed to the echoing sound of one lonely guitar playing a very familiar chord progression. He sighed and I felt the hum on the bed underneath me from his light moan. *Our song.* His head leaned softly against mine while the music drifted into our ears.

"Funny, how we love this song so much. It's actually quite depressing—the division of humanity. It's a sad song," I replied softly. So what did that really say about us?

I rolled my head over to the side to face him. His eyes melted deep into mine, gentle but intense.

"I don't think it's sad at all," he said tenderly. "It's a song of hope. You see, there may actually be a wall and there may actually be division and sadness... all of those things, but he doesn't believe that the bad will win in the end. Listen."

We listened a moment longer. I had heard the song a million times— all my life and never had noticed the optimism in it before. Sure enough, the singer wasn't giving up hope. The song wasn't sad at all. Bittersweet, perhaps.

"Don't dream it's o-ver...." We sang the words together in a whisper with the singer; I, grasping the truth of the lyrics for the first time ever, as Broderick had countless times before.

"Exactly." Broderick gave a small smile. "I can see why many view this song as a political statement, but I see the story of an unconditional love. He's in love and trying to plead his case with this amazing girl." I was intrigued with his analysis. "He wants her to see that he's not willing to give up on her—even through their struggles. He truly loves her for everything she is and everything she's going to be. She is his soul mate."

As he spoke, his hand drifted over to grasp mine. I subconsciously held my breath as he pressed the palm of his hand to the palm of mine. He slowly curled his fingers into my palm and then stretched them out to match my hand, brushing his fingertips softly against my fingers. My fingers tingled beneath his touch.

Breathe, Jules. Breathe.

He remained in his lyrical reasoning. "He'd fight through it all for what is right—their love. It's fate and he knows it. He just needs her to see all of this as well," he said as he continued tracing his fingers across my hand.

I fought through the strong choking sensation in my throat. My head was spinning with the possibility of his double meaning.

"Maybe these are all promises she's heard before," I stepped into his two way mirror of words.

"It's fated. They fit together perfectly. No matter what goes wrong between them, he will still love her. Always love her," he replied.

"Can she really trust in that?" I asked, begging for his reassurance.

"Yes, she can." He emitted a small smile, allowing a dimple to escape from his smooth cheek. "You'll never see the end of the road while you're traveling with me," he spoke along with the lyrics being sung.

It felt as though my body became void of any organ—aside from my hammering heart—and was instead filled with air. He then curled my fingers into a soft fist and enveloped my small hand into his warm, oversized hand. His eyes bore into mine and in that very second I saw my life tie into his.

"She could lose her dignity in hopes to be with him," my last attempt to stay strong.

"He loses without her." He paused for what felt like minutes. At last he broke the silence with a small whisper, "Only one question remains now."

I gulped, trembling with anticipation, my voice barely above a whisper. "What question is that?"

"Does he ever get the girl?" he asked.

"She wants him to."

He squeezed my hand gently as he pulled in closer to me, hesitating ever so slightly. I couldn't tell if it was him or me trembling. Maybe both of us? I closed my eyes in anticipation of the bliss I was about to encounter— something I had dreamt of over a hundred times. His breath blew warmly against my lips and I could literally feel the energy radiating from him. Closer, closer, and closer he came to me.

Then the music ended and the moment was gone.

My heart ached and I squeezed my eyes tighter to rid myself of any visible anguish. As I opened my eyes, I could see the frustration drawn on his face. He stared, concentrating on my face. I squeezed my eyes shut again and blushed with the humiliation of the moment, knowing that he had just caught himself before he made a huge mistake with me. The dramatic moment was led by nothing substantial. Just the emotional guidance of a stupid song.

"I've gotta go," he growled with anger. He seemed too anxious to put space between us. Shoving his feet into his shoes and sliding the window open, he couldn't get out of my room quick enough.

"Thanks for letting me come over tonight." He didn't look so angry anymore just embarrassed and regretful.

"Sure," I said avoiding eye contact, my embarrassment just as plain. My face felt hot, and I was sure my neck and chest were red and blotchy.

He caught his breath, apparently ready to say something, but changed his mind quickly. He ducked out onto the roof, and I silently shut the window behind him.

How could I be so stupid? I stormed off into the bathroom to wash my face and brush my teeth wishing I had the energy to take a shower, but was too wretched and emotionally exhausted to continue on with that idea. Sleep was my only hope of ridding myself of this terrible feeling of rejection. I could have sworn that there was a double meaning in that entire conversation! That he had been referring to us and that he wanted to be with me. I had practically admitted that I wanted him. But maybe I assumed wrongly. He was regretful and I was miserable.

"This is what happens when you're honest about your feelings, dumbass," I said to myself as I scrubbed my face and neck so harshly out of frustration. "You are such an idiot!"

Slipping into my pajamas, I heard a rustling sound against the outside of my bedroom wall. Seconds later a tapping at the window beckoned to me. In spite of my pounding heart and knowing it was him again, I flaunted indifference as I strolled over to the window and opened it. Casually, I took a few steps back and leaned against the wall, arms folded across my chest and an expressionless face. *The way a friend was supposed to look, right?*

"D'you forget something?" I asked as he briskly ducked through the window.

He stepped into the room far enough so that he could stand straight up from under the slanted ceiling by the window. His face was fierce and it made me nervous.

"Broderick?" My tone wasn't as calm now.

He sucked in a ragged breath—quick and shallow—then charged me, taking two long strides. My face suddenly in his hands, he crushed his firm lips desperately to mine. Maddeningly, he kissed me hard and held me so tight, that I no longer needed my legs for support. His lips never let up. His throat emitted a low growl causing my body to burn for more. My mind raced frantically, mildly aware of how my mouth easily moved with his. I curled my hands around his biceps to pull him closer to me. As the built up tension was finally released through our lips, he began to ease his grip on me, caressing my lips with such assurance, no hint of regret, his tongue softly entering into my mouth. Still holding my face he began kissing the corners of my mouth trailing to my chin and to my neck, finally allowing me to catch my breath from the initial shock of the advance.

The thought of him regretting this moment began tugging at the back of my mind, and I tried to find the will power to pull away from his embrace. He pressed harder against me, prohibiting any retreat. My voice shook uncontrollably from the tremors that captured my body. "I never intended for this to happen."

He pulled back to look at me with severe eyes. "I did."

And with that he kissed me fervently, leaving me absolutely breathless.

It was unbelievable and completely forbidden—alone in my room in the arms of Broderick Cooper. His lips moving feverishly with mine, feeling his tongue occasionally dip in between my lips and his teeth gently nibble on my bottom lip. Whatever kind of kissing I had done before could never compare nor never prepare me for such perfection. He kissed me in a way

I could have only dreamed of, had I only known of its blissful existence. His fingers eased in tension and gently pawed at my face, while his lips became soft with deep affection, kissing me slowly, letting our every touch and every caress of our lips linger. I could have remained a prisoner of his kisses forever.

"Are you okay?" He held my face, tilting it up to face him. A cross between satisfaction and apprehension covered his face.

Completely speechless from shock, I fought a smile from spreading on my face. My cheeks burned with guilty pleasure and my lips felt swollen. Never in my life had I felt so small and yet so grand at the same time.

"I have waited for this moment for too long. Just tell me I'm not wrong in thinking you want me, too. I'm not imagining it, am I?" He searched my face urgently for a hint of encouragement.

"I… I thought…" I stammered, viciously looking for the right words in my currently empty brain. I could only think of Broderick and his perfect, earth shattering kisses. As my lips parted to speak, I felt the confusion pull my brows together. "I thought you just wanted to be friends and I didn't —"

He placed a finger over my lips and frowned. "Are you really that blind, Jules Taylor?"

My shoulders slumped forward in a resigned manner. "A girl like me could never and should never delude herself into believing that it could happen. As far I knew, I had a snowball's chance in hell with you…"

"Are you kidding?" He closed the gap between us. "I was terrified you would reject me." He drew me near to him. "Jules, these insecurities need to stop. You're far more beautiful when you're confident." He playfully brushed my nose with his fingers. "Listen to me: This is going to happen, Jules. Stop questioning it, and if things go bad at times, have faith that I will fight for you—for us."

I smiled at his vow and let him pull me in for a few more kisses.

Finally he drew back and began walking to the window as he continued to hold my hand.

"Are you leaving me?" I asked, wishing he wouldn't.

He emitted the smile he gave when it seemed he was withholding a secret from me and the rest of the world. "I have a feeling that I'm finally going to get a good night's sleep tonight, and I want to get started on it." He let go of my hand to open the window and began climbing out. He leaned his face closer to mine again, "One more time before I have to leave you for the night." He pressed his warm lips to mine bringing on that tight unfamiliar feeling in my body again as he uttered a low moan.

"Bye" he whispered, gently pressing his forehead to mine and he disappeared into his shadows.

Life was perfect for that final week of our summer break as we fell madly in love with one another.

And then school began.

School

I SAT STIFFLY IN the passenger's seat as I heard a few random people greeting Broderick through my window, then rubbernecking as they caught a glimpse of me sitting in his jeep. This was it. He was going to open the door and people were going to twist their faces in scrutiny at me, or I was going to take it a step further and trip out of the jeep, altogether. Either way, I wasn't going to win. The pencil I was holding was clenched tightly in my fist, ready to snap in two pieces from the pressure. The door swung open, and Broderick gave me a confident smile.

"Jules, step away from the pencil," he teased.

"I'm okay," I said more for myself to hear than for him.

"Come out here and hold my hand." While holding his hand out for me to take, he tucked his lips in and his dimples appeared. Dimples that I had no power against.

Carefully stepping out so I wouldn't trip, I took his hand. His fingers intertwined with mine, and he pulled me protectively close beside him as we walked to the school. A few people stopped and stared, but for the most part, he was right; it didn't matter what anyone else thought of us. We were here, together. And he loved me. He loved being seen with me!

My first class was marching band, so he walked me to the F-wing at the back of the school and through the breezeway. He leaned casually against the wall near the door of the class, taking time to wave or say hi to all the people who called out to him. Cari passed and pinched him playfully in the arm and then knocked the backs of my knees, causing my legs to buckle.

Our close friends were not surprised by our pairing. They had all warmed up to the idea long before we had caved to it ourselves. They were just happy to finally have it out in the open.

"I was originally supposed to have honors English, but I've got to go to the office so I can get that changed to another time. The yearbook staff meets back on this wing first period." He winked before he quickly kissed my cheek. "I'll come back here to walk you to your next class," he said as he walked away.

"Good luck," I called out to him as he rounded the corner and out of the building.

Inside, many of the girls in the flag corps were grinning widely at me as I walked over to join them in the flag closet. "What?" I asked innocently, a bright smile betraying my own excitement.

Emma Rose, our flag captain, was the first to grab my arm. "Are you two dating, now?"

"Yes." My cheeks ached already from so much smiling.

"Is it serious?" Ashley, our co-captain, pressed.

"Have you kissed yet?" one of the sophomores asked.

Cari interrupted as she walked over to us. "Oh, they've kissed. Just look at her. It's written all over her face," she pointed to me, laughing obnoxiously as I blushed.

Broderick was already waiting for me by the time I walked out of the door to go to my Geometry class.

"Did you get your schedule taken care of?" I asked as I approached him.

"What do you think?" He held out the paper in his hand for me to see his new schedule. "The only classes I need this year to graduate are a few electives and English." I was impressed. "See? It pays to work and study hard your first three years of high school. You can lollygag during your senior year. I don't even need to be here next semester to graduate," he said proudly. "Where are you going next?"

"Geometry with Muir."

He grabbed my hand again, interlocking our fingers and walked me to the next class. Mr. Muir leaned outside his door frame welcoming each student dryly as they entered. When he saw me and Broderick approach, he lifted an eyebrow.

"Well, well, well—Mr. Cooper and Miss Taylor." He smiled as he narrowed his eyes, studying us closely. "Why am I not surprised to see this union?"

I simply shrugged, feeling awkward that a teacher would comment on mine and Broderick's relationship—or any student relationship for that matter. Broderick simply smiled with pride, which set me at ease.

"Took you two long enough," Mr. Muir quipped as I slipped past him and into his room. "You don't plan on provoking her into any conniption fits in my class, do you, Cooper?"

Why hasn't he dropped that already? I thought to myself.

"Never," I heard Broderick's voice playfully echo from down the hall.

My eyes scanned the room quickly for a friendly face so I could sit and divert attention from the conversation that had started outside.

"Jules! Over here!" I caught sight of Taryn Green and joined her and her two friends that sat on each side of her, one of them being Lindsey Harris. She grabbed her purse from the chair in front of her. "Sit here. I saw you on the class list and I was saving this seat for you." She smiled. "So, I heard that *someone* finally made his move. How did it happen? I want details." She leaned closer to me.

The brunette to her right slapped her arm, "Nosy!"

Taryn rubbed her bare arm as it was already turning pink. "I was just asking," she whined at her friend. "Jules, this is Jill and this is Lindsey," Taryn motioned to the brunette and then the redhead.

"Hi." Jill, the brunette, wriggled her fingers at me in a small wave.

"I heard about that sucker punch you gave Erik. Nice job." Lindsey smiled like a sly fox. "It's a shame you couldn't do the same to Gavin Williams," she muttered bitterly.

Taryn waved her off, "Forget him already, will you?" She then focused on me again, "So? How did it happen?"

"Isn't it a little creepy for her to be swapping love stories about the same guy you dated not even a year before?" Jill frowned at her.

"No way," Taryn blew her off.

"It's creepy, Taryn. Totally not cool," Lindsey affirmed as she tossed her fiery red hair behind her shoulder.

Taryn waved both girls off and focused on me. "So?" she grinned excitedly.

I had to think quickly. No one needed to know that he had been in my room at all. With my luck, that information would somehow make its way to my parents.

"It happened on Black Mountain," I finally answered.

Lindsey and Jill exchanged wary glances and Taryn's eyes widened. Jill leaned close to me across the aisle. "That's ballsy. Did you *see* anything?"

Taryn sensed my confusion and shushed her, "You'll freak her out."

"It freaks *me* out," Lindsey admitted.

"What?" I was completely lost in their conversation.

"It *should* freak her out if she's going up there," Jill said.

"*What?*" I asked again.

Taryn shifted in her seat to huddle closer. "Some people have gone there and they weren't the same when they came back. As beautiful as it is, it's dangerous at *night*," she warned.

"Devil worshipping is practiced on Black Mountain. A friend and I once found skinned animals up there," Lindsey whispered.

"I've always heard about devil worshippers too," Jill chimed in.

A shiver ran down my spine. "Are you kidding?" My lie was taking on problems of its own already.

Taryn took control of the conversation again. Jill and Lindsey were clearly creeped out and Taryn had a way of remaining calm. "Hey, we're only trying to keep you from getting into a whole heap of trouble up there and I am not talking the regular kind. Things will follow you home. And when I say things, I mean *things—not people*. It actually happened to me. Black Mountain is beautiful so by all means, if you want to see some pretty scenery, go up there and walk the trails, but only the ones that are marked and don't ever go after sundown... But hey! Broderick probably kept you safe."

Mr. Muir started class and gave me the relief out of my corner. Though their fear was palpable and should have concerned me, I found their reports intriguing. I'd already heard different accounts of what these girls were telling me. Just about every town had its similar "ghost stories", but I wanted to ask Taryn about her own personal account on Black Mountain after class. Unfortunately, when we started walking out together, she immediately darted to Jackson when she saw he was waiting for her.

Jackson's dark eyes simply looked past her and saw me. "Rumor has it my boy has a thing for you." He lifted his brows playfully at me.

I nodded quietly, hopeless of preventing a smile just as Broderick came around the corner toward us.

"He's crazy about you," Jackson said secretly just before he approached.

He seemed slightly winded as if he had been jogging from his class to get here. I was willing to bet that's exactly what he had been doing, since he was here so soon. He wrapped his arm around my shoulders this time, and we started walking with them to the main hall—Taryn and I in the middle of our foursome. We parted at the next hall intersection after comparing our schedules to determine when we'd meet up again, which looked like after fourth period.

Only a few paces down the hall, and I saw Loni Schubert and Casey Barnes heading from the opposite direction. Loni zeroed in on me in an instant.

"Bitch!" Loni blurted, knocking into my shoulder. I spun around and watched her and Casey giggle. There was beginning to be too much hostility, though I surely deserved it. Still, I wanted to snap into what felt normal to me and confront them with my wrath, however I decided against it. Today was a fresh start, and I was resolved to ignoring them.

I waited restlessly for every chance to be with Broderick again as the day progressed, completely unable to get to Broderick soon enough to satisfy me. Never had I felt such a need to be with someone. It was as if this invisible rope was tied tightly around my waist and he was on the other end pulling.

After our first few weeks of school, we were finally given the opportunity to trade out our last class block of homeroom for tutoring, a school club, an extra-curricular activity, or to leave early from school for dual classes at the local community college. Because Broderick was on the football team, he was already committed to practice—which they considered "homeroom"—and therefore, wouldn't get to move classes. The same was set for Student Council, Class Officers, and Cheerleaders.

I was going to sign up for the Jet Theatrix group, headed by the Drama/English teacher, Andrea Davis. She came to our school last year and brought her eccentric teaching tactics with her. For starters, she never allowed us to call her Miss Davis. She preferred the unconventional approach—a first name basis. She often spoke candidly about her time as a touring stage actress. The artistic crowd in the drama department appreciated how she easily fit in with all of us. Regardless of her approach, she knew what she was doing when it came to theater.

I drifted to the F-wing breezeway to drop off my books in my locker before I joined the rest of the school inside the gymnasium for sixth period sign up. I stopped short before entering into the F-wing building to watch Broderick, Jackson, and Joey walk across the parking lot to the weight room that was located near the stadium. I burst with pride with the fact that Broderick Cooper was *my* boyfriend: tall, lean, absolutely beautiful inside and out. By the time he turned the corner and was no longer visible, I became keenly aware of the foolish grin on my face and quickly readjusted my composure before continuing into the F-wing.

Through the abundance of chatter in the echoing halls and the slamming of lockers, I could hear the sound of a piano from one of the practice rooms down the hall. Like gentle bells, it continued to climb the scale in a melancholy minor key. The sadness of the song drifted serenely down the hall and swept me up in a need to find the source. Beckoning to me, I switched out my books and stepped down the hall to the haunting yet beautiful music.

Squeezing by the rush of students who hurried to the gymnasium for homeroom signups, I was the only one in the hall who seemed to be aware of it. Drawing closer to the door, the music boomed in a dramatic crescendo. Through the window of the door I saw the shiny black hair of a tanned individual moving his fingers gracefully along with the music. He sat at the piano and glided his fingers over the ivory keys with such passion and ease. I pulled a strand of hair behind my ear as it fell into my face—my eyes unable to break away from the entrancing music that captivated me at the window. His fingers moved quickly, yet gently over the keys with a strong purpose, then he suddenly stopped. I held my breath, wanting him to continue.

He straightened his back and turned his cheek toward the door. Staring straight at me, a familiar devilish grin spread across his face. My eyes widened as I realized that I'd been caught gawking at him. He slowly curled his finger at me, inviting me in the practice room. I could only stand and stare back. Then he leaned forward and opened the door just a crack. My tiny fingers slipped through the crack and I pulled the door open a little further.

"I'm sorry. I didn't mean to interrupt." I softly began shutting the door to give him privacy again, but he used his foot to push the door open wider.

"You didn't interrupt." His voice was as soothing as his music. "Why don't you join me?" he invited.

Mindlessly, I began walking into the room and closed the door behind me. "That was beautiful," I marveled, quietly kicking myself for complimenting him.

"Thank you. I've been playing piano for a *very* long time," he assured me. Then he held out his hand to introduce himself. "I'm Isaac Philetos."

I took his hand and shook it as I tried to act as though I had never heard of him before—to knock him down a peg or two. "I haven't seen you around before. Do you play any other instruments as well as piano?"

He narrowed his eyes and grinned. "You know very well that I play guitar. You saw me play at the Fourth of July celebration at the park," he arrogantly spoke.

Firm in my determination to play dumb, I changed my act as though he had just reminded me of who he was. "Oh, yes! Now I remember. Great set, by the way," I reluctantly conceded.

"I'm glad you enjoyed it." He pointed to the piano. "Are you a musician?" But before I could answer he jumped in, "Let me guess... the banjo?" He smirked, obviously attempting to make a joke because we were in Tennessee.

I didn't find it remotely funny. I was annoyed with his superior manner. "Actually, I'm a singer."

He looked unimpressed, which made my blood boil. He began playing a classical piece that was familiar to me. He continued to talk, without missing a single cue on the white keys. His beautiful, yet smug grin was practically blinding me with a vicious envy.

"So, where do you sing? In the car? Shower?" he pressed on in a belittling fashion; I tried to ignore it.

"I had a band last year, but I've decided to focus my efforts on theater this year instead. It's far more demanding than *just singing*," I explained in a haughty manner.

Suddenly, I was hit with a great idea to prove myself to him. Inviting him to audition for the school play would teach him firsthand that I was every bit as talented as he was.

"Hey, you ought to audition for the Jet Theatrix —"

"As an artist, I couldn't share a stage with others who aren't up to my level," he interrupted.

With that comment I was dumbstruck. *Is anybody really that rude? That conceited?* I hated his pompous attitude and questioned how Cari could be so infatuated with him. Obviously, he had not shown this side of himself to her or he would be breathing through a tube in his neck today.

As quickly as these thoughts ran through my mind, he changed his tone. "But on second thought… are all the girls in this Jet Theatrix as pretty as you?" He bore his icy blue eyes into mine as he continued to play.

I shouldn't have been so thrilled with his compliment, but somehow I was. How could I hate him and still be affected by his flirting? No doubt, he was not at all sincere, but merely teasing me.

I decided to act oblivious and use reverse-snobbery. "My boyfriend will tell you 'no', but I guess it all depends on your preference."

He quit playing and leaned over the keys of the piano, closer to me. His smooth, fleshy lips pulled back into a smile like a predator, alluring his prey. "A boyfriend, huh? I guess I can't win them all."

The instant I began blushing I internally kicked myself for enjoying the flattery again when he was clearly just toying with me.

"What do you think my chances are of landing a decent role?" He asked.

I wanted to lie to him—tell him he would be placed in the ensemble because there was already so much talent involved, but he and I both knew that he'd be placed in an appropriate and glorious role. I got the feeling that he wanted me to admit that to him, too. Instead of completely giving in to the idea, I would give him an insight to his opportunity, but I would make it clear to him that he and I were on the same playing field.

"Well, in all honesty, the talent level here is pretty low, but you'll have your share of challenges," I warned him in a faux friendly way.

"Like who?" he asked.

"Well, there's Mark Hines. He's almost considered a triple threat. He's been studying acting and dance since he could walk and talk."

He was unmoved. "That's it? *He's* my only competition?"

"No. *I* am." My mouth curled to one side, emitting a vindictive smirk. Isaac nodded, as if to accept the challenge. "I'll consider it."

I wanted to punch his lights out. "I better get to the gym and sign up for sixth period. I didn't hear the bell ring, but I bet I'm late."

"You never did give me your name," Isaac reminded me and I spun around on my heel.

"Jules. Jules Taylor," I replied conceitedly, as if my name should have already been branded into his brain since the minute he set foot in our town.

"Jules. Short for *Juliana?*" he almost purred, causing me to tremble in a young-girl's-crush sort of way.

I shook it off and bit back. "Maybe," I said with a smug chuckle as I dramatically spun on the ball of my foot and walked away.

In the gym, Cari and Savannah were chatting in a far corner.

"How good of you to join us, Jules," Cari said as she leaned casually against the wall with her arms folded. "Where's Boy Scout? I thought for sure the two of you would be signing up for sixth period together."

"He's already committed to football. Have you signed up for anything yet?"

"Yup. I condemned my soul to pit work for the Jet Theatrix production." Cari said. "Mr. Grayson was hell-bent to get me in there this year, so I'll be joining you ladies in your theater adventures yet again."

Cari tagged along with me and Savannah as we walked over to the Jet Theatrix table to sign up, and while I was adding my name to the roster, I noticed that Isaac's name was at the top of the list. He had already signed on before I ever spoke to him.

The egotistical bastard! He just wanted me to beg him to join the play!

I already hated him.

Haunted

THE CAST LIST WAS posted online a few days after the school musical audition. Granted, I was slightly disappointed at the revelation that the show required lead roles to be filled by males, but by late Saturday evening, my dreams were confirmed I had landed the role my heart was set on.

Scanning the page and whispering a quick prayer that the person playing opposite of me would be made of real talent, I knew exactly who was best suited for it, but detested admitting to it in the privacy of my own mind. My prayer was answered as I saw Isaac's name placed beside the role that would be opposite of mine. As much as I didn't like him, I knew we would be dynamic together.

Anxiously, I waited to tell Broderick the exciting news. The wait seemed like hours and still he never showed up on my roof like he usually did. He didn't even call. Assuming he was either overloaded with homework or sleeping, I retired to my bed for the night, snuggling under the covers to catch the last bit of *Nightmare Theater* on the Horror Channel which was hosting the movie, *The Fog*. Broderick would probably come over tomorrow. Emotionally exhausted from the school week, the auditions, and the anticipation of the audition outcome, my body crashed before the movie ended.

High pitch screams and a raucous chainsaw woke me to shock in my bed. The previous movie was no longer playing and had been replaced by torture porn—something I was not at all drawn to. I wondered if Broderick had come to my window and left when I didn't answer.

Curiosity got the best of me. I dressed in dark jeans and my red hoodie and set out to see him. As I reached the ground, I contemplated over what route to take to his house. The sidewalk seemed relatively safer despite the risk of being seen by a neighbor or worse yet, a cop driving through our neighborhood. Without Broderick beside me, the woods were horrifying with the black abyss beyond the outside barrier of trees. The woods had the presence of being alive with the sound of rustling leaves and the wind pitching the limbs. The overwhelming notion of chainsaws and madmen were quickly being replaced with real life dangers. My mind went into overdrive as I tried to forget about the howling sound I heard this past summer.

The seemingly full moon projected a comforting light. It would keep the path partially visible to me in the chasm of shadows being tossed about. As I stepped into the foliage I was trying to think good thoughts, like: *the full moon was meant for lovers*. I hesitated and also remembered that the full moon was a sign of ...

"It's not real, Jules," I reminded myself with a gulp. "Grow a pair...." Determined once again, and careful to stay on the path, I stared down at my feet. My eyes gradually adjusted to the moonlight filtering through the trees above me. I shuddered every time a branch brushed against me and nearly had a conniption fit when I walked through a spider web. I didn't scream, but uttered a deep moaning sound that sounded like a zombie as I stomped my feet in a dance-like motion. The creek—I reached the half-way point. The moon had a direct hit on the area and gave an unobstructed path to where I should step. A faint light emitted from Broderick's front windows and I breathed a sigh of relief. *Almost there*. Hopping cautiously across the creek, I allowed a quick moment to let my eyes readjust to the filtered moonlight again. Not soon enough, I darted out of the woods and ran across the yard feeling the safety of the Cooper property. The fear of the woods escaped the back of my mind and crept forward.

I took several deep breaths and jogged up the stairs to Broderick's door. I tapped quietly but no one came to open it. The jeep was in the driveway, so I assumed he was in his room. I twisted the knob to find it unlocked, and pushed the door open. Like previous times, the chilly breeze of the cranked-up air unit gave me gooseflesh.

Sleeping peacefully in a sitting position on the bed was Broderick, a pad of paper in his lap. I tip toed over to him. In a deep sleep, the pencil he had apparently been holding had rolled onto the bed and I cocked my head to see what he had been working on. As I pulled the pad of paper from his hand I could see that he had been drawing a picture of me struggling in the lake—my hair entangling all around me. My old white hoodie still in one piece.

"Why in the world would you draw this?" I laughed softly to myself, remembering the embarrassment of that Fourth of July.

Throwing his eyes open, Broderick startled awake. He looked up to see me sitting on the edge of his bed and his fear slowly changed to a smile.

"You really should lock your doors. You never know when a crazy girl from next door will come in to watch you sleep… or steal your art work." I grinned as I waved the sketch pad in my hand.

"Oh, *that*. I was just…" He frowned at the drawing as he tried snatching it from me, but I was too quick for him this time. He changed the subject. "How did you get here?"

"I grew legs, and praise the Lord, I can walk!" I whispered excitedly. He chuckled at my dry humor. "I came through the woods," I announced boldly, hoping he wouldn't notice any lingering fear.

"Brave, Jules," he said as he began stretching. Like a striking cobra, he seized the sketch pad from my fingers and tossed it to the other side of the room. He shifted to sit on the edge of the bed beside me. "I'm sorry I didn't come over. I must've fallen asleep."

"Don't apologize! I wasn't too worried about it. I just wanted to come over and make sure you were sleeping well."

He stood up, stretched again and looked down at me. He quickly became animated. "Oh! I totally forgot! You were supposed to find out about the casting today! How'd you do?"

I tried arranging my face so that I could fool him with disappointment. "It's not good."

"Seriously?" He was hurt for me.

"Yes. It's *great* news!" I squealed with wide, eager eyes.

"What part did you get?" he smiled eagerly.

I could hardly contain myself, and I squealed the name of my role out to him.

"Is it anything like the book?" he asked.

I rolled my eyes. "How would I know? I hate reading. All I can tell you is that my role totally kicks ass. And the songs I get to sing are fantastic!" I said excitedly as we high-fived.

Broderick said, "I'm going to brush my teeth and put on some shoes. You wanna go out for a drive and celebrate?"

"That would be nice." I smiled with appreciation. "And while you drive, you can tell me all about that drawing you just did."

His smile went limp. "It was just a nightmare."

"About me drowning? But that already happened."

He shrugged as he squeezed toothpaste on his toothbrush. "It was just a basic nightmare about something in the past."

"And it could be a premonition…"

"Doubt it, because, like you said—it has already happened." Broderick was firm in his decision to believe it was dream and ended the conversation by bringing the toothbrush to his mouth.

As we drove, I filled him in on every detail about the songs I would be singing and the rehearsal schedule. We decided star gazing on the bluffs of Black Mountain was where we should celebrate. I pushed the horror stories I had heard from Taryn and her two friends to the back of my mind. I was safe with Broderick.

He parked the jeep and we walked slowly along the trail to the lookout. The moon was so high now that it didn't project the same sort of light it offered earlier when I was trudging through the woods. I noticed the oncoming clouds that masked its brightness.

Just don't go after sundown.' Taryn's voice echoed in my mind, but I pushed the warning to the back of my mind. This place was beautiful and Broderick was here to protect me. Broderick held my hand as he guided me down into a sitting position and then sat closely beside me, wrapping his arms around my shoulders and pulling me close.

"I've missed you."

"I'm right here," I said sarcastically, a bit uncomfortable with his romantic words.

"No. I mean, I miss being with you so much, the way things were before school started."

I bobbed my head, though I understood what he meant from the start. "I miss those days, too." I turned my head to look at him and he gently guided my chin with his fingers and pulled me to his lips.

It was true. I, too, felt a void when we were apart, needing the boy from a world of fantasy, where prophetic dreams and supernatural gifts were common. To me, he was extraordinary, and yet, perfectly normal. I secretly wished I was as gifted and special as he was.

I concentrated on every touch as his fingertips grazed my face, slid down my shoulders and wrapped around me tightly and every breath that escaped his lips as our mouths moved together. My head fell back as his lips trailed down my neck, and I opened my eyes to see a brightly lit moon, doomed to the dark clouds that were sweeping the sky—it, like the stars, would soon be covered.

"It's almost a full moon," I said drenched in a sinister tone as I looked to the sky while he continued to kiss my neck.

He pulled back to chuckle at me. Apparently, I had just killed the mood. "In two more nights," he verified.

A sly grin covered my face. "It's kinda eerie up here on the mountain under the *almost* full moon."

He nodded in acknowledgement, unfazed by the change of pace in our evening. Instead he took part in it. "There's a church near the base of the mountain. Supposedly, it's haunted. I think its private property, so we'd have to go after dark sometime."

My eyes wide in excitement, I gasped. Not that I believed in ghosts, but the essence of believing was intriguing. I was excited at the prospect of visiting a haunted church.

"It's dark now…" I hinted.

Broderick looked uneasy. "Maybe another night."

"What's the difference between ghost-hunting late at night and making out on an eerie mountain late at night?" I cleverly asked him.

He thought about it for a quick few seconds before giving in, "I'd rather kiss you under the moon than hunt ghosts."

After a pleading expression, he soon gave in.

He drove us to the base of Black Mountain, then took random back roads that apparently led to the part of the hollow where the church was located. He drove slowly down old, abandoned roads so narrow and rough I found it hard to believe they were ever considered roads. Broderick maneuvered the jeep expertly over the washed out and rutted paths. There was no way I would ever be able to find these roads again. Finally, he seemed satisfied with a small dirt road that led into a thick, overgrown forest. He took the road and drove less than a mile before pulling off to the side.

"We have to go on foot the rest of the way," he explained.

Our little quest was already giving me a buzz. Venturing through the woods, and up the side of a small mountain, we began noticing a faint orange blaze, silhouetting the side of Black Mountain.

"What do you think that is?" I asked.

He stared at the sky with furrowed brows. "I don't know. Probably a bonfire on some redneck's property?" He blinked a few times as he tried studying the faintly lit sky. He finally looked down at me and smiled devilishly. "We still have a bit more to go," he encouraged me to keep moving.

We rejoined hands and began to pick up the pace. The closer we got to our assumed destination, we started hearing voices, laughing and talking as they echoed off the mountains. We hurried through a cornfield, which reminded me of a horror movie I had seen when I was younger, causing my imagination to swing into overdrive. Throughout our journey, Broderick's flesh became a wall of dancing shadows on his face and hands, allowing his shifting nature to take power over his body. I wasn't sure if he allowed this to entertain me, or if he was losing his sense of calm and peace.

Approaching an old cemetery with a neglected church house, I was increasingly thrilled with our quest, continually feeding off of my own needless fear and turning it into a rush of high-octane adrenaline. I eyed the old and broken tombstones that surrounded us. It looked like a set from a scary movie with low hanging tree limbs and rustling leaves on the ground.

"Wow. The only thing missing now is Michael Jackson and a horde of dancing zombies," I giggled in nervous tension. "Can we go inside the church?" I was dying to go in, but scared out of my wits! I knew I would regret it tomorrow morning if this was as far as I got.

Broderick remained obsessed with the orange glow in the sky. We had come closer to it. It was maybe a little over two hundred yards, in a thick of woods, behind the church.

"A redneck bonfire," I reminded him of his own theory.

Partially covered in a shadow, he snapped his head in my direction and smiled for a short moment before phasing back into his fleshy skin color again. "We'll check the church out real quick. I'd like to have you home before breakfast."

"What time is it *now*?" I was alarmed that he mentioned breakfast.

We both crowded around his phone as he squeezed the sides to illuminate the face. "It's 2:30 AM."

I punched his arm playfully for alarming me. "Don't scare me like that!" I laughed.

"I can't see." I was stretched up as far as my neck and toes would allow me, trying to peek through the windows, but was unable to obtain a clear view. The dirty stained glass was partly to blame, but it was almost as if the windows were being blocked—like someone had boarded them up from the inside.

Broderick made his way up the few steps and to the double doors. Sniffing the air, he looked revolted and disturbed. He peeked between the cracks as something caught his eye. "There's a light on, I think."

"You think it's a ghost?" My voice trembled in hysterical delight. He emitted a smile of incredulity as I continued to giggle. Grabbing my hand, he helped me up the stairs of the church.

"Be careful," he cautioned as he pushed open the unlocked double doors of the church. "The floor looks pretty rotted and I have no idea how much this floor will hold, we might fall through."

"Whoa!" I pulled back when a sulfuric odor slammed into me. The nauseous fumes filled the small lobby that led to another set of doors.

Broderick sniffed the air again, this time gagging. "What is that smell?"

The quietness of the church was overwhelming, and we felt compelled to whisper. He pulled the neck of his shirt up around the bridge of his nose to elude the stench.

"Smells like…" I sniffed once more before I covered my nose and mouth with my hand. "…burnt hair."

"How would you know what burnt hair smells like?" he asked humorously through his shirt.

Plugging my nose, my voice was nasally, "Let's just say it would have been nice to have had someone hold my hair back last year when I blew out the candles on my birthday cake." I saw him quaking in silent laughter.

I glanced over at the windows and saw they were boarded up from the inside, just as I had suspected. A light shined through the open doors before us, and Broderick cautiously treaded over to the doors to open them further for a better view.

He gasped and I scurried over to him, "What is it?"

He didn't answer, so I pulled the doors open to look inside only to be bombarded with a stronger odor of burnt hair. The scene was unsettling. Timber from the roof was caving in through parts of the ceiling where rain had weakened the frame of the building. The pews were lined up on each side of the isle, waiting for warm bodies to return to them. The old wood from the pews had been desecrated with strange carvings on them—carvings I knew in my heart were not meant for the same God I served on Sunday mornings at my church. The song books, deteriorating and covered in cobwebs were still tucked away in the back slots behind each pew—untouched for a countless number of years. The lectern behind the altar was tipped over to the side where I could only assume an organ or piano once sat; but in its original place sat an altar. The church was dimly lit by a few candles on the rail that bordered the altar, and in the center of the altar was a silver chalice trimmed with engravings, some of the same engravings that covered the pews.

He paled around his lips and his eyes glazed over. "This church hasn't been abandoned… This is wrong… Let's get out of here." In urgency, he grabbed my hand and jerked me back through the two sets of doors, nearly pulling my arm out of socket.

The smell of the distant campfire was welcoming compared to the ghastly stench that overwhelmed us inside the church. We took several deep breaths of the cleaner air, and then froze as we heard a muffled scream from the woods.

"What the…?" Broderick choked.

Ignorant curiosity inviting me to investigate, I didn't even give it a second thought, before I trudged toward the sound.

"Jules! No!" Broderick called out in a hush and followed me over to the woods at the back of the church.

Hand in hand, we pushed through the path leading us to a massive bonfire that was set in the middle of a large clearing. A crowd of people swarmed around the fire. A small group in black cloaks danced around the flames while others seemed to mingle aimlessly. Watching attentively, captivated by the festivities around the fire, I studied their faces but couldn't detect distress from anyone. Had the scream been simple amusement?

Broderick nudged me. "Jules, we need to get out of here. I've got a really bad feeling about this." He was high on alert.

"Why do you say that?"

"Look how they're *dressed!*" he urgently pointed out. Broderick was nervous and trying to pry me from my spot. "Come on, Jules. Let's *go.*"

I was more intrigued than afraid, but an unhealthy combination of both. "What do you think they're going to do?"

"Sacrifice a dog? Cat? A pet fish? It doesn't matter because I don't plan on being here when it happens."

"What if they're not having a sacrifice and it's just a bunch of locals having a good time like you thought before?" I asked him.

He emitted an incredulous sneer. "Really, Jules? Did you not just see the church? Look what they are *wearing!* If this was some random group of local rednecks we'd be hearing *Lynyrd Skynyrd* blaring from some piece of shit truck parked in the middle of..."

"You're not afraid of a bunch of stupid hillbillies are you, Broderick?"

"Do the words, '*squeal like a pig, boy*' mean anything to you?" He asked rhetorically as he began to stand up, morphing into a full shadow. It was obvious his shadowshifting was caused by fear—I could see that now.

I grabbed his shirt and pulled him down beside me again. "Wait! Just a second or two longer..."

Five people separated from the rest and started for the far end of the clearing. On the extreme edge of the clearing, stood a tall, ramshackle barn with a small light glowing from inside. The five walked out of the illuminating boundary of the bonfire and into the shadows that separated the barn and the gathering around the bonfire. I stared at the patch of blackness, waiting for my eyes to adjust and continue watching them, to follow where they were going. I was drinking it all in.

Broderick's words distracted me. "This isn't a movie, Jules."

He was right. The adrenaline rush I normally had during a horror movie couldn't compare to the charge I currently felt. It was both terrifying and electrifying.

The people that remained near the bonfire began to line up in some formation and speak in a hushed monotone. *Chanting!* As I opened my mouth to speak, I caught sight of the five that had disappeared in the dark patch of the field. They had emerged in the subtle glow of the moon that had broken through the clouds and from the dim light of the barn they were closely approaching.

They entered into the barn as Broderick leaned closely to my ear and whispered furiously, "We. Are. Done. Here. I'm hauling our asses back to the jeep."

"We're over two hundred yards from them; they don't even know we're here. What could possibly happen? If they're doing something illegal, we'll be here to witness it and we can turn them in!" I smiled, hoping that I was reeling him in by using his own hero-complex.

"Jules, the only crime I can see, is having you out of your house *way past* curfew."

"What is your problem? I thought you liked being the hero. Didn't we just hear someone scream from over here?"

He sternly cut me off, "The problem is this; if by some chance a crime is committed here tonight, something really bad in the pit of my stomach tells me that you and I are going to be the victims. My job is to keep you safe. That's all I care about right now." His voice was grave and I felt like I had put him through enough worry already, not to mention that his concern was now settling in my brain as a planted seed and making me worry. I began to stand when the five reemerged from the barn with a sixth person in tow—dressed in a red cape.

"*That. Is. It.*" Broderick spoke commandingly, shifting back to his regular self and began pulling me away from our hideout behind the bushes.

His strength easily overpowered mine and he jerked my body harshly to him and walked softly away from the fire with his arms tightly wrapped around me, my feet unable to touch ground as I remained upright. I didn't protest for fear of bringing attention to us. He walked me like that until we reached the church cemetery.

"Never, and I mean *never*, will I take you out this late again," He spoke angrily as he dashed ahead of me through the cemetery.

"Are you mad at me?"

He reached behind to take my hand. "No, Jules. I'm angry with myself. I should have put my foot down the minute I saw what was inside the church. I should have taken you home right then. That was dangerous back there," he spat.

"It wasn't really *dangerous*," I argued as I tried to catch up to him. "It was just a little risky; totally different."

"I'm not going to argue that point with you right now. All I want to do is get you home, safely." Under his breath, I could hear him say a short prayer for our safety. He reached further back to me as he continued to stomp through the cemetery. "Please take my hand, Jules."

His fear wouldn't allow him to slow his pace so I double stepped to grab his hand, trying to catch up. Just as our fingers grazed, I tripped in a hole, and buckled forward, my hands hitting the ground first to break the fall, and then my face planted into the moist ground. A sharp pain pierced my left hand between my thumb and index finger and I gasped loudly.

Broderick was quick to my side. "What happened? Are you okay?"

I winced in pain as I felt the warm blood rush down my arm. "My hand…"

His voice was tense, "I can't see it; it's too dark. What's wrong? Is it broke?"

He tried pulling me up, but I resisted due to the pain and remained in the hole. Cradling my hurt hand, I fought the urge to cry. With my other hand I squeezed tightly, just below the point of injury hoping to somehow cut off the supply of pain.

"Let me see your hand." He pulled my hand into the moonlight and looking like Superman's kryptonite, was a glowing green shard of glass jutting out of the skin between my thumb and index finger, blood still pumping out and running down my arm. He held my wrist gently yet firmly and quickly pulled the foreign object out and tossed it over in the grass, creating a small ping sound as it ricocheted off a headstone. The blood flowed and I sucked in my breath through gritted teeth as he ripped the pocket off his jacket and pressed it to my wound. "Squeeze it tightly to stop the bleeding."

We had become accustom to the chanting from through the woods so when it came to an abrupt halt, the silence seemed louder and *eerier*. Broderick looked anxious.

"I guess this is what I get for putting you through all of that," I whimpered in a joking manner to ease my own fear of the silence.

"Don't say that. We seriously need to concentrate on getting you out of here. You're going to need stitches for that."

I tried to stand but was unable to maneuver to my feet with both hands preoccupied. He grabbed my elbow and assisted me to my feet.

"Oh, shit!" Broderick rapidly phased into a dark shadow and grabbed me, viciously slamming my back into a nearby tombstone and curling my body into a tight ball beneath him.

"Stay still." He was barely audible. All I could really hear from him was the movement of his teeth when pronouncing consonants and his ragged breathing while he prayed.

Although I was unable to see anything with Broderick using his body as a shield around me, I could hear a mass of eager footsteps rustling by us no more than two or three graves over. Their movements sounded indomitable and quick of an aberrant nature. No one spoke. Just the long, never ending sound of shuffling feet pushing through the cold night air in the cemetery. I shook uncontrollably as I cringed from the pain and fear.

As the noise of their march faded, I heard Broderick emit a low groan and relax his body on mine. The interior of the church came alive as they began chanting again.

Facing me, he pulled my red hood on top of my head and quickly began tucking the strands of my hair inside the hood. "Keep your face down. If they catch sight of us, I don't want them to recognize you." He squatted down before me, and thumbed his back. "Hop on, Jules."

I did as he asked. As he rose to his feet I felt him shiver beneath me. He remained shifted into the shadowy. Like the hero he was, he jogged steadily, with me on his back as I whimpered in pain. Through the woods he ran, never once uttering a complaint. Soon we reached the desolate farmland with the tiny house that looked as though a stiff wind could knock it to its foundation. He reached around to his back and scooped me up in his arms to lower me softly yet hastily to the ground.

"What time is it?" I asked, my hand throbbing excruciatingly.

He stretched out his arms and legs, then glanced at his phone. "It's after 3 AM."

"What if we don't get home by the time my dad gets up? He gets up between four and five in the morning almost every day!" I raised my voice.

He pulled my chin up to look at me. "Don't worry about it. I'm going to get you home. *Safely.*" He leaned in and kissed my forehead.

"What do you think those people are doing?"

"Probably a cult of some sort. No doubt about it. God, I really thought it was all just local stories. I thought Taryn was exaggerating," he said under his breath. A shiver ran up my spine causing the hairs on my neck to stiffen. He rubbed his hands up and down my arms as he glanced over to the woods where, deep in its vegetation, the cult congregated inside the church.

He swallowed hard. "I'd heard stories about strange goings-on around this area. Unexplainable things…"

A piercing scream echoed from behind us. Clouded over with darkness, the moon provided no light. Broderick was quick to his feet. My heart felt like it would jump from my throat and into my lap. I tried to stand, but was weak with fear. He reached down, his eyes never pulling away from the direction we'd come, and helped me up. His arms wrapped around me tightly. Suddenly, another scream echoed, closer this time. We held our breaths, terrified the cult would find us.

But nothing could prepare us for the blood chilling howl that resonated in the mountain wind.

"Oh, shit!" I frantically whispered.

He stared silently and stiff; a heightened sense. Like a predator.

Another scream, muffled this time, was accompanied by the low rumble of chanting. I couldn't make out the words.

"Do you see something?" I asked him nervously, hoping that his height or his shadowshifting would play as an advantage to visually penetrate the darkness.

"*Broderick!*" I whispered loudly and gritted my teeth.

Placating that he was calm and collected by breathing slowly and standing sure and strong by my side, it was clear by his alarmed expression that he was unsettled by the commotion making its way toward us.

He grabbed my hand and hastily pulled me behind him. "They're following us! We have to get out of here!"

Voices were definitely growing louder.

"How close are they?" I was in a full-blown panic now. He ignored my question and pulled me even faster.

"Can you run the rest of the way or do I need to carry you?" To assist my decision he added, "It's probably another mile or so."

I set my jaw in determination, ready to take on the challenge despite the incessant throbbing of my hand. "I think I can keep up with you."

We immediately broke into a full dash across the clearing and into a cornfield—away from the oncoming chants. Cutting back across the cornfield was easy enough as long as we stayed between the rows, but as soon as we reentered the woods on the other side our progress was hindered by the overgrowth.

He stopped before entering the road and onto the dirt path that would lead us to the jeep. Without a second's hesitation, he slung me onto his back again. It didn't sound as if we had made a large enough gap between us and the stalking chanters. They were so fast!

We knew we were losing ground by the obvious, growing volume of chanting. I grew increasingly concerned when Broderick started taking staggering breaths. Fearing his carrying me was leaching his strength; his breathing became even more ragged as his own fear burst with each uniform crescendo of chanting. I chanced a glance behind us and my heart jackhammered as I saw three or four hooded bodies no more than fifty yards behind us and gaining space in their strange glide. Stifling a scream against Broderick's shoulder, I knew we couldn't outrun them when I felt him slow down his pace. A whimper escaped my lips as we stopped.

I felt him adjust my weight to one side as he reached for the handle of the door

The jeep!

It let loose a small squeaking sound which made us both stop breathing for a short second and then, like a flash, I heard the door squeak the rest of the way open and he tore me off of his back like a backpack and threw me like a rag doll across the seat and against the passenger's side door. I caught a glimpse of him jumping in and slamming the door as my head banged against the window. He fumbled his keys and then stabbed them into the ignition. The chanting stopped and as soon as the engine roared, wild screeching began. As the ear piercing shrieks came closer through the woods at us, Broderick hurriedly turned the jeep around and sped down the dirt path. I closed my eyes as I buckled my seatbelt. His driving was so erratic it nauseated me. I was also feeling faint. I hoped I hadn't lost too much blood.

Broderick was now in high volume. "Are you alright?"

I nodded and gulped as I kept my eyes closed. "What time is it?"

"*Time?* Are you kidding me?" he yelled as he took a sharp turn. "I'll tell you what time it is! It's time I get you to the damn hospital! You're still bleeding!" When I didn't respond, he glanced over at me. "You're not going out on me are you? Jules? *Jules!*"

"No," I muttered. "Your driving is making me car sick." I gulped back the acid forming in the back of my throat.

"I'll slow down as soon as I see a hint of civilization." The intensity was solid in his voice. "I need to call your parents and tell them that I'm taking you to the ER." He pulled out his cell phone. "I think you're going to need stitches."

"No!" My mind was suddenly a whirlwind of parental threats and consequences. I shouldn't have placed myself in this situation. *Poor judgment. Trust. Broderick being blamed.*

I moaned, "They'll never let me see you again!"

"Do you think I care about that right now? You need a doctor, Jules! We'll worry about the rest later," he yelled.

"Please don't scream at me," I begged him, weeping more over the situation and the pain than the fact that he had raised his voice.

His demeanor changed immediately. "Oh, Jules! I didn't mean to... I'm sorry... I was just scared back there. I still am! D'you see me shaking over here?" He held out his hand for me to see it visibly trembling.

He began dialing and I felt numb with the ultimate knowledge that my dad was going to kill me. I refused to let this happen. My brain was quickly conjuring up a solid story for us to go by.

"Shit! No signal!"

"I have a plan," I announced, a tad lightheaded.

"I'm listening."

"Take me home and I'll set it up to look like I cut myself in my bedroom," I said.

He shook his head, "I hate lying."

"I *hate* the idea of not seeing you again. My parents *will* make sure of that if they find out we were sneaking out at night..."

He said nothing for the longest time as he debated. We were finally reaching the overpass to the interstate and he sighed as he sent me an uneasy glance.

"*Please,* Broderick?"

He conceded with a silent nod. My nerves were completely shot and it took the entire drive home for me to gain at least some bearing of safety. Broderick helped me sneak back through my window and kissed me intensely before leaving.

Quickly, I changed into my pajamas and took the glass picture frame of me, Cari, Savannah, and Sydney and shattered it on the floor. I hastily (and painfully) squeezed a few drops of blood on the floor, on the glass, and on my shirt, giving the wound permission to start the bleeding again after I had finally got it to stop.

I screamed out and unlocked my bedroom door. Running down the stairs, I met my mom halfway to her room.

"What was that noise?" she gasped.

Finally I could weep the way I needed to, from the wound and the horror we had just encountered.

"I accidently knocked over the picture by my bed while I was sleeping and cut myself."

"Jules, how do you manage…?" She turned the light on at the landing and studied my hand, shaking her head incredulously. "You're going to need stitches."

At the emergency room, I finally got to meet Dr. Renata Kowalski, my mother's employer. She was the on-call doctor for the weekend. My mother filled out paper work in the waiting room as the young and attractive doctor cleaned my wound then numbed my hand with the most painful shot I'd ever had! She asked in her foreign accent how and when the injury occurred. Repeating my lie to her, I felt the blood rushing from my face. Her looks of skepticism left me cold and I worried she may voice the concern to my mother that I was lying to her. The dirt in and around the wound was a dead giveaway, for sure.

After seven stitches, I was cleared to return home at five in the morning. Walking out with my mother to her car, I saw out of the corner of my eye, a red jeep that was parked inconspicuously in the back row. I smiled to myself, knowing that the *hero* continued without rest until he was sure I was mended and safe.

Little Red Riding Hood

WE KEPT THE ENCOUNTER of that chilling night between us. There was no need to scare others or to let people—especially my parents—know we had made a habit of being out after curfew.

My hand injury kept me from participating with the flag corps and marching band for several weeks. Natalie and I both made our full returns to our respective teams on the same weekend. Out of her sling after a few weeks of therapy and a regaining of muscle strength, Natalie was glad to be taking an active role in cheering again, no longer coupled with the gigantic megaphone that she despised. Although my hand didn't receive the same attention as her broken clavicle had, I was left with a permanent reminder of that night. The scar from the cut in my hand was shaped like a cross. Strange, as I had obtained it during an evil encounter.

Autumn's preview came in late September with crisp and cool evenings, setting the Friday night football games in a wonderful seasonal ambience. Although I was never a big fan of the sport, I always enjoyed the mood and cooler weather that came with this time of year. It invigorated me. Watching Broderick on the field could almost make me a true fan, though.

Mom and Dad made it to every game in support of not only me and Natalie, but also Broderick and Joey. Despite the tension that had increased between Joey and Natalie, he was still thought of as one of the family. Natalie was spending more and more time with her friend, Amber—who she had bizarrely nicknamed "Berta"—in an attempt to distance herself from Joey. Still, whenever Natalie and Joey were together, they easily fell into old habits: inside jokes, teasing, and flirting. I just couldn't understand her or their situation.

Savannah would always be found sitting in the stands, snuggling close to Tripp. Sometimes Syd would be with them when she came home for the weekend. Taryn would frequently take a breather from her social routine to sit next to me at the top bleachers where the band was designated to sit. She somehow managed to stay undetected by Mr. Grayson and though Taryn and Cari didn't chatter along like old buddies, they were cordial and accepting of the other. Taryn, like always, would try plowing her way through our conversations with a constant interruption of her own obsessive cheering for Jackson who consistently played a great game.

When I wasn't in school or having a midnight rendezvous with Broderick—now strictly confined to our neighborhood—I was in rehearsals almost every day. Rehearsals started slowly, but as we neared the opening of the show, they became rushed and chaotic. By mid-month, we moved our rehearsals from the school to the theater downtown. The excitement was buzzing through the week as we plunged ourselves into full dress rehearsals.

Many of the cast was sick of one another from all the time we were spending together. Mark Hines regularly threw himself into some diva-like tantrum about the lack of professionalism from the cast. Mr. Greyson's fuse became shorter while working longer hours with us students. Cari and Savannah became more enthralled with Isaac as time progressed; all the while, my hatred for him grew…but so did my admiration of his talent.

Gossip and backstabbing had become regular theme, causing tensions to run high on stage, and the root of most of the trouble was Mark. His jealousies were getting the best of him in terms of Isaac and apparently Isaac was too intimidating to butt heads with, so instead Mark would take his frustrations out on his other rival—*me*. Mark would find the smallest things about me to complain about, and I, in return, would lash out horribly.

When the show finally opened, I was thankful. I was even more thankful when it closed, as tensions among the cast didn't subside.

Andrea's sixth period class changed from Jet Theatrix to Creative Studies immediately after the show's closing late September. Savannah and Cari were able to be reassigned to their respective choices of student council and work-study program for sixth period. Unfortunately, I couldn't find any other sixth period class I was interested in that had an opening. Isaac must have had the same problem, because he, too, remained in the Creative Studies workshop.

The week before we were dismissed for fall break, our class was assigned to analyze an old tale or nursery rhyme as a project. Andrea gave us the entire class period to decide our tale and choose our partner. With my friends no longer in this class, I couldn't find a partner for this project, so by default I was paired off with Isaac. *Of all people…*

Isaac and I thumbed quickly through the printed list of her suggestions, everything from *The Three Little Pigs* to *Little Miss Muffett*. I definitely didn't want to do a Nursery Rhyme. Andrea spoke to Mark Hines and his partner about a book of The Brothers Grimm fairy tales that she owned—highly recommending it to them as an option. They politely declined as they had already chosen to do their project on *Hansel & Gretel*.

"Andrea, could we see the book?" I raised my hand.

"But of course!" she exclaimed in an overdramatic fashion as she crossed the room to our desks.

She handed the tattered, hardback book to me. With every familiar tale, I'd call it out in suggestion.

"*Cinderella*."

Isaac rolled his eyes. "Have you ever read the story? It's not Disney, you know."

"*Snow White*, then."

"Again…" he started as I finished his sentence with him, oozing a derogatory tone.

"…It's not *Disney*." I pouted. "Fine. I get it."

Isaac pored over the pages of titles and I stood up from my desk to stretch my legs. He flipped through the pages until an illustration caught my eye.

"Wait, wait! Go back."

He thumbed back a few pages and came to the sepia toned illustration of a girl—a young teen—walking cautiously through the woods. Catching my eye was the one vibrant color on the page, a blood red cape and hood that was draped over her head and shoulders.

"*Little Red Riding Hood*," I said, feeling the deep sense of familiarity that went beyond just the story.

"*Little Red Cap*," he corrected with superiority.

We skimmed the few pages of the short story as Andrea made her rounds in the class to collect everyone's chosen assignment.

"And what story do you two plan to research?" she asked as she approached our conjoined desks.

"*Little Red Riding Hood*," I spoke without consulting Isaac.

"Cap," he corrected me again. I wanted to smack him.

She seemed pleased as she penciled our choice in a notebook and continued to the last two tables before standing at the front of the class. I cringed with the oncoming dread to spend time alone with Isaac to conjure up some sort of project for an A in this class.

During Fall Break, when Broderick and I weren't together watching a movie or taking long walks, he was mysteriously working on a project in our woods. He begged me not to enter into the woods until he was finished. I would sit in my room with the windows open, taking in the fresh and cool autumn breezes, and could hear him hammering and sawing. The fallen leaves would make it easy for me to sneak a peek through the woods and see what he was up to, but I decided to give him the chance to actually surprise me.

My birthday fell on a Saturday and I should have known that something was brewing by the way my mom had been bustling secretively around for several days. Broderick showed up that morning determined to keep me away from the house. For the first time in over a year he pulled his four-wheeler out of his garage.

I watched as he knocked cobwebs and layers of dirt and grime off. "Is it safe?" I asked nervously.

He smirked, exposing a small dimple in his cheek. "You're not scared are you?" he taunted while he pushed up his sleeves, cleaning the all-terrain vehicle.

"No," I chuckled quietly at my lie. "Where are we going?"

"Into the woods," he grinned suspiciously.

"Do I get to see what you've been working on?" I asked enthusiastically.

His dimples deepened as he walked over and tweaked my nose. "Soon. Be patient, Jules."

I pretended to pout as he finished cleaning and then tossed the dirty rag on the garage floor.

"You ready to climb on?"

I nodded excitedly. He walked over to me and put his hands on my hips. He swiftly swept me up into his arms and sat me on the back of the four-wheeler. He handed me a helmet and I groaned. This would only make me look stupid.

"Don't give me that," he said of my attitude. "I'd rather see it on your head than have something tear up that beautiful face of yours."

"What about *your* helmet?" I challenged.

"I only have one and I'd rather *you* wear it." I rolled my eyes and sighed as I shoved the oversized helmet onto my head. He climbed on and grabbed my arms, wrapping them around his chest. "I want you to hold on to me tightly."

"Are you going to go fast?"

"No. I just want you to hold onto me tightly for my own selfish reasons," he laughed as he started the motor and tore off through the open field behind his house that ran along the perimeter of woods separating our properties.

Like I was asked, but without much coaxing, I held onto him tightly. My hands pressed to his chest and feeling the thundering beat of his heart through the vibrations of our bodies from the ATV. Despite his vow to drive slowly, I felt as though we were speeding roughly through the pasture. Passing bales of hay, he finally jerked onto a path that led into a part of the woods I was completely unfamiliar with.

We left the morning sun behind us as we plunged ahead. Autumn leaves flew into the air as we shot through them—causing a swirl of browns, oranges, reds, and yellows to twist recklessly in the air until they fluttered serenely back to rest on the ground. Sunlight filtered through the vacant branches of the trees giving me a sense of peace and safety. The cool morning air was filled with the scent of decaying leaves. I despised the helmet preventing me from resting my cheek against his back as I pulled myself as close to him as possible. He let go of one of the handles and placed his hand over mine.

I was totally lost and unaware of where we were. Within minutes we crossed a gravel road that opened up to a rock quarry. He darted around machinery and flew over dirt mounds that caused me to squeal in delight. Zooming through the quarry he reentered the woods on the other side.

We drove miles from our homes. Isolated. The woods became thicker and thicker with trees, causing the area to appear dark and eerie—appealing for the time of year, in my opinion. I could see the sun fighting its way on the faded path ahead as he pulled the four-wheeler beside a large oak tree and turned off the engine.

He twisted off of the vehicle and pulled the helmet from my head and dropping it to the ground he grabbed me gently by my face and kissed me long and hard. His soft lips moved anxiously with mine as he would dip his tongue into my mouth with a rhythmic and seductive motion. I ran my fingers through his shaggy hair and tugged on the ends, practically begging him not to stop.

He stepped back with a smile and untied the blanket from the back rack of the four-wheeler and as he tucked it under his arm he held his hand out for me to take. "Happy birthday, Jules. I love you."

I grabbed his hand and hopped from the four-wheeler. "The jig is up, Broderick. I know you guys have a surprise party planned for me today."

He laughed as we walked out of the shadows of the woods and into the sunlight. "Did Natalie spill?"

"No. I'm just not that stupid."

He shook out the blanket and laid it out. He patted the spot next to him as he sat down. "We need to start planning our future."

My head began spinning and my eyes flew open in curiosity, eager to hear his thoughts. "How so?"

"I'm graduating in just a few more months and honestly, Jules, I don't want to leave you." I smiled with selfishness. "We need to decide what we're going to do about that."

"Any ideas?" I waited. I was open for anything as long as it included being with Broderick.

"I'm going to enroll at Tennessee Tech University. That's just thirty minutes away so we won't be far apart. Then, when you graduate..." he hesitated, bouncing his leg nervously. "I want to go with you, wherever you want go. It doesn't matter. That is, if you want to keep me around..."

Rendered breathless, I couldn't make out if he was proposing. "What are you saying?"

He was quick in an explanation, trying hard not to scare me, "I'm not talking about marriage yet, Jules. I just want to be with you if that's what you want, too. After you graduate we'll be free to go anywhere you want to go." He tucked in his lips, allowing his dimples to make a quick appearance.

I was confused even further. "You mean run away with you?"

He laughed at both my question and his own desperate tone he had just used. "I know you want to do theater and as far as me making a living, I can do photography or paint anywhere! I can even finish school online. Nashville, New York, L.A... *Ireland*. You could be near your grandmother again. It wouldn't be like running away because we'd tell everyone where we're going. It would be more like *me* running away with *you*," he explained as he moved closer to me. "I just want to be with you." He leaned in closer to lock eyes. His seriousness was powerful.

Unbelievable! This wonderful man was declaring his love for me. In just a matter of months our feelings for each other had grown to similar heights. I was ready to return that love openly after I offered one last insecure overture. "I-if-if you're sure that's what you really want..." I stammered.

He sighed in relief as he lay back onto the blanket and pulled me to him, resting my head on his chest. We lay there in pure delight as the sunlight danced across the treetops and time passed over us in long breezes, fallen leaves, and moving clouds overhead.

I chuckled as an old memory swept through my mind.

"What are you thinking about?" he asked, his voice echoing within the confines of his chest, my ear pressed against it.

I stifled my chuckle. "I was thinking about how my grandmother would have turned over in her grave if that was a proposal and I had just said yes."

"Why? You don't think she would have liked me?" His voice was troubled.

"Not that it would matter. Your grandmother doesn't like me and that hasn't stopped you any," I reminded him. "My grandmother encouraged me to hold off until I was well into my twenties before even thinking about marriage. She told me to be extremely careful with whom I chose to spend the rest of my life with."

"Well, that should be a given," Broderick replied in agreement.

"Yeah, but there was a sense of intense seriousness when she said it— like it was a matter of life or death." I laughed in recollection. "She was practically terrified that I would make a mistake."

He twisted his face in amusement. "I can't believe you'd openly talk about that kind of stuff with your grandmother... or with anyone, for that matter."

I nodded. "True. That sort of conversation would be awkward and yet it wasn't like a one on one chat. It was *different*."

"Different? How?" he asked.

"Well, if you promise not to laugh…" I warned.

He held up his fingers in a scout's honor.

I licked my lips in preparation. "It happened about a year ago." I took a deep breath to continue with the impending embarrassing confession. "She never exactly had a sit down talk with me over the matter. In fact, I'm pretty sure it was just my way of coping with her illness. It happened just before she passed away, when she slipped into a coma." I looked away, humiliated, and even laughed at myself a bit. I sighed. "The night before she died, I had a dream about her telling me that. It's silly; I feel stupid for telling you this." I waved it off.

He tenderly scolded, "It's not silly and you're not stupid. At least you know that your dreams are just that…*dreams.*"

"I rarely *ever* remember the dreams I have at night. I know I have them and I remember how I feel in them, because that feeling is usually lingering as I wake, but they never have any lasting impact on me. Maybe I sleep too hard. But that night, I dreamt I was with her, sitting in her kitchen drinking sweet tea and nibbling on her homemade cinnamon rolls like we always did. We talked about things I'd never openly discuss with anyone. But I wasn't embarrassed at all. She was giving me all sorts of advice." I closed my eyes remembering how grave her warning. "It was then she told me to be careful with my decisions on whom I should spend the rest of my life with. She said that I shouldn't rush into a relationship without fully knowing who they are."

I paused, focusing on a peculiar phrase that has haunted me since the moment I heard it.

"She also made a comment about how the devil will patiently pace back and forth until I leave even the smallest invitation or crack in my door for him to enter… or something like that… something creepy." I shook off the eeriness of the memory and the melancholy mood with another light chuckle.

At my last comment, Broderick's face could have easily mirrored mine the night I had heard it myself for the first time. "Why would you dream something like that?"

I shrugged. "It's good advice regardless of how creepy she sounded as she said it. I can't remember the exact words but I spent weeks after that night trying to remember them." I quieted momentarily. "I know she and I never really had that conversation, but in the past year, I have deluded myself to believe it would have really happened if only she'd had time and take it to heart."

He frowned, frustration bleeding through. "I haven't had a premonition dream in over a month. Not since that night near Black Mountain. I'm starting to second guess everything I'd seen before…the visions that haven't come to pass…"

"Maybe you should write everything you've dreamt before down so that you don't forget? That way you can refer back to the dreams if and when they actually happen," I suggested as he stared at the woods. I reached over and took his hand and he turned to look at me. "You can even share some of them with me…"

He collected his thoughts before he began speaking. "That following night after what we saw near Black Mountain, I had a dream about a car in the middle of a crime scene. Like I said, it's been over a month since I've had this dream, or any dream. It's probably nothing. It's not even a familiar car…" He changed his mind. "It probably *isn't* a crime scene at all. There are just a few policemen looking at it, walking around it."

"Broderick, what are you hiding? You wouldn't have brought it up if it was someone you didn't know."

"A white hooded shirt—like the one I bought you—is in the car," he whispered.

"You think *I'm* in danger?" I gulped.

"No! It's probably something else." I could hear in his voice how he was still trying to get a full understanding of his vision. "You don't even have a car right now, so don't worry about it," he consoled me. "I wish I had never said anything," he mumbled to himself.

"Do you *see* me in the vision?" I asked.

"No." He paused, debating on another thought. I looked to him with pleading eyes to share his secret. "The last time I saw you in any of my visions was when you were drowning in the lake."

"But you saw me with Erik and that happened *after* the lake incident…"

"Actually, I had the drowning dream again a few nights after Black Mountain. I think the original dream might have scared me more last summer than I realized and the memory has stuck around. It's like an echo."

"Has that happened before?" Worry was growing within me.

"No. I think it was actually just a nightmare. Like I said, an echo of another dream I had in the past. I haven't seen anything useful in over a month. Something has changed in me and I can't dream premonitions anymore…" In a course of a few seconds he came to a conclusion. "I'm partly relieved by this." The liberation in his face was valid. "Jules, I'm not going to let anything bad happen to you."

"You can't play God like that, Broderick."

"God wouldn't have given me this gift if he didn't want me to use it, would he?"

"I thought you said it was a curse?" I teased.

"Not if it keeps you safe." He thought for a moment, "Do you trust me?"

"Of course, I do."

Broderick checked his watch. "Let's get you back home. Remember, act surprised."

My party was small, but everyone I cared about was in attendance—save Isaac who Cari brought along. My dad was eager for me to open presents and as soon as I finished eating cake, he ushered me over to the table that was loaded gifts.

I ripped through the paper and boxes finding everything from a karaoke machine to jewelry.

"Next," Cari said ushering in her oversized box. I worried she spent too much money on me. Instead, she had stuffed a movie gift card into a box full of tissue paper. "Your little movie buddy was dying for an excuse to talk to me the other night, so I purchased a gift card from him to shut him up," she groaned dryly.

Isaac quickly scooped up the last present on the table and handed it to me. "It's not much, but as soon as I saw it, I immediately thought of you."

I didn't want to seem appreciative, but I was truly humbled that someone who had shown up uninvited to my party was kind enough to at least offer a gift. I pulled the beautifully wrapped paper from the box and pulled the lid open to find an old worn hardback titled *Brothers Grimm and other Faery Tales*. Identical to the book Andrea had in class.

I forced a small smile, "Thanks."

"Alright, now for the big surprise," my dad boomed with pride. "It should be outside in the driveway right now."

With wide eyes, I ran to the back door squealing in delight, "No. Freakin'. Way!"

"Jules…" My mom warned of my use of the word *freakin'*. She hated euphemisms.

Anxious to see the new vehicle, I ran up a half flight of stairs from our family room and stopped at the front door. The party guests trailed behind. I stepped out on the front porch to see an old, faded red Mini Cooper parked on our circular driveway.

I squealed, "Holy, crap! Daddy, it's beautiful!"

Dad proudly announced, "It's about eight years old, but I thought you'd rather stick to the classics." With a quick wink, he added, "But you have to be careful and take care of it and—"

I ran over and hugged him tightly. "Thanks so much, Daddy. I promise to take really good care of it."

"I know you will, Pumpkin." He kissed me on the cheek and walked back inside with my mom.

"Looks like you're going to be *riding* Cooper, now," Cari remarked cheekily as soon as my parents disappeared into the house, causing me to blush and setting off the chain reaction of more laughter.

I looked over at Broderick to see his reaction to her distasteful witticism but he was like stone. Pale, he stared at the faded red vehicle with two white racing stripes. It was clear that he was terrified and I was determined to ask Broderick if my Mini Cooper was, in fact, the same car he saw in his dream.

After a few hours of karaoke, everyone left. Cari was the last to leave and if it weren't for her evening shift at the super market, she wouldn't have left at all. I was so desperate to talk to Broderick that I hastily agreed to meet Isaac at the library after school that next Monday to work on our project. Normally, I would have protested until I was blue in the face, but I knew the sooner I agreed, the sooner he would leave.

We waved to everyone as they filed out of the circular driveway, careful to avoid hitting my new car. He placed his arm around me, "Go get a light jacket on; it's going to be cold. I get you for the rest of the evening. Your birthday is far from over," he smiled secretively.

I didn't want to go anywhere or do anything until he explained his rigid and pale reaction to my car. "That's the car, isn't it?"

He glance over at the Mini with casual eyes, placating that he was unaffected by its presence. "Like I said before, Jules, I'm fairly sure it's not a crime scene. It's just police walking around your car and your white hoodie crumpled up on the passenger seat. I didn't see *you*. Your car probably gets stolen."

The fact that I wasn't lying dead somewhere in the vision was almost enough for me. I just needed some reassurance. "Do you really believe that? That it gets stolen?"

The light bulb seemed to click on. "I wouldn't be surprised if that's exactly what it is, with the way the crime in this area has increased. My premonition is more than likely a warning that you should keep it locked up."

I laughed at how feasible it sounded. "I wish there was a better way to know if what you're seeing is the future or just some random picture in your brain," I admitted.

He winked at me. "I felt nothing urgent or dangerous with the vision. Keep your car doors locked, though."

"You got it." I winked back.

I went to retrieve my red hooded shirt. When I came back down the stairs, my parents wished us a fun evening, allowing an extended curfew. As soon as we walked out of the house, he pulled me into the woods.

"Close your eyes," he said.

With my eyes closed, I let him lead me down our well-worn path, making it through the trail with little difficulty. It had become such a regular routine, traipsing back and forth through the woods between mine and Broderick's homes, that I was accustomed to the feel of the ground beneath my feet and every slight turn of the path. The vegetation would swat at my ankles and arms, giving me physical clues as to where I was.

He stopped me just before we reached the creek—I could hear it rushing by—and he placed his hand over my eyes.

"Are your eyes still shut?" I nodded. He moved his hand and whispered into my ear, "Open them."

Connecting our two properties, arched over the creek, was a small bridge with railing on both sides.

"It'll be safer for you to cross now," he said with a smile as I walked over to it and timidly stepped onto it."

I laughed. "You made this for me?"

"Of course! I don't mind the idea of you coming over at night so much if I know you're going to safely make it across the creek. I would hate for you to fall in and get wet, especially in this cooler weather."

"But you'd get a good laugh out of it. Admit it," I replied smartly. His smiled widened at the truth of it.

I looked over to the large scrub oak on the other side of the bridge. He had tied an old tire to a thick and strong branch.

"A tire swing!" I enthused as if I were seven and not seventeen.

I didn't hesitate shoving my legs into the hole of the tire and kick off from the ground to gain enough momentum to get closer to the tree and eventually kick off from it for an even greater drive into the air.

"Are you surprised?" He asked as he strolled over to me. He stopped my swinging motion against the tree and instead began pushing me parallel to the tree.

"Totally! I love it!" I smiled as I leaned back and basked in the autumn breeze that loosened the leaves from the trees around me and let them flow gently to the ground. I watched the tree tops sway back and forth for minutes on end as Broderick pushed me in the swing.

"So this is what you had been working on this whole week," I said with a carefree chuckle. "I love it!"

"I have one more present," he said quietly.

I skidded my feet to an abrupt stop. "*More?*"

"I wanted to give this to you in private. Come here." He walked to the middle of the bridge and motioned for me to follow him.

I pulled my legs out from the tire and skipped over to him like an eager child. He began digging into the pocket of his brown leather jacket.

"Turn around." He motioned his finger in a spinning motion.

Facing the small dogwood tree, I shut my eyes as I drew a long deep breath. I felt Broderick move close behind me and sweep my long hair over one shoulder. He lay something cold against my chest and fastened the chain in the back.

"This was mine. It was a gift from my mother. She had it made for me just before she died."

He exhaled a staggering breath and my eyes fluttered open. Looking down at the silver medallion, I picked it up from my chest to read the inscription.

"*Life's greatest challenge is becoming who you were meant to be*," I read aloud. "But this belongs to *you*; it's from your mom. I can't take this," I said as I reached in the back to unfasten it. He stopped me with his hand on mine.

"I want you to have it. It'll hurt my feelings if you don't take it. Besides, I'm allergic to the metal. Please, wear it. It'll keep you safe," he pleaded.

Sighing, I looked down at it remembering his vision of the red car and the nightmare he had of me drowning. I understood his intentions of keeping me safe. Even though he didn't fully believe I was in danger, he wanted to be sure, and this was the best way for him to feel comfort. Staking my safety on a medallion passed on to him from his mother—now to me.

I flipped it over to see his initials engraved on the back. I found it more beautiful than any jewelry I owned, and I grasped it tightly in my fist. "I love it. Thank you so much for everything you do for me."

He held my hand, rubbing the cross-shaped scar from where my stitches had been removed weeks ago. "You know," he began "That night, just before you fell; I prayed to God that if anything happens, He save *you*. That you would get out of there alive. Then a second later you were on the ground. I thought He had struck you down out of my selfish plea, and I felt He had betrayed me. I saw that, even though you were alive and okay, you were injured. But, now I see this." He continued to trace the cross on my hand with his finger. "It's as if He put His mark on you, to protect you."

I kindly smiled at Broderick. "He gave me you, to protect me."

He cupped my face in his hands. "And I'm going to keep you safe. That's why I want you to take the medallion. It's like *my* mark on you."

I nodded, fully trusting in his vow, there wasn't anything in this world that could pose a threat to my existence. I was safe with Broderick; he could protect me from anything.

The only thing he *couldn't* protect me from was my obligation to my partnered project with Isaac. As agreed, Monday after school, I met Isaac at the library. Isaac was waiting for me at a corner table, wearing a pair of faded jeans and a black leather jacket that perfectly matched his disheveled, black hair.

I sluggishly threw my book down on the table where he sat causing a small raucous in the silent library. Receiving a not-so-friendly look from the librarian at the front counter, I dropped in the seat across from him.

"So what are your ideas on our girl, *Little Red Cap*?" he plunged in immediately.

I groaned at the impending obligation to tell him that I still hadn't read anything in that book. Isaac saw right through my groan and didn't seem to mind the fact that I was a procrastinating slacker, for he offered to read it aloud to me at the table where we sat.

"It's been a while since I've read it anyway," he claimed, as if I needed any of his excuses to *not* do my homework.

I rested my head on the comfort of my folded arms on the table and tried to give an honest ear to the story. Isaac grabbed the book and began reading the story of *Little Red Cap* by Jacob and Wilhelm Grimm. The story was short and I was familiar with it, but Isaac brought a certain reality to it. His voice, dark and smooth, I closed my eyes and imagined what Little Red Cap would look like in today's world. I expected her to resemble a girl more like me, sort of a tomboy, unafraid of the wolf, and stubborn.

"So what's our angle on the interpretation?" I asked as I deeply listened to his slow rhythmic breathing. "Obey your parents?"

"I think we should go with the sexual awakening angle," he said bluntly.

I chuckled to hide my embarrassment. "What sexual awakening?"

"Well, there are theories out there that the red cape symbolizes a young girl entering into sexual maturity. Her menstrual cycle." He was unashamed and frank as he spoke the words, whereas I wanted to crawl under the table and die at the shame of my own nature.

Still, I wanted to prove my own maturity over the discussion so I engaged. I cleared my shaky throat. "Really?"

He perked up immediately at my sudden change of mood. "Of course, the French saw the symbolization of the red cloak as prostitution, but I don't like thinking of the young girl in that manner. She was her grandmother's pride and joy. No grandmother would take pride in a hooker for a granddaughter," he laughed.

"True that." I jotted his thoughts down.

"The red definitely resembles a sexual awakening, but not in a crude and experienced sense. The red cape indicates her menstrual cycle. Quite innocent and natural. It marks the beginning of her questions and curiosities. She's young and innocent…like you."

I blushed when he mentioned it again and singled me out with it. "What else?" I was desperate to change the focus of our discussion.

"I think we should get another version of the story."

"Ugh! Why? Can't we just get this done and over with?"

"We should see if there's a different angle or interpretation that we might be overlooking." Isaac jumped up and walked over to the children's books.

I lazily sat in my seat to let him do all the work. He quickly retrieved two other books with similar short stories on Little Red and read them aloud as well. Again, I relaxed in the comfort of his engaging voice, flowing through the storyline in my mind—myself as Little Red. With every reading, I became more intrigued with the story and the girl, that for my seventeen years of life, had seemed so simplistic. He took a deep breath as he finished reading.

"Well," he thought out loud for my benefit, "apparently only the newer versions of this story clarify it was her cloak that was red. According to reference points and research in this book." He pointed to an open page. "It's speculated that her hair is red, because there's even an older story where she's actually golden hooded. But I prefer to think of her with the red cloak and golden hair. Though stereotypically speaking, redheads are stubborn, aggressive, unafraid, and even have a short fuse for a temper— just how I imagine our Little Red was. Maybe she's disguised as a blond, covering her natural red hair color?" He bit his bottom lip as he tugged at a tress of my brassy hair.

"What the hell!" I jerked away from him, mouth agape. I was surprised at his observation to details. Was he that perceptive to see that my hair was indeed not natural and constantly fighting the red and brassy tones? Or had Cari told him? She was the only one outside of my family who knew.

Unable to deny the truth, but resolved to ignore his prying, I was desperate to move the focus again. "What about the wolf? He's in the story, too, you know. It's not all about the girl."

"The wolf threatens the girl's purity."

I laughed aloud. "You're so absurd. He's *hungry*. This story has nothing to do with sex. You're trying to embarrass me and it's not working. You're just... just... *horny*!" The librarian hushed me from across the room and I blushed at my volume gaffe.

"Ah," he began, resisting my accusation that he was horny. "But that's where you're wrong. The mother clearly warns her not to wander from the path or to break the bottle. She's telling her not to lose her virginity. When the wolf sees her, he's aroused."

"*Hungry!*" I corrected and the librarian shushed me again.

"*Aroused*," he countered in a low tone. "It's a story about seduction."

"It's a story warning girls to stay away from dangers in the woods like wolves." I stated, firm in my conviction as I recalled the night when Broderick and I faced danger in the woods.

"But if it was a story about that, then the mother would have probably told her to stay away from wolves in particular. Instead she said to not wander from the *path*. She's not referring to dangers in the woods; she's referring to the dangers of leaving your innocence, leaving your upbringing. Sex can be a dangerous game, Juliana, yet we all look beyond that and only see the appeal. How will it feel? Will I like it? Does it make me sexy? Does it make me dirty? Is it love? How many different ways can we —?"

"Stop!" I warned him, deep crimson flowing from my chest and bursting in flames at my neck. "Don't talk like that in front of me. It's disrespectful."

He grinned at my mortification. He was very mindful of the discomfort his words had brought me and took a sick pleasure from it. "Men, in general, are like animals when it comes to sex—wild beasts, if you will—which is why there's a wolf in the story. The wolf speaks soothingly and gently to her, coercing her into a childlike game, figuratively inviting her into his world, making her believe that their worlds are merging, giving her a sense of safety so he can dominate her. Men are driven by sex and the excitement of being the one to steal a young woman's innocence, to dominate a virgin, it's empowering. A prize. I'm not ashamed to admit it."

My mouth became so dry; I couldn't swallow the lump that had formed in my flaring throat. I looked up into his eyes, blue like ice. My eyes felt glassy. "Maybe you *should* be."

"The wolf wants to take her virginity. The wolf symbolizes a lover or a sexual predator... a man. Women tend not to be scared of men, because they bring them a false sense of comfort and safety. A man can be a young girl's greatest love as well as her greatest nightmare. Little Red was never afraid of the wolf."

"But how do you explain the ending? He eats her anyway."

"The woodsman frees them from the wolf's belly. It symbolizes an artificial way of dealing with her trauma, if you ask me. Clearly, the girl is ruined. The memory will haunt her till her death; haunt her grandmother, too, but she finds something to make her believe that she's faced her fears and ready to move on with her life. Realistically, she never faced what happened. She won't recover."

I was displeased with his assessment and grabbed his book of *"theories"* from him and scanned the page.

"Ha!" I laughed arrogantly at him as I pointed in the book, "It says: 'she places rocks in his belly, leaving him immobile and he dies, exacting revenge for his obscene and insulting portrayal of a woman—her grandmother. Smiting the offending organ, Little Red throws rocks in his belly, where the wolf was keeping her and her grandmother.' The womb! The woman's empowerment! Only a woman—and I mean a *real woman*, not some dressed up drag queen of a wolf—can bear a child." I leaned into him with fierce eyes, fighting for the control of power between us… and of our project.

He leaned into me bringing his face just inches from mine and I slightly pulled back, disappointed that I had lost the unspoken "stare down" battle.

"Do I make you nervous, Juliana?"

I chuckled as though his attempt of seduction was poorly executed. "*Hardly.*"

"Just like Little Red, you see no harm or danger in me."

"Because, you're not scary."

"But, that's exactly what makes me so dangerous. I could easily be your own personal sexual predator and here you sit alone, with me and you wouldn't even know how close you are to losing yourself with me." He bit his lip again causing me to shudder in unwelcomed delight.

I stuck out my chin conceitedly. "We're not alone, moron. We're in a library. Besides, Broderick would kick your ass. That's why I'm not scared."

"Speaking of Broderick… you don't find your purity in danger with him, either? You don't see your innocence being recklessly threatened by the chivalrous and heroic Broderick Cooper?" he provoked.

"Not at all. And I'm done talking about this with you." I unsteadily gathered my belongings and stood up, but Isaac grabbed me by the arm and looked sternly into my eyes.

He whispered in a grave tone, "That guy is a danger to you, Juliana. You better be on your guard."

"Let go of me," I hissed.

"He is not only determined to take what is precious to you but he's going to turn your life inside out and you'll never fully gain the potential you— "

His words jolted me like an electric current, leaving me both freaked out and furious. "That is *my* decision. *My* business. So, piss off!" I rushed out of the library as the librarian hushed me for a third time. "Yeah, yeah. Don't worry. I'm leaving," I spoke curtly to her as I stormed out of the library; my legs wobbling as though they were filled with jelly.

I gauchely fumbled with my keys to unlock my doors. I threw my book and notebook in the passenger's side with my backpack purse and slammed the door as I dropped into the driver's seat and lay my head on the steering wheel. The church bells from across the street began to chime an old hymn, calming my monster down a bit. Finally, I drove home.

From that point on until the day we turned in our final work, I washed my hands of our pairing as far as any further study being needed, simply telling Isaac to do what he wanted to with the information we collected. I agreed to find photos and illustrations to justify my name joined with his on the project. I didn't want to fail the stupid class over my hatred for him. He wasn't worth it. Luckily, he agreed to my terms.

The only good thing I had walked away with was an awesome Halloween costume idea—*Little Red Riding Hood.*

Homecoming

HOMECOMING WEEK BROUGHT ABOUT an insurmountable excitement to the school. The student council went overboard with festivities for the week, but that just added to the anticipation of Friday's ultimate events: the parade, the pep rally, the game and the dance! Homecoming queen nominations were announced early that week. Jill Lawson was nominated for the seniors and Lindsey Harris was our junior class nomination. Though I liked both girls and couldn't show any favoritism to either of them during Geometry, I had already cast my biased vote for the sophomore class representative. *Natalie!* With Natalie in the running, I didn't care that I didn't know the freshmen queen nomination.

Mr. Grayson announced that the football and cheerleading seniors would be escorted during pregame and that band seniors and the rest of the ceremonial students, like the class representatives and homecoming court, would be during half time. He also informed us that only the seniors were allowed to change into formal attire for the half time escort. Everyone else slated to escort a senior would have to remain in their band uniform or flag uniform. I groaned at my vision of walking next to Broderick in his football jersey while I wore my geeky flag corps uniform, once again proving our division of class and league.

I waited rather impatiently for Broderick to call me that night so I could tell him the bad news of escort attire. His practice went on until seven and I thought for sure he would call me or come over the minute he got home as he usually did, but he never showed, and my phone never rang. Natalie's phone, however, rang off the hook. Since her nomination as the sophomore class homecoming representative, her popularity throughout the school had skyrocketed considerably within those six hours since the nomination was first announced. Many of the phone calls were her friends from the cheering squad, asking and offering advice for homecoming attire. So far, Nat had four prospects for borrowed dresses and only one real prospect for an escort. However, she refused to allow it the minute any of us mentioned his name. *Joey.*

As eight rolled around, her phone finally stopped ringing—Joey being the last caller of the evening. We all quietly listened from the living room as Natalie squirmed uncomfortably on the phone with him in the kitchen. I could only imagine the silence on the other end of the phone, as he waited for her to ask him to escort her. Things between them had been slowly deteriorating. Every kind word and loving glance he made her way was received with a scowl and a snide remark. It would be hard for anyone aside from family to understand how Natalie wasn't exactly being callous. She simply felt betrayed by his feelings toward her.

After everyone had gone to bed, I stayed up only an hour later, waiting for Broderick. Still, he never came.

He didn't show up to pick us up the next morning, either. Obsessively, I called his cell phone but he never answered. Driving by his home on the way to school, I saw his jeep parked in the driveway and I was disheartened with thoughts that he either had lost interest in me or that he had come down with some illness.

After first period practice with the marching band, I collected all of the flags and took them back to the flag closet in the band room. Although our guard captain, Emma Rose, insisted on helping, I refused. I needed to be alone so I could collect my thoughts. I walked along the back entrance of the band room as I heard the bell ring. I rolled my eyes, knowing I would have to face Mr. Muir and his excessive aggravating for my tardiness. This day was getting worse by the minute.

Handling the heavy load of flags, I fumbled for the door knob and dropped three of them when I swatted at what felt like a large June bug flying into the back of my head. The impact stung a bit.

I stopped moving and cocked my head when I thought I heard a distinct "Psst" sound come from behind me. I perked my ears for a moment, but heard nothing. Convinced the sound, too, was a bug buzzing my ear as it flew past me, I tried reaching through the unrolled flag fabrics to get a good grasp on the rusty door knob again. This time something small popped me on the shoulder blade and was quickly followed with a loud and clear, "Psst!"

I dropped all the flags as I spun around this time, rubbing my back to ease the sting. There was only a cluster of trees lining our empty practice field at the backside of our school.

"Jules!" I heard a loud whisper and shielded my eyes from the morning sun. Something moved in the woods. I took several steps across the dewy practice field and closer to the street and found Broderick crouching behind a thick bush and waving to get my attention.

I was somewhat irritated, but full of relief to finally lay my eyes on him. "Broderick! Where were you this morning?" I stepped closer and noticed that he wasn't wearing a shirt. My face twisted in confusion as I took note of my surroundings to make sure no one was watching us. "Where's your *shirt*?"

He hardened his face, filling his expression with uncertainty. "*I. Don't. Know.*" He took a deep breath. "I don't know where *any* of my clothes are," he admitted embarrassed.

His words sent me in a spiral—a whirlwind of confusion and anxiety. Nothing was going to convince me that this was explainable. I crossed my arms, demanding an answer. "What is going on? And *why* are you naked?"

"I think I might have sleepwalked here." He was plainly unsure if he, himself, could believe that.

Shaking my head, I was unable to grasp his predicament. "You *slept* out here? *Here*? Broderick, what the hell...?"

"I crashed as soon as I got home last night and then I woke up over on the football field. That's all I can remember. I've been waiting out here in the bushes hoping I'd get your attention during practice this morning. Jules, you gotta help me," he begged.

Stumped. I had no clue as to how I was going to get him out of here and home safely without him being arrested for indecent exposure. Not to mention the worry of getting my first detention ever for skipping Geometry was tugging at the back of my mind. My head actually began to hurt from all the thinking I was currently doing that I rubbed my head furiously with my hand. Broderick waited helplessly, probably spending most of his brain power on how he got there as opposed to how he was going to get out of there. Then, almost as if a light bulb had clicked on inside my head, I had an idea.

"Wait right here," I said as I jogged back to pick up the flags and get inside the band room.

"I'm not going anywhere," he replied with dry humor, trying to cover his confusion and fear.

I pushed the door open and sloppily re-bundled the flags together, cradling them in my arms. What I dropped, I simply kicked the rest of the way over to the flag closet.

I pulled a chair from the band room and into the storage closet where Mr. Grayson kept the band uniforms and began sifting through the ugly blue and white uniforms on hangers, searching for one with a tag that said extra-large. I nervously would peek around the door and kept my ears alert for anyone who might enter the band room. There was only one large enough uniform for him and I yanked it off the hanger. Before heading back out the door, I grabbed the car keys from my purse.

With the white and blue band uniform in my hands, I ran out, careful to give him as much privacy as the woods would allow. He caught the polyester bundle and as he pulled the pieces apart to look at them I saw the dread grow on his face.

"It's all I could get my hands on. It could have been worse. I could have given you one of our retired flag uniforms—a white southern belle looking skirt and a gold sequined vest." He groaned and he slid his legs into the blue pants with white suspenders.

"Oh yeah…here," I said remembering my car keys as I chucked them over to him. "You can drive my car home. It's parked on the other side of the stadium by the Jet where all of us late birds have to park."

I watched him angrily shove his arms into the white and blue jacket with brass buttons and ropes on the shoulders. He looked down at himself and sighed heavily before he looked up at me in frustration. His perfectly sculpted torso was easily seen with the jacket unbuttoned and despite the complex nature of the current situation I couldn't help but feel excited at his appearance. He was undeniably sexy.

He caught my eyes tracing his chest, down to his abs and I giggled nervously hoping that by joking, it would lighten the mood and possibly divert his attention to something other than my weakness for him. "I do have a thing for guys in uniforms."

"A *band* uniform?"

I just shrugged in response and looked at the time on my phone. "I better get to class before I get suspended like last year. I'd rather not waste another summer with Muir." I started walking backwards as I saw the boy I so normally found sexy and heroic dressed in an ill-fitting marching band uniform. Under any other circumstance, this would have been funny.

"I'll talk to you when I pick you up today," he said and I watched him jog down the road.

The bulk of my troubles had only started.

After getting a tardy slip, I found that I had missed most of Geometry. Mr. Muir gave me my assignment that I would unfortunately have to do as homework.

"Where's Broderick at today, Jules?" Taryn asked as I sat down.

"He's a little under the weather." I lied.

Lindsey leaned in from the other side and tapped my desk with her pencil. "Can I talk to you after class? It's kind of important," she whispered.

It alarmed me that Lindsey Harris would have anything to talk to me about. But as the bell rang she bounced up and practically joined me at the hip.

"This is kind of awkward, but I thought you'd be easier to talk to than Natalie."

"What is it?" I asked her cautiously.

She tossed her fiery red hair behind her shoulders as we walked down the hall slowly. "Is there something going on between your sister and Joey Burnett?"

"No. They're just friends. Why?"

"But you girls are close with him, right?" I nodded. "Do you think he'd be willing to escort me at Homecoming during half time?"

I gasped, literally choking on my own inhalation. "What?"

"I was hoping he would escort me and maybe be my date to the homecoming dance this Friday," she reiterated confidently.

My hopes for Joey and Natalie completely faded at that single moment. I wanted to hunt my sister down in the halls and strangle her for being so foolish and blind.

"There's only one way to find out," I said.

"Would *you* do that for me?" she pleaded.

I felt queasy as she threw me into a position equal to the seventh level of hell. Natalie would never forgive me. But on second thought, she had her fair shot and she blew it. She had obviously made her choice.

"I can put a good word in for you," I offered.

"Thank you so much, Jules!" she squealed as she scurried down the hall to meet up with her other friends.

I wanted to throw up as I passed Natalie in the hall. She waved at me and all I could do was give her a lopsided grin. Secretly, I was angry with Natalie for being so fickle and selfish. It only made sense to stay loyal to the innocent party, which was Joey. I felt compelled to steer him in the right direction at this point so he would no longer waste his time.

The rest of the day was equal to my morning. I scored horribly on my Economics test, and I misplaced my lunch money therefore, I skipped lunch. Assuming I would get to sing the National Anthem at the Homecoming game like I did last year, I was completely taken aback when Mr. Grayson informed me that he had already tapped someone else to do it. Because everything else about the day had sucked, I felt like my dosage of hate from Loni and Casey had tripled. Without Broderick at my side, they were over flowing with the need to call me a bitch at every passing.

Finding Broderick waiting to drive us home—dressed in his own clothes—was a nice change of pace after school. I didn't hesitate placing my lips on his as I climbed into the jeep. The kiss I gave him was a tense kiss, for I could feel that something enigmatic was upon us. Something was wrong. Things were changing all around us—*with* us—and it was out of our control. The fear for our future was abundant within me.

And ultimately, it had been a really crappy day.

"I missed you, too, Jules," he said as Natalie and Joey buckled up in the back seat.

"Hey, Jules?" Joey called out from the back seat. "I was wondering what all you could tell me about Lindsey Harris?"

I grimaced as he spoke of her in front of Natalie and brought me in on it. Broderick shot me a double take, then peered into the rearview mirror. I twisted around in my seat to look at Joey and to catch a glance of Natalie's reaction. It was just as I expected, too. Her usually wide and innocent eyes narrowed in question at me, sensing the betrayal and the guilt I radiated.

"Why are we talking about Lindsey?" Natalie pressed for answers.

Joey saw the opportunity to make her jealous and ran with it. "Word is that she's waiting for me to ask her to the homecoming dance."

Natalie said nothing, but turned beet red in the face.

Joey played as though he was indifferent. "I'm not sure if I'm going to ask her, though. I'm still debating if I even want to go to the dance."

"Joey, homecoming is three days away. You need to be nailing down your plans," Broderick chuckled. It was nice to see the worries disappear from his face and get a small amusement out of the petty, trivial matters concerning normal high school students.

Natalie's tongue was sharp. "Well, you don't want to keep her waiting. It would be rude."

I could see the hurt on my sister's face, but I couldn't fully understand why it was bothering her now. *She had her chance!*

He shot her a glance of duplicity. "I think I will. Thank you."

"Good," she said with a carefree lilt.

After dropping Joey off at his house, we drove to my house. Broderick and I walked through the woods to his house as we left Natalie home to do her homework. I followed him up the steps to his room and set my book bag down just inside the door as he dropped his keys on the table.

"So, Joey and Lindsey, huh?" he asked. "I miss one day and it seems like the whole school is in chaos," he laughed.

"Forget that crap. What's happening to *you*? And don't tell me you were sleepwalking."

He pursed his lips and frowned, turning his back on me. Broderick rocked his head back and let out a huge annoyed sigh. "I've already told you. I don't know what happened so, let's just drop it."

"No." I was firm. "If something is happening to you, it's happening to me. That's how this works. We're a team. Got it?"

He turned to face me. His temper suddenly flared and he angrily stomped toward me causing me to recoil. It was not at all what I had expected.

"What do you want me to tell you, Jules? That the nightmares have returned and are more terrifying than ever? You want me to tell you that I'm so exhausted from lack of sleep and school and football that I feel like I'm falling apart?" The shock at his confessions, made me speechless. I had been too wrapped up in our silly little romance to realize that he, as a human being with unexplainable supernatural capabilities, was struggling internally. I was ashamed. He began to raise his voice at me and like a mad man, his eyes raged with fire. "You want to hear how my mind is so screwed up I don't really know who I am anymore?" He grabbed me by my arms and shook me, shaking the tears loose from the corners of my eyes and letting them spill down onto my cheeks. "Will that make you happy enough to get you to shut up? Will it?" he screamed.

I trembled uncontrollably with fear and hurt. My face felt hard with the contortion of my sobbing as it slowly turned my emotions to anger. I pulled out of his grasp and looked away from him as my nose began to run and mix with the tears that were falling to the floor. He tried to pull me into an embrace, but I pushed him away, causing me to cry harder. I badly wanted to be in his arms and be comforted, but I was livid with his harsh anger toward me. Never, had I seen this side of him before and its appearance shook me to my core.

"Stay the hell away from me," I warned him as I wiped my face and made my way to the door.

"Jules, please. I'm so sorry. I don't know what just happened." He grabbed at me and I pulled away determined to walk out on him. "Stay with me please, I need you! Oh, God! What's happening to me?"

I heard him drop to his knees behind me as I bent down to reach for my belongings. Putting my hand on the door knob, I looked over my shoulder and saw him crumble before my very eyes; pounding his fist on the hard wood floor with all the strength he had left. Something inside of him was tearing him apart. It was killing him and I had been oblivious to it. I let go of my bag and cautiously walked over to him. As soon as I came within reach of him, he gathered me into his arms, grabbing me by the waist and he cried in torture.

Still shaken by his outburst, I tried to take control of my own emotions. I combed my fingers through his hair, softly pawing at his face as I let him cry into my chest. I whispered, "Please, let me help you."

He looked up at me like a lost young boy with bloodshot eyes. "I don't know what's wrong with me. Something in me has changed."

My mind wandered to his nightmares—his premonitions. During my birthday he claimed that he hadn't had a premonition since that night we were chased near Black Mountain.

A lot of people have gone there and not come back the same, Taryn had said. Had a curse been put on him?

"Are they premonitions? What are you seeing?"

"They're just horrible nightmares. I can't make out anything useful in them. They're just terrifying…evil!"

I knelt down to face him, though it only recreated our normal height difference. I held tight to his arms and stared right into his eyes. "We'll figure it out together."

We held onto each other for as long as time would allow, while he continued to whisper apologetically to me.

The apologies were squeezed in throughout the week, in between classes as we walked hand in hand or every evening when we said goodnight to one another in between kisses. His guilt practically suffocated me. I could see unprovoked anger brewing behind his normally calm and loving eyes and would shudder at the next possible release, hoping I would never be the target again. He would never harm me, I was convinced of it. In fact, I could never imagine him raising a hand to anybody. But he was nothing like the boy next door I met and grew to love over the summer, and it wasn't as if he had kept his true nature hidden from me all this time; he was changing before my very eyes. He could see it, too. But it was inescapable and out of his control.

By Friday, he had eased up a little on apologizing and instead to promising me an amazing night after the game, moving us into a more positive direction again in our relationship. However, at that same time, Joey made his friendship no longer available to Natalie. He made it clear to Broderick and me that there were no hard feelings toward us, but that he was now getting a ride to and from school with someone else. That someone else turned out to be Lindsey Harris.

Natalie played indifferent to her loss. And as far as needing an escort for Homecoming, Dad and Broderick offered their services to her, but she declined both of their offers when Cari asked Isaac to do it. I was livid; Natalie, however, was ecstatic. This only made Joey's plan to get her jealous of Lindsey to backfire on him. To compensate for his bruised ego he, in turn, affectionately doted on Lindsey whenever he was sure that Natalie was watching.

Many of us signed out of school early after the homecoming parade. Natalie, Cari, and I had early appointments at Pamela Patterson's salon for the night's occasion. Natalie had her hair elegantly twisted in a mature up-do. I needed to have my roots touched up and Cari had her mom put some pink highlights in her hair, though she wasn't planning on attending the dance afterward. She claimed to have better plans than what the school could ever offer.

The football stadium was packed full of the regular spectators as well as the not-so-regular ones who were simply there to watch their senior son or daughter be escorted for either band, football, cheerleading, or homecoming court. We marched our regular pregame show, but instead of leaving the field at the end of the routine, we awkwardly marched into our new positions on either side of the fifty yard line creating a path to escort the seniors of the football team and the cheerleading squad. I left my flag with Emma Rose and walked to the track in the back of the field where the senior football players and cheerleaders were standing and waiting for their escorts. Some of the escorts, who weren't involved in the other activities were already standing beside their senior companion.

Taryn was standing next to Jackson in a little black dress, dolled up in a ton of makeup, speaking spiritedly. Savannah and Tripp were handing out corsages made from ribbons of the school colors for us to pin on the seniors at the end of the ceremony. I went up and quickly grabbed one and searched the crowd for Broderick. I walked through the mob without much success.

"Jackson, where's Broderick?" I approached him and Taryn after a few minutes of an unsuccessful search.

Jackson looked around in confusion. "I thought he was out here with us."

"I'll keep looking," I said.

"He better hurry up. He's right after me," Jackson warned.

I walked along the line of seniors and their escorts looking for Broderick. When I reached the back of the line I twisted around to skim over the line again. Still nothing. Not only was I quickly becoming disappointed in missing the opportunity to escort Broderick, but I was increasingly getting worried about where he was—for the second time this week.

"Hey, sexy lady," I heard the familiar voice purr very unfamiliar words in my ear, and felt two strong arms curl around my waist from behind me. Fighting the notion to melt in that very moment, I decided to play hard to get and spun around to see Broderick looking down at me with his helmet on. Tall, lean, with the number 86 printed on the chest of his jersey. I noticed that his hair was getting a little too long and shaggy, for it was spilling out a bit from the edges of his helmet. I just couldn't see his face.

"Take your helmet off so I can see you." I smiled up at him.

"Not right now. Give me a minute," he said with faltering composure.

Something was wrong. I lifted up on my toes to get a closer look, only to find a dark face. His face was completely enveloped in shadow.

I gasped in horror and he rubbed my arms, obviously in an attempt to relax me. "It'll be okay. Just give it a minute."

"What are you going to do?"

I heard him chuckle from underneath the helmet. "I'm going to hang here with you and hopefully get control of the matter. Maybe being with you will give me enough peace to manage it. If not, you'll just escort me while I wear my helmet. Not the end of the world, Jules."

I wrapped my arms around his waist, feeling hopeless. My face pressed against the hard padding of his football uniform.

The announcer then invited everyone to stand and remove their hats for the national anthem. I shot a look at Broderick, panicking.

"Relax," he laughed. "No one's going to arrest me or shoot me for leaving my helmet on. It's just this one time of disrespect."

They introduced Isaac Philetos to sing the anthem and I snarled. "*Him?* What the hell? I hate that guy!"

Broderick began to laugh harder at me as Isaac warbled the first line of the song—perfectly, of course.

"Take it easy, Jules. You can't be everywhere. Your job is to make me look like the luckiest guy on the field tonight, not to sing the national anthem." I scowled at his statement and he removed his helmet. His face was very visible and striking as always. He gave me his dimpled grin and winked at me.

"That was quick. How can you tell when you're not in a shadow if you can't see?" I asked as Isaac continued to annoy me with his singing.

He chewed on his thoughts about how to describe it. "It's a tingly sensation. Pins and needles. Like when your foot or arm falls asleep. When I feel that over a particular part of my body, I know I've shifted into a shadow."

"And somehow I bring you enough *peace* to control it?"

"Maybe it's wrong of me, but something about the way you get jealous and pouty entertains me," he chuckled lightheartedly.

"They don't call me Jealous Jules for nothing. Glad to be of service." I rolled my eyes as I faced the center field where Isaac stood singing.

Broderick placed one of his large hands on my shoulder as he stood behind me and leaned in to whisper, "You look beautiful tonight, by the way." His hand slid down my arm, along my back, and then slipped smoothly onto my butt to give a gentle pinch. He had never touched me in such a way! I was shocked at his behavior but even more shocked at the fact that I wasn't too upset, just embarrassed at the prospect that someone else might have seen him do it. Possibly my parents, who were sitting up at the stands!

My lips were parted into a partial smile and my eyes were wide in astonishment as I tried to sternly discipline him. "What the heck has gotten into you?" I fought an onslaught of giggles.

He leaned in again with a confident smirk on his face, "You didn't like that?"

My mouth dropped open as I blushed, "I'm not talking about this with you here." I walked shyly away and led him to where he needed to be in line. Directly behind Jackson and Taryn; I hoped that around company it would enforce better behavior.

"Can we talk about it later tonight, then?" I could practically hear the teasing smile on his face as he walked closely behind me.

"I'm not going to talk about *that* at all," I laughed with embarrassment.

"Good, because I find that actions speak louder than words, anyway."

His behavior was outrageous! I released an awkward bellow as I peered around to see if anyone was eavesdropping on our very personal conversation. This was so unlike him! I was so embarrassed I couldn't even face him.

"So what do you think?" he asked as Isaac left the field and the announcer began the ceremony for the pinning of the seniors.

"I think... that I would have done a better job at the National Anthem," I said tartly.

"You know what I'm talking about."

Broderick and I linked arms and strolled to the center. I pretended to listen intently for his name over the loud speaker, but finally decided that the mature thing would be to face him.

"Broderick..." I began as I turned to him.

"Number eighty-six, Broderick Adam Cooper is the grandson of Evelyn Cooper...." The man announced loudly as we reached the center of the field.

I held my thoughts long enough for his introduction and until we reached our positions next to Jackson and Taryn on the sidelines again. The announcer began to introduce the senior player that was lined up behind us.

Broderick turned to me with a sudden change of heart and smiled in shame. "I'm sorry, Jules. I don't know what's gotten into me. That was vulgar, back there," he motioned his head in reference to the conversation he pressed upon me just seconds before he was announced.

"It just caught me off guard," I consoled him. I didn't want him to feel guilty, I actually enjoyed his advances, but I just wasn't quite sure if I was ready to meet the terms.

"I'm in a weird, frisky mood. Maybe it's the cooler weather or the stress we've been under, but it's far from your fault, unless you take under consideration how unbelievably sexy I find you," he added.

"Please, I'm wearing a blue and gold leotard. There is nothing sexy about this," I begged him off, blushing.

He stared deeply into my eyes, making it impossible for me to look away. "I'm serious, Jules. You don't know what you do to me. I love you, Jules and I would do anything to keep you from shedding another tear... especially the ones I've caused you lately. I want us to be together forever. You need to know these things. I can't tell you enough..." his voice trembled as he broke off and looked into the stadium. I saw his warm breath dissipate into smoke as he exhaled deeply into the cold night air. He composed his nerves then returned to me again. "I want to show you how I feel," he spoke slowly and clearly so I would understand what he was referring to. He blushed as he uttered the words.

I couldn't deny my desire to give in, not that I felt pressured. Naturally, I was intensely curious about sex. Would having sex with him cure the throbbing ache I persistently felt during our most intimate moments together? I wondered if it would hurt as bad as so many of the girls at school swore it did. Would I hate it? Like it? I knew I wanted Broderick to take my virginity; I only warred with the question of *when*. I was supposed to wait until after marriage, but I never really wanted to get married. If I did marry, it wouldn't be anytime soon. Convinced that it would be Broderick I would spend the rest of my life with, what could it possibly hurt to bend the rules a bit? It felt impossible to wait until marriage.

He immediately dropped his helmet that he had tucked under his arm and grabbed me by my face and kissed me zealously in front of the entire stadium. I nervously giggled while he kissed me, as I heard a few whistles and playful jeers come from the stands, wondering if my parents were watching us at this very moment. *Of course they were! Oh, how embarrassing!*

Broderick pulled away smiling eagerly at me.

After the pinning ceremony, I made my way back to the top of the stands where the band sat. I sat alone, watching the game for a long while, sure that my face was glowing from the words Broderick had just spoke to me. I quivered with anticipation at the possibility of when it would happen. My mind raced through scene after scene of my own conjured imaginations, all of which played me out to be sexier and more mature than I really was.

The concern over my original plan to be married before I had sex would trickle in from time to time, but it all vanished when I got the eerie feeling someone was staring at me. I didn't want to be obvious in my paranoia, so I refused to turn my head to the side to see if someone was. I settled instead for my blurry peripheral, only able to make out a tall figure leaning against the rail several rows over and blatantly staring in my direction.

Cari plopped down beside me and immediately began to rattle off something upbeat about homecoming, which was out of her character.

I stared at her blankly. "What are you rambling about?"

"Homecoming! Isn't it just dreamy?" A smile plastered on her face.

"Where is this coming from?"

She then whispered, "I'm saving your ass. Just go with it."

With that she shot a threatening look at the side where I felt I was being watched. I began to turn to see who she was watching, but she punched my arm.

"Don't you dare give him the satisfaction!" she growled.

I frowned with confusion. *Him?*

Again, dependent on my peripheral, I could see that the figure had moved in closer to me.

"He doesn't have the balls to come near me. He knows I'd rip them off," she said with a vile and superior pleasure.

"Oh my gosh! Who in the hell are you talking about?"

"Your favorite ex-boyfriend." She gritted her teeth.

Gavin! My stomach fell flat for only a short moment out of habit before I realized the lack of power he now had over me and the lack of interest I had in him.

"Just ignore him," I said to her. "That *kills* him. He thrives on drama. If we notice him, it'll stroke his ego."

Cari sat with me as we continued to watch a very heated game. It was close and it looked as though tensions were high on the field. A small insecurity began tugging at me. I worried about how Broderick was handling the stress on the field.

At halftime, the remaining band members marched the alternate show and lined up along the fifty yard line as we had practiced. They started with announcing the senior band members for their pinning ceremony. After they were pinned, the homecoming court was ushered in on the floats. First the freshmen girl came in, then Natalie for the sophomores. Isaac was suave in every movement, helping her down from the float and walking her over to her designated position. She beamed with arrogance that the untouchable heartthrob of our school was her escort until Lindsey made her grand entrance. This only proved to me, and everyone else who was paying attention, that not even the perfect Isaac Philetos could stack up against regular guy, Joey Burnett. Not in Natalie's eyes, anyway. I saw the flaming daggers from my sister being stared at Lindsey, who proudly held onto Joey's arm. Natalie set her mouth and stuck out her chin in false conceit. She would never give Joey the satisfaction of knowing that he had, indeed, made her jealous. She would never even admit to herself she felt that way, either.

Lindsey was announced as Homecoming Queen and the crowd cheered, but Natalie didn't seem any more disappointed at her loss of the crown than she did at her loss of Joey. The announcement didn't even affect her.

Cari rejoined me at the hip when the game resumed. She was determined to keep Gavin away from me, though I saw his presence at the game as very nonthreatening. My world revolved around Broderick Cooper and I refused to give the past another look back.

I was preoccupied with the heated competition happening on the field, anyway. Tempers were flaring and there were a few scuffles that needed to be broken up by the referees. I watched Broderick closely as he played fairly, in spite of the unwarranted attempts by the other team to lure him into a fight. The game was too close, and he knew they were simply trying to get all of our good players kicked out of the game for fighting. Erik Peterson was booted out of the game by the third quarter. Joey was even tangled up in a rough shouting match in the fourth quarter. Whatever the other team was doing to antagonize our guys was working.

Things were down to the wire, as the clock had only a few seconds left. The score was tied and our team was desperate to win their homecoming game. Jackson threw the pass to Broderick who caught it with ease, then darted to the goal post. He ducked past several oncoming players and even leaped over two who were tackled to the ground in his path. I watched in bewilderment at how fast his legs moved and with such power, then shook with the recognition that I couldn't see the flesh of his legs at all from where they should be exposed. Moreover, I couldn't see his arms or the hand that tucked the ball tightly to him.

"Oh shit," I whispered in fear, listening for the slightest gasp or scream from someone in the stadium, indicating that I wasn't the only one who had noticed. The roaring cheers made me restless and I climbed over the rail behind me, leaving my flag behind with Cari.

"Hey, where're you going?" she shouted at me.

I ignored her and ran quickly to the same end of the stadium that he was running to on the field. I wasn't even sure what I was going to do, or if I could help him if he was caught, but I had to get to him. I pushed through people that blocked the walkway and finally gave up when I lost sight of Broderick since I stood close to a foot shorter than the sea of bodies that surrounded me.

The home crowd went wild as I heard over the loud speaker, "Jets win! Jets win!!"

I climbed over the rail again and clumsily hopped down the steps to the field. When I reached the light blue rail at the bottom I looked to the end zone and saw a small pile up of players. I gasped, worried if he was hurt and if he was even visible.

Tripping as I climbed over the bottom rail, I scuffed my palms on the paved surface of the track as I tried to break fall with my hands. I brushed my stinging palms on my pants and started running to the field. Soon, I was joined at the flanks by a few obnoxious boys with their faces and chests painted in our school colors. They blew past me and I stopped running when I saw Joey and Jackson help up a very visible Broderick, giving him high fives and congratulatory pats on his backside, as guys do. As I sighed with relief I felt the pain in my side from running so hard and held my hand to it as if it would make the pain go away. I bent over to catch my breath and almost cried in relief that our secret was still safe.

Many other students ran past me and out to the field as I made my way back to the seats to retrieve my flag. Natalie caught my eye and held up her hands in question as if to ask what crazy thing I was doing now. I shook my head at her to let her know that everything was fine.

Cari was waiting for me on the track by the stadium exit with her snare drum strapped to her and my flag in her hand. She laughed, shaking her head at me. "Storming the field. You just had to initiate it didn't you?"

I just shrugged and went along with her assumption. Too exhausted to come up with some other lie.

Knowing Broderick was safe and normal looking at the moment, gave me enough peace of mind to return to my earlier thoughts. The homecoming dance, the flashy red dress, and losing my virginity to Broderick—I was fully consumed.

Upon reaching the F-wing, I slipped into a private stall of the girls' bathroom to shimmy into the dress I had borrowed from Savannah. I quickly did my touch ups, dabbing a bit more blush on my cheeks and gloss on my lips. My hair, miraculously, was still in place, even after my panic-induced run to the field at the end of the game.

I strolled peacefully to the other end of the parking lot and listened to the music from the gymnasium where the dance had already started. I smiled quietly to myself at the impending excitement for the night. Things were perfect again. Everything was falling into place.

Waiting for Broderick, I opened the jeep door and sat inside to keep warm. Ten minutes later, when he still hadn't showed, I became restless. Fewer and fewer students had walked from the stadium to the dance and I began to worry about the condition Broderick was in, imagining his legs or arms or his face completely shadowed over and nowhere to hide but in the locker room. I sat a few minutes longer, until I saw a straggling familiar couple walk from the steps of the stadium and over to the dance.

"Have either of you two seen Broderick?" I asked them.

The girl shook her head.

"I haven't seen him since we left the field. Sorry, Jules," the guy said.

I climbed out of the jeep and walked over to the stadium. Quietly stepping inside the gates, I saw a few custodians cleaning up the stands. I gave a small wave to one of them and directed myself to the locker room. As I approached the door, I debated on whether I should actually enter or not. Instead, I tapped quietly on the door and poked my head through.

"Broderick?" I called with a small voice. "Broderick?" I called again, making the echo louder this time. The only thing I heard was the dripping water from a showerhead or a faucet.

I started to pull the door shut.

"Jules!" he suddenly called out and I flew the door open again. His voice was alarming and I rushed inside to find him.

"Where are you?"

"I'm in the second shower stall on the right."

"Shake the lead out. We're going to miss the dance."

"Uh…" He paused. "I'm sort of having an issue."

I followed his voice down to a row of shower stalls, and sure enough in the second one on the right, there was Broderick in a towel, his entire body as one dark grey mass.

"Broderick!" My eyes became like saucers.

"It's okay. I'm okay," he assured me. "It's just a little out of control right now…."

"It happened on the field, too."

He laughed, "I know. That's why I allowed those guys to sack me, but only *after* I scored."

"I don't find this comical at all."

"Well, stressing out will only make it worse, so humor me please?" he begged.

I stomped to the bench in the center of the room that divided the two rows of shower stalls. "So," I changed my tone, "What do you want to talk about?"

He chuckled at my decision to lighten up and I waited patiently for him to rid himself of the shadow. "Well, for starters… you look beautiful." His voice quietly reverberated in the empty shower hall of the locker room. "I'm sorry for ruining your evening," he said. "But I promise to get it together, just give me a little more time."

"I don't hold you accountable." I gave a lopsided grin.

"You should."

"Broderick, this is just some circumstance. It's not you. This…" —I made one big motion with my arms at him, referring to his shadowshifting— "is not who you are," I explained and then giggled as I caught sight of his fleshy colored toes.

He wriggled them at me. "Keep talking," he urged as his ankles became visible.

"About what?" I felt under pressure.

"Anything. Just let me hear your voice."

"My voice…?" I sat for a moment trying to come up with some sort of dialogue that wouldn't cause him stress. I started to sing our song; it was the first thing that came to my mind. And like magic, the shadow completely lifted before I even reached the chorus. Broderick was leaning his head against the stall as he stood smiling at me. I stopped singing as the visual reality of his captivated attention made me self-conscious.

He walked over and put his arms around me. He didn't look as lanky as he had over the summer. He was bigger now, more sculpted and stronger looking. I blinked several times at the image of him, astounded at the change I had somewhat failed to notice until now.

He pulled me tightly to him and lay his lips on mine, pressing himself hard against me and without any second guessing I grabbed him by the towel and pulled him closer, my fingers lightly tracing the soft skin of his waist and lower back. Regardless of my apprehension as to whether I was fully ready, I knew where this was leading. He moaned through his kissing and slid one of his hands down my torso being sure to graze the side of my breast, but he immediately grabbed me by the waist and pushed me away.

"Did I do something wrong?" I panicked with hurt.

He readjusted his towel and cleared his throat. "Not here. Not right now. You're better than this."

"But, but I thought you… you said… you still *want* me, right?" My insecurity bled through.

His voice shook with edgy enthusiasm as his eyes widened and his face brightened. "Yes, I want you; just not *here*. I want it planned perfectly; just you and me, no interruptions, romantic and in the comfort and sanctity of a bedroom. I don't want it to be some mistake or something unplanned and irresponsible—something that could be talked about in the school halls. Do you understand?" He placed his arms back around me.

He leaned in to kiss me softly and to tease my lips with his tongue. Jumping back again with a secretive smile, accentuating his dimples, he chuckled, "You need to go."

He walked over to his locker and retrieved his black suit as I walked slowly to the door, grinning at my newly discovered power over Broderick Cooper.

"Go, before I violate you," he laughed at his own vulnerability. "I'll meet you at the jeep in a few." He shoved his arms through the crisp white, button up shirt and then rushed over to me for another kiss.

"I'll be there," I giggled.

I heard him joyfully whistling our song as I stepped out of the locker room and walked the steps back up through the stadium. I was once again on cloud nine. Like Broderick, I began humming the same song since I couldn't whistle. He had me so hot in the locker room that the cold air felt energizing against my bare skin. Swinging my arms enthusiastically as I skipped into the parking lot and walked toward the jeep, I could hear a song being played in the gymnasium and it conflicted with my song that I was humming, so I stopped. Looking over at the low lights of the gym, I smiled. As my eyes shifted over to the jeep I became startled that someone was waiting for me beside the jeep. I stopped to look around for other familiar faces to gain some sort of security but saw no one. Clearly a man, the figure was drinking from a bottle and sloppily leaning against the jeep.

I walked a few more paces until I recognized the car parked three spots down from the jeep. *Gavin*!

To prove my strength and bravery, I was going to face Gavin head on. Squaring my shoulders as I walked closer, I groaned loud enough for him to hear me. I closed my eyes, dreading my eventual approach to him. I set my jaw and folded my arms as I approached him. The smell of alcohol on him drifted in the air from more than three feet away.

"What the hell are you doing here, Gavin?"

His eyes softened and he shook his head with a sigh. "You're just as beautiful as I remember... even more."

I could see that he had his confidence buzz right now and wasn't quite drunk yet. "Oh, my gosh! Do you ever quit?"

"I had to see you. I can't get you off of my mind; it was wrong to let you go," he slurred.

"Go home, Gavin. Go home to *Morgan*." My dry tone bled annoyance.

"That last time I saw you... You really hurt me..."

He took a step toward me and I held up a finger as I took a step back. "You stay right there. Do not come any closer if you know what's good for you." I warned. I wasn't really referring to Broderick as much as I was to myself. I was already getting the feeling that left me with the notion to punch his nose in and I didn't have any doubt that I would do it or go down swinging.

"Okay, okay." He held up his hands, still holding the beer bottle in one hand. "Let's just talk. How have you been?"

My face twisted in disbelief. "How's *Morgan*? How's *married* life?" I reminded him curtly again of the girl he left me for.

"We've separated." He lowered his head in shame. "I didn't love her."

Drenched in sarcasm, "Well, stop the presses."

"Please, Jules, you were right and I was wrong. What do you want me to say?"

"'Goodbye' would be great." My patience was wearing thin.

Gavin narrowed his lazy eyes, jealousy brewing within him. "What's the story with you and Cooper, anyway? I saw you escorting him tonight. Could he not get a date?"

"We're together."

"Really? When did that happen?" he sneered.

"On your wedding day." A malicious smile spread across my face. It wasn't entirely true, but I do remember that day as our turning point. That day changed our lives forever.

"Now, if you'll excuse me." I tried to walk past Gavin to hide out inside the jeep until Broderick showed up.

Gavin grabbed me by the arm and swung me around. "He's a rebound for you, Jules. You can't honestly tell me you feel nothing for me, can you?"

"I feel nothing but disgust. How's that for an answer? Now, let go of my arm before I scream," I threatened in a loud voice.

"You need a real man. Someone who knows what he's doing. Cooper is as inexperienced as you are. You need *me*," he boasted.

"Funny, that he's so *inexperienced*. He must be a natural then," I bit back.

He studied my face good and hard, and started shaking his head slowly. "No... you two haven't...no way..." He toyed with the idea that Broderick and I had slept together. It wasn't a rumor I particularly wanted circulating, but couldn't see much harm with it since I had the intention of fulfilling it someday.

"You let him in your pants?" He rudely inquired. I folded my arms stubbornly and stuck out my chin, refusing to answer. "Wow. I can't begin to imagine that train wreck. Virgin on virgin. Do either of you even know where everything's supposed to go?" He derided in a pathetic manner. "A little advice for you, Jules. Use protection, because you don't want to get knocked up when —"

A low growl from behind me startled us and stopped him midsentence. A second later, a massive force came barreling out of nowhere, slamming Gavin's unprepared body harshly against the red Jeep. I shrilled from the initial shock until I saw Broderick pulling back his fist numerous times and smashing it against Gavin's face.

Gavin held up his hands to block the punches as Broderick showed no mercy. Blood gushed out of what appeared to be a very broken nose and busted lip.

My heart raced with fear. "Broderick stop! You'll kill him!"

He grabbed Gavin by the shirt collar and slammed him into the jeep again, calling over his shoulder to me. "You think he cared about how much it hurt you last spring when he was screwing around behind your back? That's bullshit, Jules!"

"I'm over it, Broderick! I don't even care now! Just let him go!" I begged.

Broderick threw him to the ground and kicked him in the ribs. He stood over him and pointed in his face. "Don't you ever speak about her again, you got that? Don't talk to her. Don't even look at her or I will *kill* you."

Gavin lay in the parking lot chuckling at the threat, clearly drunk now—or brain damaged.

Broderick brushed himself off and straightened his tie as he pulled me into the street light to get a look at me. "Did he hurt you?"

Too traumatized with what had just occurred, I just shook my head.

"Hey, Cooper!"

Broderick spun around on his heels to look back and unexpectedly caught the last second of Gavin rocking back and meeting his face with Gavin's fist, busting his lip.

Gavin grabbed his own hand and held it close to his body as he wailed. "Aw, shit! I think I broke my hand!"

I saw the blood drip from Broderick's busted lip and the dazed look in his eyes. He gave his head a quick shake and snapped out of his short-lived daze. He began charging after Gavin again. "Son of a bitch…"

I threw myself on Broderick with every bit of my weight—like a flea on a dog—to keep him from doing any more damage to Gavin. It was terrifying to see him so angry and violent. He was nothing like who I thought he was. In fact, it reminded me more of *my* uncontrollable anger. The only thing that stopped me from acting on most of my fury was my small size.

"Let him go. He's not worth your energy," I spoke quickly as Gavin hobbled cowardly back to his car. "You are better than him, you're better than him." He continued to stare off as Gavin drove away and I pulled his face to look at me. "Let it go. I need you to be calm. For me? Please, Broderick. *Broderick!*"

His cold, hard eyes softened as though he was just made aware of whom he was looking at—noticing me for the first time. He licked the cut on his bottom lip. As he tasted the blood, he reached up and wiped it, holding it away from his face to verify that he was undeniably bleeding.

"Are you okay?" he asked.

"Absolutely not..." My voice trembled.

"Did he hurt you?"

"No! He was only harassing me."

He fumed, "I meant every word I said. I'll kill him if I —"

"*That* is why I'm not okay, Broderick! What has gotten into you?" I asked bewildered. "One minute you're a completely normal guy, next you're naked in the woods behind the school, then you're horny, and next thing, you snap at the smallest irritation, sometimes completely unprovoked, you can't control your shadow anymore... I'm frightened for you. *Of* you."

My words stung him and he dropped his head in defeat. "I just wanted to protect you."

"Right now, the only protection I feel I need is *from* you!"

"Jules, I would never hurt you."

"*I* don't know that. When you get angry like that, it's like you're not even aware of what you're doing. You become a completely different person. I find no comfort in that, you know?" I tried to relay my concerns to him in the most sensitive way possible.

"I'm sorry for scaring you, but I am *not sorry* for protecting you," he said firmly.

I pulled his hand into the light that beamed from the stadium behind us and inspected the cuts on his knuckles from the constant pounding against Gavin's face. "We should probably go home and get ice on your hand and your lip," I said.

"What about the dance?" he asked.

Recoiling at the idea, I lamely shook my head. "Are you insane? I don't wanna go to the dance now." I tucked in my lips remorsefully at the truth of my words. He sighed and put his arm around my shoulders as we started for the jeep.

My chest rattled endlessly with nervous tension during the fifteen minute drive home. I didn't want to judge Broderick for his frenzied behavior, for daily I resisted the temptation to fight back against everyone I felt threatened by: Loni, Casey, Gavin, Isaac. Instead, I wanted to find an excuse for him. He was different than the person I grew to love this summer, and it wasn't of his own accord. It was something out of his control. Like a split personality.

Gavin never pressed charges against Broderick for the assault. My guess was he was drinking underage and didn't want the police involved with that aspect. Whatever the case, I was grateful. According to Taryn and Savannah—the eyes and ears of Crossville—he left town shortly after homecoming.

Broderick turned in his jersey the Monday after Homecoming, declaring that basketball and baseball were no longer future activities for him either. As everyone practically mourned and speculated over the loss of him on the teams, he seemed indifferent and completely unaffected. I thought back to our earlier times in the summer and remembered how he said he would quit if ever it made him unhappy. Apparently, football now made him unhappy.

Worried, I wondered how long it would be before *I* made him unhappy.

Loni Schubert

To MAKE UP FOR interrupting our plans to attend the Homecoming dance, Broderick insisted on taking me to the Halloween Festival downtown on Main Street, particularly the costume dance party for the town teens. He knew the way to my heart was celebrating my all-time favorite holiday.

In my Little Red Riding Hood costume, I walked over to his house where we planned to leave. As I walked up to his house, I could hear Evelyn's voice viciously spewing her unexplainable distaste for me. I stood quietly on the front porch to listen, my cheeks getting hotter by the second.

"She will slip up and this whole town will find out. Is that what you want, Broderick? For people to find out about you? About our family?"

"She's not like that, grandma. She doesn't care about any of it. It doesn't even phase her when I shift," he calmly argued with her.

"Your mother entrusted me with your well-being. How do you think she would feel about that girl if she were still alive today?" She spoke in short, quick flicks of the tongue, making her sound brusque.

I despised being referred to as *that girl*. It made me feel like some sort of tramp, unworthy of a name.

"I think she would love her like I do. Why is it so hard for *you* to accept her?" A lump began forming in my throat, but I wasn't sure if it was because of her coldness toward me or his defensive words.

"She's trouble. Mark my word, Broderick; she's dangerous to you and me both. Being with her is wrong—wrong for *you*, wrong for her."

"Grandma…" I could hear his weary voice drift off.

"It just can't happen." She dropped her voice just enough that I had to lean in closer to the door. "She belongs with someone she can spend the rest of her life with, without any complications."

Her disapproval was crushing. My chest became sore from the heart breaking beneath my ribs.

Broderick immediately countered, "What kind of complications? Will our kids shift, too? Who cares? You make it sound like I'm a disease. What if I told you that we *do* plan to spend the rest of our lives together? What would you say to that?"

I waited for the answer, as I'm sure Broderick was waiting as well, but nothing came. It was silent for several long beats, and then he spoke again, "I love her, grandma, and nothing you say or do will change that." He sighed heavily, I could tell that he was wrapping up his talk with Evelyn, so I bolted back to the driveway to appear as though I was just arriving.

As soon as they opened the door and stepped out onto the porch, I saw Evelyn Cooper standing angrily behind Broderick. The red color on my cheeks surely betrayed me, but I remained nonchalant—as if I knew nothing.

"Happy Halloween!" I cheerily squeaked through the constriction in my throat, greeting the two.

Broderick smiled sweetly at me as Evelyn shut the door without uttering a word in my direction.

He sprinted to my side at my deteriorating spirit. "She hasn't been feeling well lately. Don't let her get to you." He put his arm around me.

Puffing out a quick frustrating breath, "You know what kills me? I *want* to hate her for hating me first. I *want* to act like I don't care she doesn't like me. But honestly, I would do almost anything to get her to approve of me."

I looked up at Broderick to apologize for speaking those words and saw the tall boy standing over me in a flannel lumberjack-like shirt, a toboggan, and holding a plastic axe over one shoulder. My face contorted in incomprehension. "Wait a minute… What are you supposed to be?"

"The woodsman," he announced proudly.

"No! You're supposed to be the wolf! The wolf! Not the woodsman. No one's going to get it!"

He crouched down to get better eye contact with me. "Jules, is it that important to you?"

"It was," I snipped. "Why didn't you just dress up like the wolf to begin with?"

He pulled back a corner of his sooth lips. "Because I'm not the bad guy. I'm the woodsman—your hero. I'm here to *protect* you from the wolf."

I studied him with a pouty look, but a smile slowly crept upon my face. He wasn't the bad guy and he was very much my hero; I couldn't argue with that. I loved the boyish charm he emitted standing proudly as my woodsman.

"You may as well be the wolf, with your shaggy hair, though," I quipped teasingly as I climbed into his jeep.

In the corner of my eye I saw him self-consciously reach up to feel the ends of his hair jutting out from the cap he wore on his head as he muttered, "I just had it cut last week."

"Let's go, hero," I said to him out the open driver's side window.

Parking three blocks away from the old warehouse that the dance was going to be held in, my "woodsman" and I walked hand in hand through the festival full of costumed children on Main Street. I caught myself involuntarily shuddering as I saw Lucas Reiser and Ingrid Silivasi with a few of their Goth-looking friends standing nearby. Something about seeing them on the eve of Halloween as they blended under the shadows of the business awnings with their dark clothes and black hair made my skin crawl. The only thing that jumped out to me from their dark group was their bleak white skin, unimaginably pale. Ingrid was the only one with some sort of color to her skin. As we passed the haunted house and made our way to the warehouse dance, my neck felt strained as I twisted around to keep my eye on them.

The music was booming through the walls and windows as we approached the old warehouse. The room was filled with a synthetic fog and an occasional strobe light effect. Bales of hay were placed all over for people to sit. The décor looked like the rejects from the haunted house one block over, but I was delighted with the atmosphere.

Despite the thundering music, I could hear Savannah squeal the moment she saw us enter.

"Isn't this so cool?" She ran to me with a wide grin on her face. Tripp trailed behind her; I was beginning to wonder if he had a personality beyond just being her lap dog.

I was about to agree when a costumed jester approached us, causing me to flinch and recoil. Although I knew it was Cari, the painted face alarmed me. She looked too much like a clown. Clowns rank number one in my list of creepiness.

"Well, well, well," Cari began. "If it isn't Little Red Riding Hood and... Paul Bunyan?"

I punched Broderick gently in the arm. "I told you no one would get it."

He smirked playfully at Cari. "I'm Little Red's hero, the woodsman. And you are... The Joker?" he playfully lashed back at her.

"Touché." Cari gave a small laugh as she rolled her eyes and leaned in to Savannah. "Jules and her Boy Scout."

Savannah's attention was directed elsewhere to someone behind me. We all turned around to stare, not fully realizing that we were far from inconspicuous, and saw Erik Peterson walk in with Loni Schubert. He was clad in a werewolf costume, the same one I had envisioned Broderick wearing. Loni was a Little Red Riding Hood of her own style. Unlike my modest, child's size dress with a blood red cloak to match, tights and black loafers, she was wearing the same idea but styled more like a French maid's uniform and her fishnet panty hose perfectly matched her much smaller version of my cloak that was the exact same color of her three inch heels. The sexiest thing about my costume was the black bodice laced from the outside of the blouse; I only wish I had the boobs to need that kind of support. She was the embodiment of Isaac's analysis of the sexual awakening of Little Red Riding Hood. My Little Red probably hadn't even had a boyfriend as of yet. *My* Little Red still believed that boys had cooties.

Loni narrowed her eyes at me when she took note of us staring. As she and Erik walked past our nosy crowd, she leaned toward and whispered, "Bitch!" Her apple red lips glistened with gloss, reflecting off of the disco ball in the center of the room. She over enunciated, curling back her lips and showing her perfectly straight and white teeth.

Cari threw down her merotte and began to charge. "Oh, that is it! She is going down hard!" Savannah and I reached to grab her, but Broderick stopped her instead.

"Let go of me, Boy Scout!" she seethed.

"Cool down, Patterson," he said, as his own face flushed a raging tomato red from anger.

I didn't have the balls to inform Cari or Broderick that since the beginning of this school year, Loni had singled me out in the hall, every time we would pass each other, uttering that same term of loathing to me.

Cari straightened out her costume, apparently giving up the idea of attacking Loni at this moment. I had no doubts she would follow through with her threat at another time, another place.

The mood changed with the song in an instant.

"Ooh! I love this song! Let's dance!" Savannah pulled Tripp onto the dance floor, before he could object, leaving the three of us behind.

"So, where's twisted sister tonight?" Cari asked as she bent over to pick up her merotte to complete her costume again.

"She's out rolling yards with Berta and some of their other friends. Hope Sheriff Burnett doesn't catch them," I said.

"Your dad would skin her alive," Broderick added.

We looked around to observe all of the creative costumes flowing through the room. Taryn and Jackson were dressed as Dorothy and the

Scarecrow from the Wizard of Oz, and I wondered if he had simply lost a bet with her. As usual, I saw tons of princesses, rockers and movie characters; Cari had a snide comment for every one of them until Isaac entered into the room dressed as a vampire, in a simple black suit, nothing cheesy like a cape.

"Now, *that* is *hot*." Cari grinned hungrily at him.

He looked beautiful and sexier with his fangs, as much as I hated admitting it. Isaac scanned the room, and when our eyes met, the corner of his lip pulled back in a pleasing smirk. I scowled in return.

"It's unoriginal," I stated flatly as the song changed again. I turned to Broderick to ask him to dance with me, but saw that his brow was beaded in sweat and he swiftly became as pale as a vampire. "Are you okay?"

He shook his head and removed his cap. "I'm not feeling very well all of the sudden."

"Well, then let's leave. We can just go home and hand out candy and watch scary movies. I love doing that…"

"I want you to have fun." He then motioned his head to behind me. "Joey'll dance with you."

Joey, dressed as a devil, slid up behind me and wrapped his arms around my shoulders and bounced erratically with the beat. "Wanna dance with the best?"

Lindsey stepped beside me wearing an angel costume and an encouraging smile. "He's all yours," she said with a wild look in her eyes, obviously glad she wouldn't have to join him for this song.

Joey jerked me onto the dance floor, clumsily spinning me around. He was uncoordinated and obnoxious, but loads of fun. He took none of his gangly moves seriously, which was perfect for me. Next to him, I looked graceful. When the DJ slowed the music down I began to thank Joey for the dance, but he grabbed me by the wrist and held up his finger at Lindsey who patiently waited next to Savannah, Tripp, and Cari. Broderick was nowhere to be found. I squeezed my eyes tighter to try and filter through the synthetic fog and dim red lighting, looking for him.

Gone.

"I need to talk to you for a quick minute, Jules."

"Sure, Joey."

He paused uneasily, before continuing. "Has Nat said anything to you about me? Lately? *Anything?*"

I gave him a sympathetic smile. "I can see that she misses you."

He looked at me disbelievingly. "Sure, she does."

"Joey, she's my sister. I know her better than anyone else in this world. *She misses you.*" It was quiet for a moment between us as I tried to gather some sound advice. None would come. "Talk to her, Joey."

He was clearly defeated. "I'm with Lindsey now."

"Apparently your heart isn't! Not if you're still asking me about my sister."

"You know as well as I do that she would have dropped me like a bad habit, the minute my feelings became clear. Hell, that's exactly what happened! Somehow, she figured it out," he lamented loudly. He pressed his lips together in clear contemplation over something that was eating at him.

"I think Lindsey's a wonderful person. Really I do, but you and Natalie…" I began to debate out loud. There was something undeniably fated about Joey and my sister. "… the two of you had this amazing chemistry and—"

"I dream about her all the time," he whispered into my ear, barely audible over the soaring music.

I was uneasy with the direction our conversation had turned. Between Broderick's precognition and the common joke of a male's routine of wet dreams, I didn't want any part of Joey's nightly subconscious. "Look, Joey, you should probably keep this kind of stuff to yourself. Start a journal or something."

He continued anyway, "Everything about her eyes says that she loves me, too. I can practically hear her saying the words with her glances. That look, I see it in the halls every day and —"

I frowned at his delusion. "It's just a dream. As much as she misses you, she would never admit that she loves you. She would flat out deny it."

He nodded slowly. "I would wait for Nat, if I knew for sure that she would eventually come to me. But she isn't going to, so I need to…" he searched for the right word.

"*Settle?*" I asked with a cringe.

"Yeah," he remorsefully agreed. "I like Lindsey a lot. But I'd rather be with Nat."

"I know." The song was winding down and Lindsey was fast approaching.

"Thanks, for listening, Jules; I just needed to get it off my chest."

"Any time you need to talk, Joey…"

Lindsey grinned sheepishly. "Enjoy the dance?" She was laughing with her eyebrows raised, waiting for me to make a snide remark about Joey's dancing.

"Yeah, thanks for lending me your boyfriend," I chimed.

The music remained slow and Joey pulled her into a clumsy embrace. "The pleasure was all mine, *really*." She rolled her eyes giggling in delight as he dragged her into the middle of the dance floor.

I walked over to Savannah and Tripp. "Have either of you two seen Broderick?"

"Not since he left for the restroom a few minutes ago. Have you seen the ghoulies?" Savannah pointed over to a dark corner of the room.

Looking over to where Savannah pointed, I gasped to find Lucas Reiser, Ingrid Silivasi, and their group of friends standing quietly, watching everyone. They *did* look like ghouls. All were unmoving, like they had been earlier outside under the awning. Watching closely. Calculating, as if every one of us on the dance floor was their prey. A chill ran up my spine and I released a hard shiver.

"Happy Halloween, freaks," I muttered. Lucas stared directly at me as if he heard my cruel words over the booming music. Savannah and Tripp just laughed at the coincidence. I shook from another chill that ran up my spine.

I jumped back to my previous thought quickly. "I'm going to look for Broderick. If you see him, tell him I'm looking for him."

Pushing my way through swaying couples, Lucas's group of ghouls was so motionless they captured my stare—contrasting with the moving crowd of the room. I watched the chilling crew closely as I inched nearer to the corridor where the restroom signs pointed down a dark hallway. Their eyes trailed along with my movement. A shiver ran through my body as I found their behavior beyond unnatural.

I strolled to the beat of the music down the dark hallway till I reached the restrooms. I waited only a few seconds to see if Broderick would emerge from the men's room before I realized that I needed to use the facilities as well. Four girls, all dressed in sexy super hero costumes, exited the restroom giggling, allowing enough light in the hall to motivate me to dash through and out of the darkness and into the supposed safety of the well-lit restroom.

I crept in and quietly went about my business. One of the toilets continued to run as a faucet dripped, echoing the sound. It was unsettling to be in such a quiet room when down the hall it sounded like thunder. Eerie, as the memory of Lucas's cold stare crept back into my mind.

The music from down the hall became louder all of a sudden then quieted as the door creaked, alerting me that someone had just walked in the restroom. I heard shuffling two stalls down and out of sheer curiosity, I leaned far over as I sat on the toilet, to look under the stall. Standing toe to toe were a pair of red, three inch heels with white fishnet stockings and a pair of black shoes with black slacks.

Shit! It's Loni! I drew my feet up and crouched quietly on the toilet seat as I pulled up my panties. I heard low whispers and then a zipper. Waiting quietly, I steadied my breathing, abhorring the entrapment of my situation. *So awkward!* A few banging noises, grunts, and several moans later, I heard the stall door open and one set of feet walk out the door, allowing the loud music to bleed into the room momentarily again. I set my feet down and saw the lonely red heels with the fishnets laden legs standing in the stall, motionless. Unsure of the "after-sex" activities she probably need to do, I figured that it would buy me enough time to quickly wash my hands and bolt out of there.

Grimacing, I tried to sneak out undetected but dropped my shoulders with the realization that I was going to have to flush. I flushed the toilet and hurried out the stall to wash my hands. The coast was clear as I washed and dried my hands. As I turned the faucet off and looked up into the mirror, I saw Sleazy Red Riding Hood staring back at me with daggers in her eyes. I gasped out of the initial shock of seeing another's face behind my reflection and spun around to confront her.

"Loni." I gulped.

She pressed her lips together in a superior smile as she looked me up and down. "Did you snoop around to find out what I'd be wearing?"

Her look and tone were cunning and despite the fear and nervousness I felt in the pit of my stomach, I was filling with anger. *Don't cry, don't cry, don't cry...* I wouldn't give her the satisfaction of my tears and I was determined to put her in her place, though my voice was shaky.

"No! Not at all!" I exclaimed with a faux-innocence. "I'm dressed as Little Red Riding Hood, not a hooker."

My mouth began to mimic her superiority while I was clenching my teeth, bracing myself. I was ready to fight. I didn't want her to hit first, but I didn't want to start it, either. I waited observantly to see if she would shift her body in attack mode. I would just have to be quicker, although the end result would probably still be me hitting the floor.

"Cute." She tightened her eyes and leaned in close to my face. My fists clenched tightly at this point, ready to throw the first punch. "I want you to know I have every intention of making your last two years of school here miserable. A complete living hell." Her words were crisp and clear.

"Well, you're off to a good start; your breath is making me nauseous." I released a cheeky laugh with my response.

Like a viper, Loni's assault was swift and precise. The stinging sensation of her five fingers and palm burned on my left cheek before I even realized what had happened. I was looking in her blue eyes one minute, then the next I was looking at the dirty bathroom floor to my right. Slapping me so hard, she had knocked my head to one side; my brains and teeth felt as though they were vibrating from the contact.

I wanted to rub my cheek to ease the pain, but was too stubborn to give her the pleasure of seeing any sort of reaction. Instead, I set my jaw and slowly turned my face to gain eye contact with her again. I had seen it in so many movies, and the dramatic approach had always given the effect of strength and grit.

The monster that had settled quietly inside of me for months was slowly awakening. "You touch me again and *I will kill you.*"

She smiled smugly and walked away. As she paraded over to the bathroom exit, I saw three familiar girls from school dressed in poodle skirts watching us from the door. I wondered how long they had been standing there. I didn't even notice the loud music creep in to announce the door's breach. Loni rudely pushed through the girls and swept out of the door and down the long dark hallway. One of the girls cursed at her.

I turned to the sink to avoid eye contact with these girls. Everything inside me shook from anger. I took several deep breaths trying to calm myself until I could hear the girls go into their respective stalls and continue talking.

Setting out again to find Broderick, I walked slowly down the long, dark hall listening to every one of my small echoing steps that walked in beat to the music from the dance hall. It was an eerie electric guitar playing broken minor chords. Unsettling, yet appealing; perfect for Halloween, but obnoxiously loud, even where I stood. The voice slowly crept through the lyrics like a dark moan. When the song smashed into a full heavy metal piece, it completely rattled my nerves. I closed my eyes momentarily to drown out the noise with my own thoughtful concentration. My cheek continued to burn from where Loni had slapped me.

Despite the crowded room down the hall, I felt alone and defenseless in the silent shadows. My steps soon were accompanied with a low panting and I stopped walking to listen carefully. My heart was racing wildly out of control, but my breathing was calm. The sound seemed to be coming from only a few paces behind me. The room became colder, and I shivered in one sudden jerk. Pulling the red cape around my arms for warmth, I felt something faintly brush against my hair that was pulled together over my shoulder. I jumped, twisting around to face the empty darkness of the room.

"Broderick?" Giving time for my eyes to adjust, I searched for a small outline of Broderick in case he had shifted in a shadow. Nothing. He wasn't there and there was no comfort in this darkness either. The presence I felt was evil incarnate. I could sense its madness. Its hunger to inflict pain. Grabbing Broderick's medallion that hung around my neck for protection, I blindly searched the hall behind me for a hint of some existence, but froze as I felt a cold solid mass move in close to the nape of my exposed neck. I was too scared to move until I heard air being sucked away from me, like a small wind tunnel. The sound of someone inhaling, smelling me.

Unbridled fear shot through my veins and a scream climbed into my throat as I turned to run into the dance hall. The cold mass remained close. *Oh God! I'm not going to make it!* I could sense it reaching out for me! *Feel* its cold grasp close in around me. The sound of clothing or hairs on its body—or *something*—was bristling only inches away from me. I could faintly hear it!

The door to the restroom swung open on the other end of the hall, more light breaking through, and the three girls in poodle skirts emerged, walking out of the restroom, bellowing in laughter. Almost simultaneously, a gust of wind blew past me in an upward motion, causing me to look over my shoulder, my cape twisting with the sudden breeze. I heaved a large sigh at the relief of no longer being alone in the dark and rushed headlong into the crowded swaying bodies.

I scanned the room for Broderick and Cari. Instead, I bumped into Casey Barnes, who was standing in the doorway that divided the dark hallway from the dance floor. Dressed as a rocker, she turned to face me, and I quickly ducked behind someone else to prevent having a confrontation with her. The one I had just had with Loni was enough for one night, and I couldn't put enough distance between me and the dark hallway.

Walking through the crowded dance hall, someone grabbed me gently by the wrist and swung me around into an embrace. I relaxed with the assumption that it was Broderick, until I faced the culprit. Isaac slid his free arm around my tiny waist and pressed his body close to mine.

In spite of my relief to be with someone I believed would protect me, though I preferred my own boyfriend, I groaned. "You are so annoying!"

He grinned. "Dance with me, Little Red Riding Hood," he gently charmed.

"I'm looking for Broderick," I said, pulling my hand out of his and trying to turn away from his grasp from around my waist. I searched the room urgently for Broderick, shaken from what I had just experienced in the hall. *What did I just experience?*

"He'll get you soon enough. Right now, it's my turn." He smoothly recaptured and enveloped my hand with his again as we swayed to the music, though I was hardly in the mindset of dancing. "When do you think you'll give up this charade of hating me?" he teased.

"Who said it was a charade?"

He laughed gleefully at my remark, curling his lips into a dazzling smile with his costume fangs. He must have spent good money on them, because they weren't like the plastic mouthpieces you find in supermarkets. They were probably porcelain and had temporary cement to hold them in place. Effective, they appeared real.

Pouting, I wanted him to let me go so I could find Broderick. Isaac reached over and brushed his fingers lightly against my raw cheek. His cold fingers felt good against the offense that remained but I recoiled in a jerking motion as a result of Isaac feeling the invitation to ever touch me in such a way.

"What the hell...?" I frowned.

"Someone has hurt you," he growled with eyes of fury as he stared at Loni's hand imprint on my face. "*Who* was it? Was it Broderick?"

"Of course not!" I reached up to lightly rub the mark on my cheek.

"Your tenacity intrigues me," he said.

I twisted out of his grasp and walked away. I heard his laugh drift farther and farther away as I made it off the dance floor. There were more important things on my mind than keeping Isaac Philetos entertained.

"Where have you been?" Cari's voice barely carried over the music and I spun around to see her unsettling, painted face.

"Where have *I* been? Where have *you* been? I danced with Joey and came back and you and Broderick were gone."

She held up her hands to claim her innocence. "Not that I thought I had to run it by you, 'Mom', but I left for a bit to go to the haunted house down the block, which, by the way, was totally lame." She tapped her merotte against my forehead causing it to sting. "And I'm not Boy Scout's keeper."

She skimmed the room and froze as she caught sight of Lucas and Ingrid's line of zombies watching everyone. "God, that's enough to make even *my* blood run cold." She looked back at me and her mouth dropped. "What the…." I grimaced knowing she could see the hand print. "Loni," she seethed through gritted teeth. "Where the hell is she?"

Despite my plea for her to forget about it, she scanned the room for Loni Schubert and walked off to continue her search.

This night was becoming a bust. Joey was obviously heartbroken over Natalie, and in return could break Lindsey's heart, and I didn't want that, either. Savannah was so far up Tripp's butt lately, she had practically become an imaginary friend. Loni Schubert was out for my blood, which meant Cari was out for hers. I had to dance with Isaac Philetos, the world's biggest asshole. And my boyfriend was missing in action. I was scared shitless in the back hall and still hadn't figured out what precisely had happened.

The bale of hay that I was sitting on made my thighs itchy as I continued examining the room for Broderick. I wanted to be angry with him, but more than anything I was worried. It was just like the time when he failed to show and found himself naked in the woods behind our school.

Suddenly, my eyes were veiled by two hands from behind me. Before he could speak, I smelled his familiar and pleasant scent… and something else? There was a twinge of difference in his scent, I was positive. Almost earthy, like the clean air in a pine forest. Still, I knew it was him and smiled.

"Guess who," he whispered sweetly behind me.

"Paul Bunyan!" I spun around laughing.

"I prefer sexy woodsman." Broderick smiled crookedly. He climbed on the bale and sat next to me. "Sorry I had to leave for a minute. I wasn't feeling too good."

"Do I need to take you home?" I was worried.

He shook his head. "It's just a headache. I stepped outside to get some fresh air, but I came back just in time to see Isaac Philetos pawing my girlfriend." He sounded quite unhappy.

"Sorry. He pulled me on the floor with him. I think he does these things to annoy me."

"And to annoy me." He frowned. "I don't trust him."

"And I don't like him, so there shouldn't be a problem," I said.

Broderick sat quietly for a moment then turned to smile at me. "Dance with me."

He grabbed my hand and I followed him onto the dance floor. He held me close to his thick chest and I listened to every beat of his heart as we joined the mass of swaying couples.

At the end of the song, I shouted to Broderick through the loud music. "I should try to find Cari. She's on the warpath again, and I need to stop her before she does anything stupid."

"Loni?" he asked. I nodded and did my usual lip snarl.

"Erik's right over there; she should still be here somewhere." Broderick pointed to the angry looking Erik Peterson. Among the mass on the dance floor, Erik seemed to be inconvenienced by a desperate hunt, looking for somebody.

Because of the current song selection, the strobe lights flickered fiercely, and Broderick squeezed his eyes tightly. I called to him over the music. "Are you okay?"

He looked as though he was in pain as he pinched the bridge of his nose and rubbed his finger and thumb outward to massage his eyes. I stared and waited for an answer until he nodded.

The music continued to build, pounding my ears with harsh guitar licks and screams. I saw several tall boys standing around Savannah and Tripp. They listened attentively to someone not within my sight. Blotted out by all the larger bodies that circled around her, I pressed closer as I tried to concentrate through the insufferable music to hear what they were saying.

"She was supposed to meet me over there," I heard the girl's high pitched whine as she pointed over to the dark corridor that led to the restrooms. I stretched up on my toes to see a worried Casey Barnes.

"Maybe she left already," Tripp suggested to her.

"No. She came here with Erik, and he hasn't seen her since she went to the restroom. She was supposed to meet me so we could go to the haunted house together, but she never showed," Casey explained.

"I'm sorry, Casey. We haven't seen her," Savannah said sympathetically. I hate it when my friends are friendly to the people I despise.

"Well, if you see her, tell her I'm looking for her, *please?*"

The group nodded as Casey ran over to the next crowd of people.

"Who's missing?" I asked Broderick, though I was pretty sure I knew who it was.

"Your favorite person, Loni," he said with a dry chuckle.

"Good. Maybe she'll stay missing," I spat. Broderick began looking pale again and I took his hand and pleaded in his case. "Let's go home." Finally, he agreed.

Shadows

LONI SCHUBERT NEVER CAME home. Her eerie disappearance left the school feeling numb. Erik and Casey were pulled from classes on and off throughout the week to answer questions in hopes to find her whereabouts. Our town became filled with uncertainty. By the end of that first week in November, our uncertainty was increased to a level of utter dread when her body was found crammed in a dumpster behind a local diner.

Being Sheriff Burnett's son, Joey shared what details he had acquired with the rest of us. He had probably been snooping around for details of her search at every chance he got. He was too much like his father. He called our small group of friends to meet him early one morning before school.

Pulling up next to the blue angel jet, erected on a concrete slab near the football field, Savannah and Tripp showed up only seconds after us. This parking lot was separate from the main one and was rarely used— usually when students arrived late and the main lot was already full. We waited together in bundled nerves until we saw Joey in his old truck with

Lindsey sitting close by him, burying her head in his chest as he pulled in. Natalie's head dropped as she saw him wrap his arms around her for comfort.

Standing next to me, Broderick was stoic still didn't look well. He was pale and his face was drawn from stress, exhaustion, and still... something else. Something I couldn't quite put my finger on. Beyond what was currently happening in our quiet little town, something in his eyes wasn't matching up to the boy I thought I knew. The twinkle was gone. No longer able to provoke the pull of his lips that allowed me a glimpse at his dimples, I watched him carefully hide the secret laying within his eyes as he drove us to school. The disappearance of Loni Schubert had overshadowed the tense nature that had become our relationship in the last few days. Whatever it was that was bothering him, I prayed he would tell me or that it would simply go away.

Joey stepped out of his truck and helped Lindsey out of her side as well.

"Joey, what exactly happened?" Natalie could clearly see the devastation on his face and she ran to him. Broderick held tightly to my hand as we approached our friends.

Joey shook his head. "Wait till the others get here. Jackson and Taryn aren't coming to school today. Taryn's a freakin' mess."

Cari suddenly pulled her little sedan in next to Tripp's SUV. Then a short few seconds later, Isaac on his motorcycle.

Who invited him? I thought sourly.

"What's the story?" Cari whispered as she stepped to my side. I only shrugged.

Joey shivered in a cold sweat and became white around the lips. Lindsey collapsed, covering her face, shivering and crying as she sat on the cold concrete base that held the plane. He stood near her, reaching over to place his hand on her shoulders as he spoke. The rest of us huddled together to stay warm against the cold, late-autumn morning breeze.

"My dad will kill me if he finds out I said anything to y'all, so I need to know right now that we're all at an understanding. None of this gets out to anyone else—not our families, our friends... *Nobody*. Anything said, stays right here." We all nodded in agreement and Joey started. "The call came last night." His voice was soft as he shook his head in denial. "… She had been beaten, violated… completely ripped open—drained of all her blood. She's been dead for days."

Joey's voice, verbally confirming that the girl I hated was dead, drained me of any feeling or liveliness my body could obtain. I stood entranced at the Blue Angel's jet, wondering what Loni's last remaining minutes were like. Who she saw, what they did to her… did she think of Erik or her family? Was she scared or completely unaware of what was going to happen to her?

"Her decaying stench was detected when a diner employee was throwing out the garbage at closing time. It was an unfamiliar smell—said it was worse than any rotting food that had accumulated in there, so he immediately investigated the garbage bin with a flashlight and decided it was time for the local authorities to take over when he came across her feet, one of them missing a shoe." Joey continued, but I phased out of the present and into the past. All I could think about were her red high heels, seeing them in the stall of the restroom. Oddly, the shoes made it all so realistic to me. One of them was missing, left behind somewhere, never to be in Loni's closet or worn again. That shoe became as lifeless as Loni.

The police are going to start pulling witnesses from the school today for questioning. They have already detained Erik."

My eyes widened. "Is he a suspect?"

"He's a person of interest," Joey said gravely.

My initial reaction was shock, now beyond that I was being bombarded with many feelings. At the top of them was fear. I have never personally known a murder victim. That fact gave me the uncanny feeling and put truth to the age old theory that it could've easily been me, especially as I thought through that night at the dance. I was thankful to be alive and well, that I just had a full week of breathing, eating left over Halloween candy, spending time with my family, and struggling through a deteriorating relationship with my boyfriend. These things I naturally took for granted. And considering those very things, I felt sad for Loni and her family. She was taken from them brutally and suddenly; too young. Statistically speaking, she hadn't even lived half of her life yet.

Guilt was also matted together with shock. Not for anything I personally had to do with her disappearance or murder, but for feeling a little relieved that my days of enduring her hatred were over. I wanted to convince myself I would endure them a hundred fold for her to have her life again, but I couldn't fool myself. I was thankful I would never hear her call me a bitch again or to have her fierce blue eyes burn through me, full of loathing. She could no longer remind me of how insensitive I was to her feelings last year when I started dating Gavin behind her back.

I looked around at my friends for a clue as to how I should react. They were each taking this hard in their own way. Natalie remained frozen, unable to speak. Her eyes were wide in shock and her skin, which was usually a sun kissed glow, was ashen—white as a ghost. And Broderick. He was… *blank*. I could no longer read him, and it frustrated me to no end. It also scared me.

Furiously trembling with the knowledge of what had become of Loni Schubert, I realized the possibility I may have been one of the last few people to see her alive. Casey and Erik last saw her when she left the restroom. Loni had made it to the restroom that night, my cheek could attest to that. My brain began piecing it all together. *She never made it out of the hall!* I remembered bumping into Casey after I left the restroom just outside the hall. I became nauseous as I realized that I could very well be a person of interest, especially after our heated argument that night!

My guilty eyes shot up to see if anyone was looking at me accusingly, but instead I found Cari slowly straighten out of our tightly formed huddle, her shameful eyes darted at mine then shifting dreadfully around at the others. Isaac didn't appear as solid and arrogant as usual, either.

"Shit! Shit!" Cari angrily repeated under her breath countless times as she restlessly paced back and forth from outside our huddle.

"I need to call my dad," I whispered to Broderick, pulling out my cell phone.

"I'll call him," he said. "I need to call my grandmother, anyway, and fill her in on what's going on." He began dialing quickly.

I climbed to my feet and strolled over to Cari. Through gritted teeth, quietly to keep the others from over hearing, I asked heatedly, "Where the heck were you that night after you left me to look for her?"

"Smoking outside. Why? Did you need a cigarette, too?" she remarked sardonically.

"Quit joking," I snapped.

Cari threw down her newly lit cigarette and stomped on it. "Damn it, I'm not joking. I went out for a smoke."

"Did you ever find her?" I pursed my lips accusingly.

Cari put her hand on her hip and narrowed her eyes. "What are you implying, Jules? That *I* had something to do with her disappearance? That *I* killed her? You can believe anything you want to, but if that's what you truly believe then you apparently don't know me at all. I couldn't find the little shit. I looked high and low; all over the damn place for her. After she slapped you…"

"She *hit* you?" Broderick hadn't gone far when he heard this and furiously stepped around to stand tall behind Cari to get my full undivided attention.

I was flabbergasted, never wanting him to know. "Uh… well, yeah, but…."

Cari continued her alibi, more seriously now. "I never found her. I thought she was hiding from me."

"Why didn't you come and get me when she hit you?" Broderick demanded.

Cari was standing between us, completely forgotten now.

"I couldn't find you. And she didn't hit me; she *slapped* me," I corrected.

"Jules, what's the difference?"

I looked over at our friends; silence fell where they stood. All of them were staring at us with speculative and confused expressions.

Broderick stood over me, studied me, and then let out a deep sigh. "Loni knew the minute Cari found out about this, she was in big trouble.

She was scared of Cari catching her, or *me* catching her." Broderick shook with anger, his recent unreadable eyes filled with rage—very readable now.

"I was outside smoking," Cari lamely stated again, this time with sincerity, adamant about convincing us of her innocence. "I swear, Jules. I couldn't find her."

I searched her face for the slightest trace of truth to her words.

"Jules, you don't really think I could do something so sadistic, do you?" she pleaded for my loyalty in believing her.

"No," I breathed. I knew her well enough to know that she wasn't some brutal monster. She was just grumpy all the time.

"Thank you," she sighed in relief as she began digging in her purse for another cigarette, which she quickly lit up and began puffing away on.

Joey came barreling toward me with a grim look. "Jules, you had a run in with Loni that night?"

I nodded slowly. "Shortly after you and I danced."

He shot a glance to Broderick, who immediately wrapped a protective arm around me. "Don't you even look at her that way," he threatened.

"Guys, this is not the time to start pointing fingers at one another!" Natalie yelled.

"Yeah! Let the police do their jobs." Savannah brushed off the dirt from her jeans.

"It wasn't me!" I defended myself. "I was with someone almost every second that night. I don't even have it in me to do something like that. Maybe it *was* Erik? It's usually the boyfriend that does this sort of thing, right?""

Joey stayed focused on me, causing Broderick to tense. His arms became like metal vises around my shoulders. "Jules, we have to be careful about what we say; the rest of Erik's life could depend on it." Joey was not Erik's biggest fan, so the fact he was watching out for his best interest was interesting. Joey didn't believe he was guilty.

"But Erik is lying! He saw her *after* she left for the restroom! I saw Erik and Loni together that night!"

"Everybody saw them together that night. So what?" Tripp questioned.

"No, I mean I saw them *to-ge-ther*," I tried explaining in such a general sense, hoping everyone would just catch on without me having to fully explain what I meant.

"What do you mean *to-ge-ther*?" Joey asked.

"I went to look for Broderick at the restrooms and while I was there, I had to go to the restroom. Right after you and I danced. At first, I was the only one there… until I heard someone step in two stalls down from me. When I looked under the stall, I saw two sets of feet: hers and Erik's. I hid out in my stall while they had sex," I whispered embarrassingly.

Cari and Natalie groaned in disgust, and Savannah covered her opened mouth with her hand in shock. Lindsey continued to stare at me through her puffy, wet eyes.

I continued. "I tried sneaking out after he left her in the stall and that's when she found me. We argued, and she slapped me—"

"How do you know it was Erik?" Natalie quietly asked.

"Well, who the hell else would it have been?" I said, not really expecting a response.

Joey made his way to me, his eyes wide in fear. "Does anyone else know about your fight with her?"

"I knew that Loni had slapped Jules," Cari said quietly as she raised her hand, her cigarette laced lazily between her fingers.

Isaac lifted his head and looked straight into my eyes baring his secret. "I assumed it was Loni, too." My mouth dropped open and I couldn't tear my eyes away from his. *Isaac knew!*

"Were there any witnesses, though?" Joey asked.

Broderick stepped in, peeved. "Wait, wait, wait! What's going on here? What are you trying to say, Joey? That *Jules* killed Loni?" He stood tall over Joey. "You know her, man; you know she would never harm anyone. Jules stood there and allowed that girl to hit her! She's lucky I didn't find her after that!"

"Broderick, shut up!" I panicked, fearful that he was now incriminating himself.

"I'm sorry, Jules, but do you really think I'm just going to sit back and let these people we call our *friends*, accuse you of murder?"

"Broderick, stop! *Shut up!*" Screaming, I grabbed him by the arm as he continued to stare Joey down.

"I didn't say that," Joey calmly pointed out.

"No one is accusing her of that, Broderick." Savannah tried reasoning with him.

"There *were* witnesses. Three girls walked in on us. I don't know how much they saw or heard, but they caught the end of our argument." I quickly explained before Joey and Broderick got into a heated match.

Joey looked torn. "Jules. You could very well be the last person to have seen Loni before she was killed. And the fact that the two of you fought that very night... it's not going to look good..."

I thought back to my harsh words: *You touch me again... and I will kill you* and *Good, maybe she'll stay missing.* My voice, clear in my memory, suddenly made me feel like vomiting.

The faint ringing of the school bell over a hundred yards away wiped away some of the overwrought air between us and our group began to disperse; everyone eyeing me as they made their way beside the stadium and through the parking lot.

"We're late," I heard Savannah sigh aloud as she grabbed her book bag.

"I'm always late," Cari grumbled as she quickly flanked Isaac.

I stayed behind with Broderick and Nat, feeling seriously ill with my final acknowledgment, "I'm in a lot of trouble."

The school canceled classes, but only after they held an assembly in the gymnasium led by our counselors. They wanted to explain to us the grieving process and welcome anyone who needed to talk.

Like a coward, I chose to wait and see if I was going to be accused by one of the girls that witnessed mine and Loni's argument before I came forward to the sheriff's department. It didn't take them long at all to identify me.

First thing, early the next morning, Sheriff Burnett was in my family's dining room questioning me. I held Broderick's medallion tightly in my fist and said a silent prayer.

My dad was sitting across the table from the sheriff talking quietly as they sipped coffee. He looked like a wreck, like someone who hadn't slept all night.

The middle aged and heavyset sheriff gave a tight smile through his blond and gray moustache. "I decided to come here myself and save you the trouble of coming down to the station. Joey speaks so fondly of you and your sister…" he said in a calm and inviting manner, crinkling his old eyes that set behind two thick eyebrows.

He pulled out a notepad and a pen and before he said another word, he scribbled some words down which looked like my name, but were upside down from where I was sitting so, I wasn't sure.

He finally dove in questioning me about our argument.

"Mitch," my dad broke in, "Should we be getting a lawyer? I'm asking you as a friend."

The sheriff held up his hand. "Your daughter is not a suspect, Mike; she has an alibi. We have several witnesses accounting for her whereabouts throughout the evening and also that she left the party with Broderick Cooper."

"Broderick?" I asked wide-eyed.

The sheriff nodded. "I unofficially questioned him this morning when he came over for breakfast and he confirmed that the two of you were together after leaving the party."

My mom patted me on the hand, clearly seeing I was terrified.

"Jules, if you can think of anything that may help lead us in the right direction, this town would really appreciate it. I know this is hard for you, but I have a job to do, and I want to do it quickly before we lose another young life in this town."

I conceded, clearing my throat and hoarsely began at the beginning— the background story for why Loni hated me so much. Sure to leave nothing significant out, I told him everything that went on between Loni and me, up through our confrontation in the bathroom. I was partly worried I was digging myself deeper into a criminal file. I admitted to my hair-brained attempt to threaten Loni during our confrontation and swore that I never saw her again after she left the restroom. I was terribly apologetic for the threat; never would I have seriously wished for anyone to die. My mom seemed disappointed, but not surprised that I threatened anyone in such a way. Sheriff Burnett seemed to believe me, which was a great relief.

"Do you know of anyone who may have been considered an enemy to Loni Schubert?" The sheriff waited for my answer.

My head ran through the names, leaving me to wince. Cari hated her, but then again, Cari pretty much hated everybody. Isaac—he was a tough one to figure out, but I didn't know him well enough to make an honest assumption. He genuinely seemed upset that Loni had been killed, but the persistent niggling in the back of my mind was unnerving, reminding me of the shock I felt when I realized he knew it was Loni who had slapped me all along. I don't know how he knew, but he did, and he knew that night! However, it wasn't really a secret that Loni hated me.

And then there was Broderick. I closed my eyes, determined not to think about Broderick's temper flares and fury. The fact he had been missing for a while that night... and his shadowshifting... his anger.

The shadowshifting!

Brought to the forefront of my mind, was the terror of what I had experienced in the hall after leaving the restroom in the same time frame Loni had been taken. Something was following me. Taunting me; terrifying me. Hiding in the shadows and hiding well.

"No, sir," I swallowed the omission hard.

Unlike Broderick, a small lie never made *me* uncomfortable, but this afternoon... I felt like I had sold my soul to Satan. I believed in Cari. I questioned Isaac, because even in his secretive ways, he indeed was shaken with the news of her death. It seemed nearly impossible for him to be such a beast. And Broderick was so tender and gentle, until recently.

Of all of my friends, Broderick was most likely to be a suspect. He was missing at the time of her supposed disappearance, was protective of me (which gave him a motive), and had no control of his temper as of late. I couldn't fully grasp the idea he could kill anyone or anything, but the truth remained, he had become a loose cannon.

"How well do you know Erik Peterson?" The sheriff asked finally.

I frowned. "Not too well. I went on a date with him this last summer but, it was just one date."

"What can you tell me about him?" he asked.

My mom and dad and I all three spoke, "Why?"

Again, Sheriff Mitchell Burnett held up his hands in defense. "I just need character assessments of the boy. That's all. I think Jules could help us out in that respect, can't you Jules?"

I sighed. "He was inconsiderate through the entire evening. He made a rude advance on me, and I ended the date early. That's about it."

"A rude advance? You mean he made a sexual advance toward you?"

I blushed, but pushed ahead, "Yes, sir." I whispered the word and twisted my mouth sheepishly. Funny enough, what I found embarrassing was openly talking about it in front of my parents, not Sheriff Burnett.

"And what was your response?"

I answered frankly, "I decked him."

The sheriff tightened his lips as a smile began creeping onto his face. "That's the best thing I've heard all week."

I pulled my lips back and saw my parents, too, were resisting a light hearted smile. It was a nice change of pace even if only for a few seconds.

The sheriff turned serious again. "Was he violent with you in any way? Did he push himself onto you?"

"He was pushy, but he wasn't violent. And he really wasn't any pushier than any other guy I had dated before." As I said it, I saw my dad tense, clearly unhappy either one of his daughters would ever be pressured into something they were not ready for or what would be considered immoral. "He didn't force himself on me, if that's what you're asking."

The sheriff seemed troubled. "Jules, was he aggravated over your physical assault?"

"Well, yeah. He wasn't exactly happy about it. I planted my fist into his face in front of the entire theater! And I wasn't quiet about it, either."

"Did you see Erik Peterson that night at the dance?"

Here it is the moment of truth. The words boomed in my head.

"Yes, sir. I saw him arrive with Loni." I squeezed my eyes shut and blew out a long distressed breath as I dropped my final bomb. "And I also saw him with Loni later *in* the restroom, two stalls down from me before she and I had our confrontation. Before the witnesses showed up."

"Really?" The Sheriff has set down his pen and had his full undivided attention on me. "In the *ladies'* restroom?"

"Yes, sir. I heard the two of them having sex, and I just hid in the stall I was in. It was a bit of an uncomfortable situation, as you might imagine. He left the room before I even stepped out of my stall. That's when she and I had our altercation, and the other girls showed up."

Mitchell Burnett nodded in confirmation of something he had already assumed, something I apparently knew nothing about. At that moment, I nailed Erik Peterson's coffin shut.

"Sir..." I stayed calm. "I'll come right out and tell you, Erik Peterson is a complete butthole. But..." I leaned into everyone at the table to make my point clear. "...he is not a killer, and he didn't force himself on her either. Loni sounded..." I gulped uneasily. "...she sounded as though she were enjoying it."

The only sound in the house was the sound of Sheriff Burnett scribbling his pen in his notes and the television being turned on and immediately turned down to a low volume in the next room. *Natalie must be out of bed now and eavesdropping.*

He shuffled uncomfortably in his seat. "I think that's all we need for now. I appreciate you facing this head on and talking to me, Jules. Joey always said you and your sister were two tough girls." I nodded slowly to accept the remark as a compliment. I only wish I was as tough as Joey had made me out to be. "If you wouldn't mind, now Jules, I'd like a moment alone with your mom and dad."

I could tell he had information he wanted to share with my parents, and I wasn't about to pass on not knowing. I walked out of the kitchen and around the corner, planting myself just outside the door, next to where Natalie was hiding out. A perfect spot for eavesdropping. The kitchen provided wonderful acoustics and their voices carried with ease. She held a finger to her lips for me not to speak. I pressed my cheek against the sage painted wall to concentrate on the words they exchanged at the table. Natalie leaned her face near mine and steadied her breathing to a slow pace, careful not to be too noisy.

"Jules isn't in any trouble is she?" My mother's concerned voice rang through.

"No, not at all." I sighed in relief. The sheriff's voice sounded tired and strained. "I think she's probably been one of the most honest of all the kids we've questioned. The others are more concerned with us finding out who was getting high, which ones were drinking under age, who was sleeping with who—the kind of crap our office busied ourselves with before these murders started occurring. It all seems like nonsense now."

He stopped talking long enough for my mom to offer more coffee. Natalie and I froze as we heard her move closer to the door where we listened. The coffee pot clanked against three different cups and then back to the counter beside the doorway. The sheriff muttered a quiet thanks, and then waited for her to return to her seat.

"You said *murders*. Plural." My dad's voice had never scared me so much. "Mitch, what are you trying to tell us?"

"This incident isn't isolated. Damn it, I could lose my job for sharing this information with you, Mike." He drew in a deep breath, "That Schubert girl—the official autopsy is being done today, but that girl was completely drained of blood. Not a drop was left in her. Her heart is still missing; we can't find it. She was ripped wide open as if a lion had gotten a hold of her."

Natalie gasped the same time my mother did, so everyone remained unaware of our presence. Still, I kicked at her for her gaffe. She shrugged at me, silently explaining it was an involuntary reaction.

"We are positive that this murder was done by the same person who murdered another girl by the county line after the Fourth of July weekend. Since then, there have been other girls from surrounding counties and states that have been found dead. There was a girl in Georgia and another in Mississippi done the same way a month before it started here. Each one of those girls were found in a similar state, hair missing or cut considerably shorter, blood drained from their bodies, missing their hearts. But they were all found almost a week after their deaths actually occurred. The Schubert girl is a game-changer though. Hell, the monster that got a hold of her practically scalped her and was off their usual schedule which makes us wonder if it's a copycat."

"What schedule?" my mom asked.

"At the station, we're calling them the Full Moon Murders. Every one of these acts we've been able to link back to occurring during a full moon. It's almost as if it's a ritual killing. But the Schubert girl was taken about two weeks too early." He dropped his voice to a whisper as he realized how loud he had gotten, "Mike, I'm telling the two of you this because young women like your daughters are being targeted, and we haven't been able to figure out a link between the women. I don't want anything happening to those two girls of yours." His voice became barely a whisper, "What the Schubert family now has to endure... Your girls are mighty special, especially to my son."

I simply couldn't listen anymore. I didn't say anything as I despairingly walked away from the door and back up to my bedroom. Natalie was close on my heels. "Jules, Erik's in a lot of trouble, unless he has an alibi for those nights when the others were taken. Are you *absolutely positive* about what you saw?" she asked.

Insulted with her question, I looked at her with incredulity as I shut the door in her face. The truth had been told, and I didn't need her guilt trip.

My own body had been beaten so far down with all the shaking and sobbing I had done through the night that I was too tired to shower or dress out of my pajamas. In fact, by late afternoon, I was actually ready to retire for the day. I just wanted to rest. I didn't want to sleep. Didn't want to dream.

After locking myself inside my bedroom, I closed the blinds and curtains, turned off the lights for privacy, and lit a candle before curling up in my bed. I felt numb, like a hollow shell as I stared at the flickering glow on the ceiling. The licking flame of the candle whipped and whirred as if a draft was forewarning its end, causing me to look over at it. It held my gaze, unwilling to let go. What little energy was left, lingered in my thoughts, running my mind tirelessly. Don't let me fall asleep. My body was motionless; I couldn't move. The stiff silence in my room left me with nothing to listen to but the smallest crackling of the flame on the wick, the ticking of my watch and the steady beating of my heart. I fought to keep my eyes open. *Please, God! Don't let me fall asleep!* I dreaded the nightmares that waited for me in the prison cell of my own subconsciousness. Nothing could save me from them as my lids slowly came to a close. *No!* My heart raced frantically as I flew them open again. The flare continued to dance slowly, reminding me of the strobe lights... *Stop!* I didn't want to set out a welcome mat for the horrific visions that awaited me, but that didn't prevent my eyes from losing focus on depth and distance as I stared at the candle. It seemed to sit right at the tip of my nose one second, then slowly move across the room as the area grew and lengthened. *My eyes were shutting!* I clawed my way to the light, desperate to avoid the hell that lingered at the back of my mind...

My eyes sprung open, though I knew immediately it was too late.

I stood high over a crowd. Not a soul moved and everyone's back was to me, like mannequins, they stared—not breathing, abnormal, in shock; frozen in time. Looking down at the black loafers on my feet, as I stood on top of a bale of hay, I dared not move. Instinct warned me to remain still like the others, for death was watching me from the dark hall behind the lifeless body laying limp on the hall floor like a torn rag doll. I wanted my heart to stop beating so death wouldn't be able to hear it or smell my blood, like it had Loni Schubert. I could feel it in my bones. Whatever had slaughtered Loni and was watching and waiting for me to make a false move. It was the same predator that had taunted me in the black shadows that night at the dance.

My peripheral caught a small movement at the entrance of the warehouse. Slowly, I turned my head to catch a better glimpse of what was trying to get my attention. The young blonde waved at me, motioning for me to come outside and join her. *Should I move? Would death shred me if I did?* Dressed in a CCHS cheerleader T-shirt and pajama bottoms with sock monkey designs, Natalie gave an encouraging smile and beckoned me to follow her.

"Nat?" I called out to her in confusion.

I climbed down from the hay stack. As I crossed the frozen crowd, a low growl emitted from the black hall.

Outside the building was just as disturbing. Though the streets were still clad with Halloween décor and littered with the popcorn cones and caramel apple sticks and candy wrappers, Natalie was the only person there. The world was empty of life outside of just the two of us.

"Jules, Erik's in a lot of trouble, unless he has an alibi for those nights when the others were taken. Are you *absolutely positive* about what you saw?" she asked without moving her lips. Her voice sounded different, more mature. Not hers.

She lifted her arm and pointed a finger to inside the warehouse.

Just inside the door, frozen in time, was Cari flicking out her cigarette. The cigarette was far from finished. I walked back in and this time carefully looked over every single person. The growl was like a low hum in the hall. Subconsciously, the danger must have guided me to a place where I always felt safe.

Broderick stood near Savannah and Tripp and their circle of friends. I walked to him and stood before him. Focusing on Broderick's flawless face, his hair longer than usual jutting out from the wool cap he wore on his head. I reached up and brushed my fingers across his unmoving lips. He remained motionless. I would give anything right now to feel his arms around me and take me away from this nightmare. I pressed my cheek to his heart. There was nothing to be heard but the rumble from the hall rising to a low and testy howl. His scent was gone, too. There was nothing real about him. I stepped back and opened my eyes as I turned to find Natalie again, but she was gone.

The low rumble of the howl became unsteady, and agitated. The evil waited for me in the shadows. I hastily twisted around to run out of the building, but my feet became entangled plunging me forward to my hands and knees. As I began to climb to my feet, I was distracted with the feet standing in front of me. It was Erik's motionless feet and desperate pose, clad in earth tones for his wolf man costume. *Brown! He was wearing brown that night whereas the shoes I saw in the stall with Loni were black!*

Abruptly, the howl grew to an earsplitting racket. Quickly, I ran mindlessly to a bale of hay. As I ran, I heard the beast beating its heavy feet in the hall, the sound getting louder and louder with every pant from my own chest. I scurried up the hay and stood, facing the dark hall. I drew a quick breath and before I could exhale, the beast flew from the hall, soaring over the crowd and straight at me. Like a flash, it was so quick, my eyes couldn't register the revelation.

My scream was soundless as I sat up in bed. My stomach felt as though it was sitting in my chest while a cold sweat covered my body. I jumped up and dashed to the small bathroom and kneeling at the toilet. In no time, I was releasing my heart wrenching anxiety into it then rinsed my mouth. The impending doom that waited in the dark hall of my nightmare was squeezing my breath from me. We were all in danger and it was crushing in on me. Was this the same feeling Broderick had with his visions?

I tore down the stairs and into the kitchen to find my mom cutting coupons at the bar. "Mom, we have to call Sheriff Burnett. I was wrong about something!"

The Stranger

ERIK WAS CLEARED OF any charges. He had four solid alibis for the past six months on the nights the Full Moon Murders occurred. After I adjusted my eyewitness account, the law officials had nothing to pin on him—especially after another body in similar condition was found days after the recent full moon.

This time it was a male in his thirties; a well-known drug addict, according to Joey. He was found on the east end of the county in the trunk of his car. It baffled the sheriff's department because it was the first male victim, and he was over the age of twenty. The only connection police had now among all the murder victims, was that they had occurred during a full moon and the condition of the body: cut hair, practically shredded, and missing a heart. Joey confessed that his dad was at his whit's end. He felt as though they had been going around in circles for months with very little clues surfacing, even as they worked with other nearby authorities.

The Full Moon Murders were causing all sorts of other problems as well. Angry citizens—vigilantes—were now casing the neighborhoods like lynch mobs in search of the serial killer. Sheriff Burnett feared someone would be wrongfully accused and hung by the masses before ever getting a trial. People of the back woods—rednecks, hillbillies, whatever we all chose to call them—lived by their own structure of justice.

Parents limited social activities for their children, and with good cause. My trips to the Java House had become near nonexistent, unless Savannah *and* Cari *and* Natalie *and* preferably a guy, whether it was Broderick, Tripp, or Joey—preferably *all three*—came with me. With all of our busy lives, it was impossible to get a big enough group together to suffice my parents. On the days Natalie cheered at a basketball game or had practice, I was to come home immediately and lock the doors. My mom would call our cell phones on a regular basis to check in. If we didn't answer the phone by the fourth ring, it was like a signal for her to call the National Guard.

Although I was aware of the dangers we were facing, I remained unaffected. My concern was more personal—a matter that would be deemed trivial by the masses. The relationship I had with Broderick was quickly dying.

Seeing Broderick anymore was all but comforting. He rarely made any attempts to call me or see me, breaking my heart in a million pieces. I kept those pieces swept under a rug and pressed a smile on my face for my school peers though. His face—it was no longer his. All I could see was the numbing pain and fury of a complete stranger. Apprehensive to be near him, I worried that somehow I had caused this. He seemed void of any emotion. Instead of asking him what was wrong, I suffered a path of egg shells and continued as if nothing had changed. As we walked together from class to class, our fingers were lazily woven with the others' barely even touching. Hardly considered holding hands, despite my best effort. Eventually, he became "too busy" to even drive me and Natalie, and coldly suggested that I may need to start driving myself to school instead. On top of my nervousness around him and the permeating realization that things were bad between us, I was embarrassed the school may notice our negative shift.

An unsettling feeling, that I was hanging on the edge of a cliff and waiting for that moment to plummet—to jump or be pushed off—lingered for weeks. Broderick became more reclusive and absolutely unpredictable.

Sometimes he wouldn't show up for school at all. Jackson, Taryn, Joey and I always made regular phone calls to check on him and find out the story behind his absence, but Evelyn thwarted all questions and speculations like a pro, claiming he was "very ill and probably contagious", preventing us from even a short visit.

Nothing was important to me anymore. When Mr. Grayson made the announcement about the band trip to Destin, Florida in early January for a competition, I couldn't even pretend I was excited as the class celebrated, whooping and hollering. I just smiled wryly and thought: *Why bother? We suck; it's not like we actually have a chance at winning. It'll be too cold to even enjoy the beach. And it's miles from Broderick.*

Few things were able to divert my attention from my crumbling relationship with Broderick, one of them being my meandering obsession with the night of Loni's disappearance. In my heart, I knew that night I was inches away from being the victim and was just lucky Loni had only been steps ahead of me. She left the restroom and entered the dark hall, but she never rejoined the dance. Being only minutes behind her that night, I shivered every time I did a recount of the taunting predator and the haunted feeling as I made my way to safety.

Should I have mentioned this to the sheriff? And just *what* would I have told him? That there was an evil presence in the hall with me? That I thought it was that same evil presence that killed Loni? That the evil presence was hiding in the shadows? That my estranged boyfriend could shadowshift and could possibly *be* the evil presence I spoke of?

The autopsy concluded Loni was killed days after her abduction, which meant she had been kept hidden from the world somewhere before she was murdered. Scared. Tortured. I often wondered what she must have been thinking and how she felt in her last days. Did she try fighting her way back, or did she simply give up? Did she comply with their wishes, or did she emit her fiery personality as she stubbornly refused to go out without a fight?

An additional diversion was Casey Barnes, another constant reminder of that night. Though not as verbally vicious as her late friend, she made sure to continue carrying Loni's torch in her own way. As we passed in the halls she would stare coldly at me, probably resentful that I wasn't the one found in the dumpster instead.

My life had become lonely and numb. Loneliness was making me more aware of those around me. A blur of pictures and time, like the way some movie scenes are filmed. The kind of scenes that warned the end was near. A shit storm.

Casey's cold stares. Broderick's empty eyes and apathetic body language. Joey following Natalie with his eyes as he sat with his arm around an oblivious Lindsey. The affectionate play between Savannah and Tripp. Cari's continual gripe about social injustices and her judgments of those who reaped the benefits. I even paid more attention to how much of a loner Isaac was.

Always, he sat alone at lunch, reading or looking over sheet music, all the while having girls walk up to him and flirt for a few moments before taking the hint that they were not making any progress with him. Unaware of spectators, Isaac came across as intelligent and sensitive. Isaac Philetos should have been a model with the way he looked. Masculine but angelic. He was always polite and was actually a bit on the chivalrous side. The way he would open doors for girls as they giggled past him and sometimes I would see him walk some random girl to her car after school, carrying her books; even the less desirable girls. His dark olive skin and black hair gave a perfect background for his stunning bright smile and his piercing blue eyes—a pale blue, clearer than any eyes I have ever seen. He was tall and well built. I still didn't think he looked to be any younger than twenty, but no one else seemed to question it.

The Wednesday before Thanksgiving, I made up my mind to get out of my relationship-limbo. It was all I could do to keep from screaming. If Broderick was to break up with me, I wanted it done and over with. It had to be easier than the limbo we had been in, though it was far from what I wanted. I wanted things back to normal—the way they were this last summer.

I waited until dark to slip out of the house that night. Creeping through the dark, shady woods; crossing over the bridge and passing the tire swing, making my way to the dimly lit loft over the garage, I stood at the edge of the barren trees and watched for several minutes, hoping I would catch a glimpse of him or at least his shadow through the glass, but the room seemed abandoned.

"What are you doing in the woods, Jules?" I heard his gruff, strained voice from behind me and I jumped in surprise. It had been so long since I last heard his voice. It was almost alien to me.

He wasn't completely visible. Covered in black as he stood in the faint moonlight, even in the way he stood, which seemed off for some reason; I could see that he was not happy to see me.

My throat felt jittery as I tried to find my voice and speak, "I came to see you."

He lunged forward with a grunt and I flinched in fear of being a target for his unexpected wrath. He grabbed me violently by the arms and shook me. "What the hell were you thinking, sneaking through the woods after dark? After what happened to Loni?" His voice was thick with both anger and alarm, "Jules you're so stupid sometimes!"

I stammered unthinkingly, "I-I'm sorry, I didn't mean to…"

He let go, slightly pushing me away. He turned around to thoughtfully look into the woods.

"Broderick?"

Broderick cleared his throat and turned to talk to me as his shadow faded. "Jules, we need to talk," he said quietly. His mouth was set in determination, through his tired face. But his eyes were… something else. Whatever he wanted to talk about, it wasn't good.

I drew in a staggering breath, "Okay."

He took my hand and pulled me swiftly back through to the other side of the path. Back home.

Here it comes. He no longer loves me.

He sat down on the brick steps of my house and patted a place next to him, clearly at a distance from where he sat.

"What is it?" My stomach was already tightening in heaps of knots as I read each sign of oncoming bitterness.

He rested his elbows on his knees and fidgeted while staring at the dark shadows on the ground. The silence seemed to last hours, but in reality was probably no more than a few seconds. "I don't know if I can do this..." I barely heard him mutter breathlessly.

The sheer curiosity to ask him what he wanted to tell me was tempting, but I was scared that it was going to be something I never wanted to hear. He took a deep breath causing a roll of fog from his warm breath in the cold night air. I began to shake, though I wasn't sure if it was caused more by the weather or my mounting emotions.

He finally turned to me, but couldn't look me straight in the eye. Our glances would touch, but never lock.

"We need to take a break from each other," he finally said.

The words knocked the wind out of me. It should have been a relief to hear those words; after all, I was on my way to deliver pretty much the same speech. Only now, I didn't want to hear them.

"Why?" I choked back as much as I possibly could without begging him for a reason.

He stared off into the shadows of my front yard and spoke softly, "Because I'm afraid I'll hurt you."

"You're hurting me now," I whimpered.

"No, I'm doing you a damn favor." He turned to me and grabbed me by the arms, jerking me up to him. He stared furiously into my eyes, trying to convey something to me; I couldn't read it. "*This*—what you're feeling right now—wouldn't even compare to the pain you would feel by staying with me, Jules."

Had his grandmother finally convinced him to get rid of me? We were supposed to be together and fight through any and all obstacles. That's what he promised! I tried swallowing, but nothing would move down, everything wanted to work its way up—the monster, the spaghetti I ate for dinner, my heart. *Everything!* My eyes felt warm with salty tears. I closed them to prevent anything from spilling out onto my cheeks, but that just seemed to squeeze the tears to a drizzling stream. My heart and soul burned in torment over the cruel truth of his words. I always knew that it would never last and that I was never going to be able to keep his love.

"Why are you doing this?" I wept miserably.

He pushed off from the steps. I watched him stand before me and speak off to the side as he stared into the woods between our homes, plainly trying to calm his temper before it burst. "All I know is that I can't love you. I can't. I *won't*. We need to sever our ties together so we can move on to bigger, better and more appropriate things... and people." He finally stared at me, glaring with insurmountable fury. "Please stop crying. I don't want you to be sad about this. If you feel anything, anything at all..." He thought quickly. "Let it be hatred. *Hate* me! I've screwed you over. So hate me!"

"I could never hate you," I cried.

He swiftly closed the gap between us and jerked me off of the steps and shook me in anger. "Dammit, Jules, get pissed! Get angry! Then move on! I sure as hell would!" He looked disgusted with himself and his vile words that easily matched his face now, thrusting me into more tears.

"I can't! I can't!" I trembled furiously with hard sobs.

He looked me over in a hard studious manner as he eased his grip on me. "Eventually you're going to move on and realize I did you a huge favor tonight."

My chest was thick with a boulder size lump in it. My entire body began shuddering as if I were a slowly breaking dam.

"It's better this way." He let go of my arms and stepped back, phasing into blackness. The sound of crunching leaves on the ground and his voice grew distant. I couldn't feel him, I couldn't see him, but his warning echoed from the direction of the trees. "Stay out of the woods, Jules."

He was gone. And none of it made sense to me. My knees grew weak and I felt them give way from underneath me. Running through everything I was and everything I had done in my mind, I simply wasn't good enough for him.

My legs felt too weak to climb the tree back up to my bedroom window. I needed time to compose myself, to walk off some of the pain. I made my way to the end of the pavement of my dead end road, toward the construction in our neighborhood. As my eyes adjusted to the darkness, I wondered aimlessly past the broken and cracked edges of the road and onto the cold hard dirt until I reached a familiar fallen tree. Sitting and staring into the woods—the same woods that would bring me to Broderick—I released as much emotion as I could. *Get it all out, Jules.*

As my crying eased, I drew up my knees to keep the pain from splitting my chest wide open. The ache was still very much present and I wondered if it always would be there. I could sense his presence, for I knew his bed was only yards away through the woods—yet I couldn't see him anymore... Like his shadowshifting. I wanted to say that I didn't want him near me if I couldn't be in his arms, but my real desire was more acquainted with a masochistic nature: I would spend the rest of my life unable to touch him, or be with him, as long as my eyes could always hold him. Just to see him.

My nose was running from breathing the chilly night air, so I started back to my house, looking obsessively at the possibilities that waited on the other side of the woods. Suddenly a branch fell to the left of me causing my head to whip back in that direction. The sound crackled out of the darkness of the trees and thumped hard on the ground. The sheer strength of the limb falling and the crashing noise had shattered my resolve. Uncertainty over my safety, I shuddered and tried convincing myself that it was a faulty branch—old and rotten—ready to give up. Much like myself.

After a few more steps closer to the pavement, I began humming a song for distraction as if it were a cloak of protection over me. No boogeyman, no chainsaw-wielding madman. My voice quavered with every note and my eyes converted into restless darts as I watched every angle around me. My imagination was wild with sounds of footsteps that followed along with me from the woods, heavy and gruff. I stopped after a few steps, to verify I was indeed being followed, but I heard nothing.

A few more steps, now on the pavement and my ears weren't deceiving me. Footsteps could be heard, clearly. I pondered the idea of calling out to whoever it was trying to scare me, but the unforgettable memory of Loni loomed through my mind. My thoughts settled on the culprit in the shadows of the hall that taunted me, inching me closer to my death. The steps were too heavy to be human.

My heart thrashed against the confines of my chest, my lungs burning from the incessant panting of the cold air that filled them as I broke into a frantic run. Breathing became hollow as my footsteps beat against the pavement. I heard the grunting and crunching of leaves beneath another's feet from the blackness running along the side of the road, something much larger than me.

God, help me make it home! I prayed just before I reached the corner where my house stood. Little comfort came with the house standing between me and the thing that followed me from the woods. It could cut me off, coming around the other side of the house! I would never reach the tree! I didn't know what was waiting for me around the corner in front of the house that shook me to a trembling squeal. As I pumped my legs harder, I planned ahead before reaching the front lawn. If whatever it was that was following me was in the front yard waiting for me, I would run to the back yard and into my car for some sort of protection until daylight. If it wasn't there, I would take the tree and fast.

The front lawn was clear as I rounded the corner. My legs shook with weakness as they sprung me to an efficient jump, allowing me to grab a lower branch and pull myself up the tree. Never had I climb so fast! I swung off the overhang and onto the roof. Never missing a beat, I scampered across the roof and slipped into my bedroom window. I twisted around hastily at my opened window and looked out to the ground below. I needed to see it! I needed proof that there was something chasing me and that it wasn't all in my head!

Nothing.

"What the hell?" I grumbled in frustration over my overactive imagination as I sank into a slouch at the window seat. I reconsidered my fears. "I'm not going crazy. Something is out there," I whispered.

I took another glimpse out the window. Faintly in the trees across the street, I saw a man standing in the shadows. Narrowing my eyes at the figure, I studied it closely. He wasn't hiding behind a tree or using the shadows to duck into. He *was* the shadow!

Broderick was watching me. I took from it the only thing it could possibly mean: he still loved me. He was watching me like he used to, before we had become friends. He wasn't over me any more than I was over him. So why was he so intent on being apart from me? Was he trying to protect me from something?

Pretending as though I couldn't see him, I walked away from the window and turned on my TV and changed into my pajamas. With each pass by the window, I would steal a glance through the blinds, to see if he was still there. I don't think he had moved so much as an inch. I shut blinds and curtains and after turning off the lamp on my nightstand, I crawled into bed.

The sun screamed in my face Thanksgiving morning as it ricocheted off of the mirrors and television screen and anything else with a shiny surface. An extremely harsh awakening.

Going Solo

I HAD NEVER SKIPPED school before, but was desperate to give it a try today—anything to avoid the unwanted questions about Broderick. The Thanksgiving holiday had been spent in peace from those questions, though my family was well aware of my depression over the matter. Even my mom was considerate enough to eliminate any mother-daughter advice time.

I dressed and rushed around as if I was in a hurry to get to school. My purse couldn't be found in its usual spot on my desk. Luckily I found a few crumpled up dollar bills on my dresser, so I could get a coffee this morning after dropping Natalie off. I would just have to drive carefully and not get pulled over since my license was in my purse.

Natalie was taken aback when I took her through the car-rider lane at school instead of the parking lot. "You're not going to school today?"

"No," I said, numbly staring ahead. "I need to be alone today."

She nodded in sympathy before shutting the door.

As I drove through the parking lot, I twisted my head around, looking for his jeep, but failed to see it anywhere.

I pulled up to the Java House and grabbed my purse from the passenger's side floor board. Climbing out of my car, I slammed the door and stopped as I reached the sidewalk, uneasy that all of the sudden I was in possession of my purse again. I shook the confusion off, and instead, welcomed back my overwhelming misery of losing Broderick.

Chase greeted me immediately and informed the guy working the espresso machine of my usual drink. "So, how's it been going, Jules?" he asked brightly.

I stood at the counter and couldn't decide what I wanted to tell him. I opened my mouth to speak, but the contracting tightness in my stomach squeezed harder and instead of words, I grabbed my stomach and hunched over, sharing with him my bile and last night's dinner.

"Holy shit! Nick, run and get a mop!" Chase was swift to get behind me and hold my hair, though a few strands had already been chunked. Annoyingly, he rubbed my back as I growled with violent heaves.

When I finished hurling, he walked me over to a seat at a corner table. A small group of people stood up and walked out complaining. Nick pushed in an industrial mop and bucket on wheels, and Chase told him to take care of any customers who might walk in and he would clean up my mess.

I was grateful for the kindness Chase showed. He never once complained. Instead, he was whistling a familiar tune cheerfully as he slopped the mop across the floor. I fought through my wretchedness as I tried placing the title to the song he whistled. Although it was drenched in sweetness with his high pitched whistle, I was almost certain it was some heavy metal song. When he finished, he slid the wheeled bucket around to the back, reappearing shortly thereafter.

"Jules, are you sick? Do you need me to take you home?" he offered.

I shook my head and swallowed hard. I knew it was just my shot nerves that were just shot at this point. A terrible taste of acid and last night's turkey leftovers was thick on my tongue. I smacked my mouth and curled my awkward upper lip in revulsion.

He grinned at me, part in sympathy and partly amused. "Would you like your drink now?"

His thick black rimmed glasses didn't do his blue eyes justice. I nodded and then lay my head on the table, uncaring of how unsanitary it was. I just threw up on the counter and the floor for goodness sake!

Chase ran to the sink to wash his hands, then grabbed my latte from the counter. He sat in the chair across from me and smiled as I warmed my hands on the cup and sniffed my drink, but not even the aroma of the coffee could relax me.

I'm lost. I grabbed the piece of precious metal that still dangled around my neck. It should be returned to Broderick now. I grabbed it and held it tightly in my fist. How will I ever be able to part with it?

"Everything okay with you and Broderick?"

My chin trembled as I shook my head.

"You want to talk about it?" he asked.

I shrugged, ignoring the rush of tension that climbed up my spine as the reality was sinking in. He reached over and patted my hand, like my mother would have if she were sitting with me.

Chase decided to take another route of conversation, "I saw your friend in here on Black Friday."

"Cari?" It took every bit of energy just to raise an eyebrow and speak. I was emotionally and physically drained, and it wasn't even nine in the morning.

He grinned with blissful recollection then frowned in debate as he put his elbows on the table. "She's not too fond of me, is she?"

"She's not fond of anybody," I said lamely. I wasn't in the mood to play matchmaker.

"She just looks like my type of girl…" he said thoughtfully.

I looked cynically at him. Cari was right; there wasn't anything about him that would accommodate her or her choice of lifestyle. He was clean cut, mellow, and as much as I hated thinking it, too nice for her.

A couple walked in the café and looked over the menu. Apparently they couldn't smell the stench of bile lingering in the air like I still could. Then I looked down and saw that some of the regurgitation was in my hair. I blushed as I pulled my hair around, to hide it behind my back.

"I've got to go wait on those two." Chase stood up from the table. "Stay as long as you like, Jules. You're not bothering me. I'll keep the drinks coming if you'd like," he winked. "On the house today."

I sat at the table, drumming my nails to the beat of *The William Tale Overture*. My nails had gotten longer than I realized, reminding me that I hadn't played guitar in weeks. I had been too absorbed with watching the unraveling thread that held Broderick and me together. Battling the urge to weep, I recounted the break up all over again in my head.

If this were a bar, Chase would have already taken my keys and called a cab for me. I continued to order and reorder my warm beverage of choice until late afternoon, only leaving my seat to go to the restroom. I left to pick up Natalie just before three. I couldn't wait to see her; if I could be around anyone, it would be my sister. Aside from her knack for knowing when to give me silent comfort, she was probably hurt, too, with the awareness that she was wrong about Broderick. That he *wasn't* different.

Natalie was treading across the parking lot when I drove up. Savannah and Cari stared with confusion from their vehicles as I pulled along side my sister.

"What are you doing here?" Nat asked, her pom-poms in her hands.

"I'm picking you up."

"I have practice." Her apologetic expression was enough to convey that she knew I wanted her company. "Come back around five," she said. "We'll watch a horror movie tonight. Your pick." She smiled and continued toward the school.

Savannah was already calling my name by the time I put my car back into drive. Resigned, I held up a finger and pulled into an empty parking spot nearby. She quickly came over to the passenger window that was rolled down and I turned the heat up to keep warm.

"Where were you today?" She grinned slyly. "Did you skip with a certain someone who decided to not be here today either?"

I shook my head sadly and battled the tingling warmth that entered my nose and shot through my cheeks and into my eyes. Savannah immediately took notice of my crushing demeanor.

"Jules! What's wrong?" she gasped.

Cari approached us and ducked her head inside the window beside Savannah. "What's going on? Why are you crying? Who died?"

Shuddering from the silent wailing, I lost all composure.

"Oh, shit!" Cari muttered as she ran to the driver's side of the car and forced me to unbuckle my seatbelt and scoot into the passenger's seat just before Savannah climbed into the backseat. She drove us to the F-wing building by the band room. Upon jerking the keys out of the ignition, she hurried me out of the car, into the wing and through the hall until she found a private rehearsal room to sit me down in. Savannah, of course, followed.

My two good friends spent close to an hour trying to console me and talk me through my grief. I appreciated their efforts, but would have been fine with a simple "I'm sorry" then left to be alone. They were reluctant to leave, even when I was temporarily done crying for the most part. Isaac's appearance easily changed the atmosphere. He had been two rooms over practicing the piano and must have heard me weeping through the door as he passed. He tapped quietly on the door and stuck his angelic face in the narrow window for us to see him. Cari, unwittingly betrayed me and waved him in.

"What is that smell?" he blurted out as soon as he entered the room.

I tried to ignore him and keep my nose planted in my hands, but wondered if maybe he smelled the vomit that was still matted in my hair. I must have gotten used to the smell and the two girls must have been compassionate enough to ignore it.

Peeking through my fingers, Isaac looked at me with superior glares, then finally pointed at my hair. "What is in your hair, Juliana?"

As mad as I was with Isaac, I couldn't deny that I was disgusting. I felt like a waste of human skin. I dropped my hands in my lap and looked down in shame at my confession. "I threw up at the Java House and that's barf in my hair."

Cari and Savannah looked horrified at my confession as they both said, "Ew."

Composed, he shook his head at me. "You beat all, Juliana."

With that, Cari and Savannah agreed to let me leave and go home so I could take a shower. Cari stayed behind till five to take Natalie home from practice.

Sitting at my window every night, I would see the shadowy figure in the same place, unmoving and watching the house. It quickly became obvious that he was never going to leave his post and come to me. It then became insulting, hopeless, and worse yet, maddening. I slowly felt my sanity slipping away as I tried to wrap my head around the reasoning. I questioned whether I was sure it was even him, and why he was doing it.

Even in the freezing rain one night, he waited and watched. He never moved.

The beast inside of me insisted I was being treated unfairly and should fight back, not to win him over, but to reclaim my pride and my dignity! I fought the monster for weeks as it clawed up out of my stomach and nestled in my chest, waiting for the right moment to make its appearance.

Isaac finally gave the beast ammunition.

I jerked my locker door open as I sifted through the mess of wadded papers and tattered books looking for something to make me look busy as I saw him walk in my direction.

"Wow. Clean your locker much?" He peeked in over my shoulder and observed with sarcasm at my locker's condition.

I grabbed a random book from my locker—I wasn't even sure if it was the one I needed—and I slammed the door as I tried to storm off, but he quickly caught up to me and placed his arm around me and began walking along. As he pulled me in close to him with a chuckle, I slouched, and then shortly pushed his hand off of my shoulder.

"You act as though you dislike me, but I've yet to figure out why. All I can conclude is that you're jealous."

Astonished with the allegation, I stopped and dropped my jaw.

"Aw, now, don't act so surprised. This has been going on since that day at the park."

"Shut up." I tried walking faster, but he kept my pace with ease.

"I think you have sort of a thing for me, too."

My face turned sour. "That *thing* is called hate."

He chuckled at my insult. *Why can't I hurt his feelings?*

"I believe you *want* to hate me, but it's the impossibility to do so that really eats at you. You were never willing to give me a chance for two reasons."

I turned the corner of the hall, hoping I would lose him, but he remained close. I groaned, "And what are those two reasons. I'd love to hear them."

He laughed again at my bland tone. "Well first off, you *are* jealous and rightfully so. I have stolen your thunder around here."

"*That's* what you did," I spoke in dry sarcasm. No satisfaction would I give him, no matter how close to the truth he might touch.

"And you felt threatened for your boyfriend." My face became hot as he leaned in to whisper in my ear. "We both know he ended things with you because of a dirty secret he's trying to hide."

I tried to keep walking, but the eventual pull of the truth I had been avoiding for so long slowed me to a full stop. I turned around to see Isaac, waiting for my reaction, several paces back from where he had whispered. The rage started to build, but the astonishment of his knowledge shook me.

"What?" I breathed, my mind jumbled in a million thoughts, none which were coherent.

Isaac made his way toward me then gently wrapped his fingers around my tiny arm and pulled me off to the side so we could speak in private without slowing the traffic in the hall.

His piercing blue eyes bore into mine. "He was completely unaccounted for when Loni was abducted, and you've done everything you can to ignore that."

Speechless, I tried desperately to tear away from his eyes. I could feel the speculation humming all around us from the observers who passed us by.

"I'm not saying he's guilty, but I know you question his innocence." I felt horrible at the truth he spoke. His gravity struck a hard chord with me. "You and I are more alike than you can imagine, Juliana. I know how you would have done anything to keep him around, even if it was just his memory. You've believed since the beginning that he was too good for you and that it wouldn't last. Have you ever considered the fact that maybe he wasn't good enough for *you*?"

I grabbed onto what little self-sufficiency I had left and used it to walk away from him. The second our eye contact broke, I felt free and capable of fighting back. I walked backwards down the hall as I turned to Isaac who continued to lean against the wall with a casual look upon his angelic face.

"There are two days left before Christmas break, Isaac. Do me a favor and stay the hell away from me." My eyes narrowed while I grit my teeth.

"I love you too, Juliana!" he called joyfully down the hall, entirely unaffected by my offense.

His words did more than just anger me; they lingered recklessly in my mind. Everything Isaac had said made wonderful sense to me. Broderick was on a pedestal he didn't deserve to be.

Remembering back to his warning about Broderick when we were in the library, I picked up *The Brothers Grim and Other Faery Tales* book sitting on my desk, and read the tale of *Little Red Cap* three times before I fell asleep that night.

Natalie was waiting for me by the car when I walked outside the next morning. Impatient, she shifted her weight and put her hand on her hip. "Since when have you started locking the car doors? I'm freezing out here."

Stumped, I reached into my purse for my keys. "I'm losing my mind or something," I mumbled while unlocking and opening the doors. "I must have accidently hit the lock button yesterday when…" I trailed off as I stared hauntingly at the book in the driver's side seat that I knew I had left on the bed. *The Brother's Grim and other Faery Tales!*

Natalie situated her stuff in the back seat of the car then poked her head back out of the car to look at me in question. "What's up with you, Jules? You look like you've just seen a ghost."

As I drove to school, I proceeded to tell her about the book and why it should still be upstairs in my room. I also told her about the time I thought I left my purse in the house and instead found it out in the car. She looked nervous, plainly wondering on something terrifying.

"Under a normal circumstance…" she began

"There's nothing normal about this," I said to her, frantically.

"You're right. Let me rephrase. If our town wasn't under a full watch right now, and it was happening to someone else, I would find this extremely funny, but…" she thought for a moment. "I'm totally freaked out right now. Jules, we need to tell Mom and Dad."

"No!" I blurted.

"Why not?" She was as confused as I was at my response.

"Because," I became quick on my feet. "What if I'm wrong and I'm losing my mind? What if I'm wrong?"

Natalie's pale appearance and low voice was grave as we pulled into the parking lot of the school. "Jules, I think we need to tell Mom and Dad. You really don't think you're wrong because you would have never brought it up in the first place if you did… But I'll keep my mouth shut about it if that's what you really want."

I sighed, nervously, "That's what I really want."

One of Natalie's friends, Amber, yelled from across the parking lot to come and join her.

"I don't like this, but we'll think of something," she said quickly to me as she ran off to join her friend.

My mind was finally made up just before the Christmas holiday break that I wanted to move on from Broderick. I was going to be fine solo, but going forward, I needed to get a few things off my chest. I fell into a hard sleep that night before our last day of classes, clear of any further worries now that I was making an effort to let go and finally move on from Broderick.

I awoke with clattering teeth at three in the morning. My room temperature had dropped significantly; I didn't know how long I had been so cold. My body was bone weary from staying in a rolled up position and clutching my blankets tightly to stay warm. Knowing that my cold spot was still considerably warmer than the rest of my room, I was reluctant to pull back the blankets and check the thermostat. My bare feet touched the icy-cold wood of the floor, and my eyes shot open from the shock of the coolness. With a spring in each step to prevent any prolonged touch to the floor, I made my way to the door, only to stop when I saw in my peripheral that my curtains were blowing inward from the wintery morning breeze. With a racing heart I ran to the window and slammed it shut, quickly locking it. I spun around as I took into a late consideration that an intruder may still be present in my room. With bated breath, I dashed out of my room and down the hall into Natalie's room, locking the door behind me and curling up next to her.

I never fell back asleep.

Regardless of my exhaustion, I was a woman on a mission as I stomped through the halls looking for Broderick the following morning. Determined to show him no mercy, just as he did with my heart.

He was cleaning out his locker down the hall. His face, drawn and somber. I plowed ahead, paying no attention to the sadness that he bled. My body trembled with uncontrollable rage and the beast inside smiled as I approached him. His size was no obstacle for me nor was it intimidating. I pulled him around to face me and his eyes widened in shock. When he saw that it was me, his eyes soften. My monster tore into him as I shoved his medallion in his hands.

"I will never forgive you for what you've done to me. There is nothing salvageable of our relationship. I didn't even want this relationship to begin with and yet you pushed and you pushed!" I yelled at him, drawing the attention of every student in the hall.

He drew in a small shuddering breath and tried turning away from me to continue cleaning out his locker, but I denied him any escape and spun him around again.

"You coward! You can't even look at me!"

"Jules," he said sadly. The edge he carried as he spoke my name tormented me. I stepped back and covered my ears.

"No! Don't! You have no right to say my name. Stay away from me and stay away from my house. You think I don't know what you're doing? You're trying to make me crazy.... You're messing with the wrong redhead!"

A student nearby gasped in revelation as another whispered to her friend, "I *knew* she colored her hair!"

"I hate you." My weak voice trembled, and I bounced away from him quickly, so he wouldn't get the satisfaction of seeing me cry any more.

On the way to the parking lot, I stopped by Natalie's locker to tell her that I was going to go home instead of finish out the two hour day at school. She turned to her friends and told them that she, too, was going home and we left together.

At home, I wasn't much company for my sister. I lay on the couch and cried for a few hours on and off, then finally retired to my room to do the same thing before my parents got home from work. The grey afternoon fast turned to darkness and before long, Natalie was at my door, inviting me to the Christmas parade downtown. Though I was unenthusiastic, I still desired something cheerful to divert my attention. Our parents agreed to let us meet a full group of friends there.

She and I arrived to the throng of bundled people and families, but I was far from distracted from my broken heart. My eyes did a thorough scan of the area in search for Broderick.

"You're looking for him," she said.

"I know." I swallowed the lump that lay in wait for another weeping frenzy.

Savannah called to us from the sidewalk. She sat on the curb, snuggled tightly in a blanket she shared with Tripp. Cari sat next to her, sipping a warm coffee with the Java House logo on the cup.

Cari, deep with sympathy, looked up at me. "I heard what happened today. You okay?"

I nodded.

"You don't look it," she said with a wry look on her face.

"I don't *feel* it, either," I replied hoarsely.

She climbed to her feet and brushed the sidewalk debris off of her butt. "Come on. You need some coffee. Coffee makes *everything* better."

Natalie stayed behind with Savannah looking for Amber, while Cari and I headed toward a small temporary coffee stand.

"I don't really like *coffee*-coffee, you know. It has to be sweetened up," I reminded her of my high maintenance taste.

"Then I'll order you a hot chocolate." She put her arm around my shoulders and chuckled. "I'm not going to give you the I-told-you-so speech," she said finally. "I wanted you to know that I'm really sorry things didn't work out between you and Boy Scout."

Throughout the crowded street there were young children giggling with anticipation and lovers cuddling underneath warm blankets, waiting for the parade to pass by. From the singers who sang joyous carols on the floats that represented the local churches to the candy being tossed by the elves accompanying Santa Claus in the fire truck at the end, I searched for the happiness I had felt during times like these in the past, but saw no pleasure.

The short-lived joy of the season was soon diminished when days later the news of a missing college student from Kentucky soon surfaced. Her body was yet to be discovered, but authorities already believed her to be dead. Our last full moon was the night before the Christmas parade.

On Christmas Eve, my mother took the day off to bake cookies with me and Natalie. She took on the actual baking duty while Nat and I decorated with icing and nibbled on the cookie dough. I was consumed with the colors of icing I would add to each cookie, creating a unique piece of art with each one. We listened to the local radio station, which was dedicating the next 48 hours to Christmas music, and the three of us sang along cheerfully to every song. We had the music at a high volume and were singing so loudly that only my mom heard the knock at the front door. She left us for a moment to answer the door as Natalie continued singing *Santa Baby* in an overdramatic and breathy voice, causing me to giggle.

My mom came around the corner again and spoke to me softly as she turned the volume down on the radio. "Jules, Jackson's here. He wants to speak to you."

I twisted around in my chair. "*Jackson?*"

Natalie shrugged, clearly as confused with his visit as I was.

I walked to the foyer of our house to find Jackson, alone, wearing a toboggan and a heavy coat. It was freezing outside, but no snow. Our chances for a white Christmas were pretty good this year, though.

As I approached, he smiled kindly. "Hi, Jules! Are you having a good vacation?"

I gave a small smile. "About as well as can be expected."

He nodded quietly and fell silent. Jackson had never come over before, aside from my birthday party, and I had never seen him without Taryn. Something was up.

"Is there somewhere we can talk privately?" he asked.

I led him down to the family room. "You wanna play some pool?"

"Sure. I'll break," he quickly claimed.

"Jerk," I muttered teasingly. "Where's Taryn?"

"She's in Knoxville shopping with her mom and aunt."

"You couldn't pay me to go out in that mess today," I laughed.

"Which is why I stayed behind." Jackson didn't start on his initial reason for being here, until after he broke. "Stripes," he claimed. "I'm sorry about what happened with Broderick."

"I'll recover." I struck a small cluster of balls to see one roll in a pocket and shrugged as if I had moved on from the heartache.

He pressed his lips together in concentration and accidently knocked one of the solid balls in a pocket. "Crap!" He whispered at his bad move. "I don't think he will recover."

"What do you mean *he* won't recover?" I asked with a twinge of anger ringing in my voice.

He must have heard the anger in my voice, because he looked sympathetically at me. "Do you really believe that *you'll* recover?"

I looked out the windows to avoid eye contact. My tough persona couldn't fight my confession for long. "I don't know… it doesn't really feel like it… Probably not."

Jackson leaned in and rammed the cue stick into the ball, letting it burst through the huddle of balls and I watched them disperse into a spill of colors on the green table. When he saw nothing was accomplished with his move, he stood up straight and stepped away from the table to allow me some space as I walked past him.

"When I first realized he was in love with you, I'll admit that I wasn't thrilled." He cocked his head in way of misgiving, "I mean, after that incident last spring over Gavin, you weren't exactly my choice as a girlfriend for my best friend. No offense."

I just chuckled at the reminder. Last spring no longer troubled me. It seemed like a different lifetime. A different person.

"But seeing the way he looked at you… I had never seen him so taken with anyone."

I scowled, fighting hard against the defeat of giving into Broderick again.

"Why are you telling me this, Jackson?" I pleaded. My aching heart was breaking yet again as I heard an eyewitness account of the love and affection I had been convinced of and was so sure about up until a little over a month ago.

"Because that look was still there in his eyes as he watched you from across the street during the Christmas Parade over a week ago."

My mouth dropped. I had no idea Broderick had been watching me there. I looked for him, but never saw him.

"I offered to go and talk to you for him, but he refused to let me. Believe it or not, even Taryn has told me to mind my own business."

I laughed. "I *do* find that hard to believe."

"She's on your side with this one. She said you had put up with enough of his crap. I think she's also speaking as a girl who had put up with his crap before…"

"And whose side are you on?" I asked him, cringing with the possibility that he was against me.

"I'm on Broderick's side, of course. But I think Broderick's side *is* your side. This mess—this just isn't right; it doesn't make sense. You two belong together."

"So why are you here? Broderick would kill you if he knew you were here and Taryn thinks it's a bad idea, too."

"Because this morning, before she left for Knoxville, she and I discussed it at length and we believe that if the three of us could have an intervention with him, we can fix it. It wasn't you that messed things up. There's something wrong with *him*. We'd all be blind to not realize that. There's got to be a way we can help him and fix it so the two of you would see you're meant to be together. I've lost him too, Jules. I want my best friend back—well and happy again. Jules, *you* make him happy."

"I've noticed the change, too." Relief washed over me, knowing I wasn't the only person to recognize the difference in Broderick. "I've been so worried about him…"

"We'd like for you to be there during the intervention. We're scheduling it sometime after the New Year. No need to ruin the holidays since this could heat up to World War III."

"I'll be on a band trip and won't get back until the third day of school. But I'll do it with you then, if you guys wait for me."

"Thank you, Jules!" he exclaimed in relief. "I'll talk to Evelyn, too, and see when she will allow us over. Joey's taking part, as well."

"Great." I thought of Evelyn and how I was going to have to endure her scrutiny. It would be worth it if it meant getting Broderick well, though.

Christmas came and went with little excitement. That night, we actually got flurries and I sat in my bedroom window in a hypnotic state as I watched it fall to the ground by the street light, at the feet of the shadowy figure.

Exhausted from my broken heart, my sad eyes begged for one last release. *This will be the last cry, so get it all out tonight.* I made my silent vow.

I sobbed with such force my bed shook as I lay down on it. Crying quietly proved to be an immense undertaking, for I couldn't tell if it was me or something outside—maybe the wind—that howled.

I rang in the New Year just the same.

The Witching Hour

WE WERE SCHEDULED TO meet at six in the morning by the band room for the trip to Destin. Procrastination being one of my biggest flaws, I packed the night before. Since fashion hadn't ever been a top priority of mine, I just threw in a bunch of T-shirts and jeans. I wasn't sure what kind of weather I would find in Florida this time of year. Hoping the winters down there was more like a Tennessee autumn, I grabbed a few hoodies. With all the jeans and shirts I planned to bring there was hardly any room left in my suitcase.

I tried to not let it get the best of me when I found the suitcase I had left just inside my bedroom door the night before waiting patiently for me in my car the following morning. Whoever it was, and I was positive it was Broderick trying to scare me, I wasn't going to give him the satisfaction; ignoring it altogether as if I was completely unaware.

My luggage was already loaded under the bus when Cari arrived at the school. She was late, as usual, but came bearing a vanilla latte from the Java House.

As she handed me the large cup, she said, "My stalker told me to tell you hi."

I laughed as she snidely referred to Chase as her stalker. Cari sat in the aisle seat near the back, and I took the window. From the window I watched the towns pass by through country highways. We finally turned onto the interstate when we reached Chattanooga, leaving nothing but the bland Alabama pines to look at until we reached Florida. Their blur gave me a headache, so I closed my eyes and let a semi-restful sleep take over as I pulled off my heavy winter coat and bundled it under my head for a pillow.

When we arrived, Mr. Grayson gave us the evening to unwind from the drive, unpack and settle in our rooms. Most of Sunday was wasted on practicing for the competition, with a few breaks in between. I was so exhausted that night I crashed immediately upon entering our hotel room, falling asleep in my jeans and T-shirt.

Our competition was early Monday morning, so everyone was in a rush to get dressed and warm up. I just wanted to do the routine and go home. I secretly hoped our little hometown band wasn't qualified enough to go beyond the first round. The sooner we were done, the sooner I could go to my room and sleep. I wasn't tired, just shiftless. I didn't even feel guilty for the thought when it was announced by the judges our band, in fact, was not going on to the second round. Many were not upset. It was clear I was not the only one who felt like we had better things to do while out of school.

By getting away, I thought it would help me move on, give me a breather, but instead I was homesick. I missed my parents and Natalie. I actually missed being in class for the first day back at school. Wondering how I would react to seeing Broderick again, I felt the illness overtake me. I so badly wished I could be looking out my bedroom window at that familiar landscape as opposed to the crashing waves of the emerald green gulf.

The minute three o'clock struck, I was dialing Natalie's cell. "Nat! How was school?" I exclaimed, completely surprised at how lively I sounded after hearing her voice.

She groaned, "Blech! Don't get me started. How's Destin? Have you been in the water any?"

"Are you kidding? The water is freezing!" I laughed. "How are things at home?"

"Boring. By the way, the library called for you on Saturday. Says you have an overdue book out and they want it back."

"I don't even think I have a membership card at the library. I hate reading," I replied with a confused look upon my face.

She laughed aloud in agreement. "Also, Pam Patterson called to remind you of your hair appointment on Thursday. Finally touching up those red roots?"

"*Long* overdue."

A heavy silence fell suddenly. "They found the people behind the Full Moon Murders."

Just hearing about the Full Moon Murders jostled me and I deliberated whether I wanted to know the outcome. I trembled with bated breath, "Who was it?"

"You mean 'who were *they*'," she corrected. "They were actually right here in Crossville this whole time—right under our noses. Can you believe it? How creepy is that? Joey's dad got a tip about a group of seven people dead in an old abandoned house late last night; some mass cult suicide or something. He's pretty sure that they're the guilty party. All the evidence is pointing in their direction."

"Oh my gosh!" I gasped.

"One of them was even that weirdo Reiser guy. What was his name?"

"*Lucas?*" I asked, thinking about how spine-chilling he had become. In hindsight, it was obvious he and his gang were threatening that night at the dance.

"Yeah! That's him."

"Was Ingrid Silivasi one of the bodies they found, too?"

"No, she was actually the one who tipped off the police. According to talk around town, it messed her up pretty bad finding Lucas like that." I shook my head at the bewildering news. *Unbelievable.* "The news about it all is just now getting out to everybody. Sheriff wanted to keep it under wraps until they were sure of everything they suspected, but you know…small town."

"Wow," I breathed.

The line got quiet again suddenly. Then Natalie sighed. Her voice was uneasy, "He's not at school anymore, Jules."

"What?"

"Broderick bowed out of school this semester. He has enough credits to graduate early. He'll be back in the spring to actually walk the line with the remaining seniors, but that's it. He's done."

My heart sank. I knew it would be easier for me not to see him every day, but my heart simply couldn't accept it. I wanted to see him as much as possible, no matter how much it hurt. The pain was slowly growing to a burn again. Selfishly, I was beginning to look forward to the intervention more for my own personal gain of seeing him than to offer him help.

Selfish, as usual.

"You know he still loves you, right?"

I frowned at her know-it-all tone. "How would you know how he feels?"

"I've got fourth lunch this semester and I'm spending it with my new buddy, Jackson," she said as a matter of fact. "*He* told me."

"Great. Nothing's sacred anymore. Why didn't he just graduate early, too?" I asked sourly.

I heard her breathy chuckle. "Because Taryn didn't have enough credits to graduate with him. He qualifies, she doesn't. He's going to stick around this last semester just to be with her."

"So you and Jackson have become best friends now, huh?"

"I have stinkin' fourth lunch and all my friends have second lunch. It sucks." I smiled. I so badly wanted to hear my mom scold her in the background, but forgot that she was still at work. "Anyway, we both believe that Broderick ended things with you because of something with him personally. It actually had nothing to do with you."

I needed to change the subject again. The conversation had quickly taken the turn for the worse in respect to my broken heart. My voice had already reverted back to its desolate sound.

I asked the unthinkable, "How's Joey?" As soon as the question left my lips I winced and smacked myself on the head.

Her sigh was heavy. "How should I know? He's too good to be my friend now that he's dating *Lindsey*," she said in a sour sneer.

Before I could reply, she was off filling me in. "Apparently they spent the holiday's together *ev-er-y* day." She continued making that nasally sound, "They romantically brought in the New Year together and for Christmas he bought her a tiny diamond pendant…"

"Wow, for someone who doesn't know, you sure do know an awful lot," I pointed out.

"Berta told me. It's not like I asked for the information or anything…" She chuckled haughtily to herself, "As if I cared…"

My sister continued to prattle on about how Lindsey and Joey were a poor match as my phone beeped, warning me that the battery was running low. I reached over the other side of the bed to pull my suitcase onto the bed and unzipped the small front pocket to retrieve my phone charger. Midst the knotted mess of the phone cord, was the silver medallion that I had returned to Broderick.

It was like having the breath knocked out of me. I singled the piece out, flipped it over and held it up to my face in disbelief as the rest of the mess dangled from my hand. *Life's greatest challenge is becoming who you were meant to be.*

"Holy shit." I stared, staggered by the silver medallion that lay tangled in the palm of my hand. It didn't come across as a scare tactic and I didn't see this as a sick, obsessive torture on his part. It was a cry for help. He was trying to tell me something. Something important. Maybe he had been trying to relay this secretive message to me all along! What did it all mean?

I caught Natalie off guard. "Holy shit, what?"

Scrambled, my thoughts were trying to line with something insightful. "Nat! Have you heard anything weird at night since I've been gone?"

She sharply caught on to my nervous behavior. "No and I've been up *a lot* lately, so it's not like I've been sleeping through anything. With everything going on in this town, I've been having some horrific nightmares. Why?"

I stared obsessively at the medallion in my hand I had returned to him, but somehow it had made its way back to me. The decision was made. "You're right, Nat. I need to fight for him."

"Yes!" Natalie cheered. "Tell me what I have to do, Jules."

A burst of energy shot through my body. "Right now, I just need your support."

"You got it." She was on the edge of squeals, I could hear them climbing up her throat. "Are you going to go see him as soon as you get in town?"

"Yes." My voice was sure and determined.

She finally released that squeal; I could practically see her smiling that bright, toothy grin of hers.

As we both hung up, Cari walked in and sat next to me on the bed. "Wanna go to a party on the ninth floor?"

Possessing Broderick's medallion again was surely cause for some sort of celebration. It was the happiest I had been in months! "Sure, just give me a second."

I placed my phone on the charger and fastened the medallion around my neck.

A short explosion of air circulate my lungs at I took a glimpse into the mirror at the sight of the medallion resting high on my chest. He didn't want things to end any more than I did. If he needed help with something, that's exactly what I was going to do. Nothing could stop me from it now. *Nothing*.

Sneaking off to the party, we quietly tiptoed through the halls and hid behind corners where the ice machines were. The anxiety I felt only increased when I saw that the room was crammed with over thirty kids from other schools and that the party was slowly bleeding out into the hall into neighboring rooms. I was the only one not drinking—or so it felt.

I left for a few moments to get a coke from the machine down the hall and saw one of the hotel patrons knocking on the door of a chaperone of one of the other schools. I quickly made my way back to Cari.

"This party is about to be busted; we better go!" I pulled her to the back stairwell that led to the outdoor pool. She and I walked out the doors and through the gates leading to the beach. We strolled over to an endless row of blue reclining chairs supplied by the hotel.

Curling our legs up to stay warm, Cari and I sat peacefully, listening to the crashing waves and watching the starry sky. The large white moon shimmered magnificently off the black waters. She began talking about prom dresses and though I was pleasantly surprised to hear her speak of prom as if she planned to go, I got the distinct feeling that she was eyeing someone in particular as a prom date. Someone I did *not* like.

"Is it Isaac?" I asked.

She looked hurt, played off as though I was crazy. "What? No way! We're just friends."

"Okay." I accepted her defense verbally, but was still skeptical.

The crisp night air was sobering her up quickly. "Did you have sex with him? Boy Scout?"

I chuckled at her directness and blushed. "No. And I'm so thankful we didn't. I gave him my heart and soul. If I had given him my virginity, I would be an even bigger mess now," I admitted to her.

She was silent for a few moments then shocked me with her sudden revelation. "Isaac and I have been having sex for a few months now."

I jerked my head in her direction with my eyes wide and mouth open. "Shut up! No freakin' way!"

She laughed at my reaction. "I knew I could count on you to freak out on me like that."

"Are you *still* sleeping with him?"

She wrinkled her nose and shook her head indifferently.

"Why would you do it with him in the first place?"

She was direct and plain in her explanation. "It was like a friends-with-benefits thing. He wanted to get it on and I was curious. Besides, if you're going to be curious enough to do it, you might as well do it with someone hot, right?"

I was disappointed in her. "I guess."

"It really wasn't a big deal, Jules," she defended. "There were no strings attached, no feelings involved." She said the words in determination, and I couldn't see anything on her face that would say otherwise.

"So?" I waited for her to answer but she looked at me as though she didn't know what I was asking. "What was it like?"

She bellowed out in laughter.

"Don't laugh at me," I said in giggles. "I'm just as curious as you are— or *were*!" I corrected.

She finally gained control and turned to face me. "He was so gentle. He made it romantic for me every time, even though we were just friends."

"Go on…" I really was interested. In spite of the fact I always knew Isaac was a scoundrel, I was deeply curious as to what it was like.

"It got erotic at times," she tempted with information.

"Like what?" My voice dripped in innocent anticipation.

Punching me in the arm, she laugh heartily again. "I'm not your personal porn pal! I'm not giving you details." She gained control of herself again. "But it felt good. Of course it hurt like hell the first time, even though he tried to be easy with me. But after that… wow! All I can say is *wow*!"

"*Wow*," I repeated, still bowled over at the knowledge that she had been sleeping with Isaac all along and I didn't even know.

She then became serious again and looked out to the water, "You're smart to wait."

I silently nodded.

"Did you hear that they found the killers back home?" She asked.

I nodded solemnly. "Natalie told me just before you showed up today."

She sighed with relief. "Glad that shit is over."

Just the waves and our slow, steady breathing filled the air around us.

"Waxing Gibbous," she said suddenly

"Huh?"

She pointed to the sky. "Waxing Gibbous. The moon. It's over 70% full. We can finally enjoy the full moon again."

"Yeah," I calmly agreed.

We stayed there for hours until we both fell asleep, only to find ourselves waking at the first sign of the sun. Like Cari, most of our band and flag corps members were hung over, and therefore, our bus didn't leave until much later than planned. I was restless to get home and the three hour delay agitated me. Our schedule progressively got further behind throughout the trip home, and I wondered if there was going to be a way for me to stop by Broderick's house on the way home. It would be after midnight—closer to one. Surely he'd be awake, and surely he'd at least let me in long enough to plead my case. I called my parents and told them of the massive delays. They agreed to take my car to the school and leave it so I could drive home alone. This worked perfectly to my advantage where seeing Broderick was concerned, and there was no way they were going to be able to stay up that late to pick me up, anyway.

We finally pulled into our high school parking lot at two o'clock in the morning. After the luggage was all unloaded from the buses, I wheeled my suitcase over to my car that had been parked near the front row of the school parking lot. It was surrounded by cars belonging to other marching band members. I dug around in my purse for my keys until I heard them jingle in my coat pocket. I unlocked the trunk and slung my suitcase in and shut the door.

"Jules! Can you help with the flag equipment?" Emma Rose yelled from the F-wing breezeway. Her voice cut through the quiet night, and the sudden noise made me feel edgy.

"Yeah, sure! Hang on a second," I groaned with the notion that I would have to be right back here for school in just a matter of hours. I wondered if Mom and Dad would let me skip class on the account of no sleep, because I felt like crap already.

With all the activity I was going to be doing with unloading equipment, the last thing I needed was a purse and a bulky winter jacket hindering me so, I unlocked my front doors and threw my purse in the passenger's side seat along with my winter jacket, then shut the door and locked it again. For the first time in months, I was wearing the red hoodie. I pulled its hood over my head to keep my ears warm, but my arms still felt chilly, so I returned to my suitcase in the trunk and retrieved my white hoodie as well, layering in on top of the red one.

I helped Emma gather the two sets of show flags from the bus, and brought them into the band room to remove the flags from the poles and fold them up. Flag season was officially over and we wouldn't be using them again until spring tryouts. Little by little, the crowd of students left until it was just eight of us—Mr. Grayson, the flag captains, drum majors, a majorette, and me. I was so tired a light buzzing sensation flooded my body. I had been this tired before, like after the night Broderick and I had been out to that haunted church. How shaky I'd felt the entire next day! Only a good long sleep can cure that. As Emma counted every item I would viciously rub my eyes and nose to stay awake. She looked up and chuckled.

"Play freeze-out on the way home," she said suddenly as she grabbed the clipboard from me.

I was too tired to grasp what she was saying. "Say what?"

She patted me on the back. "Freeze-out on the way home to stay awake. Roll down your windows to get cold. It'll keep you awake long enough to make it home safely. Go home and go to bed."

"Thanks." I walked over to the conductor's stand where I thought I'd left my keys but saw nothing. "Uh, Em, do you remember where I put my keys?" I laughed at my sleep deprived brain.

She ducked her head out of the flag room. "You didn't lock them in your car did you?"

I groaned at first, but then remembered that I locked my doors from the outside. I shook my head.

Emma stopped inventory for a few minutes to help me find my keys. One of the majorettes found them on the bathroom sink. I rolled my eyes at my own stupidity and thanked her.

The parking lot was practically vacant now. Very few vehicles remained, and my row was completely empty, save my car. Trotting across the dark parking lot, I was trying to get a skip in my step to wake me up a bit before I got behind the wheel. Emma was right, the wintry air was stimulating. I made a strong mental note as I pulled the handle of my door not to turn on the heat in my car and instead turn on the cool air and roll down my windows. I was feeling just tired enough to crash behind the wheel, so freeze-out was the only way I knew to make the fifteen minute drive home without any trouble.

Without traffic, maybe I can make it home in ten minutes. Maybe five?

I hopped inside my car and jammed the key in the ignition bringing the vehicle to life. The seat was so cold it felt like sitting on ice through my jeans. Shrugging out of the white hoodie and draping it over the back of the passenger seat, I let the car engine warm up a bit and turned on the radio just after flipping on the air. I finally found something descent on the radio and began pulling out of the parking lot.

As I drove through town, I found it ghostly that I couldn't find a living soul on the sidewalks or driving along the streets. The Christmas décor of snowflakes and lighted angels blowing their trumpets were still up on the streetlamps.

I rolled down my window, allowing the unpleasant cold wind into the chilly confines of my car. Coming to the stop light at the library, I groaned to myself. This light was notorious for taking its time to change.

As I turned the radio up, a gust of wind blew through and I shivered myself to a short wakeful state again. I tried warming my fingers up as I blew on them with my warm breath and the breath ricocheted off from my hand and back into my face, causing me to pull my face away.

"Ew," I curled my upper lip and smacked my lips and moved my tongue in a repulsed manner. My mouth felt tired and sticky and I badly wanted to brush my teeth. There was a pack of gum was in my purse. Or was it in my coat pocket? I reached over to the passenger seat to search them while waiting at the red light, but saw that the seat was empty. Sitting up to let my eyes focus, I caught something large in the backseat in my peripheral, directly behind the passenger's seat. I jerked my head around to see my suitcase behind the passenger's seat.

"Way to freak yourself out there, Jules," I weakly laughed.

Now obsessed in finding the pack of gum, I looked on the floorboard to see if maybe my purse and coat had slipped off the seat at some point while I was driving. It was too dark to make out anything. I looked debatably at the light and at the crossroads. I couldn't see anyone coming and I played with the idea of just running the stupid light.

No. With my luck, a cop will pull up, just in time to see me do it.

Leaning far over the gear shift to feel for my purse in the shadow of the floorboard, my foot let up off the brake and I started to roll. Quickly, I sat up and slammed on my brake with a nervous heave. *I'm awake!* I pushed the gear shift in park as another icy wind blew through; causing me to shiver so harshly my back began to ache. I unbuckled my seat belt when I saw that the light was still red, and this time, reached far over to the floorboard on the passenger's side to retrieve my purse and jacket, but the space felt completely empty. Nothing was there. I lay there across the gear shift for a moment and second guessed myself. *Did I put them in the backseat?*

My heart slammed hard into my chest suddenly as I realized a major displacement. I had put my suitcase in the trunk and here it was in my backseat. The more I thought about it, the more I also realized I had locked my car before I went back in the band room to help Emma. When I came back out, *I never used my keys to unlock it, did I?* And I know for a fact my purse and jacket were left in the passenger's seat.

My heart began to race, and I shivered in unprecedented fear. The nearby church bells began to chime a familiar hymn into the night.

Intense, I began to sit back up and then prepared to slam on the gas when suddenly a horn honked from behind me, causing me to jump in my seat and scream. I looked in the rearview to see two bright headlights blinding me from any other reflection but my own and... A shadowy figure was seated directly behind me. Just as I gasped, it reached out and clamped a cold, hard hand over my mouth. I fought to pull the hand off of me but he was too strong and he pressed my head forcefully against the back of the seat. Kicking, reaching for anything that could help me. My mind raced in a million directions but couldn't focus. My foot stomped on the gas pedal, only revving up the engine because I had it in park. Outside my window, I heard car doors being opened and feet pattering on the pavement. All too soon, hands reached in the open window and began pulling me, grabbing at me.

Slithering out from under the hold of the person behind me, I screamed. I threw myself over to the passenger's seat and tried pulling myself away from the window, but felt cold hands effortlessly take hold of my legs and feet. I kicked hopelessly, grabbing at the open window of the passenger door trying to pull away again, but the door flew open, and icy fingers wrapped into my hair, pulling it out by the handfuls and scratching at my face and neck.

"God, help me!" I heard my voice cry out as the church bells continued to chime.

I heard the driver's door open and was violently yanked by my ankles out onto the pavement. I couldn't count how many people were attacking me—Six? Seven? My efforts were all in vain. I was powerless against so many. I continued to scream in climbing volumes and began scratching for something to hold onto on the cold blacktop of the road. I felt a small crevice and latched on for dear life as they tried pulling me away. What started as a ripping sensation at the tip of my middle finger gave way and popped. An onslaught of new pain shot through my finger and then my hand as they dragged me across the pavement. The rough street scratched at my torso like a cheese grater until it burned. They yanked harder and my head dropped fast at the motion, clipping my chin. My car was quickly becoming distant and they were pulling me to the brightly lit vehicle behind me.

"Help me!" I screamed

I ferociously began another kicking frenzy and tried twisting away, the street shredding my back and sides all the way up to my shoulders. I used every bit of energy trying to try to sit up as they lugged me to their vehicle, thinking it would allow me more control. As I tried sitting up, someone kicked the side of my face with their boot, slamming the back of my head to the pavement. The blinding bright light swiftly became dim with fog, and I felt my eyes roll to the back of my head.

God, don't let me die this way! My prayer was quickly fading as the whole world turned to black. I struggled to open my eyes again, just in time to see the split-second whirlwind of images—tree tops, power lines, a street lamp, a church steeple, the dark sky, and the moon—flash in my vision as though I were flying. I dropped hard on a cold slab of metal, making a booming sound, but that didn't compare to the thundering crash of the sliding door. My eye lids were closing yet again, making the church on the corner disappear before my very eyes.

Broderick, help me!

I was fading uncontrollably in blackness!

God, help me!

The church bells went silent.

Entombed

ROLLING OVER ON THE soft pillow, I looked over to see Broderick lying next to me and watching me with soft eyes. He had been waiting for me to wake up.

"Good morning, sleepyhead." He smiled affectionately.

I blinked frantically to adjust my eyes to the bright room with purple walls. "How did I get home? I —"

Sitting beside my bed, Natalie spoke, "We found you lying in a ditch somewhere."

I couldn't help but stifle a chuckle. She sounded like Mom when I didn't check in with her.

"Lying in a ditch somewhere," I repeated in a tired giggle.

My body was sore and I started remembering flashes of a struggle from the night before. I remembered nothing since then... something was wrong.

"What happened last night?" I asked as I tried to stretch, but couldn't figure out how to make my limbs move. I tried swinging my leg over to the edge of the bed and wriggle my toes out from under the blanket, but I couldn't. My toes and legs began feeling frigid under this blanket, too. In fact, my whole body was freezing cold!

"You never came home," Natalie answered.

"You're missing," Broderick replied.

Frustrated with my own immobile limbs and an oncoming killer-headache, I only caught a bit of what they had said so I stopped my battle to move and listened instead.

Did Broderick just use the present tense?

"Jules, you're in danger." Broderick was grave. Immediately, the sun went out as if someone had pulled the switch and shadows fell all along the room.

My right cheek began throbbing in pain and shot through to the back of my head. I wanted to place my hands on my face, to press in the pain, maybe make it stop, but my hands wouldn't move. My whole body began to sting excessively.

The pain caused me to whimper and Natalie reached through the darkness to grab me. Urgently pleading, "Jules, you need to get out of there before it's too late."

I gasped, and everything went pitch black.

Am I awake? Are my eyes open? I was positive they were after I sporadically blinked them for a bit, yet I saw nothing. The persistent throbbing on my right cheek bone and my head was enough reason to scream, but I couldn't find the courage to utter a sound.

The fresh memory of the struggle I had incurred was lucid and vivid. My body was shaking in tight, violent motions—cold and achy. I was certain that my tendons would snap from the stress of my flexed muscles. I slowly moved my hand to my tender face and head, dragging it across a cold ground of dirt and gravel. The tip of my middle finger was throbbing so I curled it slowly for my thumb to feel. It rubbed gently over raw flesh where a fingernail once was and my body tightened in shock. My hand flew up to my face and I quaked in an airy, high pitched sob, careful to keep myself quiet.

My eyes couldn't adjust to the darkness and I was horrified by my lack of orientation. I had no idea where I was, except that I was on a cold and dirty ground in the dark. *Black!* My throat started to tickle, but I didn't dare grunt or cough. I didn't want anyone to know I was alive, in fear of being brutally murdered or worse yet, tortured and left for dead.

My mind reeled in a thousand different directions. *What is happening? Who would want to hurt me? Mom and Dad will know soon enough that I didn't come home, and they'll come looking for me.*

I remembered seeing my red Mini Cooper sitting at the four ways stop light with the doors open and headlights on. The light had finally turned green as I was being pulled away from it. Someone had to come across the idle car shortly after that! I had no idea what time it was, it could have been fifteen minutes later or... Maybe an hour? Possibly *hours.* Natalie could have waited up for me, as she was so eager to find out what happened between Broderick and me. Maybe she noticed I wasn't home long before I was even taken, and people were already out looking for me. The sooner it was realized I was missing, the better the chances of me being found, right?

But my tears whispered hopelessness as they stung the abrasions on my face. I wanted to sit up, off the cold, hard ground but didn't want anyone to detect my movements. I couldn't see, but I wondered if there was someone in here with me, and I questioned whether they could see. Drawing my feet up slowly, I pictured myself resembling an inch worm as I placed my hand underneath my stinging torso with tired and shaking arms, walking myself up into a sitting position with my palms.

My eyes were wet with tears, and I was so cold I wondered if they would freeze on my lashes. I crossed my arms and rubbed them with my hands to warm myself, but it provided little warmth and no comfort. The shaking was beyond my control, and I knew it was due to fear, cold, shock, and pain. My whole body hurt. There was a ringing in my ears and a steady vibration coursing throughout my body. I brushed the left side of my face and felt a few pebbles drop to the ground that were embedded into my skin from where I lay on them. It was my only clue I had been here for a while.

My heart ached for my home and my family. For Broderick. I shuddered in sobs again as I recognized the danger I was in and that I might never see them again. Looking back in regret, I conjured up ways I could have prevented this from happening and deflected my brain from wondering what would happen to me next.

If I had just stayed home and not gone to Florida with the band... If I hadn't stayed to help Emma... If I had found my keys sooner... If I had my doors locked and windows up... if I had taken the back roads to my house instead of downtown... If I had only asked for a ride home from Cari instead of having my parents drop my car off to drive home alone... If I had stayed in my hotel room the night before, getting a good night's sleep, I would have been strong enough to fight them all off and possible run away!

My crying had remained silent, but I so desperately wanted to call out for help. My throat was still tickling, and felt dry and itchy, probably from all the screaming I had done. I didn't want to get the attention of those who held me captive, though. Testing the atmosphere, I let out an audible sigh and waited to see the response I would get. I listened carefully, for it was the only useful sense I had that was useful at this point. I heard nothing but my trembling breath. A blanket of silence covered the space giving to the notion that even if I were to scream, it would somehow be muffled. Snow did that. Though it was light and I could still hear my surroundings well, it felt insulated and crisp. This location was like a box, even muffling the sound of my breathing.

The quiet area, though eerily disconcerting, gave me some relief that maybe I didn't have company in the room. *I wish I could see!* Making a louder sound, I softly cleared my throat and waited for a response again. This time I counted to three hundred, thinking that approximately five minutes would be ample enough time for a reaction if someone was listening.

When the minutes passed, I felt at ease enough to move around on the ground and get my bearings, repositioning myself on my knees to crawl. My arms felt mushy from the fear and exhaustion. I would crawl a foot forward, then tap my hand lightly around me. The ground felt the same, cold and dirty with tiny pieces of gravel. Then I moved a foot or so to my right and felt a thin and lumpy cotton mattress; it reeked of vomit and urine and a familiar metallic smell. Another two feet from that was a blanket, with the same rancid scent.

I continued my blind search pattern countless times when I finally felt a solid wall, but lined with something cold, thin and with a feel of fiber. I pressed hard on the lining to get a better understanding as to what I was touching. It felt familiar and sounded familiar as I ran my hand slowly over it. I tilted my thumbnail and forced down on what felt like a weak spot, the material gave way with a small popping sound and I flinched. *Paper?* I blindly picked at the new hole with my thumbnail, making my middle finger sore as I clumsily rubbed it against the makeshift wall. Finally, I got a solid piece between my fingers and pulled, feeling a ridged pattern inside, made of the same material. Not just paper. *Cardboard.* Like a broken down box. Strangely, the familiarity of the material gave me a sad sense of comfort. I tore at the hole until I found the solidity of the wall. With my left hand, I scratched at it, feeling the matter build up under my fingernails. *Dirt.*

Am I underground? Like a grave! I panicked.

It was time to make an even louder noise to test the area again. Coughing loudly, I waited, bracing myself against the cardboard wall and crying. I wondered when I would become so dehydrated that the tears would no longer flow, and my weeping would be dry like a heaving drought. My crying couldn't be audible, though. My stubborn personality told me not to give the perpetrators the satisfaction of making me cry, though I knew if I had a choice right now, I would beg and plead to be released. I counted to three hundred again, and nothing happened; no one came.

There had to be a way out of here. After crawling around for what seemed like hours, I found a door. I firmly grasped the knob and turned… it was locked. As I felt around its hinges, I realized that it wasn't really attached to the room I was in, that it was hinged onto whatever frame was on the other side of the door. *Maybe I could dig my way out?*

Returning to the walls, I quietly started ripping the cardboard away from the dirt and instantly felt a noticeable drop in temperature from the holes I was creating. The cardboard was my only insulation, so I stopped. I'd die of exposure before I ever dug my way out. I was shivering again and curled into a ball with my back facing up, rubbing my hands together, breathing on them with my hot sticky breath so my breath would bounce from my palms onto my face to try and warm my nose. I curled my body inward, tighter and tighter, until my back felt too chilly. Then I repositioned myself on my side, pressing my cold back against the cardboard, lying on the thin cot and curling up in the smelly blanket. The stench persistently gagged me. I held myself tightly, ignoring my need to pee.

I prayed that God would somehow get me home to my family, negotiating promises in exchange for that chance. I promised I would never tell another lie, that I would never say another cuss word, would never watch another vulgar movie, wouldn't watch any sacrilegious horror movies, that I would never have sex before I was married, that I wouldn't even think of sex...

My promises fell flat, and I felt as if God was no longer listening to me, that I was hidden so deep into the earth that it was impossible for Him to hear. I considered that maybe He wasn't listening because my promises were unrealistic. I would never be able to hold up my end of the bargain. All I could do was ask for forgiveness at this point and hope He would have a change of heart toward me. I told him I was sorry for all of the evil and selfish things I had done in my life, but as I tried to make a mental list of it all, I felt myself drifting into another realm of lonely darkness.

I shuddered awake at the noisy entry of two bodies, verbally silent. My eyes were definitely open now, because I was blinded by the light. My vision couldn't adjust quickly enough to grasp the full picture in front of me. I felt worse than before—sore and stiff—and I winced in pain and horror as the two bodies jerked me harshly off from the ground by my arms and dragged me into the light. My shaky legs hindered me from putting up a strong fight and my knees scrapped against the uneven ground, causing me to bounce around as the two roughly held onto me. My throat was dry and tight, and I began to weep.

"Where are you taking me? Where are you taking me?" I repeated over and over. My insides became tight and jittery with anxiety.

The bodies didn't answer, disturbing me even more. Their cold, hard hands clamped callously around my thin arms, and I concluded that by the size of their hands and by their strength, they were men.

My voice grew louder and screechy. "Talk to me! Where am I going? Please don't do this. Please don't do this…" I shook violently from the bawling and thrashed with all my might. I needed to free myself somehow and run for help, but I couldn't think beyond just getting their hands off of me.

My eyes still weren't fully adjusted, but I was starting to make out a few shapes as they dragged me through the long, dimly lit hall. The lights seemed brighter in certain spots just above my head to the right. As I passed each essence of brightness, I could feel the warmth and smell the fire. It reminded me of a dungeon beneath a castle, with torches to provide light along the way. Finally, the brightness began dying off and gave way for me to see what was ahead. I saw a flight of stairs that led to an old door at the end of the dirt tunnel. The instinctual horror that filled me as we drew closer to the door propelled me into frantic screams.

"I don't wanna die! Please, someone help me! Help!"

I thrashed from side to side again trying to pull away from the end of the hall as my voice shrieked hysterically—quickly exhausting myself, using the last of my energy. I hadn't had anything to eat or drink since I was on the bus, and I didn't even know how long ago that was. My body went limp and I continued to snivel through my tears and running nose.

"Please don't do this. You don't have to do this. I just wanna go home. Please! I'll do anything. My parents will pay you! They'll give you all of their money…."

The guy on my right opened the door and they started hauling me up the stairs. My arms felt as if they were ripping from the sockets as they drug me. I saw a light glowing at the top of the stairs. I heard a faint voice speaking. Then, after a few more slow steps up the wooden stairs, I could hear a rhythmic chant from a mass of voices. The familiar smell of incense and sulfur filled my lungs. A second burst of panic and adrenaline coursed through me quickly as I understood why it was all too familiar. *The church!*

I closed my eyes in fear of what I would see—what awaited me on the other side of the doorway. Whipping my body in violent throws again, I hoped that it would cause the three of us to fall down the stairs and give me a chance to escape. The screaming hysterics gave way again. My own voice was alien to me. It was one that belonged to a mad woman. I even heard wild laughter squeeze from my constricted throat as I sobbed. My reckless mind went blank. *Hopeless.*

A tall, blonde woman came near to stand behind me. I begged her to help me, but like the others, she spoke not a word and continued on her mission. She reached around my head with the handkerchief and tried wrapping it around my mouth. I slung my head around to keep her from succeeding, but another girl came forward and held my head tightly with her two stone cold hands. The woman behind me began gagging me, tying it tightly in the back. My eyes were raw and wet from crying, but I tried to focus into the eyes of the girl who stood before me. Despite the slight blindness I had, I found it unfathomable as to how black her eyes were. They weren't a dark brown, but a solid black with a small red ring around the iris. She stared blankly at me and I wondered if she could see me at all with eyes like that. My tongue was pressed back by the gag and my mouth was already exhausted from the discomfort.

"Bring her to the altar," a soothing voice beckoned and the girl in front of me smiled in eager pleasure. Even in the small glow of the candles, providing very little light, I could see her face was as white as her teeth. A chill ran up my spine, and all I could sense around me was evil.

As the two men dragged me into the sanctuary of the church, I saw the same set up of flickering candles, like the night Broderick and I had visited, but what stood behind the altar shook me to my crumbling core. Lucas Reiser stood tall in a black suit—very much alive. He had changed since I last saw him. He wasn't pale like before, but dark—almost gray, reminding me of a mushroom color—sickly and cadaveric. It resembled alabaster. His body looked gaunt and his black hair had thinned considerably.

His presence was incomprehensible to me.

Uncontrollably shaking, I tried screaming but the gag had my mouth bound with my tongue pressed to the back of my throat. All I could produce were muffled squeals. Lucas came toward me, almost as if he were floating and I could smell death on him. With a fluid and graceful motion, he reached out and touched my face, causing me to tremble harder. His hand was hard like plastic and cold like ice. He cocked his head from side to side and studied me. His eyes were different from the girl who held my head in the side corridor. The irises were pitch-black, but instead of the outer red ring, his pupil was silver. Then, like a flash of lightning, he quickly leaned into me and inhaled deeply, running his fingers through my hair and I suddenly peed all over myself as the tears flowed down my stinging face.

He took in my scent with intensity, then pulled back with a sinful smile. He drifted back a few feet and looked to the congregation behind me and opened his skeletal arms wide in a welcomingly manner.

"The circle is complete with this offering," he announced in crisp enunciations.

"The circle is complete," they repeated in a low hum.

"We will submit our burnt offerings tonight on the eve, as we prepare for our feast of blood," Lucas said.

"Life is in the blood!" The voices of the mass rose.

"Immortality will be complete when the beast dines at our table during the full moon."

"The promise will be fulfilled!" They chanted.

The men clutching to my arms twisted me around, and I saw the congregation of about thirty people ranging from my age to the same age as my parents. Everyone was wearing black. The two girls from the corridor entered the sanctuary. The young girl held a silver bowl with several engravings on it, one of the engravings being a pentagram. The older woman held a silver dagger on a red velvet pillow. My eyes enlarged as they drew closer to me, and I screamed as loud as I could through the knotted cloth in my mouth. The man on my left produced a red cable from his jacket pocket and began winding it around my wrist while the man on my right held my wrists together. I tried jumping and bouncing to get away, but their strength was amazing against mine.

The silence of it all became a nightmare to my ears.

The man finished tying my wrists together and effortlessly lifted me off the ground to carry me closer to the altar where Lucas stood. I twisted and jerked my body awkwardly to resist as they placed me on the altar and tied me to it.

The two girls knelt at the altar I was tied to, bowing their heads as Lucas stood over me. He looked up to the sky and in a lifeless and croaking voice spoke words I had never heard before. A different language, but not like a language from another country. More like a language from another place entirely—another world! Then he, too, knelt beside me. I quaked in mortal fear as he placed his heavy, cold hands to my stomach and looked at me.

"You will bring us life immortal and become our saving mother. Feel honored you have been found and chosen. He smiled at me, and my throat became so tight I felt as if I could no longer breathe. He leaned in close to my face again to inhale, this time opening his mouth to literally taste me. As I saw the jagged teeth behind his deep red lips, I shrieked. He smelled of rot and I gagged, fighting the urge to vomit.

He looked to the older woman and requested with authority, "The athame."

She held up the velvet pillow holding the dagger. He gracefully wrapped his fingers around it. His other hand swept up under my neck and began stroking his long, bony fingers through my matted hair, painfully combing it through tangles and away from my face. Then as if he were trying to tie it in a ponytail, he pulled it all back. I felt like fainting, knowing that my life was coming to an end. I close my eyes and tried to brace myself for the stabbing pain, forcing peace into my mind.

And all I could see was Broderick. But like a flash of light, his serene face disappeared and my eyes flew open at the stinging sensation on my scalp. I felt the sawing motion of the dagger against my thick hair as Lucas pulled it away from my head. Writhing in pain and causing myself to choke on the ties around my neck, I felt the air lift out of me and my face became hot and firm. Quickly, the pain subsided and Lucas held up the dagger in one hand and my long brassy tresses in another. The mass spoke in a foreign chant, as he placed what looked like nine inches of my hair in the silver bowl.

He pulled up my bound hands and twisted them upward, so he could look at my palms. The candles beside the altar reflected in the dagger as he slashed both of my palms. I cried out in pain, and he squeezed the wounds, allowing the blood to flow and then drip in the silver bowl. Lucas delicately placed the dagger back onto the velvet pillow and took the bowl from the young girl. I watched him through teary eyes as he laid the bowl on the table and took a long, thin purple candle with inscriptions on it. He tilted the fire down into the bowl and I immediately smelled the burning hair. He pinched something out of another bowl and dusted the fire, causing it to burst into a blue flame. As the flame decreased, he held up the bowl under his nose and inhaled. I could see the bright blue smoke drift into his nostrils. He rolled his eyes shut, then leaned his head back and slowly blew the smoke back out in a billowy black fog.

"Our Lord, we beseech you. Accept our offering," he said in a hush.

Lucas glided around the altar and stood between me and the others while holding the silver bowl. One by one, the mass stood and eerily made their way to the blue flame. Each inhaled the blue smoke and puffed the black cloud from within them, whispering their foreign language. Then they filed out of the front of the church.

When almost everyone had inhaled the smoke and exited, Lucas placed the bowl back on the table and instructed the two men to untie me. I didn't fight them for I felt comatose—lifeless. My heart continued to thunder in my chest, but all sense of life had seeped out of me. Like a ragdoll they removed my gag and began dragging me back to the side corridor that led to the stairs.

Lucas called to them, "Make sure she is given water. We need her alive for the full moon."

The two men carried me back down the stairs through the long tunnel. My head felt lighter without my thick, long mane and I let my head roll with the motion of their walking. My eyes had adjusted to the light and I was able to see better this time. The ground was clearly dirt, as if the tunnel had been dug out and the ceiling and walls had been reinforced with lumber. It reminded me of the tunnels that were made in *The Great Escape*, but these were large enough to stand and walk in. We passed another corridor to the left. I twisted my head around to get a better look at it, but they were walking too fast.

Hope was becoming distant, especially after the two men dropped me into the dirt tomb again and shut the door. I lay on the ground for a few minutes as I readjusted to the desolate blackness of my confines. Just as I felt my body shutting down, I made my way back to the cot I had laid on earlier, feeling around for the smelly blanket. I pulled it over me and curled up tightly underneath it to stay warm as I wore urine-drenched jeans in the cold underground.

I slept in short, jumpy bouts throughout the night.

The sound of footsteps above woke me the next morning and I sat up, pushing the smelly blanket off of me. A wobbly buzz was all over my body and I warred with my own exhaustion to grasp the newest revelation that I was underneath a wooden floor. Fixing my eyes above me, I saw light through the wooden cracks. The light was diminutive but still blinding since my eyes had become so used to utter blackness. I turned away to blink, then faced the light again, allowing my eyes to get used to the brightness a bit at a time. I could slightly see a shadow moving above through the cracks as I continued to hear footsteps.

It would be impossible to reach up to the possible exit. Along with the stiffening soreness from my attack and the exhaustion from all of my struggling, I had battled muscled cramps and stomach pangs all night long. I was in no shape to greet anyone. But deep within myself, I found a spark of combat, willing to fight to stay alive and would do anything to succeed.

"Help!" I shouted as loud as I could through a dry throat and mouth. I tried to swallow, but couldn't muster up enough saliva to do so. It felt as though with each contraction to swallow, the sides of my throat would stick together. "Hello! I'm down here! Someone please! My name is Juliana Irene Taylor and I've been kidnapped. My parents are Leah and Mike Taylor and they live at 46 Creeksi…."

I heard jingling of keys against something metal, located over the floor.

"Yes! Yes! I'm down here and I need to get home!" Excitement grew like a flash within me.

The door was pulled open and the light from above made it impossible to see who was saving me. All I could make out was a figure wearing a hooded cloak peering down from above. I could see locks of her hair swinging down from the cloak and I felt as though she resembled Mary, the mother of Jesus. It was the perfect image of my salvation!

"Thank God, you've found me." I began to cry without tears. "I don't know how long I've been down here, but they're going to kill me if you don't get me out—"

Her low monotone voice echoed down from a few feet above me where she leaned in. "Here's water for you to drink."

Earth shattering disappointment knocked the breath out of me as I realized she was far from any salvation. I was defeated. She dropped a bottle of water down to the ground. As I watched it fall, I prayed it wouldn't burst upon impact. Never had I been so excited to have water! My human nature—my physical *need* for it—took precedence over the disappointment I was not going to escape. I scampered clumsily to grab the bottled water. Just as my fingertips rolled over it, the overhead door slammed shut and I heard the keys jingling again.

Seizing the water, I held it protectively to my chest and reached up. "No! No! Come back! You don't wanna do this! Please!"

The tears would no longer come, though I continued to cry. My face was stinging from all of the scratches I had incurred the night I was kidnapped; my skin was raw from where I had obsessively wiped tears away in the cold underground. I opened the bottle and after a long swig to ease my throat and quench my thirst, I poured a tiny handful into my palm and wiped it all over my face to stop the stinging. It was a regular size bottle so I knew the water was limited and that I should try to conserve it, but that plan was impossible. My body yearned for the water—*needed* it—and no amount of willpower was going to keep me from devouring every last drop.

A small speck of light glimmered through from the above door. Capturing my gaze, it hypnotized me. I placed the cap back on the bottle and lay down. Drained, I felt myself drifting further away from the speck and deeper into the darkness.

The second the speck disappeared and I strained my eyes harder, but realized that I had closed them. I opened them quickly to see Natalie sitting at Grandma Taylor's kitchen table. Everything in her house was how it had been before she died. I stepped forward into the cinnamon scented kitchen and sat in the empty seat at the table. It was here I last spoke to my grandmother in a dream. Only this time it was Natalie who sat across from me. She looked up from the coffee cup, looking weary and miserable.

"Where's Grandma? And when did you start drinking coffee?" I asked trivially, unable to have power over my words like so many of my dreams.

"Maybe I've always liked coffee. Have you ever thought of that?" she said smartly.

I concentrated hard on my self-control, gathering meaningful words to speak to my sister. "Natalie, I think I'm going to die soon."

She reached over and grabbed my hand. Her thin fingers, like mine, felt breakable and gentle. She said sternly with her brows furrowed. "We're coming for you! Fight to stay alive! We are coming!"

I shook my head and began feeling the stomach and muscle cramps again. "I can't figure out a way to get free, and I don't have a lot of time left. Whatever they have planned for me tonight will push me closer to death. And I'm so tired. I just want to rest."

"Damn it, Jules! You have to fight it!" She yelled as she slammed her fists down on the yellow table. Her nostrils were flared and for the first time I saw that she, too, had the same awkward upper lip I did, and that it was curled in determination. In fact, we looked very much the same.

She breathed deeply as her eyes glazed over. "Salvation is in the shadows. But be wary of the darkest ones."

I shook myself awake at that moment, and drank a bit more water, feeling the need to pee again. I inched my way to the other side of the hole I was in and pulled my pants down to relieve myself—only a trickle, and nothing close to relief as I felt that I needed to pee some more. No more would come.

On the cot, I sat with my knees drawn up to my chest. Natalie had started a fire underneath me. My blood began to boil at the threat of my own life. Maybe it was the water, too, that gave me enough energy for a fight to the finish I wasn't going to be taken so easily, and if I was going to be taken at all, it wasn't going to be alive, because that's what they wanted. I wasn't completely afraid of dying. As a Christian, I had full faith in the promise of the afterlife. But *my* life had been too short. I didn't want to die. I wanted to go back to my life with my mom and dad and sister. To see my friends again: Cari, Savannah, Joey…

Broderick. My heart ached for him as he flooded my memories. Whether he would ever love me again or not, I was going to do right by him and tell him that I loved him. I loved him more than I had ever loved anybody or anything in my life. I loved him and I was going to fight through this just for the solemn moment of telling him.

When the water was gone, I set the empty bottle down beside the cot. Sliding my fingers behind the hole I had started in the wall when I first arrived, I pulled on it with all of my weight, making a larger hole. The cardboard was tough and durable—thick—against my light weight and I was somehow going to make enough slits in it to climb out of this hole. I was going to see the sun today.

Motivation overtook me as I dug another hole, the size of my foot in the cardboard, this time just below eye level. Then I made another hole about two feet over my head. My arms became tired as I dug, but the adrenaline and motivation shot through me and I began work again after only a few minutes of rest. The three holes were a stretch, but my legs were long and I practiced climbing the makeshift rungs out of my confinement. At the top, near the door, I could feel the air from above seeping through the cracks. The wood was weak and crumbling, and I debated on banging on it with my fist, hoping it would give way for my escape.

Since I didn't know what waited for me above, I made the decision to lure someone down to me. I wanted to assume that only one person was guarding the trap door. If I could eliminate the girl who guarded me, I might have a chance of cutting through the woods to freedom. I hoped I could remember how to get to the dirt road that led to civilization away from the haunted church. My memory's instinct was my only hope.

"Oh, my gosh!" I screamed horrified, in my most convincing role ever. "I'm bleeding! I'm bleeding to death and I can't stop the it! Someone help!" I called as I jimmied my way up the created rungs again.

My right hand was ready in a tight fist, and I waited for the girl make her way to the door again. My head throbbed as I concentrated hard and focused on the blinding light that crept through the cracks of the frail door. I heard the keys jangle as she knelt closer to the door. With shallow breaths, I listened for a clue as to when I should attack.

God, give me strength!

The door creaked as she lifted it and let it slam open. She placed the hood over her head and stooped over carefully to observe my alleged hemorrhage. My body shook with exhaustion and nervous tension and I felt just enough power in my right arm to reach out and shove my fist in the vicinity of her nose.

She howled in pain and fell back. I thought for sure the impact had broken my hand. Still, my heart roared mightily and I desperately climbed out of the hole. My eyes were unable to adjust to the brightness of the day so I ran in the opposite direction of where she fell, tripping over the thick and wadded rug that had been laying over the trap door. I scurried back to my feet and within moments I was falling over a table, tripping over furniture and bumping into walls. I felt my way frantically, hoping I could find a window or a door that would lead outside. Despite my blindness, I knew that the brighter it was the freer I was.

I blinked furiously, hoping it would speed up the process of gaining my sight back. My hands ran across a brightness that felt like glass and I could literally taste the freedom that waited for me on the other side of the window. I rammed my injured hand through the window in determination, shattering the glass and slicing my hand more just as I heard the girl coming toward me. She grabbed me by the neck and slammed my face into the window pane with little force, just enough to make me dizzy from the collision and I cried out. I reached out for her and began scratching at her, catching my fingers on a necklace she was wearing. I held onto it as I was losing my balance and she slapped me repeatedly in the face, cutting me with a jagged edge of something on her hand—possibly a ring.

I screamed for help, but none came and my eyes were just beginning to focus better when she reared back and hit me so hard that I felt a few of my teeth crack on impact. I clenched securely around her necklace as I fell, feeling it snap just a split second before I rolled my eyes back into my head and hit the floor.

"Bitch!" I heard her hiss as I wrestled to stay conscious.

She grabbed me by the ankles and dragged me across the splintered floor. "No. No…" I dryly whimpered in weakness, unable to open my eyes.

She let go of my ankles when I felt that I was by the edge of the trap door. Giving me a violent shove, I gasped and my left arm involuntarily sprung out to prevent me from falling, but I felt the vast wind rush by as I dropped to the earthen floor below. I heard a distinct cracking sound from my wrist as my body slammed against the ground.

I screamed; writhing in pain for minutes on end until the pain and shock over took me.

My body must have been motionless for hours. I was sore. Painfully stiff in my awkward position on the dirt floor. I didn't want to move my left arm for it was attached to my wrist and the slightest movement sent me rocketing in pain. But I was also tired. Though fighting the forthcoming horror I was going to endure, I was quickly coming to the realization that I just wanted it to be over in a very final sense. I wanted to *die*. My brain wasn't sharp enough to come up with a brilliant plan for escape, and I was losing the will to see my loved ones again.

Dizzy for lack of rest and food and water, I tried to make sense out of everything that was happening to me. My first night here, they cut my hair. They burned it, inhaling its scent that was fused with my blood and some powder. I remembered the first night Broderick and I had come to the church with the smell of burnt hair. I knew the smell. They must have just had another one of their 'burnt offerings' that night as well! We were so close to the truth of the full moon murders then, if we had just investigated a little further or called the authorities or maybe if I had gone straight to the ER that night instead of lying to my parents, the truth would have come out, and I wouldn't be living this nightmare right now.

Tonight was a feast of blood. Deliberating, I wondered if they meant for me to drink someone else's blood or if they planned to use my blood for a feast. Deep down, I knew the answer. I would probably not survive this and I shuddered as I realized that these breaths may be my very last.

But, wait! There was to be a ceremony of some sort on the full moon, which was tomorrow night! They wanted me alive for that! *The beast will dine at our table.*

Thinking back to all instances of a beast, the most powerful memory of a beast to me was not some horror character from a movie like an animal or a werewolf, but a demonic being—Satan himself. *Am I to come face to face with Satan tomorrow night?* There was no doubt in my mind this tomb was full of inescapable evil. Lucas was practically the embodiment of all that was wrong in this world and otherworldly. My skin crawled in repulsion as I recalled the smell of his putrid body when he pulled himself nearer to me. It wasn't of uncleanliness; it was like rotten food, but worse! A rotten body! It smelled as if his skin and muscles and organs were literally decomposing off his bones! Worse than any garbage I had ever smelled. I would never forget the smell for as long as I lived—which was looking like a short few hours from now.

With footsteps outside the door and then the door scraping open, I shook, terrified at what lingered for me in the blindsiding light where two shadowy figures stood. All I could do was beg "no" in low, short whimpers. My tears were long dried, and I was left with just the longing for them—I needed some sort of release even though the salty liberation from my eyes was hardly going to bring about a release to my condemned spirit.

The two men grabbed me up under my arms again, making my wrist dangle loosely. I screamed from the excruciating pain shooting from my wrist up to my shoulder. Even if I had the energy to fight, I would be too hindered with the pain.

They dragged me through the dungeon-like tunnels and up the stairs, bringing us to the side corridor of the church again. Keeping my eyes shut, I didn't want them to have the satisfaction of seeing the fear in my eyes, and I couldn't see anyway. The smell of my burnt hair was still thick within the walls of the ramshackle church, fused in with a musky incense smell from the mystery powder.

As the two men lay me on what felt like a table and strapped my arms down with Velcro bands, Lucas began to speak to the apparent congregation in the sanctuary.

"Our sacrificial soul has proven to be a determined soul—dire to preserve her own life instead of sharing her strength with others. This should be adequate testimony that our Lord has sent us the righteous and life sustaining blood to feast on." As he said the word feast my eyes sprung open in panic.

My thoughts scrambled rapidly as three straps were bound around each arm; I felt the same being done to my legs and ankles. I was thankful that by some merciful reason the strap did not engage at my broken wrist.

Lucas continued speaking. "Her blood will be powerful and sweeter than the others we have encountered, more so than that of the whore's we seized on Hallows Eve or the angel's we consumed before the Winter Solstice."

Loni! The thought of her brought so much sadness to me. For once, I became oblivious to my own surroundings and instead consumed myself with thoughts of her last few hours as a girl in torture. She never had a chance. No more of a chance than I had.

"With this sacrifice, I smelled that her virtue is unbroken, so make use of it and feel the beauty of her gift course through your body as she shares her life with you," he told his followers.

My eyes reached over to Lucas who lifted his arms, inviting everyone to stand. I could not make out the details of his face, but my general vision had become sufficient enough to see him drifting eerily behind me with his arms spread wide.

Several in the congregation, in one swift and audible motion, stood. I turned my head to see close to ten people line up and come toward me. The whimpering in my ears was my own voice, shaking and whining in pleas—weak. Slowly the mass circled around the table I was strapped to, wearing black cloaks with hoods over their heads. I wanted to ask what was going to happen, but I was too frightened to hear the answer. Suddenly, the church bell rang slow and loud and with every clang, my insides quaked and tightened as I anticipated my death.

On the thirteenth ring, everyone around me removed their hoods, revealing their gray skin. Theirs, too, reminded me of mushrooms. Each exposed a part of my body that was closest to them and my muscles tightened with anxiety as they drew their faces closer to me.

Lucas leaned in and whispered, "Her blood will be sweeter than anything you've ever tasted before. Fight the urge to finish her and leave just enough to sustain life. We must save her for the beast."

"Yes, master," they all replied.

I tried lifting my body off of the table as if it would free me enough to escape. Their mouths inched closer and they sniffed my body, causing me to cringe. My own smell was rancid. I hadn't bathed since I had left Florida, and I had no idea how long ago that had been. I had been lying on a dirty cot with a filthy blanket for what felt like an eternity, and I had urinated myself the night before. Still, they trailed their noses along my veins and inhaled in ecstasy.

Their teeth were normal as they raised their heads back and opened their mouths, but I saw an outlying layer of jagged teeth protrude from their gums as they dropped their heads to puncture my skin with their bite. I screamed with such excruciation that I was positive my throat had grated itself to the point of bleeding. I wanted to succumb to death, to see only the darkness behind my eyelids, but I couldn't tear my eyes away from the appalling scenery of the evil ones.

Every small movement of their mouths were felt. Their suckling and how they sank their teeth in deeper after the first few swallows of pleasure, enjoying what they tasted. They fed off my fear I was sure, for with every shriek of pain I could feel the full activity of a feeding frenzy upon me. All around me were low murmurs of slurping and humming in delight and the faster they drank the more faint I became. Drained. Their small vocal noises became distant echoes in my ears. I could feel myself drifting farther away and my eyes began to roll back until my lids closed altogether.

I was dying!

God, take me. Let it be over.

I battled for a strong grasp of my faith to overcome this agony. My sporadic brain raced to a thought of comfort, as the memory of a Sunday school lesson over Christ's crucifixion flooded my mind.

I asked myself, *what was it that Christ said on the cross at the time of his death?*

"It is finished…" I answered my memory out loud in a whisper, "That's what Christ said."

And I floated into a blackness that had no end.

Full Moon

THEY SAY THAT JUST before you die, your life flashes before you. I saw it all. Along with many other visions that were a direct result of the maddening torture I had been through, I saw my past and how I came to this solemn moment; precariously balanced on that thin line of life and death. Obscure images of scenes from my perspective were woven through it.

My plump little fingers wrapping around a green garden hose, bringing the nozzle to my lips as it flowed with cold water

My mother, beautiful and young, pregnant with Natalie, sitting on a rickety lawn chair as I rode on my red tricycle.

I saw myself looking out to the congregation of my church as I sang *Amazing Grace* at a very young age.

Then swirls of images of my overactive imagination sparked in my mind along with memories of wearing an old cornflower blue dress and screaming, while I was being burned at the stake.

I saw my grandmother sitting at her dining room table as we talked about my future—the dream I had the night before she died. Her warning.

"The devil patiently paces the floor waiting for the smallest invitation through the door."

Blended into this scene, I also saw Natalie sitting next to her at the table from my recent dream. "Salvation is in the shadows. But be wary of the darkest ones."

In a mirror's reflection, I observed myself, pale skin with my hair piled high as I wore too much make up. I was wearing a flowing gown and leaning back on an antique settee. A dashing man with black hair hovered over me, and though his face was buried in the nook of my neck, I saw the backside of him. He was cradling my body, romantically and intimately, and I could feel the burning on my neck from where he was drinking my blood.

I saw myself on a bridge crossing a rampaging river. Young and adventurous, I must have gone too close to the edge. Just before my fragile body reached the waters, I was saved, caught from behind by a bright light, so bright I couldn't lay my eyes upon its beauty for long. It gently carried me to the nearby rocky shore. Its angelic voice speaking in a whisper bringing me more comfort than I could withstand. "I love you and I will never let you go."

My heart raced harder and faster as the memories flooded my mind's eye.

I imagined my life before coming to earth as a baby—an Angel kissing the back of my right shoulder, giving me the birthmark, a joke I had so commonly used when discussing the imprinted lips on my body.

And with that memory, the floodgates were opened.

My remembrances of Broderick came in large waves, causing my heart to ache with every flash of his face. I could see clearer. How he pulled his lips back in smooth smiles, accentuating his deep dimples on each cheek.

The night he saved me from plummeting from my roof. Shadowshifting, amazing me with his breathtaking gift.

The sound of shuffling was in my ears. Weakness was my greatest adversary now. I hardly had the strength to breathe, let alone sit up or inspect my surroundings. I wasn't sure if I was awake or sleeping... Possibly dead. In limbo.

I felt one long arm curl up underneath my frail body and hold me up as another arm wrapped around the other direction. My head fell back. This memory I couldn't place.

"Jules!" his voice whispered in tears. "What have they done to you, Jules?"

He held me close to him, my wrist throbbing agonizingly more so than the bite marks and cuts and scrapes that covered my body. His soft lips gently placed on my forehead, I could smell him. *So real!* I inhaled deeply, allowing myself to be consumed in this final memory of my greatest love. Clean. Soapy. Fresh. Like my grandmother's air blown laundry, tinged with sweat and… what?… pine sap?… dirt?…

His hand swept up and brushed my choppy hair from my face, lightly touching the gash below my bottom lip. His fingers drifted along my jaw line and to my neck, where he felt the impression of teeth. He was trembling now. He traced his fingertips away from the offensive injury and searched for a pulse.

His body sighed in relief and he began rocking me, like a baby, in his arms. "Stay with me, Jules. Stay with me."

I didn't want this dream to end, but I could die in peace now. Broderick was holding me. My Broderick. I wanted so much to tell him how much I loved him and missed him, but the first words that slipped through my dry cracked lips, with air that provided very little articulation due to dehydration and my failing life was the one question that had been on my heart for months.

"Why did you leave me?"

I heard him laugh and cry at the same time as he held me tighter and squeezed me close to his chest.

"Jules, Jules." he whispered through anguished tears. "I'm so sorry. I was wrong."

The physical pain I felt was shortly forgotten as I continued to imagine myself in his arms. He kissed my right cheek and I gasped at the pain I felt, bruised from where I had been kicked during the initial attack.

"I have to go get help but I'll be right back. Don't die on me, Jules. I'm coming right back for you. I promise."

This was my end. Our time together was over, but I gave my last resistance.

"Stay," I whispered.

He gently laid me on the cold hard ground and moved his arms out from underneath me. "I *have* to go. But I promise you I will be back; I'm getting you out of here, so stay with me."

I couldn't bear the false hope in his voice nor this fantasy I had conjured up. Broderick could never love me like this, and I was never going to be saved.

"Let me go," I whimpered.

I thought I felt my eyes flutter open and I saw the door open and a rupture of light bled into the room, once again blinding me by the light.

I'm dying, I thought as the darkness overtook the room again. My wrist continued to ache and the bites on my body stung. My stomach cramps intensified to such agony, I begged God to take me. My energy to war with death was gone. I prayed for a quick release to its eternity before the torture of my captors ensued.

The Beast's feast!

My chest began to quake with dry sobs, knowing death wouldn't come for me until I was completely devoured by a nightmare so horrific I was unable to create its existence in my own mind.

My mind turned to fears that had lingered for months in my subconscious. The night Broderick and I came to this very location to play around in a church we believed to be haunted. Just for fun.

"Things will follow you home and when I say things, I mean things—not people."

Indeed, something followed us home that night, and neither Broderick nor I have been the same. It was all very clear to me now that it was too late. My fingers floated softly over the scar between my thumb and index finger. Broderick was wrong. The imprint of the cross *wasn't* enough protection from the evil we had encountered.

My arm shook like stressed rubber as I tried to push myself off the floor. My mind was continually shutting down or zigzagging through memories or creative scenarios that never have happened and never would happen. My arm felt as though it was going to buckle underneath me and so I twisted around to sit upright. I was disoriented and wondered if I was truly awake. While I curled my left arm closely to my body to protect my wrist I stretched out my other hand to brush the tips of my fingers across the ground. As I swept my hand behind me, I felt something round and metal and grabbed it. I thought it might be one of my medallions. Mine or Broderick's? I reached up and touched the medallion around my neck feeling the inscription. Broderick's engraved initials on one side with the quote on the opposite.

My hand glided across the dirt floor again until I found the chain and medallion again. It was a bit larger than a half dollar in circumference and slightly thicker than a coin. One side of it was completely smooth and the other side had ridges—some rough, some smooth. I rubbed my thumb over it slowly. Did this belong to the person who previously occupied this tomb? Little by little, I started to remember the struggle with the girl upstairs in the house from the day before. I vaguely remembered having hold of her necklace as she pushed me back into the hole. It must have fallen in with me.

Awkwardly, I lay back down as I persistently stroked the medallion.

Slowly losing consciousness again, I prayed that this darkness would be permanent. *Let me die!* The darkness became so heavy it pressed me to the ground, making it difficult to breathe. I curled up into a ball and took short shallow breaths; my thumb, tracing along the design of the medallion endlessly.

It could have been minutes or hours later, but the door opened again, waking me. My eyes hurt from the light that burst through, and I couldn't keep them open. My body quaked uncontrollably. The shaking was so hard, it hurt every inch of my already-battered body.

Why won't God just take me?

I thought back to my mother and how she always explained during hard times. That everything happens for a reason. What was *my* reason? *My* purpose? To feed a beast that brought evil to this world? If I became the life force for this evil, would that disqualify me for entry into heaven?

I didn't feel like I could make it to heaven, though. My spirit was too tired for the journey.

Broderick. I could smell him again, clearly, and I shuddered even more furiously as someone curled their arms underneath me. My body was literally beating itself up with the harsh trembling.

"Jules? Baby? Are you still with me?" his voice whispered.

"Yes," I spoke to my imagination.

He sat me up a bit higher and my head fell forward. His hand gently pulled my head back and brushed the scraggly and uneven hair out of my face. I heard the crackling of cheap, thin plastic and then felt a cool ring brought to my scabbed and cracked lips.

"Try to drink," his voice was full of tension, edged with compassion.

As the ring tilted the cool water into my mouth and soothed my throat, my stomach squeezed in rejection. I swallowed hard anyway, but the stomach won out as I threw the water up immediately. This gave me a strong sense of reality as I began choking on heaves. While I coughed hard, I felt my body being sat up at a full ninety degree angle.

Everything suddenly became very real to me.

"Are you okay, Jules?"

At the sound of his voice I inhaled as deep as my feeble lungs would allow. His scent was everywhere—even through the vile smell of urine and vomit.

"Broderick," I whispered.

He brushed his rough, stubbly cheek against mine. I could smell him and I could feel him; I just couldn't see him.

"Jules, I need to get you out of here." He was panicking, it was obvious.

I strained to speak. "They're going to kill me."

"I'm taking you home," he said. "Try to drink again?"

I tried again and struggled hard internally against the rebellion in my stomach. Eventually, I was able to keep some of it down.

"Can you walk?" he asked.

Still not certain if I was dreaming or if I was actually going to be saved, I nodded my head. He helped me to my feet, but before I could take a step, I collapsed. I never hit the ground, though; he gently caught me and held me close to him, cradling me, like a parent would hold their child, as he fumbled with the door. The blinding light was more than I could bear, and I turned my face away to bury it in Broderick's chest. Then there was the cleansing breath of fresh air! This pure refreshing air was waking me. It was making me more alert. Was this for real? If not, what a cruel joke my mind was playing on me. I'd already given up hope of survival. I'd come to terms with my imminent death. Why this awful trickery now? I felt the breeze of passing wind blow by us. He was going at a quick pace.

"Where does this path take us?" I heard him ask.

"The church," I whispered dryly.

"No, Jules, the hall to the church is straight ahead. What about this one to the right?" With the blinding lights, I had never been able to observe the tunnel well enough to know where it led. I had no memory of being in this tunnel.

I barely shook my heard in answer to his question. "I don't know," my voice croaked.

I felt the motions of him winding through the darker tunnel. It was dimly lit, less than the other tunnel, so I was able to open my eyes a little bit. I looked up and saw the beautiful outline of Broderick's face—fierce and determined like a man, with a boy's mask of worry as well. We were both in danger, and he was willing to risk his life to save mine. Nuzzling my face into his chest like a sleepy child, I wanted to cry in relief.

"Thank you," I softly said into his shirt.

"Don't thank me yet…" he trailed off and stopped moving. I, too, could hear voices being carried from the other tunnel.

Broderick broke into a fast run through the narrow passage then stopped and sat me down on the ground. I reached for him with my good arm to keep him close to me.

He held my hand and put his face close to mine. "Can you see anything, Jules?" I anxiously shook my head. He tried to keep his voice calm. "Okay, we're at a small set of stairs that leads to something like a trap door. My plan is to wait until I think the coast is clear and climb out of here. Hang on."

He moved away from me and started up the stairs. I heard him push on the door above, the lock jingling with every small thrust.

"Locked," he said nervously to himself as he shuffled back down to me.

He cupped my face in both of his hands as if he were looking directly into my eyes. I wish I could see him better, but I couldn't keep my eyes open; even the faint light burned them.

"They're going to figure out you're gone and when they do, we're going to have to move quickly."

"But it's locked," I whimpered.

"I think I can force it open. Listen to me Jules; as soon as I get you out of this tunnel, I want you to run as far west as you can go. Do you understand what I'm saying? Run away from the moon."

I understood, but I shook my head. "I won't go without you."

He put a finger to my lips. "We can't be too far from the church—do you remember how to get back to the cornfields and then back through the woods to where we parked that night?"

"I think so, but I can't see." I started to cry.

"It's dark outside. The only light you've got is the full moon..." He paused in deliberation, "You need to get your bearings and—"

All of a sudden, the two voices in the other hall began yelling.

"Shit!" Broderick whispered. "*Shit!*"

He scooped me up effortlessly, cradling me on his hip and then trudged up the stairs. I felt us being swept into the cold air as we made our way closer to the trap door. His body shifted, ready to strike, and I firmly grabbed his neck in anticipation. He rammed his body upward with such force, causing the wood of the door to split instantly upon impact. Dim light faintly glowed behind the door through the cracks and I shielded my face from its blinding brightness.

The cold air, gave me gooseflesh as it filled my lungs.

Broderick put me down and swiftly he began to rummage around, panting in between words as his voice drifted from different directions all around me. "I don't see anyone, Jules."

I kept my head down and attempted to blink, but even hiding my eyes from the partial lighting was blinding. My eyes couldn't adjust quickly enough.

Broderick grunted in strain and I heard something large being moved close to where I sat on the ground. I smelled gasoline and hay.

In one final grunt came a loud metal sounding thud and then a deep breath. "I reinforced that door with a bale of hay and some barrels to keep those guys from following us."

I heard his footsteps take him further away from me, then the sound of creaking wood. He came back quickly and he placed his hands on my knees as I sat, leaning against a wall. I shivered in the cold night air.

"I can't see," I said.

"I know you can't, Jules. Your eyes will adjust shortly. Just give it a bit more time." He paused to gulp in a quick breath. "God, I don't know if we have time," he whispered to himself. He became enthusiastic as he started to explain. "We're in a barn. That same old barn by the church. There are a few people outside in the field building a fire. We need to figure a way out of here. The police are on their way, I called them when I went back to my jeep. Now we just need to survive long enough for them to get here.

"I don't know how long we'll be safe here. They're going to come looking for us soon." His words were coming as sporadically as his thoughts. "What do you want me to do, Jules? Do you want to wait it out here or do you want me to try and run you out of here? I can't shift as well as I use to." I felt him pulling up my clothing and inspecting my body, lifting my arms gently and tilting my head from side to side. "Oh, God! What have they done to you, Jules?" I heard his teeth snap tight and grind, on the verge of tears.

I didn't know what to tell him. The answers I had for him were unbelievable.

He stroked my short and choppy hair to comfort me. "Can you see anything yet?"

I struggled to open my eyes but blinked shut soon after I was able to capture two white things on the ground before me. It was still very dark in here. "I think I saw my tennis shoes."

"Good!" he encouraged.

He was restless; he sprung up quickly and strolled several feet away. "Shit! Where are they?" He cursed again. He scurried back over to me, his tone was dire and his words were distressed. "Jules, I need to get you away from here or…"

Scratching on the metal barrels that now reinforced the shredded trap door, I could hear the hisses of those underground. Broderick jerked me up from my seat on the hay and guided me to the door of the barn. I blinked frantically, catching a glimpse of my feet in short glances as they took each stride with him.

"Jules you've got to try and get away!" Broderick urged. "Don't look at the bonfire. Your eyes will adjust faster as you get further away. Head west *away* from the moon…"

"I'm not leaving you."

"I *can't* go with you. You need to get out of here now!"

A commotion was stirring outside. It was too late for either of us to run. We were trapped. Death was imminent and my time with Broderick was gone. He cupped my face and stared intently into my eyes. I could almost see his beautiful face in the dark shadows of the barn. Before he could speak again, I interrupted. He needed to know.

"Broderick. I love you." The words spilled off of my tongue.

At the sound of the door behind him being thrown open, he dropped his hands and twisted around. Another source of light bled into the barn from the door and I fought hard to keep my eyes open. It was unbearable to go on without my sense of sight any longer; I had to see what was happening. I sensed Broderick standing and facing those that intended to harm us. Helplessly, I continued to stare blindly at my feet, blinking at my tennis shoes. My sight was coming back, but slowly.

No one spoke.

Broderick released a breathy shudder and reach behind to touch me, grabbing my shirt, almost pushing me off from him. I stumbled back to my seat on the bale of hay.

He whispered, "Jules, go."

His voice alone told me that he was terrified. I looked up to see a crowd closing in on us.

"Not without you," I said sternly, fighting back wails that were quaking in my tight chest.

"Get Lucas!" One of the evil ones hissed. At the request, I heard the barn door open again and then footsteps beating away on the ground outside.

"Look," Broderick began with a firm and assured tone, fighting for composure against his own apprehension and fear. "We don't want any trouble. I just want to take the girl home to her family."

I could tell by his tone that he was pissed, but he spoke delicately knowing we were outnumbered and that I was going to be of no help in my blind and weak condition.

"Jules, go," he spoke louder. He grabbed my broken wrist and jerked me up to my feet, causing me to scream in pain. I could only imagine the look on his face when he realized that he had caused me more pain with his action.

He lightened his tone this time; just a bit to encourage me, "Go, *please*."

A thin veil of fog blurred my vision, but I could roughly distinguish a few details where I could run to. I didn't want to leave him, but if he came to rescue me and we both died, then it would all be for nothing. But in the same breath, at least we would die together.

I took a few wobbly steps and attempted to run, but collapsed on the dirt floor before I could get more than five feet away. The evil ones laughed in sinister sneers.

I heard several steps being taken closer to Broderick and me. Broderick reached down to help me back on my feet and I ineptly scrambled to them. This time, instead of pawning me off onto a seat somewhere, he held me close to him, allowing me to lean on him. My legs were too weak to hold me up. If we were going anywhere, he was either going to carry me or drag me.

Broderick was hot and sweaty, wearing only a T-shirt, whereas I was shivering in the freezing night air in my red hoodie. I didn't understand why he was shaking so hard. It suddenly came crashing back to me. He was losing his temper. I fully remembered his bursts of rage in the past, how he shook feverishly beforehand.

His voice was testy as he took a few steps away from the throng that entrapped us, dragging me with him at his side. "Whatever it is you think you're going to accomplish by hurting her, you're wrong. Just let her go and there won't be any trouble. Take me instead."

A few of them chuckled balefully as the others hissed louder.

Broderick backed away from them a few more steps, ducking me protectively behind his body. Little by little my vision became more reliable and I could see bodies in black cloaks lining up around us in a semicircle to prevent our escape.

"I mean it!" Ironically his words came as a warning. His deep voice oddly carried an echoing rattle with a higher pitch. "You don't want to do this."

Just as I looked up to see their reaction to his impossible threat, the one on the far right moved as in a blur. He easily covered more than fifteen feet in one leap. Without a second's thought, Broderick shoved me to the side. But this was no normal shove either. With massive strength, he flung my body into the air like a rag doll. Slamming into the back wall I landed in a heap. I gasped in pain as I carelessly pushed myself to a sitting position. Blinking furiously, I saw Broderick swing at the evil one and lay him out on the floor. The others hissed at him.

"Jules, get the hell out of here!" he yelled in panic over his shoulder at me.

I twisted my head around, hoping to see a door or window that I could climb out of, but I couldn't see anything that would prove useful in an escape. Shielding my eyes from the faint glow of a lantern overhead, I noticed a loft above me. I trailed along the loft with my hindered vision until I saw a ladder leading up to the left of me. I needed to figure out a way out of here so I could find help, though I despised the idea of leaving Broderick behind to fight alone. I would only be a hindrance to him in my weakened state.

My sight was strengthening with every moment in the poorly lit barn.

Two women shrieked like banshees as they ran to Broderick. He kicked one with such force her body jack-knifed and the other latched onto his back behind him. She wasted no time as she sunk her teeth deep into his shoulder. Crying out, he reached for her blonde hair and yanked her off of him, throwing her to the ground. Her mouth was stained red and she spit a chunk of his shoulder out at him as she flipped herself back onto her feet. She lunged at him again, and he crushed his fist into her face, able to keep up with her frenzied and rapid movements. She writhed on the floor, grabbing her head, shrieking in pain. As she crawled away from him, I saw the trail of blood from her wounded head. Broderick's fury had overcome any mercy. He grabbed her by the ankles and jerked her closer to him. My hand flew to my face to hide my eyes from the violence as her crackling bones and screams echoed in the barn.

"Broderick!" I called to him.

Covered in blood, he spun around to see me. As if he'd lost track of where he was for a moment, he shook his head slightly, pulling the shroud of violence from his eyes, revealing regret and shame in them.

Distracted, two of the men jumped on him and he plummeted to the ground.

"Broderick!" I screamed for him.

I heard a low growl from the pile up, stunning me with the wild sound. Broderick struggled, ravaging his way out from under the two of them. Broderick yelped in pain as one of them, the bald one, latched onto his leg with his sharp teeth.

The blinding glow seeped in again as the barn door open narrowly, and a figure in a red cloak stood at the entrance peeking in. I squeezed my eyes a few times and blinked. It was too far a distance to see who it was by detail, but I could tell by his tall thin stature that it had to be Lucas. My feet wouldn't move any further up the ladder; the anxiety that came from his presence brought me to a crumbling halt. Lucas quietly watched the two evil ones attack Broderick through the small slit of the opened door.

A howl resonated from the nearby woods and everyone in the barn froze.

The wolf!

I gasped.

The evil one that was on top of Broderick looked up with blackened eyes and with a wide grin, exposing his fanged teeth, his mouth dripped with Broderick's blood as he hissed, "*the beast.*"

Broderick quickly grabbed the man's head and twisted it with a flick of the wrist. I heard a fierce snap noise as the body fell limply to the floor. The second evil one kicked Broderick hard in the stomach, sending him to his knees in agony. Defenseless, it jumped onto his back. Just as Broderick had done, he grabbed the back of his head and prepped himself to twist it off.

"No!" I shrieked.

Broderick pulled the evil one over his head, landing him on the floor at his feet. Just as inhumanly quick as the evil ones, he sprung to his feet and grabbed the evil one by the shoulders and thrusting him into a piece of farm machinery, ripping him open from gut to sternum.

I wailed and shook in fear of the violence. Broderick composed himself immediately upon hearing my cries and ran to me. Covered in blood—all over his shirt and jeans and tennis shoes, he knelt before me and placed his blood drenched hands on my arms.

"Jules, you've got to run. It's a full moon…." he rattled nervously as his body vibrated.

My throat, tight in constricted fright, whispered to him, "Lucas."

"*Who?*" He was close enough to my face and the barn was now dark enough that I could see his confusion.

Just as Broderick limped toward an escape, pulling me weakly along, the barn door opened wide and Lucas stood majestically before us. I shielded my eyes from the luminance of the bonfire as he pulled back the red hood of his cloak and smiled wickedly at the two of us. Mocking us—

it was clear, even to my unfocused eyes. As he removed the red garment I saw that he no longer looked like a cadaver. He was beautifully white; his hair was shiny, black and full of life.

Broderick saw him and took a few steps back in shock, tripping over the body of the blond whose head was crushed in. He steadied himself and took a few more steps back.

"*Lucas!*" he uttered alarmingly.

Lucas smiled wider in appreciation of Broderick's undignified start. Broderick pushed me behind him and shook his head, unable to grasp that Lucas was in fact alive even *after* his burial.

"I see you've found your lady friend." He motioned gracefully at me. "And I'm thoroughly impressed with your... *strength*."

Lucas was baiting Broderick. I pulled him by the shirt to follow me, to help me up the ladder that led to the loft, positive that there would be an escape of some sort. The risk of jumping was less threatening than what stood before us.

Broderick loosened my grasp on his shirt and continued to push me away from him.

"I've been watching you for a while," Lucas continued as he drifted in a space before Broderick, speaking calmly. "And I've learned a lot about you."

Broderick straightened his back up at the acknowledgement.

"Yesss..." Lucas hissed like a snake. "I *know*."

"Jules, damn it, get the hell out of here!" Broderick warned through his gritted teeth.

"I watched you that night you came to our ceremony where we acquired our strength. I followed you *closely* as you foolishly thought you gained a safe distance. I tasted her blood that she spilled in the cemetery, licking every drop that lingered on the shard of glass that you picked from her hand and I followed that trail of blood..."

I looked down to foggily see the scar of the cross on my hand.

Without warning, Broderick hunched over and grabbed his stomach in pain.

"Aaah!" Lucas was in ecstasy over Broderick's pain.

Raged-induced adrenaline flowed through my veins and my eyes grew in livid terror. "What are you doing to him?" I screamed as I hobbled feebly to Broderick.

Lucas held up his hand innocently and smirked. Broderick pushed me roughly away from him and fought to regain control as Lucas chuckled in amusement.

"I found it engagingly ironic how you dressed as her savior at the Halloween dance. But what confused me was how quick you were to abandon her afterward. Hardly what a *hero* does, don't you think?" Lucas taunted in a soothing manner.

"Shut the hell up!" Broderick seethed. His voice sounded deeper than usual and he battled with the pain in his stomach again.

"Jules, get the hell out of here! *Now!*" he growled at me as I made my way to the ladder.

Lucas's eyes grew wide with a pleasing awareness. He grinned at me, making the shiver in my spine shoot straight through my chest. "She doesn't know..."

Broderick grabbed his head in agony, grunting and pulled at his hair.

"Broderick!" I cried out as I held tightly to the rungs of the ladder, despite the unforgiving pain in my wrist. "Leave him alone!" I shrieked at Lucas angrily, shaking with the notion I could turn his focus on me instead of tormenting Broderick.

I watched Broderick writhing in pain and thought back to the biting he had just endured. *Is he to become like them? Evil?* I had been bitten and wasn't changed yet. I was still human, wasn't I? My heart shuddered as I realized that I could soon become prey to two evils within seconds in the middle of nowhere. Wobbling up my first step on the ladder, I watched in horror while Broderick gained control of the pain again.

He stood firmly prepared to attack Lucas now, ripping his shirt off and kicking off his shoes.

Lucas laughed at him gleefully. "I'm not going to fight you. I could kill you easily. The blood of my Father runs through my veins, unlike those in my coven. You're no match for me, *boy.*"

Broderick turned to me in wild fury and set his jaw. His eyes became dark and brooding.

"Get your ass up there now, Jules!" he spat, his deep voice pulled in several different frequencies all at once as it shook, just like his reddening body.

Broderick curled back over and held his head, screaming. In severe convulsions, his body began jerking and twitching.

I pushed myself to the top of the ladder, fighting through the pain in my wrist, and took several deep breaths as I climbed onto the loft. I looked down at the two men. Broderick was now on his knees. Lucas paced around him, occasionally stepping back to take in the full scene of agony. The inner workings of his mind began turning, and he leaned in one last time to speak calmly to him as Broderick howled helplessly in pain.

"I'll make a deal with you," Lucas sneered in superiority. For the first time ever in his life, he had control over our small town's golden child, Broderick Cooper. "*I'll* let her go, if *you* do us the honor tonight."

Broderick jumped to his feet and pushed Lucas with such force that he flew across the room and landed back into a dark corner. Lucas casually brushed himself off and straightened up, ready for an attack.

I froze as I looked over the scene in the barn. Lucas stood in the darkest shadows—the corner of the barn, facing off with Broderick. He opened his mouth in a hissing smile and his fangs extended further down, vicious and threatening like a lion as he faded into the shadows. *A shadowshifter! Broderick's painting!*

Heaving with deep throws of breath, Broderick poised himself like a man ready to rip something apart with his bare hands, though his eyes were wide with a boy's fear. His muscles bulged and a ripping sound emitted from his back and shoulders. He turned to look for me and saw me hanging over the edge of the loft looking down at him. My eyes suddenly focused as I saw his dark eyes roll into the back of his head. He squeezed his eyes shut tightly then they sprang open, revealing the yellow eyes of a wild animal. My hand flew to my mouth and I worked hard to swallow my terror. His set jaw started pulling forward and his beautiful teeth where being pushed back by a new row of teeth—sharp and grotesque.

"Jules!" I heard him call for me as he gurgled and growled in his own saliva. His voice was wrenched in misery and remorse, carrying the depth he had always carried when uttering my name.

Lying on the wooden loft floor, I squealed and kicked my legs in horror as if I were running with all my might.

His upper and lower jaws pulled drastically forward into an elongated snout and dark grey and brown, wiry hairs began sprouting out all over his massive body. Muscles swelled and knotted into places that allowed for his legs to gruesomely break then remold the exaggerated haunches of a large animal—a beast! He fell forward, his arms holding himself up off the ground while brown and grey hairs pushed out of his skin. His feet and hands grew astonishing sizes, and claws protruded from the tips of his fingers and toes. His ears grew to a point, and a tail developed from his coccyx simultaneously.

The colossal and bristling beast shook out the tension as it remained on all fours for only a second longer. Lucas's eyes widened in anticipation, a grin spread on his face. The wolf pushed itself up on its hind legs and stood at close to seven feet tall. It's long, oversized arms hung staunchly at his sides as it took a deep breath and released a spine chilling howl into the cold night air, echoing off the trees and the surrounding mountains nearby.

I gave out an ear splitting scream, ringing my own ears as the beast drove forward to the thin white face lingering in the dark corner. Lucas lunged in flight out of the shadows toward the wolf and the two clashed together in rapid motions. I watched in blood chilling horror as the wolf swiped at the vampire, knocking him to the ground, but the vampire was quick to gain control as he bit into the seething wolf's leg, spitting out a portion of its muscle, causing the wolf to howl in pain. While distracting it with pain, Lucas gracefully shoved the beast, making it seem effortless but apparently with enough force to send it across the room and crashing against the wall. The aged wood busted and the wolf steadied itself for another lunge. Its teeth clamped hard on the vampire's neck as it rammed him into the center beam, breaking it in two. The monsters struggled viciously on the floor, and the beast never surrendered his hold on the vampire's neck, but Lucas was not so easy to admit defeat.

In the midst of the howling and growling and hissing, I heard a loud creaking sound, like a shift in the building. The barn was old, and it wasn't going to take much to send it crashing down around us, but with the heated battle between the two horrific creatures ensuing, it was going to take us all down—*definitely* killing me. I needed to save myself. Still weak from dehydration, pain, and blood loss, I now had two monsters below me, both predators. I fought through my hysterical screams and made my way to the window of the hay loft. I pushed with all of my might to swing open the two doors. The bonfire was slowly being put out by the heavily falling snow in the middle of the empty field. The coast was clear! I just needed to get down. I looked up and found a pulley without a rope located in the overhang of the door.

"Shit!" I needed the rope to get down.

I hobbled around for a sturdy line of rope as the clatter continued below me, now sounding like thundering metal along with the snarls. I peeked through the cracks of the rickety loft, praying that the wood wouldn't give way, plummeting me into the middle of their battle. In the shape I was in, I was certain I wouldn't survive the fall.

Lucas tossed the wolf into the canisters of gasoline and they spilled out. My heart beat faster as I tried to come up with a better plan. I couldn't find a rope, and I had no way of getting out of the barn unless I jumped. Again, I worried that the landing would kill me if not break me into a million pieces. And then, even if I did survive, what would stop the vampire or wolf from getting me outside. They were both extremely fast and strong. I was weak and slow, even on my best day, compared to them. I had to jump; it was my only option, my only hope to survive. I scurried over to the broken down work station at the back of the barn and sifted through the rusty hammers and screw drivers and a pocket radio in my last attempt to find a rope. Nothing!

There was a yelp, and though my heart burned for Broderick's safety, I knew it would be impossible to escape as long as he was alive. My heart broke at the knowledge. I loved him so much. He came to rescue me and all I could do in return was leave him behind as he fought with the undead. I took a deep breath. *Push it from your mind and get out of here!*

The monsters crashing below me, I saw another beam bow in and part of the loft drop from the missing support. I felt the entire barn shift. The lantern hanging on the nail beside the ladder dropped and shattered, catching the barn on fire. Immediately I felt the heat from the fire below as the flame trailed along with the gas spill, reaching the hay.

I heard a deafening sound against the opposite wall and I turn around to see Lucas climbing up the wall with ease like a spider, reaching for the hay loft door to get to me, but the wolf jumped up and grabbed him by the ankles, jerking him to the ground.

I closed in on the loft's edge and watched in horror as the wolf tore into his flesh and devoured the thinned meat that was left on his bones. Lucas emitted an agonizing scream as the wolf pulled back the bones of his chest, causing an unforgettable crackling sound. Within seconds of ripping out his heart with his teeth, he swallowed it whole.

I had to act quickly, because as soon as it was done with Lucas, it was sure to come for me next assuming I wouldn't burn to death first.

The wolf looked up to where I stood on the loft and howled. As fast as I could, I ran to the opened window of the barn, fighting the pressing urge to collapse. I saw the wolf clambering up to where I was in mammoth bounds, bouncing from stacked bales of hay to the wall and from the ladder to the wall again. Just as I made it to my escape route I turned around to see the terrifying monster standing massively at the top of the ladder, just leaps away from me. I thought my heart was going to rupture through the confines of my chest out of fear alone, but the ache of my lost love brought me a sense of my own death.

I took in a quick breath and jumped just as the wolf drop to all fours and started driving toward me. I expected the drop to be quick, but it lasted long enough for me to panic more the closer I came to the ground. My shadow on the ground below from where the barn burst into flames projecting a great light, began to shrink and line up with my body and over my left shoulder was the wolf, hurdling after me.

The second my feet touched the ground, my legs crumbled beneath me. I smashed into the hard, cold dirt with a thud, jostling my insides. Everything went black.

I stayed in the blackness, as the unsettling notion of being in danger lingered around me. Still, there was a strange comfort in where I lay. I didn't want to move; didn't want to wake. I wanted to fade away, further into the blackness, but restlessness moved over me, causing my eyes to flutter open.

Coming to, I was instantly fear-stricken. I didn't know how long I had been out, but I whipped my head around to look for the wolf. There was only the barn. A swooshing sound grew to a roar inside the barn and a large explosion from the back caused shards of wood and debris to fly into a rage through the air. I watch hypnotically as the fire consumed the structure. Slowly, the barn collapsed. Dark black smoke billowed out of it, floating high into the sky, carried like a curtain over the full, orange moon.

I glanced over to my left seeing the beautiful, young man pushing himself off the ground slowly—barefoot and shirtless, with shredded pants, barely hanging on by their threads. Even with profusely bleeding wounds, he lifted his head to examine the grounded barn. Through the beautifully falling snow, our eyes met. Words could not explain the hurt that filled them, reaching my saddened soul. We stared at each other for what seemed like an eternity. Not moving, not speaking a word; fear, misery and regret filling the distance.

From far off I heard a convoy of motorists closing in on us.

"They're over here!" someone shouted from the woods nearby and suddenly a harsh wind blew about us and we were immersed in an overhead spotlight. The bright light blinded me from above, and I shielded my eyes to see the source of it as it drew closer in a loud beating sound.

"Juliana Taylor. Remain where you are. We will come to you," a loud voice echoed from the helicopter above.

We were saved. I wanted to see the faces and the safety of the men and women from the rescue squads, but I couldn't tear my eyes away from the boy I loved—the boy that was half man, half beast.

A werewolf.

Daybreak

RELIVING THE HORROR OF his transformation, even in the safety of my own memory, gave me a harsh shake, and I emitted a horrifying scream just as my eyes opened to a bright white light fluttering my lashes.

The scream was all in my head. I was only able to utter a shallow gasp, but my dad gasped loud enough to suffice a scream for me as I startled him with my harsh awakening.

"Jules!" My mom cried and squeezed my hand. I blinked furiously to gain focus. "You're home, sweetie."

My heart immediately began to warm at her words. More so at Natalie's dry tone. "Technically, you're in the hospital."

I looked over to see my beautiful blonde sister lounging back in an uncomfortable looking chair and shifting her eyes between the TV set mounted on the wall and me. My dad sat in a similar looking chair next to her.

"Hi, Pumpkin," he whispered as he stood and came to my bedside.

Stiff and sore, I became restless immediately, wanting to sit up and look into a mirror for my reflection. What kind of monster would I see?

Concentrating hard as I tried to swallow, my throat felt dry and sticky. I smacked my lips together preparing to speak, and my mom quickly retrieved a mug with the hospital logo and a plastic straw, full of ice water. She pressed the button on the side rail, and my head slowly began angling me up to a sitting position. Bringing the straw to my lips, I decided that water would feel good on my parched throat, so I took a small sip. Upon swallowing, I realized just how much I wanted it, so I increased my sips to huge gulps, sighing in breaths between each swallow.

When she set the mug back down on the table, I began to wriggle free of the impression I had left in the bed from my dead-like sleep, but I moved so slowly and fluidly that I wondered if I was moving at all. My wrist was now a dull ache and in a cast, resting upon a pillow that lay across my lap. My legs felt tired, almost too tired to stretch them under the hospitals thin worn sheets. Once I did move, even a little, I moaned from the pain. Slowly, as I gained visual focus, I realized how much my peripheral was hindered by a bulging cheek.

"How'd I get here?" I asked in a raspy voice. I searched around the room and saw the room filled with floral arrangements—colors brilliantly splashed throughout the room with their floral scent.

My mom and dad hovered on opposite sides of my bed. Immediately Natalie appeared at the foot of my bed.

"They found you shortly after midnight two nights ago. We've been here with you ever since you arrived." My mom's eyes welled up with tears as joy spilled from her face. "Do you remember very much?"

As if it were powered by a hamster in a wheel, I felt my brain getting a slow start. I pursed my lips together in concentration, vividly remembering the change that had occurred within Broderick and the battle that resulted between him and Lucas. The barn, how it burst into flames and how we both had leapt from the top window just before it exploded and collapsed. I vaguely remembered the rescuers arriving just as I was able to lay my eyes on a transformed Broderick.

"Not after I jumped from the barn. No," I replied as the hamster in the wheel started to pick up its pace.

"They said you passed out from shock and exhaustion before the helicopter even touched down," she said.

"A helicopter?" I vaguely remembered that flying overhead.

"They couldn't get an ambulance to you, so they air lifted you to the hospital. The county rescue squad got there by ATVs."

My mind ran rampant as I tried to collect some solid memory of the incident.

"You had three blood transfusions." Natalie smirked. *Was she impressed with that?* My mom gave her a scolding look. Apparently, she wanted the three of them to be a bit more sensitive to me. I was already feeling more comfort with Natalie, though. She made me feel at home again with her dry and humorous behavior.

"They now have you on IV fluids and antibiotics," Mom said.

"Sheriff Burnett said he'd stop by sometime later to see if you were awake enough to ask you a few questions," my dad interrupted.

"A *few* questions, my butt," Natalie scoffed; again receiving warning looks from my mother. I couldn't help but smile, which brought a vindictive smile to Nat's face. I was only encouraging her.

Mom continued, "A lot of your friends... well, practically the whole town came to the hospital yesterday to see you, but Dr. Kowalski would only allow family until you came to. She said it's critical that you rest. Cari, her mom, and Isaac stuck around the longest, until early this morning, and then he drove them home. They all said they'd come back after school today."

"What time is it?" I think they were reading my lips more than listening, because the sounds I was producing weren't enough for real verbal communication. I could barely hear myself.

"Just after lunch," she replied with a smile. "Are you hungry?"

My eyes widened at the prospect of food. "*Starved.*"

"I'll let the nurse's station know." She leaned over to press the red service button.

I had to ask, no matter how much it broke my heart to say his name. "Broderick? Is he…" I took a deep breath in anticipation for their answer, "…*okay?*"

Natalie's face twisted and her lips pulled back in misgiving. She dropped her head and walked back to her chair.

"What happened?" my voice trembled.

"Honey, he's fine. He took quite a beating, but he's home and recuperating. He refused to stay here." Mom brushed a few straggling hairs from my forehead and spoke soothingly. She pressed the button again, frustrated that she hadn't been contacted by the nurse's station yet.

"Mom, why don't you actually walk the few yards down the hall to tell them she's awake." Natalie forcefully laughed. "In fact, why don't you and Daddy both go down to the cafeteria and get something to eat. Y'all haven't eaten in days!"

They looked at each other, both were unwilling to leave, "We just got you back; I don't think I can leave you," Mom said. They appeared quite gun shy with the prospect of either one of us girls being out of their sight. Then Dad jerked his head toward the door, making the final decision. Mom kissed me on the forehead and they walked out of the room holding hands.

The minute they walked out, Natalie shut the door behind them and scurried secretively over to the bed, sitting on the corner of it. Her toothy grin quickly dropped as her face began twisting, fighting an emotional breakdown. Eventually, she lost her composure and hid her face in her hands. She held up a finger to give herself a minute to control her crying.

"I'm sorry. Hang on," she said, weeping. "I didn't think I was going to do this." Natalie wiped her tears and rubbed her eyes. "I'm sorry. I had to hold it together for Mom and Dad for so long… I couldn't wait till they were gone." She smiled, her face flushed. My sister was stronger than many of us realized.

Nodding my head to let her know I understood, my throat was still raw and my tongue too thick for speech.

"I was starting to think we'd never see you again."

"What happened?" I whispered.

She chuckled incredulously. "We should be asking *you* that question!" She suddenly became reserved. "But I guess that's not something you really want to talk about right now, is it?"

I shook my head slowly as I frowned; though staying silent about the whole ordeal was hardly going to keep it from flooding my memory. It would forever be a haunting nightmare.

"Gosh, where to start." She took a deep breath and paused. "Well, some bartender came across your car at the stop light by the library. He was on his way home when he pulled up behind it and saw that it was empty. The doors were left open and the car was still running. Lucky for you, he was honest enough to call the police instead of driving off with the thing."

"I still have a car?" I asked with a smile.

"*And* a purse! He was honest, I tell ya." She grinned in surprise. "Mom and Dad got the call just before four in the morning and from that moment on, our lives have been turned upside down.

"I called Berta that morning to tell her why I wasn't going to be in school and the news spread like wild fire. Sheriff Burnett was over at the house for the majority of the morning, asking all sorts of questions trying to figure out where you might be. Emma Rose said that she was the last person to see you at the band room before you left for home that night."

I nodded at the memory and reached for another swig of ice water.

Natalie quickly assisted in holding the glass for me. "They put out an Amber Alert for you, but I don't think anyone was hopeful to find you in time. Well, some of us were."

"Like who?" I asked.

"Well, Mom and Dad of course, silly! And I have to say, I was quite impressed with how well Mom handled it all."

"Really?"

"She mowed right on through. Determined, positive, never once cracking in front of us. She kept her deteriorating spirit under wraps and in secret. But I could hear her crying late at night as she sat in the kitchen waiting for the phone to ring. Dad was a basket case. I've decided that when our parents are old and grey, Dad needs to die before Mom. He'll never survive the grief."

I smiled at this knowledge—my intimidating father, the emotionally weaker of the two.

"*I* never lost hope." She shrugged. "Call it a hunch. I witnessed some pretty determined people who were willing to practically give their lives to find and save you. The police were amazing." She swallowed hard as she continued her thought. "Joey came over every day to check up on the family." There was palpable sadness in my sister's face. She saw her mistake with Joey.

"*Cari*, of all people," she laughed out loud, "organized a student search with Savannah's help. The sheriff was pissed about it, I might add. He didn't want anyone else getting caught up in the trouble, but after getting most of the high school involved, it kinda took on a life of its own. Soon, the parents joined the searches and teachers, then random town folk. The rescue squad led us all out in groups, of course, covering every bit of ground in the county. Some even went to surrounding counties."

"Who?"

"Everyone! Cari, Savannah, Tripp and Joey and *Lindsey*," she said in a whiny voice. "…Taryn, Jackson, Isaac, that guy from the Java House…"

"Chase, too?"

"Yeah! There were people in the search parties that I had never even seen before, Jules! Complete strangers!"

I could feel my eye brightening at the knowledge that I had so many loved ones who cared and worked hard for my safe return.

"We all went in shifts, too; meeting up at the courthouse three times daily. I think everyone was skipping school. They may as well have closed it with all of the tardiness and absences over the chaos. Even some of the teachers like Mr. Grayson and Mr. Muir, took a day off for a search shift!"

I laughed silently at her amusement.

"Oh!" She rolled her eyes. "And get this! Your two favorite ex-boyfriends even took part in looking for you. And might I say, Broderick was not thrilled about that at all. Erik said that he 'owed you one' for clearing his name in Loni's case. And Gavin; apparently, he's back.

"I told the Sheriff about how someone had been messing with you for weeks, since Thanksgiving," Natalie confessed. "So they did a thorough sweep of your bedroom, gathering fingerprints and other things that could qualify as clues."

"What did they find?"

A nurse interrupted us with a tray of food. "I have lunch for Miss Taylor."

I struggled to sit up better. Natalie came to my rescue before the nurse could even set the tray down. She grabbed the remote and began pressing buttons. It was as if she had worked in a hospital all her life and knew the most efficient way to arrange my bed. I gave her an impressive look. She shrugged, "You sleep like the dead, but Mom told me to stop playing with it during the blood transfusions." She devilishly grinned, causing me to laugh as the nurse rolled the table closer and swung it over the rails and in front of me.

"Let me know if you're still hungry when you're done, hon."

Natalie returned to her seat at the edge of the bed. She began nibbling on my food as she continued her story. "So, you want to know what they found?" she antagonized.

I gave her a wary look.

"You should be thankful that God gave you a sister who's willing to cover your butt," she said. "They found Lucas Reiser's prints all over your room—all through the house, in fact." Her face turned pale at the acknowledgement. "But they also found someone *else's* prints in your room. Pretty fresh, in fact."

I knew exactly who she was referring to.

"Broderick," I whispered sadly as I reached for small handful of fries and began nibbling.

"I told them that he had come over shortly after you left for Florida to return a few of your items and that I let him in your room." She became somber. "He wasn't well, Jules, after he got the news of your disappearance."

I dropped my head at her words.

"He was *desperately* cooperative for them to find you. He drove the police crazy, as bad as Mom and Dad did—asking questions, constantly calling with new theories, not really allowing the police to do their work." Her face twisted at a second thought. "It was strange though, he never took part in our searches; he said that he preferred to search on his own. He said that he felt hindered having to stay with a group and being told where to search. Anyway, he finally confessed to the police about how the two of you snuck out once and stirred up a hornet's nest with a cult of some sort out in the boonies. It was the only strong lead the police had. Joey said that his dad ordered Broderick to stay put, but Joey knew he was already on his way to the church when he called. He said that Broderick was freaking out because of something about it being the night of a full moon. He must've known that it was to be your last night alive." Natalie grabbed the hamburger on my plate and took a big bite.

Now that the realistic nature of the horror I had just encountered was over, I was going to have to face the wrath of my parents for the sneaking out at night, not that I was ever going to do that again.

"We got the call shortly after midnight saying that Broderick had found you and saved you. He's your hero, Jules!" She took another bite of my burger.

I couldn't even disguise my misery and confusion and fear as I turned over as much as I physically could. I wanted to remember how we were together before we got caught up in all of this mess and even when he first found me—his words were tender and loving. But all *I* could see was the wolf, evil and grotesque. Broderick was lost to me forever.

In the corner of my eye, I saw that my plate was empty and that Natalie was chewing on the last of my fries. "Well, *I* haven't eaten in days, either." She smiled sheepishly and reached over to press the red button. This time a nurse called back immediately. "We'll need another plate of food." She snickered and I forced a small chuckle wishing I could take in the enjoyment of my sister and her humor and of being home, but the hole in my heart, was now filling with fear in its cavity, overwhelming me.

"Where is he now?" I asked. I trembled with the thought of this beast roaming the halls of the hospital.

"He refused to stay in the hospital. Dr. Blythe tried looking him over in the ER as they brought the two of you in. Talk about a hissy fit! Between the doctor and the sheriff's department giving him the third degree, it was no wonder!" She paused to swallow the rest of her toast. "Finally, Dr. Kowalski was able to calm him down, and within a few minutes, he let her treat him privately. She said he was just agitated from the shock."

The same nurse came back in with another plate and quickly left, taking the previous plate. Another hamburger. I was certain that under normal circumstances, this hamburger would taste like crap, but the smell of edible food was so appealing at that very moment. But, like the talking, Natalie was also doing most of the eating.

She reiterated her last statement. "So, he let her treat him but he pretty much ignored all of the questions that the police asked him. Said he wouldn't give them a statement."

"Why?" I asked curiously.

"The doctor claimed that an explosion occurred as he jumped, and the impact of that explosion prevented him from remembering much of anything."

When Sheriff Burnett showed up later that evening, I was prepared for what I was willing to tell him—and for what I was *not* willing to tell him. Though I didn't want to get one detail wrong, I didn't want to pass off any information that I was unsure about. What had happened to me was so farfetched to my own imagination; uncertainty was thick with my recollections.

Beginning with the night Broderick and I accidently stumbled across their celebration and how we were detected and chased back to the jeep, I then filled him in on the goings on that had occurred in my room since Thanksgiving, and I was sure to give every small detail, down to the wire, of what happened when I was taken. My explanations for what took place during the ceremonies were as foggy as my memory. Lucas' cryptic words had no meaning to me, and I could only guess what the ceremony accomplished. I told of the earthen prison I had been left in, how I tried breaking free at one point and how I failed.

But somewhere in my quest to give the truth, I justified my secrets. The shadowshifting, the werewolf... none of it was ever mentioned. I knew it was unbelievable and that only more trouble would come of my complete honesty. It was the best way for me to pass "crazy" onto someone else. I was already deemed insane when I brought Lucas into the story.

Sheriff Burnett held up his hand to stop me, "Now, Jules, you are aware that we found that Reiser kid dead only about a week ago, right? In fact, we buried him the day before you were found."

"Yes sir," I answered with uncertainty.

"We also never found his body at the crime scene. That being said, are you one hundred percent positive that it was *Lucas Reiser?*"

The news plummeted me into shock. The debate warred within me. I could either push further, to reveal the truth or I could concede to the sheriff's truth as he saw it.

I shook my head.

The hardest part was acting relaxed when Broderick was brought into the story again. The eyewitness account of him becoming a werewolf moved to the tip of my tongue, but I simply couldn't put that into words.

Sheriff Burnett gathered his notebook and stopped his recorder, placing it in his coat pocket and stood up to shake hands with my parents when he had my statement.

My mom hugged his neck, and as he started walking out, I was compelled to ask one question of him. "Sheriff Burnett?"

"Yes, Miss Taylor?"

"Are *you* one hundred percent sure Lucas Reiser was dead when you buried him?" I asked. My eyebrows rose, hoping he would say no. I was beginning to feel insane over the contradiction. *Could it even be possible?* The strength and the speed the evil ones showed. *Were they really the undead? Were they vampires?*

"One hundred percent. He's dead and buried," he assured me.

"And what about the other bodies at the barn? Do we know who they were?"

He was cautious as he approached his answer to me. "The bodies at the barn were burned to a crisp. Only a few of them have been identified yet—runaways mostly. But like I said, Lucas Reiser was not counted among them."

Lost in my insanity, I didn't even thank him as he walked out.

Cari and Savannah stopped by that evening. Natalie refused to leave my side, explaining that she felt uncomfortable leaving me. I think she was hoping for Joey to show up to visit, too.

Cari pushed past Savannah and came barreling toward me. She dove in and hugged me securely. Savannah moved in for her hug when Cari finally pulled back.

Embarrassed at her sudden show of emotions, Cari ruffled my short, messy locks. "Nice hair," she said sourly.

I whined, "I'm sure I look like death warmed over."

Our private visit was short-lived as a thick foreign accent drifted into the room. "Hello? Is Juliana awake?"

"Yeah, she's up," Cari said and the tall, thin doctor walked gracefully into the room with a caring smile.

"Good evening, Juliana. How are you feeling?"

"I'm sore and tired."

"Well, you are dehydrated and suffered a substantial amount of blood loss, so that would explain why you are so tired. But your skin has some good color to it now that you've had your blood transfusions."

I gasped. "You mean I looked worse earlier?"

Natalie muttered, "You're look has improved considerably since they brought you in, Jules."

Dr. Kowalski smiled warmly. "You should be thankful to be alive, Juliana. You're resilient and are bouncing back quickly." She tilted my head up into the light to inspect my face, and then she lowered my face to look squarely at me as she pulled a small light from her white coat pocket and flashed it into my eyes. "We have you on IV fluids to hydrate you and antibiotics for a Urinary Tract Infection."

I twisted my sore face in question, blinking hard at the bright light in my eyes. "Is that why I feel the non-stop need to pee?" I had already been to the bathroom several times already and had only been able to release a trickle each time. It was annoying.

"It should clear up within a day or so," she assured. "Do you think you might feel like going home tomorrow?" I concentrated hard not to blink my eyes shut as she shined a small light in them.

"Maybe," I said, unsure if I even wanted to. My bedroom. My car. My home. My home next door to Broderick...none of it felt safe.

Dr. Kowalski pulled the light back, checked my wrist then locked eyes with me—dead on. "Juliana, your face will heal. Your wrist will be out of a cast in a few weeks, being only a crack... but I would be more concerned with the emotional and internal scarring than your physical ones. You've suffered a very traumatic ordeal."

Sighing hopelessly, there were so many layers of emotions I had to work through. I was devastated with my current looks and I was terrified of the world outside—a world that most people were unaware of. I was also confused with my feelings for Broderick. Without a doubt, I was frightened of him, but my heart ached for the boy he once was. Was it even possible to love someone you feared?

Dr. Kowalski observed the bite marks that had been left on my body, shaking her head. Savannah winced and turned away but Cari and Natalie gasped at the marks on my body.

"If the scarring bothers you so much, you can purchase an ointment at any drug store that'll help the scars fade," she said finally.

I had a hard time believing that that was all she wanted to say to me. There was something deeper behind her eyes and looked almost speculative as they locked with my eyes.

"I will schedule a follow up appointment for you at my office. We'll see how you're doing then." She then cocked her head to the side and looked pitifully at me. "Juliana, your body has suffered trauma, but also trauma here." With that, she gently touched my forehead. As she walked to the door, she announced, "I'll be back tomorrow morning to see you. If you are still stable, I'll let you go home."

"Cool! You get to go home tomorrow!" Savannah enthused as the doctor left, but I just stared out the window and watched the sky spit a few more flurries of snow.

First thing the next morning, my dad was transporting my flowers to the house as my mom listened intently to the doctor's orders. School was cancelled due to snow, so Cari and Natalie stayed close by to assist with anything my mom needed to accommodate me on my first day home.

It was weird and contradicting, really. All I had wished for, other than death when I had become hopeless for escape, was to go home and return to my old life, but nothing was the same anymore. Nothing looked or felt the same, and truth be told, I wasn't sure if I wanted it to be. For things to be like they were before, I would have to forget the past. Make it as though it never happened. I would want to go back far enough to correct my mistakes. To wipe the slate clean of Broderick so I could forget about the beast that he was, I would need to forget everyone that was connected to my memory of him. It was all impossible. Broderick would somehow, forever be branded into my life, and there was nothing I could do to escape that.

My first night home was disheartening. I wished I could absorb the comforts and reassurances I'd always felt, but before I was even able to walk into my bedroom that night, I felt my knees begin to quake in fright and apprehension. Just as I stood in the doorway, I was fighting tears, imagining Lucas looming over the foot of my bed. I swallowed hard at the vivid imagination of what probably occurred as I slept these last few months. He had been in my room—all over the house!

Walking in, I took only to glance over at the dormer window to see Broderick sitting in the window seat, waiting for me. I didn't know what to say to him. He had a tentative smile spread on his beautiful lips, happy to see me return to him. Closing my eyes, my heart broke with the reality that he wasn't here at all. When I opened my eyes, the oversized and grotesque wolf hovered in his place, seething and panting, preparing to lunge at me. Quickly, I shut my eyes again to absorb this image also. The adrenaline rush in my already weakened condition caused me to stagger against the door.

This isn't real. Not real. Not real.

I found that being in my room that night was agonizing. It was too dark, too quiet. What used to bring me peace, now brought demons. The branches from the tree outside cast menacing shadows on my wall. The wind howled, and the icy branches tapped on the roof over my bed. My room was no longer my safe haven. I was foolish to believe it had ever been.

I contemplated how I was going to escape its confines without my ankles being grabbed by the thing that hid under my bed, or have my escape route cut off by the monster in my closet. These were the kind of thoughts that I obsessed over as a young child, and even though I knew these things didn't exist, it didn't bring me much reassurance. Now, as a young adult, I knew just how real they were and all comfort was lost. Lucas had been in and out of my room for God knows how long! My security was breached in my own home and in my own bed.

Anxiety became as heavy as a boulder. I had foolishly convinced myself that hiding under a quilted piece of cotton would keep me protected or hide me from the monsters as if they would never find me. My breathing told me this was a lie as it increased and became shallow.

With just a little bit of stubbornness left in me, I squeezed my eyes shut determined to ignore it all and fall asleep, but then the house settled and my hard wood floor made a loud popping sound in the process. My eyes flew open and again, I saw Lucas standing over my bed, the lips of his sinister grin parted just enough to expose his deadly fangs. I could literally smell his decomposing body again! There was no hope for me to escape, so I hunkered down into a ball in my bed, pulling myself deep under the bundle of covers. I wanted to scream for help, but knew that with his speed, he would snuff me out before I could get a full throttled scream out. Another foolish plan flashed through my mind instead.

I motivated myself. *One, two, three!*

Throwing back the covers, I dashed to the door in one frantic move. My poor tired legs were sluggishly pumping as my feet slapped against the hard wood floors of the hall. Without fully thinking as to where I would run to, I skidded hard into Natalie's bedroom door. As soon as my hand wrapped around her door knob, I caught my breath. With a quick flick of my good wrist, I twisted the knob and pushed the door open. I flipped my body around the door and shut it fast, but quietly, careful not to wake my younger sister.

I looked over at her, snuggled deep within the blankets of her bed without a care in the world, her back toward me. Jealousy clung to me. I wanted that comfort, not just in my bed, but in everything around me. She had never suffered from insecurity or unpopularity or a real fear like being kidnapped by an evil cult, tortured, and rescued by an ex-boyfriend who turned out to be a werewolf. It all fell on me, and I resented that. I wasn't strong enough for this battle. Not physically, not emotionally. Beyond the jealousy, I was a very scared little girl, who needed the one person who knew me better than anyone else in this world, someone who shared not only a past, but the same blood. Natalie.

"Natalie?" I whispered, on the verge of weeping.

She never spoke a word, but instead lifted her blanket from where it lay across her body, inviting me into her bed. She was awake. I didn't hesitate, climbing under her covers and curving my body securely behind hers, I put my arm around her waist and hugged her tightly as I trembled with tears, pressing my face into her back. She put her arm over mine and held my hand, in a silent consent to cry myself to sleep.

I never went back into my room.

Natalie never once complained about sharing her bed or how I would wake her up every night in one of my horrified gasps for a scream, or in the way I kicked in a subconscious struggle.

Due to the unusual circumstances of my life, I was granted special permission for homeschooling to keep up in my studies. I toyed with the idea of possibly rejoining my friends in the fall for our senior year, but before then? I was resolved to sitting the rest of this school year at home. A guy named Randy Livingston, from my American History class, would come over several times a week to tutor me and keep me up to date on class requirements. I would spend most of the days doing homework while Nat was in school and my parents were at work. They were against the idea of me staying at home by myself but could hardly push the issue due to my fragile state of mind.

Being alone at home during the day was intense, but I was willing to accept it and fight through my fears during the daylight hours. I usually began freaking out with the oncoming winter darkness when Natalie was in cheerleading practice or my parent worked late. In these cases, I turned on every light in the house and resorted to a brightly lit movie—comedies; even the stupid and vulgar ones that I hated.

And I always had a large kitchen knife handy; carrying it with me from room to room as I remained dressed in my pajamas. This time I would be prepared.

I was up front about my qualms to rejoin my peers at school, dreading any form of contact with them, even my friends. My reasoning went beyond my temporary deformity though it didn't help matters either. I wasn't ready to answer questions of who took me and why and what happened. I wasn't ready to explain how I was able to escape. It was a hard enough struggle not to even think about it. My mind was constantly being flooded with images of the burning barn or the overpowering fog of my adjusting vision. Or of Broderick.

Mom and Dad begged me to reconsider joining my friends back at school in February; adamant in believing that socializing at school would prove to be helpful in my emotional recovery. My mom also urged me to go see Dr. Kowalski, stating that I needed help coping with my anxiety. I insisted that I was only being cautious and that I didn't want to take medication to make me feel or act normal. I was never going to be normal again!

Hell had allowed something evil to escape into our peaceful world, and I felt like I was the only person aware of it. The weight of that knowledge was on my shoulders alone.

My lack of improvement over time began to age my mom and dad as they were beaten down with stress. It seemed that with every visitor and phone call I would avoid, their hair would become grayer and their fine lines deepened into wrinkles. With every nightmare I would endure, their eyes would become tired. Finally, my mom took it upon herself to confront me as she sat beside me on the couch one afternoon. At first I thought she just wanted to watch television with me, but her body turned toward me, which was a huge red flag to me that she wanted to talk. I squirmed uncomfortably as I stared at the TV screen until she made her first step.

"Have any plans tonight?" she asked.

I shook my head slowly as if I wasn't much for her conversation but more involved in the storyline on TV. "Nope."

"Why not?" she came right out and asked, jostling my nerves.

"I just don't," I answered grumpily.

She hesitated then chose her words carefully. "Jules, you can't keep on like this. It's not healthy. It's not normal."

I frowned. "There's nothing normal about what happened to me, either! What do you want from me, Mom?" I finally turned away from the TV and stared coldly at her.

"This isn't you! The only emotion I ever see in you anymore is anger or fear." She spread her hands out in a sweeping motion. "I want my daughter back. I miss her so much," Her voice quaked.

"So, this is about *you?*" I asked cruelly.

"No. You're right. It's not about me. If it were, I'd do everything I could to get better." Mom stared into my eyes as if she could actually see into my very soul. I knew she wasn't going to give up. She was in fighting mode. "Jules, physically you're improving every day, but in here..." Mom duplicated Dr. Kowalski's gentle touch to my forehead, "there's no improvement. You're getting worse. I want you to see Dr. Kowalski...."

"I just need time."

My mom's voice began to shake. "Jules, I'm afraid if we give you any more time, we're going to lose you forever."

"How so?" I thought quickly as to what she referred to and flinched. "You think I'm suicidal?"

She chose her words carefully. "I think you're depressed and need help."

Jumping up in a rage, I threw the remote down. "What I need, mother, is for you to get off of my back!" I screamed. As I ran down the hall, I heard my mother faintly call to either me or pray to God in her sobs. I wasn't sure which.

"I just want my daughter back."

Survival of the Mind

THE CASE OF THE Full Moon Murders was closed before I even had the cast around my wrist removed. The case was *buried*. My questions remained unanswered; it felt as though it was just swept under the rug, so that the town could move on and simply forget.

My statement had been discredited because of the trauma I had suffered and the fact that my vision was greatly impaired. My account of what happened at the barn was never reported on, spoken of, or even printed about. It was our town's biggest cover up, bringing a quick closure and healing for our community.

I would never heal because of it. I was powerless and assumed crazy.

From the safety of the hall, I would watch my room and see the ghosts of my haunting past taunt and torture me. Lucas would smile at me from across the room, curling his boney finger, his nails dark and grey, inviting me into my bedroom. Just as frightening, I could hear the low growl of the wolf from around the corner of my door, where my closet and escape window would be, warning me in that unsteady whimper just short of becoming a howl. And in the midst of it all, I saw the boy next door lying on my bed with his head propped up by his arm, staring at me with unbound love and longing in his eyes. It was as if he and the wolf were separate entities. *Were they?*

The latter of the three ghosts tortured me the most.

Because I would never get the answers I needed from law officials, I decided to take a trip to the library to research vampires and cults and werewolves and anything else of the supernatural sort. I would get the answers myself.

It felt ridiculous really, seeing as how I should know the rules and warnings of every monster ever created with all of the horror movies I had seen in my seventeen years, but yet, this was a new playing field. What I knew was of fictional characters. What I had witnessed, was very much real. I had been with Broderick for months and never once took note of the warnings. How did I miss all the signs? Had he been a werewolf all his life or just recently? Anger and fear burned within me as I tried making sense of it all, and I was sick and tired of everyone wanting me to "talk about it". How could I possibly talk about something I couldn't understand and no one would ever believe?

The cold weather burned my nostrils as I strolled up to the library, looking over my shoulder every few seconds. The grey skies made the day much darker than it should have been, leaving me uncomfortable with my surroundings. Just before I pulled the doors open to walk inside, I stopped to look at the stop lights at the corner where I had been taken. I glanced at the tree tops, street lamps, and the steeple of the church—the last few flashes of my view before being taken as I was wrestled to the ground. My screams echoed in my mind as I stared at my surroundings. I closed my eyes, allowing the tears to seep from their creases.

Shaking my head as if I could physically shake the memory away, I walked inside to the warm and quiet building.

Upon seeing the librarian, I remembered a small detail about my last day in Florida while on the phone with Natalie. She had told me the library called to remind me about a book I had checked out.

I walked up to the frumpy, middle aged woman behind the counter as she took inventory of recently returned books.

"Can I help you?" she asked me as I approached her.

"Uh, yeah. My name is Juliana Taylor and a month ago I received a message from here about an overdue book?"

She immediately began tapping away on the keys of her computer. "Juliana Taylor. Taylor..." she mumbled. Her brows began to furrow. "Do you even have a membership with us, Miss Taylor?"

I chuckled, dumbfounded as she was. "No."

"We don't have a record of you. What did you say the name of the book was again?" she asked politely.

"I don't know," I whispered as I turned my back to her. I was completely confused with the whole debacle.

Must have been a mistake. Brushing it off, I went back to the reference file. Soon enough I had found my way to the books dealing with the supernatural, sorcery, and cult practices. One book in particular interested me—it was a book about cults. I took it back to the table with me. Skimming through the pages, I learned that most of the book was based on cults of supposed Christianity and Polygamy. Nothing of sorcery.

I returned it to the shelf and moseyed down the aisle. Nothing caught my attention. I continued to the end of that isle searching titles and authors but to no avail. The bottom shelf began with P's.

I went around the corner to see if the section would continue on the other side. When I saw the continuance, I carried on, skimming the titles for the words *vampire* and *werewolf*. The werewolf section was scarce, but the vampire books were well stocked. Too lazy to pick a few out and carry them back to the table, I sat on the floor and leaned against the opposite shelf as I skimmed the pages.

The illustrations were terrifying enough, but as I delved further into the book, my blood ran cold over the true accounts of people who believed they were indeed vampires, and willingly described their lifestyles. However, there was never any sited scientific proof of their existence beyond their own claims.

Suddenly I felt a warm and totally unexpected glow kindle my soul, bringing me an essence of comfort. Comfort I had not felt since before my abduction—since before Halloween. I was determined not to move from my spot, reminding me of when my mom used to scratch my back and it felt so good that I was afraid she'd stop if I made the slightest move. Languid with the enveloping comfort, I lifted my chin and looked to the ceiling, taking a deep sigh of relief. I didn't question where this euphoria sprang from, only that it felt right somehow.

Get a library card and borrow this book, I decided as I stretched my legs out and pushed myself to my feet. As I stepped out from the isle of books, I caught a familiar stature in the corner of my eye walking toward me from the other side of the shelf.

I slowed to a stop, my heart rate speeding up, and looked over to see Broderick standing and staring helplessly at me with a book in his hand. I flinched as he took a timid step toward me. A delayed reaction, I stepped away from him, partially twisting my body around to run away, but my ankles tangled with one another causing me to fall back. Protectively, I put my hands out to break my fall, but I still made a loud crash as I banged my elbow against a few chairs and they tumbled to the ground.

I heard the librarian gasp at my accident and I quickly repositioned myself on the floor to keep an eye on Broderick. My mouth was too dry for me to speak or scream, but my body alone revealed my fear as I shook.

In an almost debilitating state of stun and panic, I clumsily scrambled to my feet and grabbed my purse and coat, running frantically out the door and to my car. I drove erratically back home, never once fully catching my breath.

Staring inside my bedroom from the safety of the doorway became the usual agenda for me. My instincts forbid me to enter. Resting my head back on the wall and turning to face the room, I took several nervous sighs as I contemplated my entry. I just knew Lucas would be waiting for me in there. So was the werewolf.

"Jules?" I was so consumed with fearful thoughts that I didn't hear my mom's footsteps approaching. I gasped in shock from the sound of her voice.

"You scared the crap outta me!" My eyes wide with fright.

"Sorry." She made her way to the top of the stairs and then sat beside me on the floor. This time she remained quiet as I continued to stare in the brightly lit room.

I sighed again, longing for my possessions, my refuge.

"You know, your father and I are willing to switch rooms with you," she suggested.

I furrowed my brows as I debated the offer. It sounded like exactly what I needed. A change, a new setting. Surely there would be some feeling of safety in that. But just before I could answer her, I imagined Broderick sitting on my bed. He looked over at me with one of his many endearing smiles in which his dimples showed. Then he faded. My heart ached as I shook my head at her. I couldn't leave *this* ghost. I would willingly endure the other two for his appearance every once in a while.

"No, thanks. I'll be fine."

She lovingly patted me on the knee. "If you change your mind, you only need to say the word, and we will move everything for you."

"Yes, ma'am."

"Did you have plans today?" As she so often asked.

I rolled my eyes, assuming that she was about to do another intervention. My voice was testy as I answered, "No."

"Oh." She was taken aback with my answer, which I found odd. I hadn't had plans in over a month. "Because someone's here to see you."

I groaned, "I really don't want to see anybody, Mom. Not today."

She gave a misgiving smile. "He's pretty adamant about seeing you…"

"*He?*" I asked suddenly as both fear and excitement bubbled inside of me. *Broderick?* I'd panicked when I unexpectedly ran into him at the library, but strangely enough it had also given me a burst of loving remembrances as well. I wondered if my reaction to him at the library had motivated him to confront me.

I needed confirmation. I asked shakily, "Who is it?"

"It's just me," a soothingly soft voice echoed from the stairwell and I jumped to my feet to see Isaac Philetos standing directly below the rail. Just as beautiful as he ever was. His face full of concern.

"What are *you* doing here?" I asked rudely.

"Jules!" My mother scolded.

"It's okay Mrs. Taylor." He climbed the stairs gracefully to where she and I stood. He stood tall and sure. "Juliana, I just need a few minutes of your time. I really think it's something you need to hear."

Staring at him coldly, I spoke to my mom. "Mom, can I have a private word with Isaac?"

"Sure," she agreed and she walked back down the steps as Isaac climbed them to the top.

Isaac and I locked eyes for a long moment before he finally spoke. He tucked in his smooth, fleshy pink lips and then exhaled noisily. Isaac knelt on the floor facing me, his back leaning against the banister. His smile was bittersweet. "I can't even begin to understand what you've gone through...*still* going through and I'm not going to pretend to."

"Good," I said shortly. No one knew what I went through and the only person who could closely relate to me was just short of a monster himself.

He cleared his throat nervously. "But just because I can't fully understand, doesn't mean I can't listen."

I figured that he was sent here by one of my friends. Probably Cari. "Forget it," I grumbled. "Whoever sent you here, tell them they're wasting their time."

"Do you think you're the only person who has ever suffered a loss or a traumatic experience? You're not, so get over yourself!" He force-fed his words to me as he intimidatingly stared at me.

I wasn't going to take it lying down. "Why the hell did they send you anyway? Like I'd ever listen to you! I *hate* you." I rolled my eyes.

He chuckled arrogantly. "You keep saying that, but I happen to know that it's short lived. You and I are too much alike. You can't hate me because you can't really hate yourself."

"We are nothing alike."

"You're wrong." He narrowed his eyes sternly at me. "You think I don't see what you're doing to yourself and everyone around you? For some stupid reason, you feel guilty over what happened to you, like it was something you brought on yourself. Physically, you'll heal. Emotionally, you can't be the same, so you've built up a wall to protect yourself. You won't let anyone in because they wouldn't understand, and you know they deserve better than that. Have I struck a chord yet? You stop me when you think I'm wrong."

His tone felt vicious to my ears, but I couldn't stop him. My armor was being stripped away. It was uncanny how close he was in describing what I couldn't have described myself. I was stunned as he continued.

"To *you*, the safest place now is the secrecy of your own indignant thoughts. You endure your own torture now because you think that's what you deserve. It's the closest thing to death you'll allow yourself to be without disappointing those around you—as if you're doing us a favor by continuing your life like this. What you don't understand is that's the worst place you could be hiding!

"You're scared. You're a scared little girl and though it's obvious to everyone around you, you won't simply admit it to yourself and fight it. I don't know about you, Juliana, but I'd be damned before I let this ruin the rest of *my* life. It would really piss me off to allow something to control me to this extent." His harsh words hit home and *that* pissed me off to the point I felt the monster within me stir from its near-death coma.

I stayed silent and watched as Isaac clenched his fists tightly as if he were bracing himself for a fight and then he released them, wriggling the tension from his fingers.

"If this is how you want to spend the rest of your life... You're more dead than alive." He added quickly, "So why'd you bother coming back at all?"

He didn't sound malicious, but disappointed as he stormed out of the room. I heard each resounding step he made. Then he politely said goodbye to my mother and left. I was still staring into my vacant bedroom when I heard his motorcycle zoom away from the house.

How could he know so much of how I felt when I couldn't even make sense of it? I had been in such a state of confusion for so long that I couldn't organize it all into neat and precise thoughts or feelings. But somehow, he was able to come in and sweep the cobwebs away pointing out each fault, lighting a fire inside of me again. All in one sweep, I was now driven to do something. What, exactly—I didn't know. But *something* was better than *nothing*. The fire he created inside me was partly filled with anger, but it was also full of inspiration and drive. I felt an ignition of perseverance burst through.

The house was silent, except for my own breathing, and I made my first decision.

Placing my sweaty palms on the hardwood floor and rolling onto my knees, I stepped into my room and the fear began melting away. I felt so liberated in my small victory. I steadied myself back to a sitting position, now just inside the door, light as a feather for the first time in over a month.

I continued to sleep with Natalie, but the next day I was able to crawl five feet inside my room, despite the warning from the wolf and the chilling sneer of Lucas' ghost. The day after that, I sat on my bed, next to the boy who had been waiting for me to join him. By week's end I was able to enter my room for anything I wanted and needed. Now capable to pick out my own clothes and listen to my own music, I was still on edge inside the purple walls, but it was a start to what I believed was a real recovery.

The day I walked into the waiting room of Dr. Kowalski's office, my mom's eyes filled with bittersweet but prideful tears. She never said she was proud of me or that she was happy to see me there, but I knew that she was. And though the good doctor's schedule was quite full, she made a special effort to fit me in.

Dr. Kowalski checked all my old injuries and again recommended an over the counter ointment to help the scars fade—even though I was now more concerned with healing my inner scars as she had mentioned before. She pulled out a clipboard and asked me several questions about my sleeping patterns and how I felt about myself and my life. I cringed as she forwardly asked if I had any suicidal tendencies regardless of how minor I considered them. Her question only served to remind me of Isaac's declaration. *You're more dead than alive…so, why'd you bother coming back at all?* I may not have specifically considered suicide as an option, but Isaac was right. I was too cowardly for such a drastic measure, afraid to hurt my parents and friends; but I was taking an equal option by severing ties with the world and the life I was meant to live. Explaining that to Dr. Kowalski, she nodded as if she understood what I meant and prescribed an anti-depressant and something else for my anxiety.

"Will I have to take this forever?" I asked. I didn't want to be dependent for the rest of my life on a drug to help me cope.

She smiled encouragingly. "Like the cream I recommended to diminish your scars, this medication will help to diminish emotional scarring. It will take time, Juliana. In time all of your scars will diminish considerably."

I nodded and hopped off of the table, starting for the door.

"Juliana?" she called to me, causing me to turn to her before leaving. "I am aware of the odd nature of the circumstances you claim to have encountered, and I want you to know that if ever you need to talk about it, I would listen and it would remain confidential—doctor and patient. Secrets, too, can have a way of threatening your health. Don't bottle it in."

I nodded in agreement and thanked her again.

I still slept with Natalie, but found myself in my old room more and more every day. Two of the ghosts waiting for me inside the room slowly disappeared—only one remained and he would warmly smile and silently beckon me to join him for a movie as he sat on my bed, or invited me to venture out with him as he sat near my window sill. At night, he would lay his head on the pillow and look lovingly into my eyes. There was no fear of his ghost, only a dull aching need for what once was.

Eventually, I worked through enough fear and pain to return to Cumberland County High School. Natalie sat in the passenger's seat and nervously filled me in on what was happening at school, not that I truly cared about any of it, but I could see that she, too, was anxious about my reentry. My stomach was in knots as I wondered what kind of welcome I would receive. Not that I expected a banner or a committee, but I wondered who all would speak to me and who all would fish for more information on my mysterious abduction.

A dumpy sweatshirt and short hair, lazily pinned back from my face, was the look I embodied for the grand occasion. Beauty made me uncomfortable. It felt dangerous to be attractive now, and I was a hideous sight for sure, especially to everyone who watched me stroll through the parking lot alongside my gorgeous sister. As we neared the school, I would nudge her and inconspicuously eye the entrances. I felt uncertain and self-conscious.

"There's a ton of people by that door," I whispered quietly against the winter morning wind. "They're all looking at me."

"Jules, they're happy to see you back and they're curious. That's all," she explained calmly.

Natalie began guiding me to another entrance—the front of the school, where it was always congested with the bus riders. I would probably go unnoticed there. Natalie and I wove through and blended in as we slipped through the doors. Immediately I felt, and then saw, the eyes of everyone in the main hall draw toward me.

As though I had no control over my own two legs, I was unable to run back out of the building. I continued to walk, floating through the halls in a dream-like state. As Natalie and I progressed closer toward my locker, our classmates parted like the red sea to let us pass. They gawked, some smiled, but *all* stared. I'm sure they saw it as a welcoming, but to me, it was a funeral procession for a girl who no longer existed.

I kept my head down, watching my feet take each step. Unable to look up, whether it was due to embarrassment over all of the attention or maybe it was a survivor's guilt. Of all the victims of the full moon murders, *I* was the only one who came back. I was also afraid that my eyes would deceive me by looking for a face no longer present in the halls of our school. A face I both loved and feared.

Natalie reached down and linked her arm in mine like we used to when we were kids. We passed through the exit doors at the back end of the building and walked through the breezeway, then onto the F-wing at a separate building in the very back of the premises. The hall was more crowded than I had ever seen it before, full of friendly and familiar faces.

Many spoke greetings and I heard my name in short breathless whispers, but I continued marching in my funeral.

As I turned the corner, I found the people who mattered most to me, waiting for me with open arms, causing my heart to swell.

Through the applause, Savannah squealed as she ran excitedly over to embrace me, long and hard. I fought the tears that welled up in my eyes and Natalie patted my back consolably as Cari quickly approached saving me from an emotional moment with her dry and unbeatable humor.

"Your hair still looks like shit, Jules. Do all of us a favor and *call my mom.*"

Wiping the tears away, I laughed and looked up to my greatest supporters. Tripp standing close behind Savannah and smiling sweetly at me. Joey lifted his hand to say hi, and Lindsey skipped over to give me a hug along with Taryn. Jackson stood back, smiling at me. Emma and Ashley, from the flag corps, were leaning against the wall with excited grins on their faces. Natalie's friend, Amber, also stood close by with a smile. And far in the back of my little crowd of friends, alone, was Isaac Philetos.

For once, I didn't feel the hatred I wanted to feel. Deep down, I knew if it wasn't for his harsh words, I probably wouldn't be standing in the halls of our school right now. I would still be a shell of the person I once was.

I endured the same treatment all day: hugs and greetings from acquaintances and others that I was barely familiar with. Natalie stayed by my side the entire day. She took it upon herself to walk me from class to class, and she would always confirm that this person or that person—whether I knew them or not—took part in the search for me when I went missing.

For days, my friends ran circles around me, trying to get me back to normal—inviting me out for coffee, to parties, to basketball games. They just didn't understand. I declined any opportunity to hang out or talk on the phone with them.

Weeks after my return, Casey Barnes timidly approached me at my locker, which made me feel guilty that for once she wasn't verbally attacking me.

"Hi, Jules," she began softly.

"Hi," I said, uneasy with her presence.

She took a ragged, deep breath and I winced. "I just wanted you to know...that...I'm glad they found you and that you made it home safely."

I swallowed the discomfort hard. "Thanks, Casey. That means a lot." My voice echoed in a hollow box, numb with guilt.

She nodded and frowned, probably because she was thinking about her friend who wasn't so lucky. Perhaps she resented me for the outcome of it all. And who could blame her? I recognized how hard it was for her to approach me.

Settling back into my old routine at school, I no longer counted time in days or weeks or even by the breaths I took. Time was now calculated by each fear I conquered. The scars of my past were still there and my emotional wounds would still bleed, but I felt stronger every day, like a seasoned warrior. I was going to survive this, and I was going to be stronger in the outcome. Isaac was right that I should be angry with the wall I felt compelled to hide behind. At times I still held myself accountable for what had happened, but I was slowly coming to terms with the fact that I was a victim and that I could not be blamed for any of it.

The skinny and shapeless body that had once been defeated would face me in the mirror. Physical scars healing, I still looked weathered.

No longer would I accept my own physical weakness.

I found myself rolling out of Natalie's bed at five o'clock one early spring morning and dressed comfortably in layers. I wasn't fully aware of what I was doing as I walked out the front door and latched my phone into a holster around my waist I stepped onto the front porch, down the circular driveway, and into the street. Only a few casual steps before the anger over my fear within me began to build and direct its energy to my legs, my feet, and I began beating against the cold hard street. I ran.

The greatest release I had experienced. No longer running away. Not from Lucas, or the wolf, or Broderick. Not even from myself or my anxiety. I was charging ahead to face it—all of it. My insecurities were beaten into the ground. The resentment of being kidnapped and then for being allowed to survive, I crunched it beneath my toes. The ghosts—my demons—holding my memories prisoner, I converted the anger and the power in my legs into utter strength, willfully conquering them as I reached the first mile.

It couldn't all be accomplished in one day, but it slowly became a morning routine. My internal clock sparking something inside me every morning at five, and my war began. And damn, if I wasn't winning!

I knew I had crossed into the enemies' lair, invading their territory, when I woke one morning in my own bed, alone for the first time in almost three months. This gave me the motivation to take another big step in my life...

I called Cari and asked her to meet me at the Java House. The excitement in her voice alone was like pouring gasoline into a fire. She arrived within minutes.

Chase came to the table to take our order. Cari coolly waved at him and he pinched at her arm quickly in an odd greeting, then focused all of his attention on me.

"Coffee's on the house for you two today. Stay all day—until close if you want. I'll get your drinks started." He smiled and walked back behind the counter to the espresso machines.

"Thanks," Cari said politely.

I leaned in close to her and chuckled at Chase's flirtations toward her. "I see some things haven't changed."

"Huh?" she asked as I pointed over to Chase and his eager manner. "Oh, yeah... *that*." Instead of tearing into him with insults, she waved it off.

Watching my friend with questioning eyes, I was unable to put my finger on the difference I saw in her. Cari looked refreshed and light and I wondered how long she had been like that? Did I just fail to notice in the previous months? I couldn't decide if it was her clothes, her makeup, or her hair. She also seemed talkative and chipper. Everything about her was somehow out of character for her. Different.

She relayed to me that no one was angry with me over my reclusion and that Savannah had simply urged everyone to give me space. "Her dad must have given her that idea, because there's no way in a million years that she would ever leave you alone like that by her own doing."

I laughed at Cari's dry humor as she rolled her eyes at our enthusiastic friend.

"She and Tripp are still doing great though she's a bit sad with his impending graduation." I nodded as I listened and thought back to the same concern I had last fall. I missed having that concern. "I don't think Joey and Lindsey are going to make it over the summer," She added.

It was amusing how she had become my source for gossip.

Chase brought over our order and we both sipped our coffee as she studied me over. "What are we going to do with your hair? It is killing me. You look like hell," she laughed.

"I've *been* through hell," I wryly reminded her.

"So it's like a souvenir? A tattoo?" I shook my head with a limp grin. "You wanna talk about it?"

"No. I'd rather forget it," I sighed and shrugged as I pulled on the shorter layer that had fallen out of my bobby pin. My mom has been trying to smooth and even my choppy hair and create a bob. It was still a disaster. "I guess I do need to do something with this mop, don't I?"

She held up her finger as she pulled out her cell phone and hit speed dial. "Mom, you up for an afterhours visit tonight? I've got Jules with me and she needs your help desperately." I laughed at her dramatic choice of words. "We'll be there even if I have to kidnap… I mean, hogtie her. See you then. Bye." She slapped her phone shut and smiled at me.

I looked at her solemnly. "Thanks, for *everything*."

"It's nothing. But I think the secret's out that you're not a true blonde now." She wrinkled her nose as she pointed to my auburn roots.

As my hair appointment time was approaching, I decided to take a restroom break before we left for the salon. I would be in the chair for a while—color job, shampoo, and cut—and Dr. Kowalski had recommended that I try to pee often so I wouldn't get another urinary tract infection. As I walked to the Ladies restroom, ignoring the apprehension of entering a room alone, I heard Cari call across the room, "I'm leaving your tip on the table, Chase."

When have we ever left a tip? Cari and I were always broke. I didn't work and her paychecks from her part time job usually went to partying, gas, and other car necessities. As I nervously sat on the commode, worrying myself over the possibilities of being attacked while in the restroom, she tapped on the door to let me know she would wait for me in her car. After washing my hands, I started to the doors of the café when I realized that I had left my phone on the table. I turned around and went back to retrieve it. As I scooped them up, I saw the single, insulting quarter Cari had left behind for Chase's tip.

"Cari, you ass," I said under my breath as I dug in my purse for more change. *Gosh, and we didn't even have to pay for the drinks today!* I didn't know if she thought it would be funny or if she genuinely thought it was a worthwhile tip, but I didn't want to lose my friend, Chase, over the issue. It was rude.

As I dropped all the change I had left in my purse, which wasn't much, I noticed something else on the Java House napkin that the change sat on. It looked like impressions of backwards letters and I deliberated as to whether I wanted to flip the napkin over and read the words that had been scribbled on it. Watching Cari getting in her car, Chase was slammed at the counter with drink orders, and no one else was watching me.

Call me if you're going to be late from work again. — Cari

And it was completed with a smiley face shaped in a heart. I stifled a giggle as I quickly read the note again and returned it to its original position. *That explains everything!* Somehow and someway, she and Chase had hit it off.

"Chase, what time do you get off work?" I asked as I strolled past the counter.

He twisted his face in confusion but answered anyway. "Eleven. Why?"

"Just wonderin'. Thanks for the coffee," I said as I skipped out the door.

I followed Cari in my car two blocks to her mother's salon. The minute we entered the salon I took a bite.

"So after this, I was thinking about hanging out. My parents said I didn't have to be home until after midnight. You wanna go shoot some pool or something?" I asked her.

She sifted through the color swatches pretending that I hadn't hit a nerve. "I'm kind of tired and was going to go home and to bed after this."

I thought harder. "How about a slumber party, then? Savannah said we could meet up after her date with Tripp and then go to her house. Let's say around... hmmm... eleven?"

Cari's eyes started to become shifty as she fought for control over the situation. "I think I'm coming down with something and I don't want to get either of you sick."

Cari's mother came through the room from the back to lock the front doors as she and Cari shared a secretive glance. I sat in the seat at Pamela's station and saw in the reflection, Cari shaking her head slowly at her mom, warning her to keep quiet. Her discomfort was too enjoyable for me.

"Can I ask you for some advice?" I asked her finally.

"Shoot," Cari said in her normal nature.

"Since it's getting so late and I don't have a date for prom, I'm thinking about asking Chase. What do you think?" I said with a mischievous grin, letting her know that I was well aware of what was going on.

Her mouth dropped at the revelation—in both embarrassment and excitement. "Damn it! You went back to the table!"

I threw my head back in laughter. "I had to! I accidently left my phone," I explained.

"Why's it such a secret, Cari?" her mother asked as she began brushing through the tangled mess on my head.

"Because it would only confirm that I was right for once and she doesn't want to admit it." I continued to laugh.

"It's not serious," Cari claimed.

"I know that, because you *always* sign your notes to me with a smiley-faced heart, too."

Cari's face turned a bright red as she buried her head deeper into the book of swatches. She finally slammed the big book shut and slid down into her seat, reluctant to dish out her latest bit of gossip.

"Okay, I'll tell you, but I don't want to hear one 'I told you so'. Got it? Or I'll kick your ass right there in that chair."

I just laughed and held up my fingers in a scout's honor, sobering me as I thought of Broderick again. *Boy Scout.*

"We partnered up during a search party while looking for you," she said with a smile. "He got fired from the movies when he called in to volunteer that night. He was wearing worn, holey jeans and the same Metallica T-shirt that I had on. I didn't even recognize him when he showed up that night. And I nearly crapped when he took off his leather jacket! Jules, he is covered in ink!"

"Tattoos? *Really?*" I was shocked and back into rolls of laughter, giddy for my friend.

"Anyway, as guilty as I should feel about admitting this, I took advantage of the opportunity, during a search party for my missing best friend to hook up with him." I wrinkled my nose and waved her off. I wasn't resentful of her. More like I was amused at how well my disappearance had worked out for her.

"We talked nonstop as we looked for you. We have so much in common—music, movies, piercings, ink… everything but that whole religion thing. Anyway, he kept me cheerful when I was worried about you." She thought for a moment. "He's a good guy… a lot more appealing than the bad ones." She smiled and all I could do was smile approvingly back at her before Pamela interrupted.

"Are we attempting blonde again? Because I tell you, Jules, this other color coming in is gorgeous. It's more appropriate for your skin tones, too." she said.

"I don't know…" I said unconvinced.

"Jules, make it a clean slate! Besides, I always thought that the blonde looked crappy. It always came out kind of orange because you wouldn't let Mom bleach it," Cari said with a snigger.

I took a jittery breath. "Okay. Match it up."

We continued talking about Cari and Chase as Pamela found hair dye that matched my roots and started coloring my hair. Cari admitted that she wasn't ready to announce their newfound relationship because of how and when they got together. She was afraid our friends would look down on her for using a serious dilemma as an opportunity to meet a new guy. I didn't see it that way. To me, it was the only good thing to come out of the nightmare I had to endure. Still, I agreed to keep her secret safe.

It felt like a new beginning, but it now looked like one as I looked into the mirror at the slow transformation. I thought I was going to cry as Pamela began towel drying the significantly darker hair, but I found instead a radiant splendor in my mane as it reflected brilliant red tones in the lights above. Pamela immediately began sniping and razoring the uneven edges of my hair, layering it into a short, choppy, winged-shag. Hip and sexy, she swept my sleek bangs over to the side. I was speechless at the end result. I didn't even look the same. Mature and flashy, yet wholesome in my natural hair color, my eyes looked richer and my skin pinker—glowing almost. I felt beautiful.

March's full moon found me awake and restless in my room, ironically reading about werewolves and vampires until way past midnight. I could never be certain of it, but I could swear I heard the persistent howling from the woods surrounding our neighborhood. A small piece of me wanted to hide my head under the pillow and scream out to drown the night sound calling to the moon, but instead, I found myself drawn to it, unable to sleep.

I stayed in my bed and continued to read, making the small connections between Broderick and other accounts of self-proclaimed werewolves. They all had sudden outbursts of anger, and then shifted their mood drastically to something else, like love or excitement. Many claimed to have debilitating headaches—some caused by flashing lights and others from nothing at all. The pages told of extraordinary strength and speed that the wolves had when in either form—human and wolf. And with each new discovery, I relived a past memory that verified how long I could have been aware of his change if only I had paid closer attention and had an opened mind.

We received our yearbooks leading into our Spring Break. Though most of us spent the day at school passing around our books for friends to sign, our core group planned to meet at the Java House so we'd have more time to write something profound to our closest friends while we enjoyed coffee and each other's company.

It felt like old times with a few new friends as we sat drinking, chatting and laughing at the pictures in the yearbook. Joey, Jackson, and Tripp spent most of their time laughing as they pointed out our lame quotes that we wrote in the book, while Taryn, Lindsey, and Savannah gushed over the wonderful photographs on each page as well as how beautiful or ugly certain girls appeared in them. Cari and Isaac started their own battle of who's-in-the-yearbook-the-most. Taryn and Cari were the first down, then Tripp and Savannah. Jackson, Joey, Isaac, and Natalie held a strong lead until it was official that I beat them all. I was possibly the most photographed person in the yearbook. It wasn't because I was popular, involved, or an over-achiever. We all knew why, though no one said it out loud. It was an unspoken rule not to say his name—a dearly departed member of our group. Loneliness burned a hole in my broken heart, even as I sat amongst the greatest group of friends a girl could ever ask for. We passed the books around with our pens in hand. It was a mass of confusion, but we joyfully survived the madness.

I made a point only to sign the first page, and prevent any further delving into the pages. There would be too many memories in each page and I couldn't face them just yet. It wasn't until I felt like I had signed way past my quota that Jackson slid his book over for me to sign.

"You missed this one," he said.

With all the books that had been passed around, it was sure to happen that I would miss someone's yearbook.

"Take your time. I'll come by later during spring break to pick it up. Right now, Taryn and I have got to go and finish our application essays."

"What school are you two going to attend, again?" Chase asked as he set down another cup of coffee in front of Cari and she looked up to kiss him on the cheek. Cari never came right out with their relationship, but had sneakily slipped it in on all of us, just as she would have it.

"University of Memphis," Taryn said proudly as she patted Jackson on the back.

"They have an excellent law program there," Jackson explained.

"Awesome," Chase congratulated them as they gathered their books and said goodbye.

We all parted ways and went to our respective homes shortly after Taryn and Jackson left. I carried the two yearbooks straight to my room and left them on my small desk, making a mental note to sign Jackson's yearbook sometime during Spring Break.

I was nervous through most of that night in bed, waking at every sound, but gained all sense of comfort when the ghost I loved appeared, laying his head on the pillow beside me and smiling. This ghost stayed. On several occasions, I felt inclined to speak to him, but would always let reality take over, and instead, I would sadly watch him fade away into the shadows. My heart ached terribly as I fell into an unstable sleep. Missing the boy next door.

Before the end of spring break, I finally sat down with pen in hand to write a few short sentences to Jackson in his yearbook. I propped myself up with several pillows in my bed and turned on the lamp on my nightstand. Then the jolt of sadness hit me when I read the notes that were signed inside. None of the passages were addressed to Jackson.

Broderick, you make a better friend than a boyfriend. Ha, ha! I love you anyway. Stay in touch with us after graduation and we just might invite you to the wedding someday. — Taryn

Broderick, thanks for being a great friend! Don't lose touch with us after graduation. — Savannah

Boy Scout, things haven't been the same without you second semester. Good luck in your future endeavors. You are definitely one of the good guys. — Cari.

To the brother I never had. Come see us in Memphis when you get the chance. Preferably as much as possible; we'll miss your ugly face. — Jackson

Broderick, I feel blessed getting to know you this year. Wish you would have stuck around. Things aren't the same without you. I'll be praying for you. Love you, Nat

Four years of the best baseball and football games and practices. The best years of my life and all because of your friendship. Take care, man. — Joey

I read every signature on the front few pages, everything from *"stay cool"* and *"don't ever change"* to *"I'm the first to sign your crack."* I shut the book quickly, feeling like I had invaded his privacy, but shortly after shutting the book; I ran my hand over the cover and imagined him looking at it for the first time with me. The way it was supposed to be.

Jackson must have picked it up for him and passed it around for everyone to sign. I fanned through the pages and saw almost every page full of signatures and short notes, some phone numbers. Finally stopping at a dog-eared page, I opened it wide to see a large photo of Broderick and me laughing together in the parking lot, his arm around me, apparently taken by another photographer on the staff. Between the pages was a small slip of paper folded in half with sloppy writing on it.

Jules, I know you think it's done and over with, but I'm hoping that maybe you and Broderick will see what we all see in these pages and know that it's still there. One of you just has to make that first move. Please, be the one that does that. Sorry for the deception. Don't be mad. I'm on his side with this and his side is your side. Your friend, Jackson.

The book and note fell on my lap and I looked up at the ceiling, fighting the warm tears that began filling the brims of my eyes. Jackson had set me up, hoping I would be the one to deliver this book to Broderick. His heart was in the right place, he just didn't know what all was involved. Broderick now terrified me. He wasn't who we all thought he was.

And what would I say? What should I say? *Gee, I loved you more than I even realized, but you're a werewolf so it would never work out because you scare the shit out of me.*

It was insane. All of it. Broderick was a werewolf—a monster—and that was complicated enough, but what would it take to be with him. Was it even possible for me to survive a relationship like that?

One lingering reminder stood out against all logic: *He fought for me.*

I finally climbed out onto my roof that night. The answers I searched for overshadowed any fear I had left of supernatural occurrences. I looked up at the crescent moon. For so long I had looked upon her in wonder and amazement, but now I felt resentful of her. Her phases and movements were in complete control of the one I loved. Or did we have control all along?

Overcome with restlessness, I made my way back to my bedroom and found a pen. I picked up the book, and for over an hour, I debated on the right words but found nothing profound enough to suit me—to suit us.

I paced the floor in front of my dresser, eyeing the *Brothers Grimm and other Faery Tales* book as well as his medallion that set on top of it. Broderick was always big on honesty, so I decided to tell him exactly what was on my heart. I grabbed his medallion and fastened it around my neck again.

I found the picture of the two of us, this time glancing at the other signs of us on other pages. Every picture he had taken of me filled the book from cover to cover with my images. Even if I wasn't the focus of the picture, I was in the background. And I knew his photos from the others. His were always better.

Returning to the page that held the two of us at one of our happiest moments, I began writing the first thing I thought of.

Broderick, Life's greatest challenge is becoming who you were meant to be... and I love that person. Always have and always will. Yours Forever, Jules

I dropped the pen when I was done, assuming that the restlessness would cease, but it didn't, so I slammed the book shut. *I'm done.* But the adrenaline flowed through me, telling me that I was *not finished.* Never before had I felt so drawn to him! I had to see him! I had to talk to him!

The last thing I was concerned about was what moon phase it was, what shape he was in, or whether I was going to get caught. I ran to Natalie's room and shook her ecstatically.

"Nat! Nat!" I whispered.

"What?" she groaned groggily. "What is it?" She finally snapped up and began reaching for the baseball bat she now kept beside her bed, assuming that I was in danger.

"I need a favor."

"What?!" she asked incredulously. "It's... it's..." she looked over at the alarm clock with squinty eyes. "Midnight! Are you freakin' kidding me, Jules? This better be good," she warned.

"I'm going out for a bit."

"You're *what*?" She sat up alert.

"Shh!" I hushed her. "I have to see Broderick. It can't wait. I feel like I'm going to die if I don't do this right now."

"Kinda dramatic don't you think? Besides, why do you need me?"

I swallowed my fear hard as it constricted my throat. "In case I don't come back... if I'm not home in thirty minutes, get Mom and Dad."

Life was imperfect and bad things could happen when you least expected them; I knew that now. Broderick didn't worry me; I was worried about anyone else getting hold of me and no one having a clue as to where I was when it happened.

"Mom and Dad are the ones you better worry about. They are going to kill you."

"They're not going to find out, right?" She nodded and reached over for her alarm clock.

"Thirty-five minutes. I'll give you an extra five to change into something other than pajamas." She set the clock timer for thirty five minutes.

As I made my way out the door, I heard her mutter in her sleepy state, "Why do I get the feeling that you're going to get me killed over this?"

Quickly, I tossed off my pajamas and threw on a pair of dark jeans and a black turtle neck sweater with my denim jacket. The only bright giveaway on me was the white tennis shoes. I tip toed down the stairs and slipped out the back door, but not before I grabbed the spare key from under the fifth step leading up to the deck. The entire plan felt audacious as I trembled in fear while dashing through the woods with his yearbook under my arm. The crescent moon wasn't bright, but the trees were bare and opened up the path with its illumination. The bridge felt as sturdy as ever when I crossed over the bubbling creek. The dogwood tree beside the bridge was in full bloom with white blossoms and was bright against the shadowy woods. When I could see Broderick's bedroom light on with the curtains drawn I increased my pace and I felt the strength and power in each step build my confidence, which was exactly what I needed as I climbed the steps to his door.

I held my hand up to tap on it, but held off for a moment when I saw movement of his silhouette, being cast from behind the curtains as I peeked around to the front of the garage. I walked around to the windows and saw him through a small crack of the curtain. He wore only his jeans as he painted. Desperately, I tried to make out what the canvass told, but the break in the curtains wasn't wide enough. His window was cracked open to let the cool air in.

Kneeling down to the opening of the window and leaning in closer to the screen, I took a deep breath, but before I could even speak he dropped his head and shoulders and stopped painting. He knew I was here though his silhouette kept its back to me taking slow, deep breaths.

I closed my eyes and began. "I never thanked you for what you did for me that night. You saved my life... again."

I waited for a response. Silence. His silhouette hadn't moved at all. Discouraged, I double checked the moon as if it would suddenly be a full phase. *Crescent.*

Unprepared with what I really wanted to say, I felt as though I was stumbling thorough meaningless words. "There are few things I have to say to you and I wish... I wish you would listen...." I began nervously.

Slowly, I saw him step back and lean against the window, then slide down to a sitting position. Our heads were now leaning side by side on the opposite sides of the window.

"You have become everything to me, and I don't care what has happened or what's going to happen, or what you are. It's never going to change the way I feel about you." I took a deep breath. "I love you. Whether you love me back or not, I love you, and I can't ever take the chance again of leaving this world without you knowing that."

I waited for him to repeat the words back to me, but he never did. Crushed, but not hopeless, the burning within me gave me strength to carry on and give him time. My time was running short and I didn't want Natalie to wake my mom and dad when everything was fine. I would be toast if they knew I was out.

"I have your yearbook and I'm leaving it here by the door. Everyone misses you. *I* miss you." I stood and spoke over my shoulder to him. "He still gets the girl if he wants her."

Slowly, I walked down the stairs and laid the book by the door. I never once saw him move from where he sat.

The following morning as I ran, I was power driven every time my toes kicked off from the pavement. Maybe it was because a new season was apparent to me this morning. The wind still spoke of winter, but the sun was brighter, and I could see buds on the trees. The white blossoms on the dogwood trees were abundant and beautiful.

I never broke pace down the driveway, even as I scooped up the Saturday morning paper. I tossed it up to my parents who were sitting on the deck drinking coffee. I debated taking the stairs and visiting with them before taking a shower, but stopped when I saw a note attached to the door under the deck. Cautiously, I walked over to it and snatched it off the door. My nerves began to bubble as I quickly realized by the timing and handwriting who it was from.

Broderick! My heart cried out as my confidence quickly slid away from the possibility he could be requesting that I never be near him again. My fingers, red and burning from the cold morning air, pinched the paper. Nervously inhaling the crisp air, I blew out a deep breath and read.

Jules,

Meet me at the bridge at 8am.

Broderick

My stomach twisted in anxious knots. My watch read 7:30.

Nat was still sleeping, and not in the shower, so I was in and out of the shower in record time. My hair air dried for the most part by the time I finished with a quick, light application of makeup, and I arranged the short locks of my hair to give it body. The clock on my dresser said I had only five minutes left to get ready. I shoved my arms into my thin, brown leather jacket and hurried back out the door. Listening to my mom and dad ask me where I was going, I simply turned to them smiling and pointed to the woods. A smile spread on both of their faces as I dashed into the woods, pushing through the thorny bushes and branches that hung over the once well-worn path.

He stood on the bridge, patiently waiting as he glanced at his phone, then down at the creek again. He was taller than I remembered, and more striking than ever before. My heart thundered for him.

He rested his elbows on the rail of the bridge.

I slowed my pace when I realized I hadn't thoroughly considered what I was going to say to him. As I got closer, he sensed me and straightened up, shoving his hands in his pockets. His eyes were wide and eager, but anxious, and he tucked his lips in as he swallowed hard—his dimples appearing long enough to make my heart flutter. His eyes traced along my face, lingering at the short red lock on my head. I bit my lip as I approached the bridge, and I could already feel my throat shaking before I spoke.

"My name is Juliana Irene Taylor, but my friends call me Jules. I've lived here for almost three years. I began coloring my hair blonde at the age of fourteen, thinking that it would help catapult me into some sort of popularity when I started high school in a new town."

Broderick stared at me with confusion, but I continued.

"My family roots are Irish, but I was the only one in my immediate family to have red hair. I... " I thought quickly as to what else I would confess to him. "... I don't like feet. I can't let someone else's feet touch mine. I can't even let my own feet touch each other. It's like nails on a chalk board to me, so I sleep with my socks on. And I hate ice-cream. I love horror movies, and even though my life recently became a true life horror movie, I recently found that I still enjoy them, which probably makes me a little unbalanced. I love music, and I love to sing." I had to stop and take a breath.

He furrowed his brows in concentration, trying to make sense of what I was saying.

"I cheat on tests and sometimes copy my friend's homework because I'm too lazy to do it myself. I hate school. I lie when I think it'll save my tail. I'm addicted to vanilla lattes, but my favorite drink is cherry coke. I enjoy the autumn more than any other season. I'm not good in relationships. I'm very selfish and everything in life to me is a competition. I fell in love last summer for the first time ever with a boy who lived next door…" I had to breathe again. "… And I find it difficult to say the word *love*."

Broderick's face softened as he listened.

"Love. It's not only been the greatest feeling I've ever had; it's also been very scary. But I truly loved this guy. He was my soulmate and I loved everything about him. I loved how he smelled, how much of a friend he was to me,… how he would say my name. He said it like it meant something, that it was intimate to him. My heart broke into a million pieces when he left me." I took a step toward Broderick and he flinched. Calmly, I proceeded to let him know that I wasn't afraid of him or of what was to come. "I knew from the beginning that he was different from all the rest. Miraculous, even. And I am referring to his humanity and compassion, not just what he could do supernaturally or—"

He cut me off. "Why are you doing this?"

"Because, months ago you wanted us to lay our cards out on the table, and neither of us really did that. I know I didn't. I always wanted to be more than just friends with you."

I stood next to him, both of us resting our elbows on the rail of the bridge looking off into the woods. The water below was crystal clear as it bubbled around the rocks, and the white blossoms from a nearby dogwood fluttered into it, drifting down and around the bend. I sniveled from the cold breeze as I notice another white petal from the dogwood blossoms entwined with the auburn strands of my bangs.

"I'm not going to lie. You hurt me. You hurt me when you left me and you hurt me even more when I saw the truth about you that night. I couldn't understand why you didn't just tell me. You told me about the shadowshifting and about the dreams, and I believed you and I managed. But for some reason, you felt that I couldn't be trusted with… with…"

"A werewolf." He spoke bluntly with resentment, "I'm a werewolf, Jules."

I looked down at the water again, dropping my head closer to the rail as I continued. "I felt the intensity of our fate last night. I can't deny it anymore now than you could last summer and you need to know that."

Feeling a light tug on a strand of my hair, I looked over to see his fingers lovingly pinching the ends of my hair.

I turned to face him. "I *love* you. Nothing is going to ever change that, I don't care if you shadowshift or are shapeshift or if this crazy world falls down all around us. I love you and I don't want to give up on that."

"It's wrong, Jules," he said sadly as he reached up and pulled the petal from my hair, grazing his fingers in the short tress. "We can't ever be together because of what I am. Your face said it all in the library—"

"It was a fresh wound, Broderick," I explained calmly.

"Your biggest concern right now should not be whether we get back together or not, but how you can protect yourself from me. I'm a monster," he growled.

Earnestly, I looked up at him. "We each have our own monster inside of us. I battle mine on a daily basis." I placed my hand on his heart. "You're not defined by whatever takes over your body during the full moon, though. It's your heart and soul that make you who you are—what made me fall in love with you from the beginning."

His will was crumbling. "What makes you think this could ever work?"

"I have faith in us, and I think you do, too. You just don't have faith in yourself anymore."

"I can't control it like you think I can..." He stood closer to me looking down on me.

I smiled up at him. "It's a risk I'm willing to take."

He lifted his hand and gently brushed his knuckles across my cheek.

"I can't even promise you a normal relationship. So much has changed."

I reached up to touch his warm face. "We never had a normal relationship. What we have is so much greater."

"So, where do we go from here?" he asked.

"You know, I could really use a friend right now. You were always great at being a friend to me, and I'm willing to bet that you could use a friend as well."

"Just friends?"

"Just friends until you choose to take it another step." I smiled, putting the ball in his court.

We stood facing each other and then he slowly placed his arms around me. Oh, it felt so good to be held by him again. All my aching and loneliness was finally silenced. From the inside out, I could feel myself healing.

He buried his face in my hair, drawing my scent in and softly whispered. "I love your hair...It's...*unbelievable*..." He paused for a moment. "...it makes you look warmer."

My brow pulled together as I sensed he was wanting to say something else.

He became serious. "Aren't you afraid?"

"No."

"Why not? I'm a monster, Jules."

I gave him a smart smirk. "Because I'm actually more afraid of clowns."

"Seriously?"

Blushing at my confession, I nodded.

We laughed and it felt good. Neither of us had laughed for such a long time. Then he pulled me back into his arms and held me for the longest time as the winter wind blew its last breath through the spring air. The dogwood blossoms swirled and fell all around us.

Moondance

B RODERICK AND I WERE taking things slower this time. He was continually apprehensive to touch me—even as a friend. Our contact was limited to short embraces. It was a struggle at times to control my desire for more contact. And the longing in his eyes was clearly evident as well.

My parents gave us a lecture about curfews and after-hour shenanigans. My curfew remained at ten, but not so much because of our history of sneaking out as it was due to the unusual turn of circumstances our lives had taken a few months back. Even with a cell phone glued to me and a friend who was proven to be a true hero time and time again—they weren't going to take any chances. They were even looking at quotes to put a fence around our yard, like I was a toddler in danger of slipping in to traffic.

With the warmer weather, Broderick started mowing and landscaping again. If he wasn't working, he'd be found waiting in my driveway when I came home from school. Occasionally we'd head over to the school and watch the baseball games. I could see that he missed playing but also that he found it equally enjoyable to sit beside me on the bleachers and cheer for his old teammates. At other times, we would meet up with our gang of friends at the Java House. Things were definitely getting back to normal.

Two weeks was all the time Broderick gave me to prepare for prom. We agreed to go as friends. Since every girl in school already had their dress, I was left with very limited options while shopping with Mom and Natalie. My heart was set on a red slip dress. Classic and tasteful. Quickly, I became frazzled by the very scarce dress rack. Most dresses were so far from my size that alterations were not an option. Natalie and my mom concentrated their efforts in other areas of the store in hopes to find something that would not only fit, but compliment.

Finally, Natalie came across a slip dress. Although it was not red like I had originally hoped, the color flattered my hair and skin tone unlike any other. Pink. My initial response was to ignore it. Pink was too girly of a color for me, but I couldn't deny how beautiful I felt wearing it when I tried it on. It was a keeper.

While my friends were out getting their hair and makeup professionally done the day of prom, I was at home playing salon with my mom and sister. After spending hours on the internet learning how to cover tattoos with makeup, Natalie learned a method to try to cover a few bite marks that were still visible on my arms.

Never in my life had I felt so beautiful. As a final touch I put on Broderick's medallion around my neck. It may not have been "prom-worthy", but it was me. I was his for the taking when he would be ready.

Horribly nervous, I stayed in my room talking to Natalie as the front doorbell rang. I glanced at the clock on my dresser and saw the time. Five o'clock. I was already taking a hard swallow when I heard my dad's voice carry upstairs and into my room, "Jules! Broderick's here!"

My eye became larger and Natalie raised her eyebrows, giggling.

I drew a long, shaky breath. "Here we go," I said to her and she walked down the stairs first with me following close behind her.

"Hi, Broderick," she said in a sing-song manner as she took the corner into the living room

Broderick said hi to her and I walked into the room. He quickly stopped shuffling his nervous feet and fought to look strong and sure in his stance, but his face spoke a million other emotions. For the first time since before we broke up, I saw that flicker of hope in his eyes and he lifted his head and straightened his back. He was stunned with the unveiling of my dress. And I was just as equally stunned with what I saw. His tall stature in a suit and tie, his hair gelled in a classy but stylish way. He took my breath away and made my heart rattle in delight.

"*Wow*," He breathed tenderly as I came closer to him. His eyes grew wide and a grin crept onto his lips with a small chuckle. "You said you were looking for something in red."

Just a glimmer of diffidence fluttered in my stomach. "Disappointed?"

"Far from it."

We had to endure my mother's twenty minute photo shoot that could have easily extended to an hour if my dad hadn't cut her short, announcing that we needed to leave or we would miss dinner. Instead of an expensive meal at one of the finer restaurants, we opted for burgers, fries, and cherry cokes at Main Street Drug Store. It was a strange location for a pre-prom dinner, but it made perfect sense to me. I didn't want Broderick to feel any pressure, as if this was a date.

We arrived to prom late, which is apparently what you're supposed to do because everyone else was showing up at the same time. Savannah and Tripp were already on the dance floor slow dancing to every song, even the fast ones. Joey and Lindsey, and Taryn and Jackson were socializing as Cari and Chase were getting their prom pictures done—her wild, purple dress perfectly matching the purple chunks in her hair.

Broderick and I sat alone at a table for a few minutes before our friends started joining us. Now that prom was here, the excitement focused toward graduation. Tripp, Taryn, Jackson, Joey, and Broderick would be leaving us for their college destinations, whereas Cari, Savannah, Lindsey, and I would be returning next year as seniors. It felt like a defining moment but deep down, I knew would never hold any serious meaning as I grew older. The girls at the table began complimenting each other on their dresses and making snide remarks about other girls at the prom.

When the song changed to an upbeat one, Lindsey approached us and begged me to take Joey off of her hands. She was clearly avoiding any fast dances with him. I allowed him to make a fool of me as a dance partner because I knew it would be fun, as it always was.

When they announced the prom king and queen, none of us were surprised to see Jackson and Taryn take the throne. As they danced, everyone circled around them watching and waiting for their chance to begin dancing again. Broderick stood tall beside me and slid his hand into mine. I looked up at him, happy that he was touching me.

"You're not going to dance with me at all tonight, are you?" I asked him quietly.

"I don't know if it would be a good idea..." he began.

"You won't know until you *try*," I said.

And with that, he let go of my hand and walked off into the crowd, causing my heart to break. At the end of Taryn and Jackson's dance, everyone clapped and then stormed the dance floor for the slow song that just started while the DJ congratulated the king and queen again.

Our group retreated back to our table: laughing, joking, visiting, and gossiping. I was unsettled with Broderick's distant look. He sat several seats away from me on the other side of the table, just listening to Jackson and Joey talk about summer plans.

When a favorite upbeat song blared through the speakers, Lindsey, Taryn and Savannah screamed with excitement and jumped out of their seats to dance together, pulling me and a very reluctant Cari out with them to join in. Joey, Chase and Jackson followed, making our dance a large group dance. The cosmic music brought a sense of dream and fate to me, as if I had waited my whole life for this one night. Jackson took turns twirling me and Taryn around, and my eyes would shift to where Broderick sat frowning alone at our table. I continued dancing with my friends through the song and my breath was knocked out of me when I looked back at our table and saw Broderick gone.

He left me!

As the song started closing, my friends began pairing off with their dates when a chord progression to an intro of a slow song began.

Our song.

Desperately, I swung around, searching the crowd for his face one last time. I couldn't find him, so I dropped my shoulders and stared at my feet in silent debate about calling Natalie for a ride home. But something was happening; I could feel it stirring inside of me. I looked up where the DJ was and saw Broderick gallantly strolling toward me, holding out his hand. The glow in my heart began to warm again as I met him half way and fell into his strong arms. He wrapped them tightly around me with no misgivings and held me close to his warm body. I rested my head on his chest and heard his heart crying out for me alone. I took in his scent and closed my eyes as I let it bring me to another dimension while I listened to his voice in my ear.

"I want to be worthy of you. I want you to love me as I love you. I want us to spend the rest of our lives together and I want to believe it can happen," he said.

"It *can* happen." I looked up at him.

The lyrics floated between us as we swayed to the music, never losing sight of one another for the longest time.

"This is the moment I dreamt of, Jules. *This* is what I saw that night I first saw you on the roof. You, in my arms, your beautiful, auburn hair, a small scar just below your lip, and the angel's kiss here on your shoulder. Exquisite in pink." His dimples appeared as he tucked his lips in to hum. "I saw this happening over a year ago, I just started doubting if it was real."

We danced along a few moments before I heard him sing quietly in my ear. I looked up at him again.

"Those words—that's us, Jules. *This is going to happen*," he reminded me.

I was speechless as I stared up at his beautiful face and into his eyes. Suddenly, he shuddered violently. I flinched and my body became tense. He looked desperate, urgency in his expression.

"I'm starting to lose control, Jules," he said with intensity.

My heart raced violently at his admission. We were all in trouble here. I needed to be brave. "I'll get you out of here, then," I said as I started to break away from the dance floor.

He grabbed my arm. "No. Not with that."

"What?" I asked confused.

"*This.*" Before I could even comprehend what he was saying his soft warm lips were pressing against mine, and we had stopped dancing. He kissed me softly for a few short moments before giving completely into passion, his kisses becoming hopeless and consuming. He held my face close, never letting up. I became completely unaware and uncaring of the audience that surrounded us. He pulled back, and the mask of distress was no longer upon his face, I saw the boy next door for who he was—who I fell in love with.

"I love you," he whispered.

"I love you, too."

He kissed me hard again until a chaperone tapped him on the shoulder, causing him to blush and me to giggle.

"Do you want to get out of here?" He asked me and I nodded enthusiastically.

We said our goodbyes to our friends, politely begging off rejoining them at the cabins for their party, and headed for the door. They all seemed to understand, especially after our public display of affection.

I took the plunge and invited him to my house, too apprehensive to venture out at night. Shadowed out as we walked through the house, he waited for me outside of my parents' bedroom as I turned off their alarm clock before it went off at three. They must have been sleeping on pins and needles because I heard my dad sigh in relief as I tip toed back to the door.

"Did you have a good time?" My mother's groggy voice asked in the dark.

I smiled to myself. "It was perfect," I told her.

"Wonderful. G'night, Jules. You can fill me in on the details tomorrow when you wake up," she said as I heard her voice fall short of energy.

"I love you, Mom," I said as I closed the door.

Broderick was quick to take my hand as he led me to the stairs and whispered in my ear. "Perfect?"

"It always feels that way with you," I answered as we quietly stepped up the stairs.

I stayed in my dress as we climbed onto the roof through the chilly morning breezes. We lay on the roof staring at the sky until we finally resigned to my bed where he held me as I slept. We spoke very few words that night. Words could not have described our contentment with one another. At the first sign of day break, he climbed out through my opened window. In my near sleep state I whispered, "I love you." My lips barely moved from the smile on my face, and I didn't think he had heard me, but then I heard him chuckle lovingly as he escaped from the window.

A few days before our end of year rally, Savannah and Tripp approached me with a brilliant idea. Broderick's steady withdrawal from the public had cost him from being voted any superlative, which I was sure he couldn't care less about anyway, but what they had to offer was honorable. The student council was in full support of their idea as well. During the final assembly, after graduation rehearsals and in between finals, the student body would recognize him as the official hero for rescuing me in January. The more we discussed it over coffee that afternoon, the more I could see how befitting it was to recognize him.

Broderick's hero-complex. I smiled to myself

That Friday felt like déjà vu as it started. I took my English exam that morning and was waiting to take my last exam—Geometry, this time—with Mr. Muir at the end of the day. Cari was setting up her drums in the gymnasium as I waited for our friends to join us from their exams and graduation rehearsals. Cari was the first to sit next to me.

Consumed with thoughts over the comparisons between this year and last year, I laughed silently to myself.

Cari twisted her face and looked at me with exaggerated concern. "What's so funny, Looney Toon?"

I shook my head. "Just thinking."

"About going postal this year for the rally? It would be the only way you could top last year's rally," she laughed.

"No matter how convinced I am that this time is different and that this time it's real, I can't help but wonder what drama I'm going to face when I see him walk through those double doors."

"*Boy Scout?*" Cari asked as I confirmed with a definite nod. "He's solid, Jules. He's going to walk in here and search for you, and when he sees you, he's going to grin like an idiot and dash on over here to be with you. You will also be grinning like an idiot. I wouldn't expect any less. You two are stupid for each other."

My friend smirked approvingly at me, then pointed to the double doors. Just like she predicted, he walked in with eyes peeled for my face. I stood up and waved. As he located me, a wide smile grew on his face, both prideful and loving, that made his dimples so big they were clearly visible from where I sat. He made his way toward me in long strides. He put his hands on my waist and leaned in to give me a gentle kiss on the lips.

Cari groaned teasingly as she stood up to allow him the spot beside me, "Get a room."

Jackson and Taryn joined us, as well as Joey and Lindsey. When Natalie walked in, she started making her way to join us until she saw Joey. I shrugged in apology at her and she waved me off with a small smile. She, instead, joined Amber and a few of her other cheerleading friends.

Savannah, Tripp, and others of student council were taking the stage with some of the faculty as they began the assembly, recognizing the students on honor roll first. Broderick and I held hands the entire time, and with the length of time it took to run through all the categories, I would occasionally rest my head on his shoulder in boredom.

As they started the superlatives, I began to notice eyes shifting toward Broderick, and grew tense hoping he was oblivious to it. Tripp was voted *Most Likely to Succeed* and with the announcement Broderick and I used our outer hands to clap each other clumsily instead of unweaving our fingers and clapping ourselves. We clapped for all of our friends, even Erik Peterson who was *Most Attractive.* Joey was *Wittiest,* and Taryn and Jackson were selected *Mr. and Mrs. CCHS.*

On that cue, Cari and Savannah took their places on stage with Isaac at the helm of their group.

"Before we start the concert, we'd like to recognize another member of the graduating class as an outstanding citizen…" Principal Dean began.

I took a deep breath as a glowing smile crept onto my face.

"This person went beyond the call of duty at another person's time of need, proving himself worthy of being called a Town Hero. The entire senior class took time to vote on this special privilege with an amazing amount of support. So, it is my pleasure to announce our first ever Town Hero superlative winner, Broderick Cooper."

The entire gymnasium went wild in applause as his name was announced and Broderick stiffened at the realization. Stunned.

He turned to look at me in shock, and I grinned tenderly at him. "What are you waiting for, hero?"

He kissed me in haste just before he stood up and joined his friends and peers on stage. The entire gymnasium roared with applause. I was positive that I clapped the loudest for him. His face shone like the sun as he shook Principal Dean's hand and was handed the certificate. It may only have been a piece of paper, but what it stood for was priceless to him and definitely to me. Before the applause started to die down, Cari's small band began their set.

Isaac sang for thirty minutes without screaming at someone or accusing them of cheating on him—something I was unable to accomplish a year ago.

I had admit, it was a nice change to go home knowing I was not suffering a suspension from school and that summer school was definitely not on the agenda.

After school, Natalie and I spent some time getting ready for graduation. My parents were quick to get ready themselves when they got home from work and we all loaded up in the van and left for the stadium. Broderick waited for me just inside the stadium, for no other reason than just to see me before he walked across the stage.

Cari joined my family shortly after we found seats close to the center and we chatted lively waiting for the ceremony to begin. I couldn't help but notice Evelyn sitting a few rows over, staring at me with watchful eyes. She was definitely going to be an obstacle I would have to overcome someday, and I did not look forward to it. Her eyes cut me, but I tried to ignore her by watching Broderick as he spoke in a friendly manner to those who sat near him.

It was strange how emotional I felt over this rite of passage. My throat grew tight as the names I had grown familiar with were called out over the loud speaker, for I knew that the chances of hearing those names again after tonight would be slim to none.

I was emotionally exhausted by the end of the ceremony and ready to collapse into tears when the seniors tossed their caps into the air. Their era as seniors was over and change would be ushered in soon.

I immediately rushed to be by Broderick's side as the stands began to empty. Evelyn and Broderick were posing for pictures and I stood back out of view to avoid any conflict, but Broderick waved me over as soon as he saw me. My stomach tightened as I approached them, and I couldn't help but notice Evelyn's eyes narrowing. The camera was handed back to Broderick, and in turn, he handed it to Evelyn.

"Grandmother, get a picture of me and Jules," he said proudly.

Her sour look should have been a big enough hint for him, but he ignored her distaste and I definitely got the impression he was doing it on purpose to prove a point to her. She snapped the picture of the two of us snuggled closely together—much to her chagrin—and then announced that she was going home. I was glad she was gone by the time my parents approached to congratulate Broderick.

"What are the plans for tonight, kids?" my dad asked.

We became wide eyed and confused as to how to answer. Our night would be cut short because of the full moon.

"Any parties?" my mom asked.

"Jackson's family is having one," I said.

"And so is Tripp's," Broderick added.

My parents stared at us waiting for a confirmation that we would be attending either or both functions. The silence was uncomfortable.

"Oh, we're not going," I said suddenly.

"Why not?" my mother pressed.

"Because Broderick has to work." My excuse was not well thought out which wasn't a good sign since I was the one who usually felt more at ease with lying.

"*Tomorrow morning,*" Broderick quickly added. "I have to start early tomorrow morning, so I'm calling it an early night," Broderick lied nervously. He cleared his throat. "I would still like to spend some time with Jules if that's okay."

They both agreed. "Just have her home by ten," my mom said.

"*Eleven,*" My dad said as he looked at her. "Special occasion," he explained.

But the moon was in control tonight.

We arrived at his house before dark and watched a movie, holding each other tenderly. The mood swiftly darkened around us, like the evening sky. I had to let him go, give him up to the night. Not only did my heart break, but I also shuddered in fear over the impending departure as my mind raced in several different directions with questions and vivid pictures in my mind.

Broderick finally shifted his weight beneath me to sit up and the sadness seeped in. I sat up as well and gave him a few inches between us. He reached placing his trembling hand on my knee to console me.

"It's almost time, Jules," he whispered hoarsely.

Nodding in acknowledgement, I held back my tears of frustration.

"I know what will cheer you up, Red." He winked, fighting his own frustration and remaining calm for my sake. He dashed over to the closet and retrieved a brand new red hoodie to replace the one damaged in *The Incident.* I pushed my arms through the sleeves as he placed the hood on my head and smiled. We took each other's hand and walked through the woods under the twilight. All the while, I watched the full moon above as it mocked me.

Little Red Riding Hood and her wolf.

"Is it the sight of the moon that does it to you?" I was curious.

"No." He looked at his watch and took note of the time. "I know it plays some sort of controlling significance, but there's never really a set time. I sense the oncoming transformation throughout the day—all day. I just begin feeling restless and start getting really hot. Shuddering uncontrollably and headaches are an early indication that my transformation has been triggered, but I don't have to *see* the moon for any of this to begin. It just happens."

"How much time do we have left?" I asked as we crossed the bridge and entered my side of the property.

"Thirty minutes at the most. But I can't be sure," he said sorrowfully.

"Do you like it?"

He paused momentarily as he designed a well thought out explanation. "After the transformation is complete—yes. I feel invincible. *Powerful.* Every one of my human insecurities are filtered out, and only my instinct, aggression, and passion remain. I don't think like I think now, and I'm aware of it, but can't control it. Like I'm locked inside a room with only a window to look out of. And I seldom remember the images when I return to my human form."

We broke through the woods, and he walked me to the back door of the house. It was obvious my parents had already retired to bed and Natalie was out with her friends celebrating graduation at a few of the graduation parties.

"Few things guide me along while I'm in my other form."

"Like what?" I asked as we both walked into my house.

He kept his deep voice low as we made our way up the stairs and to my bedroom. "The moon, for one. It controls me in a large way when it comes to shifting. But once I'm changed, I'm driven by the hunt and instinct and the taste for blood."

I shivered as I closed the door, making note to myself how crazy it was for me to be locking myself in a room with a man—though I loved him—who was only minutes away from becoming a monster that would thirst for my flesh and blood. I tried to control my fear.

"You said you liked it after the transformation was complete. What about during it?"

He looked gravely into my eyes and spoke in dread. "The pain is unbearable, like I'm on fire. Agonizing. I feel my body ripping and breaking all at once."

He squeezed his eyes shut and pressed his feverish lips to mine, I could feel the quaking in them. As he restlessly pulled away, he opened his glassy eyes and pressed a smile to his face.

"I'm sorry, Jules. I'm out of time."

He made his way to the window and I followed him, reaching for him, wanting him to stay with me. To stay as he was. But it was impossible. I forced a smile on my face to put up a brave front for him, but the tears flowed down my cheek. He wiped them away as he spoke gently to me.

"I love you, and I'll see you tomorrow." He opened the window and stepped out onto the roof. I climbed up to his exit, pulling the red hood from my head and he kissed me once more.

"Stay inside, Jules—where it's safe. Don't come out again till dawn."

He jumped from the roof and landed lithely on the ground on all fours. As he dashed into the woods, the shadows over took him and before he completely shifted into the shadows, I saw him shifting into the monster I so feared.

And with that, he was gone into the night.

I glanced at the wicked moon, resentful over its betraying beauty and bitter with its resolve to rip me from the one I loved. Staring at her, attempting to prove my power over her, I knew I had lost when I heard the spine-chilling howl crack deep from the woods and into the night air. I frowned at my defeat, closed the windows, and locked them.

Laying my head on the pillow, I turned the nightstand lamp off just before another cry of the wolf echoed.

Coming in
2017!

Lycanthrope

Book Two

Lycanthrope

IN MY RED HOOD, I toed my way through the thick brush of the woods, following the brightly moonlit path, careful not to stray as my mother had warned. My grandmother waited for me on the other side and I was dependent on my love to show me the way, but he was lost to me so I was steadfast in my independent pursuit.

I would not give in to the fear I felt as I heard the step close behind me. The evil one that followed thirsted for my blood—for it promised him eternal life. Unable to focus on him, he was like a bolt of lightning behind me, toying with me and encouraged—feeding off from the fear I desperately tried to hide. I refused to run and instead sang quietly to myself and began to put a skip in my step, for in my mind, safety was found in oblivion.

I was consumed in my quest to remain unafraid, that I didn't notice how far I had been straying from the path. When I did notice, I begged myself to ignore it for it, too, played on the oblivious part and as I thought, it would keep me safe from any harm. At the howl of the wolf, I stumbled and my eyes shifted for a detour that would return me to the path from whence I came. This wolf was to trick me and I needed to avoid him, for he was my greatest weakness.

The evil one began closing in on me; I felt his cold hands brush against my skin—taunting me more as he ran circles around me so quickly that I couldn't see him—as I skipped fast down the path. The moon was swallowed by the dark mass in the sky and my path disappeared into the darkness. I stopped. The only sound in my ears was my panting and my thundering heart as it pumped life into my veins, beckoning the evil one.

I needed to face him. Show him that I was not afraid of him, that he would never possess me. That I—and I, alone—was given the power to conquer him. I swallowed my fear and assertively turned my heel, but the evil one was gone. I could still sense him, but he was hiding, watching me from the shadows. Instead, I heard the low rumble of the nearby wolf come from behind me.

I spun around quickly to confront him, as well, but the claws were already inches deep in my face as it swung at me and knocked me to the ground. The pain was excruciating and I tried to scream, but was choked off by the pressure of the predator throwing itself onto my body and ripping me to shreds, eating the insides of my torso, splattering my blood several feet around me—everywhere. As in a nightmare, I wouldn't die, I watched helplessly and painfully at the macabre carnage of my body. The dark wolf stared at me with its black eyes and growled ferociously in my face just before it sank its teeth deep into my throat, cutting off my scream.

I jumped up, wet and panting in my bed. Gasping for air, but finding none. My body shook violently at the shock and the fear was so intense I ached.

The room was mostly dark, allowing only a small sliver of moonlight to slither in between the sheer curtains of my windows. My body heaved as I tried to take a deep breath. My hair was soaked in sweat and I reached up to hold my heart in place, certain that it was going to rip open my chest.

"Holy shit," I croaked.

My nightmare was far from over.

For more information and dates on

upcoming releases!

go to

www.MelissaDEllis.com

About the Author

An avid fan of horror since before she was saying her alphabet, Melissa D. Ellis writes spine-tingling Young/New Adult fiction in hopes that her readers will always look under their beds before sleeping at night.

She studied Music Therapy, Theater, and English at Tennessee Technological University. When she's not writing, she's making a living as a voice instructor and musician, enjoying the outdoors, conjuring up scary ideas to write about, quoting movies, changing diapers, running carpool, being a Mom, being a wife, drinking a lot of coffee, or eating.

Melissa makes her home in Crossville, Tennessee with her husband and three boys.

To learn more about Melissa D. Ellis and her writing adventures, please visit her at www.MelissaDEllis.com.